TROUBLE *Me*

BECK ANDERSON

OMNIFIC PUBLISHING
LOS ANGELES

Omnific Publishing
1901 Avenue of the Stars, 2nd floor
Los Angeles, CA 90067
www.omnificpublishing.com

First Omnific eBook edition, May 2015
First Omnific trade paperback edition, May 2015

The characters and events in this book are fictitious.
Any similarity to real persons, living or dead,
is coincidental and not intended by the author.

Library of Congress Cataloguing-in-Publication Data

Anderson, Beck.
    Trouble Me / Beck Anderson – 1st ed.
    ISBN: 978-1-623422-20-2
    1. Contemporary Romance — Fiction. 2. Movie Industry — Fiction.
    3. Blended Family — Fiction. 4. Idaho — Fiction. I. Title

10 9 8 7 6 5 4 3 2 1

Cover Design by Micha Stone and Amy Brokaw
Interior Book Design by Coreen Montagna

Printed in the United States of America

To any woman who's ever asked,
"Does this make me look fat?"—Stop.
You're beautiful.

ON THE ROAD AGAIN

I love road trips. I love driving. I never get to drive.

Here's a secret: movie stars miss driving cars. In the heat of the spotlight, my brain has apparently turned to soft scrambled eggs, and I can't be trusted to drive a car.

Okay, that's not fair. I've been working so much (too much, Kelly would tell you) that I'm always in the middle of a press tour or on set.

Tucker Caldwell, my trusty bodyguard, drives when we work.

We work a lot.

"Are you awake? You have to be awake to drive in Oregon. They give huge tickets. Trust me." Kelly Reynolds, the best thing that ever happened to me, looks at me from the passenger seat. She's tipped her sunglasses down her nose to give me a field fatigue test and now eyes me suspiciously.

She has her feet up on the dashboard. I resist the urge to tell her to put them down. If I careened off the road and the airbag deployed, it'd be a bad deal for those toned legs of hers. She thinks she's the worrier, but I've read too many horrible true-story scripts — I'm the worrier. She doesn't even know the half of it.

I get a little lost looking at the curve of her calf, the way the tendons lead up to the knee, then the thigh leads…

"I was kidding, but, Andrew? Are you in there? Really, we can pull over, and I can drive awhile. There's no shame. I know you're all 'Andy Pettigrew, invincible bad ass,' but I like awake bad asses behind the wheel. You're allowed to rest."

I shake myself out of it. "I'm fine. I was just thinking about how much I like to drive."

I cast a glance in the rearview mirror and check on Hunter and Beau, Kelly's boys. Hunter is asleep and probably getting taller even as I watch. He's thirteen now—I remember being that age, the growth spurt days. My hips ached for a whole year from growing pains. I couldn't sleep or eat enough to feel satisfied.

Beau, the younger of Kelly's boys by two years, has his head-phones on and stares out the window, head tilted up, bobbing ever so slightly. I look back at the road and then to the side and realize he's following the sway and slope of the power lines. They swim in a lazy pattern between the poles when we're driving this fast.

I turn back to the road but keep my head facing a tiny bit away from Kelly. I can't help it; I get a little choked up. The whole "I am king of all I survey" thing? Well, I survey, and I feel full to bursting. I have a family. A beautiful family. I have this girl, this glorious woman to the right of me now, who let me into her life when I probably least deserved it. The last year and a half (plus a month, but, you know, it's close) have been richer than I ever could've hoped.

Driving ten hours across the desert with these people, it gets me misty. I don't care if my ass is sore; I don't care if Kelly packed more than Lewis and Clark probably did—and they traveled this route plus the whole trail from St. Louis.

I don't care. I have a family. I love them.

I don't know how this could get any better than it is right now.

All right. If it wasn't a mini-van I was driving, it might be a hair better. But other than that, it is the Griswold family vacation and *Full House* all rolled up into one. Without Mary-Kate and Ashley.

The abundance almost makes me scared.

I've never had so much to lose before.

SEA OF LOVE

We've reached our destination. The surf pounds into white spray, and the sea tosses restlessly, but I feel peaceful. I feel whole here on the Oregon Coast, a place that makes me happy, surrounded by my family. All my boys: Andrew, Hunter, and Beau. I love the way that sounds, all those names mashed into one sentence. My man and my sons together.

I'm in the midst of a run on the beach. I can feel sand against my ankles, the wind blasting up from the south. The big storms come in that way, up from Northern California. It's not a problem, the wind, unless I turn my head to look at something. Then I taste salt and feel grit in my teeth.

But I've taken a cue from Andrew and worn sunglasses today, even though the stormy conditions don't call for it. They save my eyes from the sand.

The Oregon coast is cold, the water's brutally icy, and the weather is often gray and windy — even now, in late June. If you turn your back to the surf, you're likely to have your neck snapped or be dragged out to sea. I make it sound terrific. The Oregon Tourism Board thanks me. This isn't some gentle breeze, warm water, sandy spit, wussy kind of Atlantic beach. Here the ocean demands respect. It's a fighting kind of beauty.

Though running is my respite, it's a slog today. The sand, even down by the water's edge, feels softer than usual, and my sneakers sink more than they should. I probably won't get far. But I want to make sure I get to Silver Point. I want to check out that house again.

I do this all the time—I'm pretty sure ever since I was a kid. Whenever I go on walks or runs, I stake out the neighborhood, figure out which house I'd claim as mine. It passes the time. It's fun to daydream about what the house looks like on the inside.

We've been coming to this part of the coast since before my husband, Peter, died. It's the Reynolds family spot. Haystack Rock and Ecola Beach with Manzanita to the south: these are the places we visit as pilgrimage to the ocean from the desert of Idaho.

When we packed up this time, the thermometer at the house in Boise was creeping up on ninety-nine. It's been a few weeks since school let out, and the weather is already settling in for a long, hot Idaho summer. So we find refuge in rain and cool green forests that meet the ocean.

Here, on the beach south of the house we've rented for the week, huge rocks climb out of the sea. Silver Point has one lone stone monument that rises from the ocean, but the mainland also is solid rock there. At high tide, the Point is impassable. And the beach on the other side is stopped by another large rock field to the south of it, so if I am ever to go to that side of the Point, I always check the tide tables. I get a bit cautious. There's something terrifying to think of the sea crawling up as the tide changes, and I would be stuck on the rocks, and probably swept out to sea. That's being overly dramatic, because the tide doesn't come up in one fell swoop, but if for some reason a person wasn't paying attention to the sea's rumbling march, it wouldn't be a good place to get stuck.

But I'm running on the "safe" side of the Point, and the headland climbs stonily out of the sea. It's a dark, wet, solid face of rock as I approach, but the house I lust after perches above it.

When I'm close enough to find it, it has a new For Sale sign on its deck. A prominent sign, plastered on the house I chose a long time ago, on a run much like this one. *My dream house on the coast has a For Sale sign on it!*

This has happened before, from time to time, with a house I've taken a shine to, in some neighborhood where I like to run. But in the past, the only allure a For Sale sign has added is the possibility of a walk through and glimpse of the inside on an open house day.

Here's what's different: The guy I happen to be dating—that nice one waiting for me with the kids back at the house we are renting this week? He could snap this house up if I asked. We haven't gotten so crass as to talk directly about his net worth, but I'm not an idiot. I know he is very good at what he does, and after winning the award he did this past January, he could ask for the price of this house as payment for a few weeks' worth of work on a movie. It's a little dazzling to think about his stardom.

This is a weird quandary. I'd love to show Andrew this house, but just to share it with him. It's like when Tessa, my best friend in Boise, brings me yet another fluffy magazine to leaf through. I like to show her dresses that are cute. It's a bonding thing. I don't expect her to go out and buy them for me.

But guys—all guys—have a weird need to show off from time to time, especially when it comes to proving how worthy and competent they are at providing. Though I'd love to have Andrew join my ogling and speculating, it's pretty clear that this house will have to stay my little secret.

This is evolution, I tell you. Some things, people are compelled to do. I had a moment where I was poised to out-earn my late husband, Peter, when he was teaching at the university because he had to take several furlough days. It cut him to the core. He even thought about picking up another teaching job on the side.

It's not sexism. It's the drive to take care of your own.

Andrew is new to the game, but he's not immune. I had to impose a Lego moratorium on Hunter and Beau a few months ago. I forbade Andrew to buy any more Legos before we were buried in them. But he liked that he could take care of what the boys wanted.

I have money of my own, but it's pretty ridiculous to even have a money discussion with Andrew. It's important to me that I still have my little nest egg. I don't like complete dependence. It makes me uneasy. And I think Andrew understands that.

Oh, but a gorgeous house like this…It'd be a grand gesture, and I think he would love to snatch this up, slap a shiny bow on it, and gift it to me.

Nonetheless, the second I start asking Andrew for things, material things, I'm afraid we'll have turned our relationship into something really cheap and really nasty, bordering on payment for services rendered. And what we have is way too precious and special to cheapen it like that.

Still, I take a break from running to stalk the house.

The roof is peaked above an A-frame with three stories of large plate-glass windows. The weathered gray roof echoes the deck that stretches across the front of the house and wraps around it on both sides. Like a lot of the houses here, there are tempered glass panels enclosing the deck, breaking the relentless wind. There's a two-sided fireplace, with Adirondack chairs surrounding it on the deck. I imagine the interior side of the fireplace has a big slate hearth and overstuffed pillows on a plush rug with a distressed leather sofa and lived-in, beaten-up side chairs. All very Ralph Lauren: tired and worn but incredibly expensive, the preppy thing goes to the beach. Nothing ostentatious. Lots of weathered gray, sun-washed blues, stormy grays, driftwood whites.

I don't know how long I've been standing, gawking at the house, when someone grabs me by the waist.

"Gah!" I jump out of my skin. "Damn it, Andrew!"

He howls with laughter, picks me up, and spins me in a circle. "Hey! What are you daydreaming about? I could have been a grizzly bear sneaking up on you." He throws an arm around me and kisses me.

"No grizzly bears on this beach. Did you follow me down here? It's kind of a trek." I know I haven't been running very fast lately, but I didn't see him tailing me.

"Naw. I took the car down to get a cup of coffee at Sleepy Monk. I needed high-octane something this morning. This gray is harder core than LA's marine layer."

I look for the coffee cup. "Where is it?"

"Oh, I downed it already. There's a tea for you in the car if you want a ride back." He dances around a little. "I parked at the beach access a block up from here."

"Are you cold, LA baby?" I can't help but tease him. He and his fellow Angelenos operate with this weird expectation that all other places in the world have the perma-weather that they do: sixty degrees, no matter what time of year. Suspended animation of the jet stream or something.

The first day we were here, he wore his hoodie and got absolutely soaked to the bone. Today he's still got his hoodie on (I swear it's his security blanket, his "wubbie"), but he's added the Merrell shell I bought him in Portland and insisted he pack.

"Come on, I'm wet and cold, and you've been running, so I can suck all the body heat off of you when we get back." He smiles at the thought.

"It's just as well. I might as well be running in oatmeal. I think I got passed by a sea tortoise."

"I'll make you some brunch. I cooked bacon for the boys already." He turns me around on the sand and points me toward the beach approach. He casts a casual look at the promontory above us before we trot to the car. "Nice house."

We hustle to the car. Andrew cranks the heater.

"This is silly," I tell him. "You basically drove down the block to get me. I could've run back, you know. I need to redeem myself for weeks of crappy runs."

"I missed you. Time to come home, pet." He grins at me.

"Stop. I'll blush." I love it when he flirts.

"I hope so. There's a nice color to your cheeks right now, though. Nothing like a little sand blasting to give you a rosy glow." He turns on the wipers. "Everyone's allowed an off week or two. Maybe you should cross train or something. Yoga, maybe."

I sigh. "Maybe this is me getting old."

He shakes his head. "Oh lord, here we go. I will now say my required line: 'You're not old, you silly gorgeous young thing you.'"

"That sounds mean." I needle him a little.

"You sound ridiculous. You're thirty-seven. That's young, and I'm tired of the 'old' thing. It's a little insulting. You're insulting my hot girlfriend." He pulls a cup from the console. "Now drink your tea."

I take it, trying to pull the warmth of the tea into my damp and stiff fingers. "Thank you."

"You're welcome. And change the subject."

"What are the boys doing?" We pull into the driveway. The rain comes down harder. Looks like it's an inside day.

"Hunter was watching TV and eating a gigantic bowl of cereal. Beau was on your computer. I think he had nuclear launch codes or something."

"Ha ha." This is part of the beach routine. Hunter and Beau laze in bed until mid-morning. Beau hasn't declared a no-pants day yet, but I suspect one of these rainy mornings, he'll decide to spend the whole day watching TV and eating cereal out of the box in the loft of the house we've rented. It's not a vacation until someone stays in PJs from sunup to sundown.

I get out of the car and make a break for the house.

Andrew follows me inside, and it hits me right away. The smell of bacon. I gag. My stomach turns over; I swallow hard.

"Mom?" Concern washes over Hunter's face for the two seconds I see it before I run for the bathroom to puke my guts out.

The cold bathroom tile floor feels so good under my hands. It's actually a relief to throw up.

There's a knock at the door. Andrew's voice filters through. "You okay?"

"Come in here." The moment of relief has passed. Something is wrong, and I start to run through what it might possibly be.

Andrew comes in, a blanket in hand. He kneels and wraps me up. "What's wrong? Flu?"

"No. I don't think it's that. I can think of two things. One is remote and horrible, and the other is less remote but kind of shocking." I let him help me stand up.

"Which one do I want to hear?" He looks at me in the mirror. I try to avoid looking at the greenish sweaty face reflected back at me. His face is all clean lines and beautiful worry. When I catch a glimpse of myself in the mirror, even when I'm not vomitous, I am a sideshow mirror of weird postures and grimaces. I don't think Mr. Movie Star has an awkward pose. I've yet to see it, and I've been staring at him a lot over the last nineteen months. (Who's counting? Oh, that's right. I am.)

"The first one can't be true. It'd be that I have cancer, like Peter did. Nausea can be caused by tumors."

"Well, that idea is shit, so let me hear the second one." Andrew is deadly serious now.

"I'm pregnant." I gulp — I hear myself do it.

"Really?" He smiles.

"My runs suck, I'm tired as all get out, and smells make me hurl." The idea starts to sink down from my brain into my body, and I feel tears begin to climb up to my eyes.

"But we always use protection." His voice sounds lighter, higher.

"There's always that percentage. Read the directions, the pamphlets, there's always the possibility. I thought my period was late because it was getting less predictable—you know, because I'm getting older. Maybe not." The more I talk, the sadder I feel.

"How late?"

I think. It's been a while since I've had to keep track of this kind of stuff. "I guess beginning of May."

He smiles. "June got away from you, huh?"

"I just never..." I trail off.

Hunter and Beau will freak. A baby. My life will be turned upside down for the next four years. And the boys have been so wonderful, such little men. So much fun to relate to.

Andrew looks at me. "Why are you crying? Isn't this a good thing?"

I shrug. "I don't know." I can't say anything. I can't.

He looks hurt. "Don't you want a baby with me?"

"We're not married. I'm almost thirty-eight. I've been done for a while with being huge and babies and diapers and tantrums and no sleep. I made it through that stage seven years ago. Seven, Andrew! The boys are eleven and thirteen. Hunter'll be fourteen in September. To go back to it now...the thought is just exhausting." I pull the blanket around myself and check to make sure the bathroom door is shut tight. I don't want either son to overhear this conversation.

Andrew is quiet for a minute. "We should make sure. We're talking about something we don't even know yet. We're talking about nothing, as far as we know."

"It could be a bug. A virus," I say, but I know it's not. The second the idea formed in my brain, every part of me had that shocking realization. When someone describes how an idea "dawns" on you, this is what she's talking about. The sun rises, and it only sets in one direction. Not the other way, not ever.

"We'll run into town for the test. Then we can have this discussion." He pats my hand. "I'll tell the boys we're going in for milk, see if they need anything. It's a rainy, lazy day anyway. They'll probably be happy not to have to get fully dressed." He sounds chipper. But as he turns, just for the briefest second, I see a look of sadness.

He's disappointed in me. I think he was excited, and I shut him down so quickly. He's never had a child.

I'm such a bitch.

"Andrew, wait." I squeeze his hand. "Listen. It'll be good, either way. No matter what."

"Remember, this is an amazing gene pool you're swimming in," he tells me. "Imagine what a kid could be like with us for parents! An astonishingly good-looking professor of literature! An Olympic runner who does soap operas!" He flashes his smile and goes to tell the boys we're going into town.

I wash my mouth out, brush my teeth, comb through my hair, and put it up in a new ponytail. In the mirror, the green tinge in my face seems to have subsided. It's been replaced with an exhausted look. My thirty-seven-almost-thirty-eight-year-old face is pale and tired.

Slow down, Kelly. Breathe. I walk out into the living room and see Beau. He's wearing an impossibly small pair of shorts and an old soccer jersey. This is what I get when I let him pack for himself. He wants the independence.

I was so close. Am I starting all over again? Really?

I give his shoulder a little squeeze and glide out to the porch, escaping the bacon smell. The rain blows sideways. I feel wet tendrils of my hair immediately crawl into my mouth, whip into my eyes, and plaster my neck, driven out of the ponytail I just reset not two minutes ago.

But the cold, wet air feels fresh on my clammy skin. I try to breathe in as much of it as I possibly can.

"Come here, pet." Andrew is behind me, and he pulls me into him, wrapping his arms around me in the sideways rain.

"I'm sorry. Let's go get the test and start over." I tell him as I turn around and hide from the salt and spray in the folds of his coat. I smell him, a little Old Spice and his unmistakable Andrew smell, a faint hint of musky sweat, feel his breath on my neck.

"Let's go." He tilts my face up to him, kisses my forehead.

We drive to the Tolovana convenience store. Elvin, the Bosnian owner, comes to the door and holds it open as we rush in from the rain.

God love him. It suddenly strikes me that if we were anywhere else in the world and Andy Pettigrew, movie star, strolled in and bought a pregnancy test with his live-in girlfriend, we'd be sunk.

But Elvin, he would never tell a soul anything. His smile is broad and warm under his spidery mustache. He's maybe twenty-two. His dad died late last year of a heart attack, and Elvin came home from

Oregon State with a new degree in marketing and a business to run all of a sudden.

"Kelly and Andrew. Why are you out in such rotten weather?" There's the tiniest trace of a foreign accent in his speech. The only other clue to his heritage is next to the "We ID under 39" sign under the glass at the counter: the bumper sticker that says "Srebrenica 1995." It's a reminder of the turmoil that brought his family here in the first place.

Andrew looks positively placid. What an actor. This might be the performance that deserves a nomination. "Junk food. Possibly doughnuts. And a few other little odds and ends."

I roam the aisles for a few moments, praying and hoping that Elvin actually carries pregnancy tests. Otherwise we'll relive this ordeal in each little market farther north on the coast of Oregon until I may possibly die of the stress.

But, thankfully, there are two, snuggled in next to condoms, adult diapers, and stacks of kindling for beach bonfires. I check the expiration dates and pick both of them up.

"Are you ready?" Andrew looks at me, smiles as he puts three Gatorades and a bag of white powdered doughnuts on the counter.

"Yep." My voice is a tiny peep. I place the tests next to his pile.

And what happens next is an absolute miracle. Elvin looks down at the tests, looks up at me, and comes around the counter to give me a hug.

"This is good, right?" He looks me right in the eye.

I start to cry, but I can feel the smile on my face, and it's true and very wide. "If we are, then, yes, it's very good." I hug him tightly.

Leave it to me to have the first bonding moment of my pregnancy with the c-store owner, not Andrew. Kelly Reynolds, the complete and total social failure, as usual.

Andrew pays and slips an arm around my shoulder. He squeezes me tightly. "Mum's the word, Elvin. It's you, me, and Kelly for now."

"I give you my word, Andrew. The Reynolds family, they've been here every summer since when I was in high school, and Hunter and Beau were just little. And you, the big movie star, we've kept your secret, right? This one's the same, I promise." He gives us a thumbs-up for good measure.

We drive back to the beach house. Andrew holds my hand the whole way. Now I do feel a little excited. There are lots of good things about this. Pregnancy is just nine months. I'd never even considered that Andrew and I could have a child together. "You know, Andrew, the path of us just got a lot longer, if this is true." I watch his eyes, which are fixed on the rain, the windshield, and the road ahead.

He grins. "And what do you think of that?"

"I think I like it."

"I think I like it too." He turns his head to look at me, and his grin is even wider. He squeezes my hand.

We get back inside to find the both boys in the kitchen. Hunter has the frying pan out, and Beau cracks eggs into a bowl.

"Hey, guys." Andrew comes to Beau, gives him a side squeeze. "What're you making?"

"Scrambled eggs, the only thing we can make." Hunter digs through the drawers for a spatula.

"Not true. I can make macaroni and toast. Speak for yourself." Beau always bristles at any hint of dependence. He's determined to be his own man.

Hunter snorts. "Yeah, you're a regular Bobby Flay."

"I don't even know who that is." Beau shoves him.

Andrew intervenes. "I like the teamwork here. Can we just stick with that and skip the fighting? I'll wash dishes if you can get along."

Andrew's found a way to help parent without parenting. The boys don't see him as a father figure, but they respect him as an adult who loves them and wants to help. He's the cool guy in the house, but he never wavers on house rules, always backs me up when the boys chafe at responsibilities. I am lucky.

He shoots me a look over the boys' heads, nodding in the direction of the master suite.

Two seconds before I ask what he's waggling his eyebrows for, I remember the tests sitting in a bag on the kitchen table.

Hunter stands at the refrigerator. "I thought you guys went into town for milk. We're still out."

Andrew stalls. "Oh, yeah, that…" Here's hoping Andrew's acting can get us out of this. I let him handle it and make for the bathroom.

I use both of the sticks and stand at the bathroom counter, staring at pink lines. There's a knock on the door.

"Yes?"

12

"Let me in. I want to see the official results." Andrew nudges the door open.

"Not much to see yet." I hold up one of the sticks. There's still nothing in the second window.

He picks up the other one. "What am I looking for? And does this have pee all over it? Because now maybe I don't want to hold it."

"I have good aim; don't be gross. You're looking for another line in the second box."

"You mean like this?" He puts an arm around me and shows me the stick in his hand. It has lines, lines in both windows, pink and clear as day.

We're pregnant. Officially. I look at him, and he picks me up in his arms. He kisses me hard, and I smile under his kiss.

Beau is at the door. "What? What's going on?" Andrew didn't shut the bathroom door. Beau stands there, curious.

Now I panic. "Umm…" Are we telling them now? How are we doing this?

Andrew takes charge. "Come on out in the living room. We have something to share with you and your brother."

"What?" Beau wants to know now.

Andrew puts a hand on his shoulder, steers him to the living room, sits next to him on the couch. Andrew's face is still completely neutral, relaxed.

Hunter has a plate of eggs and brings it to the coffee table. "What's up?"

Andrew starts. "Well, boys, I've been with you all for a while now, and I just want to tell you again how much I love both of you. And you know how much I love your mom."

Hunter looks suspicious. "But what?"

"But nothing. We have some news." Andrew looks at me. I guess it's my turn.

"Guys, I'm going to have a baby." I sit down on the other side of Beau and give him a squeeze.

Hunter smiles. "Really? Cool!"

"It's really, really early, so it'll be a while before we tell anyone."

"How come?" Hunter is still smiling.

"Sometimes babies have a hard time early in the pregnancy, so we need to make sure everything is fine before we tell a lot of people."

Beau stands up. "How come you didn't ask us first?" His brow darkens.

Uh-oh. "Oh, honey, sometimes things just happen." I don't know if I want to say that we weren't planning on the baby.

"Sometimes we have to see if things can happen before we tell you too. It's not always a sure thing when you're having a baby." Andrew smiles up at Beau.

"I don't want a little brother." Beau frowns, and tears well up in his eyes.

"Beau, it's going to be fine." I don't know what to say. It's been a long time since I've had to have a conversation like this. And Hunter was a little, little boy. Beau's got a lot more awareness than a toddler.

"No, no, it's not. I don't need a younger brother. I like the way things are right now." He runs out of the room to his bedroom.

I start to get up, but Andrew puts a hand on my knee. "Give him a minute." He turns to look at Hunter. "What about you, Hunter? How are you with this?"

Hunter shrugs. "I don't know. I think I like it. I'm happy for you guys." Something dawns on him. "You're not married. Do you need to get married? Wait. This means—never mind." He grins for a second and then picks up his plate of eggs. "I'm not thinking about that part—more than I need to know about my mom." He gives me a peck on the cheek and offers Andrew up a fist bump. "I'm going to eat in the TV room."

And he's gone.

"Andrew, poor Beau." I feel confused and cloudy, and tears threaten to choke me up.

He pats my leg. "Change is hard. This is huge. He doesn't have to love it right now. Don't push him. We'll just love him up, and when the baby comes, we'll love him up then too. It's going to be different. I promise I won't sugar-coat it for him. But I suspect when there's a little somebody who worships the ground he walks on, he'll start to feel differently about it."

"That could be true." Beau will be a spectacular big brother. I can see him now, doting on the little one. It'll be amazing to watch. "He'll love having a little brother."

Andrew chuckles. "A brother, huh?"

"Just a hunch." I feel a smile forming at the thought of another little guy toddling around.

"Or, an assumption. So, on to Hunter's question." Andrew looks at me, steady and clear blue eyes searching mine.

"What?"

"Do we need to get married?" He holds my gaze.

"I hadn't even thought about that. I don't know, Andrew."

"Well, just for the record, I'm game." He leans forward and kisses my bottom lip, gives it a little nip, sending a shiver down my spine.

"Actually, I do think I know what I want."

"Yes?" He's curious.

"I want to call a time out on this discussion. I want a real-deal proposal. I want it to be a surprise, and I want it to happen when we have time to plan whatever amazingly cool kind of wedding we want."

"If we're having this conversation, you're not going to be very surprised that I propose. Clearly it's something I want, and you don't seem opposed to it, either."

"I know that. But when Peter and I decided to get married, we had a very similar, very practical discussion, and then he took me to pick out my ring. This time, I want you to surprise me. Nothing practical. So, time out. This conversation never happened."

"I can get on board with that. I will hunt down the Eye of the Tiger and give it to you while we are in a hot air balloon above an active volcano. When you least suspect it. We're going big. Very big."

"The baby takes first priority right now. You're not allowed to propose to me while I'm huddled over the toilet, sick as a dog. And no proposing while I'm in labor. I will kill you if you do that. I guarantee."

He gets up to go do the dishes the boys have left. "I promise. None of that. Now leave me to my creative thoughts. I'm thinking about a trained monkey or possibly Donald Trump. Maybe a marching band."

I stick my fingers in my ears. "Not listening. We're not having this conversation. You're going to surprise me."

He laughs and kisses me on the forehead as he heads for dish duty. "What were we talking about? I've forgotten."

All this change coming at me so fast, and just when we were settling into being a family. It wasn't until after Andrew's rehab that we were even officially and publically a couple. That's only been about a year. So much for a nice boring stretch of just living and existing and enjoying the status quo. But I can't help but smile. Nothing ever stays neat in my life. Messy is how we do.

FIREWORK

A few days later we decide, in light of my recent frequent puking, not to go into town for the 4th of July parade. But Cannon Beach allows fireworks on the beach at night, and I'm surrounded by pyromaniacs. So, that's the grand plan for Independence Day: hang around and grill assorted meat and then light stuff on fire and watch the Oregon wind whip the flames out as soon as they're started.

"You don't have to come down with us. You could watch from the deck if you want," Hunter tells me.

He's not trying to be helpful. He's trying to get rid of me. I'm not dumb. I'm the mom that doesn't want people's fingers blown off. This tends to put a damper on all sorts of outlandish and literally explosive ideas.

"I'm coming. Nice try, though."

"Andrew's coming with. He can handle us." Beau packs up the beach chairs and the clever Oregon beach invention, the wind break. It's a portable big screen to huddle behind when the wind tries to scour off the first layer of our faces. Though at sunset, the wind seems to be calmer than it has been in a few days. The sun leaks through the gray and turns strips of ocean hot pink, streaking clouds with fuchsia and orange.

I shake my head. "I was going to take some pictures. And you don't need adult supervision; you need female supervision. Andrew's as much of a guy as you two — he wants to set stuff on fire too."

"Not true. I want to blow stuff up." Andrew walks out onto the deck with a bag stuffed with towels and blankets. A few hours ago he and Hunter dragged and lugged and carried wood for the fire down to the high, wide sand at the top of the beach.

"You're not helping." I look him up and down. I swear, he always makes an entrance. He's just wearing old, worn jeans and a red long-sleeved T-shirt, but it's the way he wears them. His broad shoulders, the ease with which he carries his lanky frame, the mischief in his blue eyes. I'm biased, but he's just so damn handsome.

"Are you going to come with us?" Beau looks annoyed.

"At least for a while, yes." I give him a little hug as he shrugs, resigned that the party pooper will be coming.

Hunter isn't so subtle. "Well, dang. There go the M-eighties."

"They're not even legal. Who bought M-eighties?" I cast a scolding look at Andrew.

"Hey, is that my cell phone ringing in the kitchen?" Andrew smiles slyly and drops the bag of stuff on the deck, making his escape.

After much hauling of chairs, blankets, fireworks, hot dogs, and s'mores supplies, the whole Pettigrew/Reynolds family unit settles down around a bonfire on the beach. Hunter obsessively stokes it, adding kindling and bits of newspaper. Beau lights sparkler after sparkler.

"Andrew! Watch this one and see what I'm spelling. See if you can guess." Beau takes a punk and touches it to the tip of the sparkler. It sets off a shower of sparks, and Beau swings the sparkler in the growing darkness.

"I think you're spelling July." Andrew sits with his arm around me. I snuggle into his warmth. The wind comes and goes, but the air cools at our ankles. I shiver at the conflicting sensation of warm and cool, the fire and the wind.

"Yes! You're good at this." Beau lets the sparkler go out.

Andrew motions to the big wrapped box of fireworks. "Why don't you and your brother get the main-attraction fireworks out?"

Hunter hears this and leaps up. He bounds like a puppy to the box. He and Beau drag it away from the circle of the bonfire, begin to tear the plastic off of it.

"Oh, boy. I may go back to the house. This part is all about you menfolk and your evolutionary obsessions."

I make a move to see if I can get up.

"Wait." Andrew pats my knee. He turns in his spot, faces me.

"What?"

He reaches in his pocket for something. "Before we blow ourselves up, I just wanted to give you this."

He pulls out the twist tie from the hot dog bun package. It's twisted in the shape of a ring. "Kelly Reynolds, will you marry me?"

I laugh and hold out my hand. "Where's the Eye of the Tiger?"

"I've arrived at a brilliant idea. I'm going to propose multiple times — so many times you can't stand it. And you won't be able to tell which is the official, last 'real' proposal. It's a perfect fake-out."

"And you're doing it this way because?"

"Because I kind of ruined the element of surprise the other day, and I feel bad about it." He holds out the twist tie. "Will you marry me?"

"Am I supposed to say no until I like the proposal or say yes all the time?" I fold my arms across my chest, give him a little grief.

"I hadn't thought that part through, to be honest."

"Well, this time, I'm saying yes. But don't count on it each time. You must woo and wow me with your novel approaches. You should remain on your toes."

"I can do that. But you have to say yes more emphatically than that."

"Okay. Yes, Andrew Pettigrew, I will be your wife." I hold my left hand out with a flourish.

He slides the twist tie on it. "Excellent. Oh, and you have to wear whatever ring it is until I give you the next version. That's a rule, too."

I shake my head. "You're crazy, but I'll do it."

"You love it."

"I love you."

He stands and helps me get up. "And I love you. Now go inside so we can blow stuff up." He kisses me, wraps the blanket around me for better walking, and gives me a playful pat on the butt to start me up the beach to the house.

HOW DO YOU SOLVE A PROBLEM LIKE MARIA

"I think it might be best to tell my mom in person." Andrew says this as he crunches on an apple in the Red Carpet Lounge of the Portland airport. It's the second week of July, we're headed to New York for rehearsals on Andrew's new movie, and he drops this bombshell on me.

"What?" I think I just choked on my ginger ale.

"My mom. Telling my mom. I think we better tell her in person."

"Are we doing that already? I didn't tell my folks about the boys until we were out of the first trimester."

"If she hears from a tabloid, I'm dead. She'll send my dad out to LA to kill me. Or hire a mafia hit squad."

"She's not like that."

"You've never met her in person. Talking to her on the phone does not count. My mom is…" He sighs, takes another bite of his apple. "Complicated."

"You hardly say anything about her. Your sisters are nice. You're mostly well-adjusted. Your dad's still married to her. She has to be at least somewhat normal."

"Look, let's you and I hash out a way to go see her."

"What, you mean now? Go see her now?"

"The boys are flying to see your folks. We've got a couple days before I absolutely have to be in New York. We could change our flights right now…"

Which is how I ended up driving a rented Prius through the Pennsylvania green farmland on this Thursday night. It's hot, sticky, and the bugs are yelling from the jungle-thick brush that lines the road. The sky is inky black, and the air smells like rain.

I'm driving so Andrew can get a hold of his folks. He tries to text his mom again.

"She has a smartphone. This is ridiculous."

"She wants you to call her. She won't text you. You're supposed to call and tell her we're here. Or she's very pissed about the late notice and is punishing you."

Andrew sighs and tosses the phone on the console in front of him. "It's probably all of that. Dad was fine with it."

"Your dad is a guy. Guys don't realize what kind of cleaning is involved in house guests. You have created a huge trauma for her."

"You mean *we*." He points a finger at me, then at him. "We're in this together."

"Yes, and I want to thank you again for that. She's going to flip out when she finds out we're having a baby. But first, she's just going to be plain mad about the inconvenience."

"I offered for us to stay in a hotel."

"No mom is going to tell you to stay at a hotel. Even if it would be easier."

"Hey, you just missed the turn."

"Hey, I've never been to your house before. Geez, Andrew!" I slow the car down, look for a wider spot in the road, whip a U-turn, and make a wild left into the development.

I drive through the neat, colonial-style subdivision. The houses all look vaguely the same: brick and white wood trim, shake roofs, everything very orderly. The macadam road gently winds its way through tall pine trees. I can't help but feel like these roads could be the same ones Peter and I drove when we were first married.

I'll admit it; the East Coast makes me break out in a cold sweat. Okay, I love New York. It's just the rest of the eastern seaboard I hate.

My time in Virginia has Peter's fingerprints all over it, and it brings back too much from my "other" life. It was the beginning of a tough road, but I didn't know it then.

Plus, the girls I knew here in college were all about pearls and flats and matching handbags and no white after Labor Day. I don't wear white, ever. It shows stains. I don't like pearls. I fit better other places. I'm more messy snow and dirt trails and running clothes.

"Are you listening?" Andrew pokes me.

"What?"

"Next house on the left. Casa Pettigrew."

I slow the car. "The beige one?"

"That's the one. There's Dad." Andrew sits up, carries his shoulders a little straighter.

Ugh, parents. How nerve-racking can they be? Peter's were very polite, and they also lived in upstate New York, which helped. Good fences make good neighbors; multiple-state buffers make good in-laws.

And my parents are very sweet. I love them very much, but everything with them takes about twenty minutes longer than it should. Talk about nerve-racking—calling them to tell them I was having a baby? They always put me on speaker, and this time, I got to hear all of their reactions in gory detail when I sprung the news. Mom started crying, and Dad wanted a detailed run-down of the risks since I was, "you know, getting up there in age." As if I needed a reminder about that. But then Mom called me Bug and got excited about making something special, maybe a quilt, for the baby and then started crying again when she realized it was Andrew's first time as a dad, and then she started reminiscing about Dad's reaction when they found out she was pregnant with me. That phone call forced me to lie down with a damp washcloth over my eyes. A rollercoaster of emotion all carried out via cell.

We park and get out. Andrew strolls to his dad, puts out a hand for a shake.

We're huggers, my family. It always makes me sad when a dad doesn't hug his son. Maybe it's just me.

"Kelly, so good to see you again. How was your flight?"

"Hi, Hugh. The trip was uneventful, so that's good." I get a little hug.

He looks at Andrew. "Your mom's so excited to see you. We were really surprised to hear from you, to hear you were coming."

I can hear the code in that: What are you doing here? You never call. You never visit.

"Is she inside?"

"Of course." Andrew's dad says this with a touch of sadness. That's what it sounds like to me, at least.

We walk in without the bags, and I resist the urge to stay out at the car and putter. We have to be a team on this announcement, this visit.

Andrew's dad opens the front door. A brown and white Papillion comes skidding around the corner and barks in little shrill yaps. Hugh scoops it up. "Hush you, Barnaby."

"New dog?" Andrew reaches out to scratch its chin. It nips at him.

"Your mom was lonely." He turns and calls to the rest of the house. "Maria! They're here!"

Andrew walks past him, strolls into the kitchen at the end of the front hall. "You painted in here. I like it."

"We had to take out that magnolia in the backyard too. It was rotten in the roots."

"Huh. I liked that tree." Andrew sifts through the mail on the table. There's a weird disconnect. He's at ease here, like he's just come in to grab a glass of milk out of the fridge, but the conversation with Hugh bumps and stalls like an old car smoking and sputtering down the road.

"Andrew!" Maria comes into the kitchen with her arms out.

"Hi, Mom." He comes to her, hugs her for a good long squeeze.

I've never actually laid eyes on her. Hugh's been out to LA for some special occasions since Andrew and I started seeing each other, but Maria has never flown on a plane. Ever. I've yet to get the story on that.

Maria has a red cable sweater over her petite frame, with pearls at the neck and khaki slacks. Her dark hair is bobbed neatly below the ears. She wears patent navy flats.

From what Andrew has said, she doesn't go out much. She doesn't like to drive. She goes to the grocery store and church and the country club—that's about it. But looking at her, you'd think we were headed to dinner downtown, even though it's more like bedtime.

"You must be Kelly." She clasps my free hand with both of hers, gives it a gentle shake. Not a hugger either, I guess.

"It's wonderful to finally meet you, Mrs. Pettigrew." I feel like a last-name basis goes with a shake over a hug.

"Please, it's Maria. Would you like a glass of water?"

She pulls out a chair at the kitchen table for me, and I sit. I am the obedient, gracious girl who just got knocked up by her son. This is going to be painful.

"That'd be great. Airplanes always dehydrate me."

"It's especially important now," Andrew says.

"What?" I shoot him a scrunched-up-face look. Give us a minute before you kill them with this news, big guy. Yikes.

"Summer in the land of humidity." He mouths "stop" to me when she turns her back to get a glass.

"How's the biz, son?" Hugh stands behind the chair next to me, but I'm the only one who has sat so far. I feel short.

"Good, Dad."

"What're you up to? Any big deals in the works?"

"You know Jeremy; he likes to keep me busy. I'm on my way to New York. We'll start shooting in a couple weeks."

Maria brings me the water and sits across from me at the table. "What will you do while Andrew is gone, Kelly?"

"She's going with me, Mom. The boys too."

"Really? How nice." She smiles, no teeth. The way that *really* just came out sounded pained.

"I couldn't pass up a chance to show the city to everybody. Re-member the first time I went with Todd and his folks? Maybe the boys will love it as much as I did."

"Uh-huh. And where are they right now?"

"In LA with my parents. Getting some quality grandparent time," I explain.

"Speaking of grandparents—"

Oh God, here he goes.

"Oh, you should see little Avery. She's adorable." This is Lizbeth's daughter, Andrew's niece. Mama Pettigrew already has grandkids.

"I bet she is, Mom. We're pregnant."

"What?" She sets her glass of water down with a plunk.

"We? Who's we?" Hugh sounds confused.

"Kelly's going to have a baby, Dad. With me."

So much for this going well. I guess Andrew decided to take the Band-Aid route. It's news that just needs to be torn off.

"When are you due?" Maria looks right at me, and I feel a chill.

"We're not super sure yet—we just found out ourselves," I tell her. "We wanted you to be one of the first to know and didn't want it to get to you some other way."

"Are you going to get married? And what about a pre-nup?" Maria's eyebrows knit together in a deep V.

Andrew just looks tired.

"Don't just go getting married because of the baby." Hugh's voice is louder, annoyed.

Guess I won't show him my hot dog twist-tie engagement ring. I feel positively frozen now.

"We're not going to do that thing where we have a conversation about someone in the room as if they're not here, are we?" Andrew stands behind me and puts a protective hand on my shoulder. "We'll get married when we want to, before or after, whatever we choose. And I'd write her a check with all my money right now if she wanted it. This is it. Kelly's the one."

He stops, and we all remain sitting or standing, quiet. I can't help but smile at his words. I really want to give him a big fat kiss. But I'm going to hold still and stay silent instead. I sure as hell won't be the one to say anything next. I'm staying as far out of this as I can.

Man, am I sick of Andrew defending me to other people. First, co-star Franca and Jeremy the agent, now his parents. Am I that much of an albatross around his neck? I guess I had to defend him to my folks and Tessa when we went through his rehab, so maybe we're almost even.

Maria picks up both water glasses and goes to put them in the sink. "We're very happy for you, son. It's a big step, that's all. I'm sure Kelly can tell you that."

"Of course. Of course it is." That's all I get out. I dazzle with my articulate speech under pressure.

"Mom, Dad, I love you both to pieces. Hear me when I say that this is good. I'm happy and healthy—the healthiest I've been since I went out to Hollywood, probably. It's been more than ten years, and I'm ready for this. And I care about you and love you, which is why we're here, telling you the news." He walks to the sink, puts his hands on his mom's shoulders.

She turns around. There are tears in her eyes. "I guess I just thought at some point you'd come back. Come back home, settle down here. Now you don't have a reason to."

"A reason to come back? I'll always come back to visit with my family, Mom. I know it's been crazy, but things will eventually slow down."

"No, they won't. Kids mean you'll be busy. Your sisters are always too busy to come home." She takes a tissue from a box on the kitchen counter, dabs at her eyes delicately.

"You could come see me, Mom. Dad's been out. Maybe it's time you get past the flying thing."

"We're not talking about me. We're talking about the fact that you're starting a family with a woman who's already been married, has already had kids, isn't in your business, doesn't have money of her own."

I swallow hard. Don't take that bait, Andrew. She's your mom; don't do it. "Maria, it's okay. This is big news for everyone. I love Andrew with all my heart. I promise." Maybe this will stop him.

"Mom, would you like us to stay or should we head on toward New York tonight?"

Her face goes blank. "What?"

"If you can't give me credit for choosing who I love, and for having a brain in my head, maybe we should move on tonight."

Hugh slaps the newspaper in his hand down on the table. "All of this is ridiculous. We've stayed by your side from the time you left for LA, through the soap opera jobs, through your ups and downs, through rehab, through all of it. Let's not get ahead of ourselves and say things we'll regret later."

"And Kelly's been with me through the worst of it too. We're a package deal. Me and Kelly and Hunter and Beau and the baby. That's the way it is." Andrew takes her hand. "We'll come visit. But you could come out to see us too."

"Andrew…" She puts her other hand on his, squeezes it.

"Please, Mom. Please." He looks at her.

"Just give me some time." She lets go and walks out of the kitchen.

Hugh looks at me. "It's a lot to digest. That's all. I'm sure it's all occurred to you too."

I think he's campaigning for some help here.

I nod. I don't know these people. I don't know the family dynamic. I do know that family is complicated. It just is.

Hugh turns to Andrew. "Son, please stay tonight. You know your mother. You brought up the flying thing. You can't expect a good outcome when you do that."

"It's been the elephant in the room forever. Now she won't even go to the mall, Lizbeth said. Someone has to say something about it."

"Well, that someone doesn't need to be the son who never comes home, unless it's to drop a bombshell like a pregnancy-out-of-wedlock on us."

"Twenty-first century, Dad. It's the twenty-first century. I don't even think the word *wedlock* is still in the dictionary."

Hugh pinches the bridge of his nose. Funny, I've seen Andrew do that too. They look a lot alike, especially through the eyes and cheekbones. I always thought he might look more like his mom. Hugh finally says something. "Let's all get some sleep. Give your mom the morning, at least. Let this sink in. Don't go storming off." He puts a hand on Andrew's shoulder, tilts his head and raises his eyebrows. "Okay?"

Andrew relents. "Okay."

"I'm going up. The sheets are clean on the bed in the guest room. See you in the morning."

Andrew sits at the table with me for a minute. "Want to leave? We can just go. Say the word."

"I'd love to take off. But you know we need to stay. They're your folks, Andrew. They always will be. You need to give them a chance."

"I knew you'd say that. Want a cup of tea?" He gets up to look through the cabinet.

"Show me around. Where's your old room?"

"Down the hall." He points.

"Let's go." I stand up and take him by the hand.

He walks me down the hall. There are tons of family pictures hanging: he and his two sisters, all towheaded, posed in a little circle in front of a fountain; the family in front of Niagara Falls; Andrew and his dad with fishing poles.

"Look at all these memories. You look like the perfect family."

"Oh, I learned to be an actor from somewhere. I'll tell you all the sordid details someday when we're trapped together in an elevator for hours or something." A trace of bitterness clings to his words.

We stop at a panel door. "Here it is, the famous lair of Andrew Pettigrew, boy wonder."

He swings the door open. I step in to a sewing room. "What?"

"I told you, my mom converted my room the second I left for LA. No shrine to Andy Pettigrew in here."

"Aw, that's kind of sad." I look at the sewing machine, the card table in the corner, the rolls of gift wrap hanging on the wall, organized by holiday.

"They had faith in my success, maybe…knew I wasn't going to come crawling back a failure."

"So much for having sex in your childhood bed." I elbow him, trying to get him to smile.

"Now that is a bummer. I could make up for all of the failed attempts in my teen years."

"Not a lot of luck with the ladies?"

"Todd was the ladies' man. I never really figured it out."

"Your fans would be shocked." I turn around, plant a kiss on his lips, and smack his butt.

"Watch it, girl! This is a wholesome and decent family's home."

"I've been corrupted by a Hollywood lothario. Can't help it."

"I'm not going to get up to no good with you in a sewing room. Not gonna do it."

"Well, let's go look for a more suitable place." I wink and lead him out the door.

I don't sleep much. A guest room in a strange house, Andrew tossing and turning next to me, and absolute terror for the awkward morning that awaits keep my eyes wide open. I can't imagine how the next talk with Andrew's parents is going to go.

I've never been much for confrontation. It's so much easier to run in the opposite direction. Andrew never seems afraid to have the big conversations, and I admire that about him. I wonder if the movie business requires a certain boldness. Andrew would be trampled by all the hungry actors looking for a break if he weren't able to hold his own and speak his mind, I suppose.

It's a relief when he sits up on his side of the double bed before seven.

"Are you up?" he whispers.

"Never really went down. Not a good night's sleep." I sit up too and cuddle into his back, strong and broad under the white T-shirt he slept in.

"Let's go down. I have an idea for the olive branch." He stands and slides on his jeans.

"Thank God for that. I spent a good chunk of the night trying to find a way to redeem myself."

"And?"

"I got nothin'."

"Get dressed, because I'm taking you and the fam-damily golfing."

"What?" Maybe I'm not awake yet, because I think Andrew just said we were golfing.

"Golf. My folks love golf. I'm going to fix this."

"I thought your mom didn't like going out."

"The country club she can manage. I try not to ask too many questions."

"I don't golf. I haven't since my grandmother got kicked out of the Sevier County Country Club."

"What was that for?"

"She said it was okay that the four-year-old French twins wore Speedos in the country club pool. The rest of the social committee thought it was immoral."

Andrew stretches and runs a hand through his messy brown hair, ruffling it more into place. "Scandal. Well, Hugh and Maria like golf, and I'm decent at it, and you can whack the ball around and drive our cart."

"And then we leave first thing tomorrow?"

"It's the best I can do. I can't push the visit any longer. I have a movie to shoot."

I stand up and give him a kiss. "Golf is a brilliant idea. Otherwise we have to stare at each other for a day. Might as well have a purpose."

Andrew can be a charming guy, and a persuasive one too. At a rather frosty breakfast, he talks his mom and dad into a round of golf at the local country club. Hugh is a member, but Andrew's called in some favors too, so we'll get a prime tee time and any other first-class perks he can think of.

We drive in Hugh's Cadillac to the club. I keep quiet, finding the Pennsylvania countryside intensely intriguing, in hopes that I can keep from making anyone cranky before we even get there.

The golf pro's arranged everything for us, so in swift succession we have clubs, carts, and arrive at the tee box for the first hole.

Maria wears a cute pink and green outfit with a matching wind-breaker. Her golf glove is worn smooth on the palm and fingers. She knows what she's doing on the course, obviously, and her straight, long drive down the fairway is further proof of that.

Andrew's good at everything, so he's next and pounds the ball down the course.

Hugh whistles. "I thought you didn't like golf, son. That was quite a drive."

"I don't like it much. But producers love it. Deals get made on LA courses." He hands me a driver from my borrowed bag of clubs, and I say a silent prayer.

I step up to the tee and try to channel my grandma's abilities. "You all might want to look alive," I joke, but for a split second I pray that I don't bean Andrew's mother. I'd be done for sure.

The club head connects with the ball, and I do that "look down the fairway" thing I've seen golfers do on television. My freshman suitemate in college watched golf when hung over; she liked it that the commentators whispered.

"Andrew, you didn't tell me Kelly played golf." Hugh seems impressed.

"She didn't tell me."

"Beginner's luck." I owe my grandma for the angelic assist.

We get in two carts and head down the fairway. Andrew drives and puts an arm around my shoulder as we follow Hugh and Maria's cart. "Okay, Miss LPGA, you may just get on my folks' good side faster than I thought."

"I have no idea what I'm doing." I suspect I will pull a muscle before day's end.

"That's fine. Keep having no clue." He hums a little tune that sounds suspiciously like the *Caddyshack* theme.

We make our way around the course, and my luck holds. I can't putt from any kind of distance, but I'm able to keep driving the ball down the course far enough to make it on the green in a decent number of swings.

Hugh loosens up at about hole number six, a long dogleg to the left with bunkers on both sides of the green. When he asks Andrew if we're naming our baby Jack Nicklaus, I think we've turned a corner with him.

But Maria stays quiet.

When we're on number fifteen, I finally start to fade. It's after lunchtime, and I'm hungry, and my back is starting to hurt. Plus, the humidity makes me queasy. The drive I'm able to manage off the tee hooks left hard.

"And it's in the water." Andrew gives me a high five.

"My streak is officially over." I rub my back.

I drop another ball and make it down the fairway this time. We go to get in the carts, and Hugh motions to his. "Kelly, come ride with me. Your boyfriend needs some time with his mother."

I do as he says. Andrew raises his eyebrows hopefully over his sunglasses.

I'm grateful for the cart ride. "I'm getting tired. The rest of this could get pretty ugly, Hugh."

He nods. "I'm sorry about last night. We were just surprised."

Thank God he's not angry. "We were too."

He looks at me. "Really?"

"I love Andrew more than anything, and now I'm excited, but I thought I was done."

Hugh nods, without looking at me, and looks out into the thick leafy forest at the edge of the fairway. "The longer you live it, the more life surprises you."

"I couldn't agree more. I figured on a long and boring life with Peter."

"Your husband. Andrew told me about him. I'm sorry, Kelly."

I'm ready to change the subject. "The universe has a lot of plans that I don't get consulted on, apparently. But the one where Andrew and I get to have a child together I never thought was in the cards. It's a gift I didn't even consider."

Hugh pats my hand. "What do you think? Can you stand us as in-laws, grandparents to your child?"

"Can you stand me as your daughter-in-law?"

He pulls the cart to the end of the path. "More than stand. Andrew loves you; we love you. And look at him."

We turn to see the other cart driving up behind us. Andrew has his arm around his mom, and he's got her laughing about something. The man's a miracle worker, I tell you. I look at Hugh. "She doesn't look mad anymore."

"She was never mad. She just had to see he was happy. And I haven't seen him stand so tall since he went out to Hollywood. You've brought him peace. I'm on board with that."

Andrew gets out of the cart and pulls a putter to go to the green. I smile at him, and he gives the brim of his Ping visor a little tip. I look at Hugh. "In that case, let's put this round out of its misery, shall we?"

He pats me on the shoulder, and we follow Maria and Andrew to the green. "Maybe you can bring the little tyke out for golf lessons when he's bigger." He says this loud enough for Andrew to hear.

"You hear that, Andrew? Your dad thinks it's a boy too."

Andrew shakes his head. "The campaigning has no effect on the outcome, Kells. This isn't the Academy Awards." He motions me to him. "Come here a minute before we finish this hole."

I walk across the spongy turf, putter in hand. "What?"

He bends down on one knee and takes out a stainless steel ball marker, attached to a ring fashioned out of grip tape. He takes my left hand, slides the twist-tie off and slides the ball marker on. "Will you marry me?"

I laugh out loud. "On a golf course?"

Maria looks confused. "What, is he proposing?"

I look at her. "It's a long story."

Andrew shakes his head. "I like to propose. I'm only getting married once, but no one said I couldn't propose lots."

Hugh rolls his eyes. "Andrew never can do something without a production. We knew from the time he was five he'd be an actor. Always the center of attention."

Maria points to the ball marker. "Is this real? Are you really going to get married?"

"Yes, Mom." Andrew stands up and kisses me. I haven't let go of my putter yet.

"That's not the ring you're giving her."

I kiss Andrew again and smile wide under his lips. "He's working up to the Eye of the Tiger."

Hugh walks over to his ball and sinks it in the hole without so much as a look. He points to the fairway behind us and walks back to the golf cart. "Time to wrap it up, kids. The Yorks want to play through."

TELL ME YOU LOVE ME

Three days later, up-and-coming actress Amanda Walters sits next to me at a long, white conference table in New York City. She has a Starbucks cup in one hand and her copy of the shooting script in the other. Her red hair tumbles down her back, and I can't help but remember my hands tangled up in it. She was amazing in bed.

But a mess everywhere else—the true definition of a hot mess.

And though I've made it crystal clear to Kelly and anyone else who will listen that I'm not interested in having anyone but Kelly in my life, Amanda Walters doesn't make anything easy. She's not a temptation for me—not in the slightest—but Amanda never lets anything go. What I'm worried about now is how this red-headed freight train of crazy will be received by my currently-very-tenderhearted Kelly.

I grew up with sisters, and it was a good way to grow up. I mean it when I say I appreciate and admire women's strength, tenderness, and instinct. But now that I've made that clear, I also have a gripe. What I hate about women is the insecurity. I can meet the most amazing girl, but she's consumed by it. I mean, I don't walk around feeling like God's gift, but I also couldn't live my life if I were a quivering mass of "Do you like me?" and "Are you mad at me?"

That's the thing that gets me. It pisses me off that Kelly still sometimes can't see how I feel about her. She can't feel how badly I want to touch her when I'm close to her. How I would take a bullet for her.

Since that first visit to Boise, I've wanted her to be mine. She is *mine*. I want to possess every inch of her, and she has the audacity to look up at me with those eyes and ask if I still like her.

Seriously? When a man says he wants to move in with you, it's not because he's wishy-washy. It's because he wants his life to be your life.

Believe it. End of story. Let it go.

Right now, if I could shut Amanda's ass in a packing crate and ship her to eastern Katmandu, I would. I'm not an idiot. She is trouble, and she is bat-shit crazy. And she could send my significant other into orbit. Around the moon. Make my life a living hell.

It certainly doesn't help that Kelly is carrying my child. You'd think the fact that she is "ripe with my heir" (too much *Game of Thrones* for me) would give her some reassurance that I want her in my life. But apparently in early pregnancy all it does is invite comparison between hers and other women's asses. Her mind tells her I will see the fertile spread of her derriere, and I will ditch her for some bounce-a-dime-on-it perky butt sashaying around dangerously close to me.

Women are exhausting.

Specifically, one particular woman named Kelly is exhausting. One maddening, amazing, soft-hearted woman who clearly does not truly get the way I feel about her. Jesus.

So, what has put me in the middle of this sure-to-be mess? Mandy and Andy, that's what.

Almost seven years ago, Amanda and I were in a movie together: *Redcoats Rising*. We were both pretty young, and it was one of the first big movies I did. She came from England; I came from a soap opera.

Neither of us was the star of the movie. We were the son and the son's love interest. But we could tell it was going to be a big deal. The movie was going to break both of us out of working-actor oblivion.

And we were right. We got some attention for our acting, but when we started dating, the attention really ramped up. Lots of pictures walking from lunch at the Ivy or outside Chateau Marmont in the early morning hours of a late, late night. It was kind of heady. It was a good six months of tabloid chatter and paparazzi mayhem. And in her native UK, we got the nickname "Mandy and Andy."

It didn't last, the attention—and our relationship either. She did a lot of yelling, I did a lot of drinking, and when we went to Cannes for the premiere of her first "serious" indie movie, she threw a plate at my head in the Majestic suite of the Hotel Barriere. I kind of took that as a hint to quit while I was ahead (or still had a head).

But ever since, Jeremy has been jonesing to get the two of us to work together again. And when the script for this movie came my way, I did like it, a lot. Even though Amanda was already attached to it.

So, I said yes. I may regret it later. I may regret it sooner than later—we'll see.

The movie—*The Bull, the Bear, and the Dragon*—is about a young trader (me) who realizes a Chinese diplomat in America is maneuvering to launch a cyber-attack on the U.S. stock markets. He also suspects the NSA may have put the Chinese spy up to the sabotage. Lots of intrigue, and I'm on screen for most of the movie.

We also get to film almost exclusively in New York. Yes, I have to put up with Amanda, but it's summertime, and as soon as I started thinking about having the boys and Kelly in Manhattan—showing them around, taking Kelly to the places I love here—I couldn't help but get excited.

I'm crazy about New York. Cheesy, I know, but I came here once on a trip with my friend Todd and his folks when we were in high school. We stayed on West 57th, did all the tourist crap, and I was hooked. I can't wait to show my family all the cool parts of the city.

Plus, I get a little privacy here in New York. It's weird, but there are just too many people living here to keep track of a movie star. Sometimes I can even wander around in relative anonymity.

But today, here I am at the first table read. Jeremy is somewhere, pacing around, yelling at some poor soul on the phone. Sandy, my publicist, even made an appearance today. I think it was mostly because she has a bit of a crush on the director, Chase McDougal.

She shouldn't. He's a douche. The first clue is that he turns any noun he can into a verb. He "tasks" the second unit director with finding the storyboard artist. He talks about us "hothousing" the script so we can "boilerplate" the themes we want to "front stage" in the movie. If I were still drinking, McDougal's verbing would make a fine drinking game. As it stands right now, I'm thinking a little on-location wager for the number of nouns that get "verbed" might be the way to go instead of shots.

Sometimes the habits from drinking are hard to forget. Since rehab, I haven't touched a drop. But I've sweated through some tough temptations. I've dreamed about drinking, and when I cross paths with a hung-over frat boy who still oozes alcohol from his pores, the smell makes me salivate like one of Pavlov's pups. It's behind me, but not far enough to make me feel comfortable. Kelly, God love her, she's been quiet and trusting and all-around inspirational about the whole thing. I dragged her into my mess, almost broke us apart for good, but we made it out the other side together, so I guess we're stronger at our broken places now.

"This is unacceptable." Amanda slaps the script down on the table.

I'm a little thankful, truthfully. My mind's been wandering for a while, and someone's probably going to notice the gigantic circle that I've drawn, shaded, and added octopus legs to on the legal pad in front of me. It must be getting pretty dire if I'm about to cheer Amanda on through a diva hissy fit.

Too bad Jeremy's wandered off. He loves to watch her throw a tantrum. She's not his client, but I suspect he has some devious plot to win her over on the shoot. The brother likes hotheaded women.

McDougal raises his head. "Amanda?" This will be interesting. They've never worked together. He may regret that she's a genuine redhead.

"I don't appear until page six. In the draft I read, I was onscreen by minute three."

McDougal licks his lips nervously. Ooh, there's something I could keep count of. I bet I could get a PA to hide one of those little silver clickers in his pocket, and we'd track the lip-licking all the way through the eleven-week shoot.

"We messengered this script over to your rep last Tuesday. You haven't had a chance to eyeball it?"

I think I counted two nouns that just got hijacked in there. I try to refocus on what McDougal actually said.

Amanda flips through the pages. "Are you saying I'm not doing my job?"

That took two seconds. She's already defensive. This shoot will either be really entertaining or really, really long.

McDougal launches into a monologue-length backtrack, trying to appease his leading lady. My mind drifts again. To sex, to be honest.

I found us a condo in Chelsea, a neighborhood that's a little boring for my tastes. But it's safe and near the water, and I think the boys will like it. The condo has a split layout. The master is set on the opposite side of the place from the boys' bedrooms. Which Kelly and I will like.

What I consider right now, while watching McDougal's lips move, is how loud Kelly and I can get without risking the boys hearing us.

Oh, come on now. I'm a guy. This is what we do. And it's pretty tame, because I could be thinking about what I want to do to Kelly, but I'm just thinking logistics right now. Tactics.

I had no idea. A family is something I've always wanted. It's a thrill to have one, and Hunter and Beau amaze me. I had no idea how much those little dudes would wrap themselves into the corners of my heart. They're like kudzu.

But sharing space with the woman I want to be with in every sense of the word *and* a tween and a bona fide teenager is a challenge I hadn't anticipated. There's a balcony in our new condo. Maybe that's a place we could sneak off to late at night. Of course, it could get mighty awkward if a nosy neighbor decided to see what the moon looked like…

Amanda stands up. "I need a minute here. I'm going to walk away from the table and figure out why I'm already being jerked around, and we haven't even started shooting yet." She stalks off. Several young women scurry after her.

She should have said "dicked" around, and she and McDougal could bond over the verb-erizing. McDougal looks like he has a headache.

He shrugs at me. "Sorry, Andy. I guess we're taking a break."

I like this. "No problem. I'll just step out to make a quick call."

So, I'm the good guy, the level-headed, amiable one. This is a healthy way to start the shoot.

I hustle out to the hall and run into Jeremy.

"Hey, hot stuff." He slaps me on the shoulder.

"You owe me five bucks."

"She already went ballistic?" He pulls out a money clip and peels off a twenty.

"I said five, J." I take the twenty anyway.

"I'm a high-roller, son. I don't have a fiver."

"Jeremy, the high-roller. Don't overcompensate so obviously. People will worry that your dick is shrinking."

"Ooh, burn." He slaps me again, hard enough to knock me to one side.

I get past him to the stairwell and out onto a fire escape. I call Kelly.

She answers right away. "Hey."

"Hey. How are you?"

"Good, and you? I thought this was the first table read. Aren't you busy?"

I want to go home and hold her. Kiss that full, wet mouth of hers. Do other stuff. "Yeah, well…"

"This is an Amanda thing, huh? Is she better or worse than Franca?"

Kelly met Franca, and Franca tried to eighty-six my relationship with Kelly before it even started. "Different, maybe? Like Dante's *Inferno*—a different level of hell."

"And you dated this woman."

"Don't remind me. I had poor taste. Until I met you, of course."

"Nice save. When will you be home?"

It thrills me to the marrow of my bones to hear her say that. Who knew the word *home* could be so sexy. "It's not looking good. You should probably eat without me."

"Bummer."

"This is why I wanted you here with me. I'll at least get to crawl into your bed every night." I run a hand through my hair and try not to think about her, in that bed, waiting for me.

"I could text nasty things to you if you want. It might make the day go faster."

"No, thank you. I'll resent Amanda for keeping me away from you that much more." There's a guy at the window in the building across from me with a cigarette in his hand. Now I want a cigarette. Great.

"I didn't get sick this morning at all." Kelly sounds proud.

"Remind me not to eat garlic at lunch today. Let's see if we can keep the streak going." We discovered garlic is not cool when I made spaghetti and she had to leave the condo until we aired it out.

I could go on and on about the pregnancy. It's been a mystery so far. Every day I figure out something new about what it's doing to Kelly. But I've only had two panic attacks about becoming a father. I think that's good, considering that I'm not exactly the role model of the year—since I'm a recovering alcoholic and brooding movie star and all that.

I can't go on and on right now, though. Jeremy steps out on the escape and waves me back in. Amanda must've calmed down.

"Gotta go, Kells. Love you."

"Have fun. Love you." She hangs up.

Jeremy rolls his eyes. "How's the missus."

"At least make it sound like a question."

"I love Kelly. I don't know how I feel about knocked-up Kelly calling you while you work. You need to stay focused, not have some Mr. Mom moment."

"I called her. And you need to cool it on the baby talk. That is a state secret until we make it out of the woods. The very last thing I need right now, if you want me to stay focused, is some craft services flunkie to tell *TMZ* what he heard Andy Pettigrew chit-chatting about on set."

Jeremy rolls his eyes again. "Point taken. I'm leaving anyway. Text me when you wrap up. Or call me from the car and let me know how the read went." He sees Amanda walking down the corridor in our direction and abruptly turns and jogs in the other. "Hasta, amigo. Enjoy the drama."

I watch as Amanda fluffs her hair and straightens her tight T-shirt before she walks back into the conference room. She's gearing up, readying for battle.

This is going to be a long day.

BACK IN THE HIGH LIFE AGAIN

After two weeks of prep for the movie, Andrew has concluded that he's not crazy about his director, Chase McDougal, but he does like the meticulous rehearsals. He tells me he's happy to be working and happy to be with me. This is the first time, really, that we've been in the same place while he filmed, and so far the time we've had here by ourselves has been blissful.

He's gone today, for a long set of rehearsals, and he's told me to expect that the days will get longer and longer when filming starts. Hunter and Beau are in LA with my mom and dad for another five days, but I'm getting used to kicking around by myself.

I feel a little better, so that's good. And when I talk to them, the boys seem to have settled more into the idea of a new sibling. I think Hunter just wants to get home to Idaho so he can see his friends. Beau, he'll be a little mad forever. He will never again be the baby, so that will always be a bone of contention.

I miss them. I've planned out these days on my own in New York to keep myself plenty busy. I go to museums. I run in Central Park. I ride the Staten Island Ferry just to ride it. I'm proud of myself. I only rode the subway out to Brooklyn mistakenly once, and a very nice lady told me how to get off and get back on to ride in the correct direction. All my experiences with New Yorkers so far have been so hospitable, not hostile at all.

Today I need to run. A car came for Andrew painfully early this morning, though he's not doing location shots yet. I'm actually looking forward to that because Tucker, my favorite bodyguard, will be in town. I miss him. I haven't seen him since January, when we all went to the Golden Globes together. If Andrew is out on the town shooting, Tucker gets to be here. I want to hog him and take him to dinner and maybe have him take me some places to go shopping. The fourteen-hour days might slow us down on that, but we'll see.

I choose an early morning run on the High Line. I walked to it from our condo a few days ago, and I love it. It's an old elevated rail line that's been converted to a greenbelt, floating above Chelsea and the Meatpacking District. The breeze comes in off the Hudson River, and the views are glittering and wide, not something I get to experience much here in New York. The Idaho part of me gets to feeling a little claustrophobic when I'm down in the concrete canyons for whole days. The High Line liberates me from the city.

I don't have huge expectations for my runs. I know girlfriends who ran hard all through their pregnancies. I wasn't much of a runner when I was pregnant with either boy, and I was young. The way my knees are already creaking and complaining to me now means the present-day Kelly will likely not get to be the bad-ass pregnant marathon runner either. I might just be a take-a-trot-every-other-day runner and stop when my knees or other parts of me start to hurt. But as long as I can still run, even if it's not for long, I'll be good. It's mental, as much as physical, for me.

I lace 'em up, tuck my phone into the pocket of my running skirt, and scoot out the door. Down in the lobby, I double check with the doorman about my directions: north on Seventh Avenue one block, west three blocks. This is easy, but I don't dare pull out my phone on the street and check my map. I don't want to be that person.

I'm tired, and my stomach still feels mildly queasy, but I promise myself I can get a tea if I run a little.

Andrew didn't even mean to, but the condo he chose for us — the very safe and very nice building with the insane rent (we're talking monthly rent that'd be close to the mortgage on my house in Boise for the *year*) — is one block from the most extravagant tea shop. I'm in green tea heaven.

The man is good, even when he's not trying.

I swing open the door of the building and feel the humid New York air. Lately I've made a very conscious effort not to breathe too deeply. Occasionally there's a whiff of overripe trash can, and though I think I'm almost out of the nauseated woods, eau de Manhattan garbage might send me back to the toilet.

"Excuse me." A sweet, high voice speaks up behind me.

I turn around, almost out the door of the lobby, to see who it is.

A young woman, dressed in running gear, stands behind me.

"I'm sorry. Did you need to get by?" I assume I'm in the way. I move on a ten-second delay compared to native New Yorkers. They know where they're headed, for one thing, but the cliché might also be a bit true: they seem to be in a perpetual hurry.

She smiles. She has pale blond hair, her bangs clipped to the side with a barrette. She has her phone out. "No, but my phone's dying. What time is it?"

"Ten after seven." I smile as she does get past me now, sliding out the door as the doorman pulls it wide.

"Thanks!" she calls over her shoulder and breaks into a confident stride. She looks like she's running in the direction of the High Line.

And I have a dorky thought — *Oh! A running friend!* — before I remember that this is a gigantic city, even if she does live in the building. I don't think it's a strike-up-a-running-friendship kind of place.

I start my run, carefully following the blocks to the stairs to the elevated railway.

When I climb, I can hear my right kneecap click a little. I've been ignoring this, but I'm not an idiot. I know that pregnancy does things to ligaments, loosens them. Something is clicking in Denmark. It doesn't hurt, yet, but I have to be careful or I could really screw something up.

At the top of the stairs, I feel the breeze first and then take in the view. The sun climbs in the sky, and the green strip of the High Line bathes in the gold light. Tall grasses wave languidly, and here, at one of the places where the thin path widens, water trickles along the side in a small fountain.

It's not crowded. No one occupies the chaises or benches dotting the deck.

I jog for a while and let my mind wander. Andrew's invited me to the set. Next week he'll be location shooting all around New York's Battery Park and in the Financial District. I'm excited. I've only spent time with Andrew on the set of *The Last Drive,* and our relationship was in its infancy.

This time, a location visit means I'll meet the infamous Amanda Walters. An ex-girlfriend. That'll be interesting.

And people will realize I'm pregnant. Maybe not everyone, but sooner or later, people will notice. I'm twelve weeks in, and the first trimester is almost over. We're going to tell Tucker when he gets here. He'd figure it out too fast anyway. He's a smart, smart guy. So far, Jeremy knows, Sandy knows, Hunter and Beau know, and our folks know.

I slow down. The girl, the one from the lobby, is up ahead. She's stretching out on one of the steps to the little amphitheater that's suspended between the High Line and Chelsea Market below. Andrew said sometimes there are concerts or plays here. The girl is doing dips, stretching her Achilles out one at a time, stepping backward off the step to lengthen the back of her calves.

She smiles at me. "Hi, again."

I take this invitation. I might actually make a friend here in New York. All by myself. "You live in my building?"

"Maybe you live in *my* building, you know. I might have been there first." She puts out a hand, steps up so that both her feet are on the same step. "Mari. Nice to meet you."

I shake her hand. "Kelly."

She stretches both arms up, grasps her hands together. Her running jacket comes up a bit on her stomach, and I have a moment of envy. She is impossibly toned, and I catch the wink of a navel ring. "What a great morning. I'm having a hard time staying focused on running. I think I need to do something to savor the day before it's too hot and sticky."

I nod. I could run more, but I feel the urge to put my feet up somewhere and relax. "Lately my runs aren't as amazing as they could be. I'm always looking for a reason to put the run and me out of our misery."

"Today is your lucky day. I'm looking for someone to have a cup of coffee with."

"Say you'll have tea with me at that place near our building, and you have a deal."

"Done." She trots up the last few steps and walks along with me, back the way we came.

"Mari. That's a nice name." We stroll, and I'm kind of pleased to not push it, force the run. My knee throbs a bit.

"It's a constant thing, though," she says. "No one who sees it on paper knows how to pronounce it. I'm always, 'Mari rhymes with sorry.' Every class I have to re-explain it nine million times."

"Class? Are you in school?" I have a moment where I really hope she's not in high school. She can't be my friend and be a juvenile; it'd just be embarrassing. She doesn't look that young. Plus she'd be at school right now if she was in high school. I breathe a little easier with that thought.

"Grad school. Design school at The Fashion Institute. My marketing degree just wasn't cutting it, and luckily, I got my dad to agree with me." She peels her running jacket off. She wears a tiny tank, revealing a tattoo on her shoulder blade: scripted initials that read *CRM*.

"You live with your folks?"

"Nah. They live on Long Island. I'm housesitting for some friends of theirs. So, I guess I can't say you moved into my building, really. But you did just move in, didn't you?"

We climb down the stairs to street level. I wince a bit. There will be ice when I get home. I say a silent apology to my abused knee. "We're just here for the summer."

"And the 'we'?"

"My boyfriend and my two sons. They're with their grandparents right now, but they're excited to be in New York for the summer."

"Most people escape if they can. To the Hamptons, or somewhere else that's not so hot with pavement."

"It's different from where I'm from, so I like the novelty. I like new adventures."

"Me too. Grad school is good for that."

"So, you're going to be a fashion designer? Like runway and Paris and all that?"

"Hopefully. I love men's fashion, which some people think is weird. I'd love to do a men's and women's line, clothes that fit with both maybe. Twiggy, Mick Jagger, skinny ties. Mod androgyny."

We come to the front of the Argo Tea, the best spot in the universe as far as I'm concerned. "Ah, sweet relief. This is the only reason I ran today—the promise of a giant iced green tea."

"I thought you'd be a sweet tea drinker."

"Really? Why?"

"Your accent is southern, isn't it? Maybe just a hint of it?" She pulls her jacket back on.

"You're good. Yeah. A while ago, though. But born and bred south of the Mason-Dixon line, that's true."

"Well, Southern Kelly, welcome to New York. Hope you have a great summer. I've got to go, but I'll see you around in the lobby, yes? Maybe we can go on a run together sometime." She gives a little wave and turns on her heels, leaves the shop before we've even ordered. I stand by myself for a second, puzzled.

I thought we were going to bond. Maybe I was too overeager and scared her off.

I get my tea and sit outside, watching the traffic and the people pass by. I'm disappointed—my first New York acquaintance might not turn out to be a buddy. Now it looks like my best shot at a new friend might be one of the doormen.

I guess I'll be executing the rest of my day alone. I decide to go to a bakery off of Houston Street next. It's another subway ride, but I want to get off and walk Greenwich Village a little. It's seemed greener, calmer, and mellower than some parts of the city. I want to get my bearings there a little more. I have a sad moment that no one will be coming with me.

I dig out my phone. I dial Andrew.

"Yes?" He picks up right away.

"I just wanted to say hi."

"Hi, and happy birthday tomorrow. Are you excited?"

"I'm ready for Tucker and the boys to be here. That's what I'm excited about. Except that we won't have the condo to ourselves anymore."

"We should've messed around in the kitchen and living room and study while we had the chance. You didn't remind me to ravish you all over the house, woman! Damn. I should leave. We could fix that now, before anyone's home."

"You need to work. You want to work. This'll be a big movie for you."

"What I want is to come home and see you. The birthday girl. The mother of my child."

"You can't leave. It's not even ten a.m. yet. Next week, we'll hang out on set. It'll be fun. This week, you work."

"Fine. At least tell me what you and the little Pettigrew are up to."

"I ran up on the High Line. It was quiet and just gorgeous. And I met someone who lives in the building. She seemed sweet."

"Really? Well, that's good." He sounds a little skeptical.

"That didn't sound like a good tone. What?"

"I wonder if she knows who we are."

"I don't think so. Do people know we're in the building?"

"At some point we'll get sold down the river. A doorman or somebody will tip off the paparazzi. A neighbor, maybe."

"I didn't tell her who you were." I feel a bit defensive.

"I know you didn't. It just got me to thinking. When location shoots start, everyone will be looking for me."

So, so many things I never think of. How will the boys react to a media circus outside our building? I've been walking from the building to all over the city. Will we not be able to do that anymore? "Will I still be able to go out and run?"

"I don't think it'll be a problem. Until they figure out you're pregnant. Then it might be for a while. There's always the treadmill."

Jesus. I hadn't thought about that, either. Getting hugely pregnant is enough of an ordeal. Now people will be keeping track of it too? Great. "You're making all of this sound really fun. Can't wait."

"Don't worry about it. Tucker will be here; he can always go out on runs with you. And you may not want to run that much longer, anyway, depending on how you feel."

My knee throbs in agreement with him. "I'll have to do something. I go crazy if I don't. You've not seen me when I don't exercise. It's not pretty."

He sighs. "I'll take your word for it. Hopefully I don't have to witness the ugliness that is Kelly Reynolds, stir-crazy pregnant lady."

I hear a voice in the background. "I have to go. McDougal needs me on set."

He hangs up. I nurse the end of my tea and try not to drown in all the new things to consider. This could get complicated.

Since meeting my neighbor and almost-friend out running almost a week ago, I haven't had too much more time to dwell on new things. I had arrivals to prepare for. The rest of my brood will be here tonight.

Andrew's gone to get Tucker and the boys, a role reversal for once. He's picking them up at JFK and has promised to text before they arrive back at the condo.

I'm so psyched, it's embarrassing. I can't wait to see them. They'll probably be two inches taller and need new shoes.

And I missed Tucker too. Yes, I know he's an employee of Andrew, but really, he's my friend. He proved that to me in Malibu the night things went south for Andrew and me. He came to get me, he helped Andrew, and he stuck by both of us through the toughest of it.

I know Andrew's safe with him, and for that, I'm grateful. I don't worry. I know Tucker makes it his job to be vigilant.

So, yes, I love this guy. All six foot four inches of him, the big lug. While Andrew may be tall, he's lanky. Tucker is a tank.

But I can't wait to see how he reacts when I tell him I'm pregnant. I suspect he'll be a big gooey mess.

I'm preparing for their arrival and for the announcement.

I add another balloon to the bazillion all over the kitchen.

This was Andrew's idea. All the balloons have a message tied to the end of their ribbons. Most of them say "Happy Birthday, Kelly." One of them has a copy of our very first ultrasound photo tied to it and a "Here Comes Baby" message.

But it doesn't stand out very much from all the other balloons. Yes, it's tied to the chair Tucker's supposed to sit in, but when I do stuff like this it never works.

"We'll probably have to tell him straight out," I say out loud, to the baby. Maybe I'm a doofus, but I talk to the baby. He can hear me. No one else is here to tease me. I like it.

My phone buzzes. Andrew texts that they're in the building. I dim the lights. I hear the key in the door in the foyer. I can hear Andrew chatting with Tucker as they come into the condo.

Hunter calls for me. "Mom, we're here!"

They all come in the kitchen. I turn on the lights.

"Surprise!"

"I thought it was your birthday? Why are you surprising us?" Beau giggles and comes to hug me.

Tucker stands there, towering over everyone, bags slung over both shoulders. As big as he is, his face is lit up like a little kid's. He looks at the balloons everywhere. "Happy birthday, Kelly!" He comes over and gives me a peck on the cheek.

Andrew laughs. "Typical Kelly to throw her own party." He comes to kiss me hello, and Hunter is not far behind. I hug him tight.

"Hunter, you did grow. I told you not to grow while you were gone."

Beau points to the door. "Can I go look around the rest of the condo? Where's my room?"

Andrew shakes his head. "Slow down, big guy. We're doing a little birthday celebration for your mom first."

Andrew pulls Tucker's chair out, the one with the news tied to the balloon.

Tucker raises an eyebrow. "What is this?"

Andrew shows him to the chair. "Have a seat." He plucks the balloon from the air and hands it to Tucker.

Tucker examines it, looks at the different message, looks at the ultrasound picture. Then he looks up at me, then at Andrew.

Andrew comes up behind him, puts a hand on his shoulder. "Well?"

Tucker gets up and hugs him. "Andrew's gonna be a dad. Wow. I think I might cry." Tucker comes over and gives me a huge squeeze. "You've been keeping a mighty big secret, Miss Kelly. Congratulations." He pats my belly gently and hugs me again.

"So, we haven't told anyone, really. Our folks, and the boys, obviously, and Jeremy—" Andrew begins.

"Unfortunately," I add. I wasn't thrilled for him to know so early, but he needs to know to protect Andrew's interests.

"You two, you're gonna be so cute!" Tucker pulls both of us close for a group hug. "And you have an advantage because Kelly actually knows what she's doing. Good thing too. Andrew's allergic to babies."

"What?" I haven't heard this before.

"Oh, yeah, he hasn't told you about him and babies?"

Beau wants in. "What, what is it? Tell us!"

Tucker grins. "On the soap opera, even before I met him, and every time he's worked with a baby since, he makes them cry."

Tucker sits back down at the island with Hunter. Andrew hands him a bottled water.

"They shriek in terror, actually." Andrew puts an arm around me. "I'm baby repellant."

"That should be fun to watch." Hunter sips his drink and smiles at the thought.

I have to come to his defense. "It'll be different than that. Babies know the sound of their families' voices. He's eavesdropping right now, you know. He'll already know Andrew before he even meets him." I can't wait to see Andrew with the baby. It's going to be amazing. There's no sexier sight than a man holding his own child.

Tucker points at me. "That's a lot of *hes* in there. Do we know it's a boy?"

"No, but the smart money's on a boy." I wink at Andrew. "Gender aside, though, Andrew'll be great."

Andrew smiles at me. "This is why I love you. Thanks for the vote of confidence." He waves Beau to the kitchen island. "Come have a seat, guys. We have birthday cake for your mom."

Everyone sits at the island, and Andrew serves up the cake. I'm about to get up to get the boys some milk when he puts a hand on my shoulder.

"You missed a balloon." He smiles and hands me a purple balloon.

"What?"

"You missed one. It's got something attached to it too."

I read the message: *Kelly, will you marry me? Happy Birthday. Love, Andrew.*

Tucker's curious. "What's it say?"

"It's another sneak-attack proposal."

Tucker tilts his head, confused. "Another? What?"

Beau perks up. "A proposal for what?"

Andrew pats him on the shoulder. "A marriage proposal. I want to marry your mom."

Beau's not impressed. "Where's the ring, then?"

Andrew grabs hold of the purple balloon and shakes it. It rattles. He arches an eyebrow. "Hmm. Sounds like there's something in there." Beau rolls his eyes, but Andrew's not done. "Cover your ears, young man." He picks up a fork and pops the balloon. He hands me the contents and the shredded latex. It's a plastic container from a gumball machine.

I open it. Inside is a plastic ring, with a pink sparkly "diamond."

Hunter looks skeptical. "Really?"

I get up and kiss Andrew, put the ring on, and set the golf marker aside. "I love it. Yes."

Andrew nods. "Awesome. I'm three for three. This proposal stuff is a piece of cake."

Tucker stands up, water in hand, and slings his bag over his shoulder. "I've missed a lot, clearly. Congrats, you two, on your confusing pending engagement, I think, and on your baby on the way." He kisses my hand, admires the plastic ring. "I'm sure the little tyke will learn to love, not fear, the baby-frightening Andrew. And now I'm going to go wash the airplane grime off of me." He gives me one more kiss on the cheek before leaving the kitchen. "Andrew Pettigrew, engaged. Andrew Pettigrew, family man. So many words I never thought would be spoken together!"

WALKING ON BROKEN GLASS

The morning after he and the boys flew in, Tucker's ready to leave with me at five a.m. for the first day of location shoots. We're going all the way the first day: closing down Wall Street proper for a fourteen-hour shoot. I didn't get much sleep. Kelly tossed and turned most of the night. She kept having charley horses in her calves—she was crying in her sleep at one point, they hurt so bad. It killed me. I do not like hearing her whimper. Morning sickness is one thing, and I sure am sympathetic, but I hope this new problem isn't a preview of more coming attractions. I worry about her, and the last thing I want is her health in jeopardy or the baby's.

And I had a nightmare. Ironic, I know. Kelly had terrible nightmares when she and I first met. The shoe's on the other foot now, I guess.

The dream started out innocently enough. I was walking down Wall Street, toward the Charging Bull sculpture. The street was quiet, but that's what it'll be like today: closed for shooting, no traffic.

But then I noticed in the dream that I was barefoot. Which was fine, but I saw a figure standing by the bull, and my heart started beating faster. The figure had a box in one hand and a pistol in the other. I came closer. I couldn't make myself turn around. I kept walking toward the person. It was a woman with a black veil over her face, and she was dressed in black, head to toe.

Suddenly I felt sharp, searing pain in my feet, and I looked down. There were shards of glass strewn over the street, everywhere, all different kinds: broken mirrors, broken light bulbs, broken wine glasses.

I looked up at the woman again, and she turned the box over, showing me that it was empty. Like she was the one who put the broken glass all over the road. I still couldn't turn around; I still walked toward her. I left a trail of wet, bloody footprints.

She dropped the empty box and raised the pistol, pointing it at my head.

And that's when I woke up.

Yeah, I didn't sleep so great. But today's a big day, nightmare or no.

So, I hurry to get ready, and then I hustle out the door with Tucker to the waiting limo. No press. No photographers. This is a good sign. They'll figure out where we're staying; it's gonna be in the next couple of days, so I'll take every moment of peace I still have. I've tried to warn Kelly. She hasn't really experienced it. I'm over the fricking moon to have her here with me, but I hope she's ready for the full-on fame game. It can get pretty damn old.

"Tuck, did you get me a tea at least?" He's not driving today. He's riding shotgun to someone from the production company's security detail named Janus. Janus is a large Filipino mountain of a man. He wears shades and a tight fade haircut.

"When have I not gotten you tea? I got in last night, all tired from the flight, and where was I this morning? That's right, out getting you tea so you can survive your movie star facial and makeup and manicure and what not, you poor, poor thing."

I can see Janus grin in the rearview mirror.

"Kelly mentioned taking you shopping sometime."

Tucker loves Kelly. Kelly loves Tucker. It's a good thing he's gay, because otherwise I might be threatened. She hasn't seemed to notice other men, but the two of them really get along. I guess it's good. They might be my two most important people.

"I would love to take her shopping. Has anyone figured out where you two are staying yet? Do they tail her?" His tone is a bit different. Protective, maybe.

"Nobody's found the building yet. And I don't know if the tabloid guys recognize her unless she's with me. They sure will, though."

"When will she start showing?"

"I don't know. Soon. She's thirteen weeks along. So far, the doctor says all is well. But pretty soon somebody will get wind of all of this. And Tucker?" I look at the rearview mirror. I kind of wish Janus wasn't here. This is an important and not-consistent-with-the-production-company's-policy conversation we're about to have.

"Yeah?"

"When they go after her, I want you with her."

"I know. She'll want me with you."

"I know. But you know what my priority is. Her."

"And the passenger." He makes the baby sound like an alien. I like his discretion, though, even though Janus has been briefed.

"Is that his codename?"

"So, you really believe he's a he?" His tone rises, just barely. Is that excitement I hear?

"Well, Kelly thinks yes. Calls it mother's intuition." I notice a glance up at me from Janus in the rearview. Time to end this conversation. I cough, clear my throat.

Tucker is a keen one. He changes the subject. "We need to go over logistics. Are you awake enough for that?"

"Go for it. I will feign concern." I hate talking security. The undercurrent here is that some jackass wants to kill me or wants my picture badly enough to kill me by accident or that some crazy middle-aged guy who lives with his mom wants a lock of my hair and is wandering the streets of New York with a sharp pair of scissors. I try very hard not to think about any of these people. The dream I had last night doesn't help.

Fear is a weird thing. FDR called it on this one. The unknown is what's terrifying. When I first experienced the frenzy of a red carpet, the eighteen hundred possible unknowns who wanted my autograph or my left pinkie finger as a souvenir melted my spine into jelly.

And I could live my life that way. There are all sorts of possibilities out there. But guess what? I could be a CPA in Kansas and get killed by a F5 twister or a bad case of sepsis from a nasty infected paper cut. Any person can stall out thinking about his eventual death. It's a waste of time.

Tucker makes it his job to think about my eventual death, though, and how to prevent it from happening on his watch. I like it that way.

He keeps most of it to himself. He trains on active-shooter scenarios while I watch reruns of *Storage Wars*. My only job is to follow his directions when it comes to my safety.

"Andrew?"

I think I'm supposed to be following his directions right now. "Go ahead. I'm with you."

"Streets of New York. Chaos. You know what this is going to be like. Pretty soon every soul south of Houston Street will know we're shooting today. So, what I need from you is predictability."

"I am the very model of predictability. I don't even know how to zig or zag."

"Trailer, makeup trailer, set, trailer. No autographs unless I vet them. Let me put them in a bullpen. It's not some field in Alabama. It's New York."

"Got it. Janus helping on this?"

Janus sits up a little straighter. "Yes, sir. Apotheosis put me and two other guys on you for the outside locations. Under Tucker's direction, of course."

Apotheosis is the baby of Chase McDougal's boss, Jordan Aaronson. Apotheosis is the production company backing this movie, with the most pretentious company name I've heard in a long time. A lot of men in the film industry spend a whole lot of their efforts and energy compensating for overbearing mothers and inadequate anatomy. No lie. Not me, of course.

Jordan is a world-class dick. While McDougal irritates the living hell out of me, he at least wants to make a good movie. I can stand a little verb-er-izing if his heart is in the right place. Jordan just uses his money to yank people around. He'd like to have more money, and that's what we—the people actually making the movie—have to capitalize on if we hope to get the movie made.

The only relief we get from his general dick attitude is that he brought on a whole boatload of overseas investors to finance this movie. Shady characters in Eastern European leather coats and gel-slicked hair show up on set, and he is occupied. Or sheiks from Dubai Skype him to get progress reports, and he disappears into a conference room or a trailer.

But I am his investment, and so Janus and assorted people like Janus will be here to help Tucker protect his potential profit.

Not that Janus is a problem. He seems like he's trying.

The limo slows, and Janus leans out of the window to a guy manning the gate to the parking lot we've commandeered. They yell at each other, and the guy swings the gate open.

"Remember, you're Mr. Predictable." Tucker gives me his mom look. I roll my eyes.

"Fine. Show me to the makeup trailer."

Tucker comes around to the door of the car and opens it. I get out, and there's a weird, far-off roar. It's a large group of people, down the block, and apparently the back of my unwashed head at almost six in the morning is cause for great celebration and gnashing of teeth.

"Ugh." I can't help it.

"Oh, come on now, Ebenezer. They're just happy to see you."

"I know, I know. But it's so damn early. No one should be enthusiastic about anything until nine."

"Mallory awaits. Let's get you inside." Tucker walks with me to the large RV marked with the Apotheosis logo and a sign that reads "Makeup."

"I wish I still smoked." I miss that part of my morning routine. I could sit tight in a makeup chair if I had nicotine in my system.

"No, you don't." Tucker nudges me, scolding.

"Yes, I do." I feel like being grumpy.

"The baby doesn't want you to smoke." He lifts an eyebrow.

"Oh God. You win. Are you going to do that a lot, bring him into arguments as the secret weapon?"

"Just getting you used to it. I think it might happen when you and the mother of your child fight too. Thought I'd get you started early."

"Tucker, you'll give me a panic attack. Thanks."

"And I think I'm going to assume that the passenger is a girl. Just to give equal billing."

"Ten bucks it's a boy."

"You're on. But make it twenty and a round of golf wherever I want."

"Done."

Mallory pushes the door open now. "Are you girls going to stand out here all day?"

I smile at her and go inside.

MANEATER

A few hours later, Amanda waves me over. "Are you coming, Andy?"
We're due on set. She's got a ridiculous "lawyer" outfit on for our
scene together. Her heels are sky-high, the suit she's wearing is low
cut, and the skirt, well, the skirt isn't a skirt. It's a napkin.

I wouldn't last a second if I was a girl in this business. It's brutal.
Amanda is smart, but if she wasn't built the way she is, didn't look
the way she does, she wouldn't be here. Sure, I know I look decent
enough, but guys in Hollywood have it easy. Take the Bechdel test.
It says look at any movie and try to find more than one woman in it.
Then see if either woman has a name and talks to the other one. And
if they talk about something besides the guys. That's how screwed up
this business is. Take a second, see if you can think of a movie…This is
why Amanda has to be Amanda. I might be ambitious, Jeremy might
be ruthless, but Amanda has to be stone cold and lethal or she's out.

In moments like this, I think Amanda's not that terrible. Okay,
she's terrible. But she doesn't seem to hate me anymore—not yet, at
least. This is an improvement from back when we dated. By the end
of that, she wanted to kill me. Maybe not kill me, just break a lot of

plates and other expensive things in our hotel room in Cannes. You know, to make the point of how much she disliked me.

"Are you ready for this?" She tosses her red hair over her shoulder and runs a finger over her teeth, checking for flecks of red lipstick.

"Game on, sister." I'm trying really hard to be on her side. The whole shoot will go better if she doesn't hate me. And she has really good aim. I remember that, so I'd rather not have anything chucked at my head.

We approach the sidewalk. We're shooting right by the bull, the one from my dream. Tucker salutes me, and it's barely a nod, which tells me he's working hard, and I need to be Mr. Predictable.

I see McDougal over at the dolly camera, and the director of photography is checking the boom cam.

My job today? To walk. In a straight line. I'm not even kidding. Oh, and at one point, I have to take Amanda's hand, and she has to look into my eyes.

We'll shoot this for two to four hours. If we really get clicking, there may be a line or two of dialogue. If we get really, really ahead of schedule, I'll get to hail a cab. And it's crazy to expect it, but we may get the blocking figured out for how Amanda gets into the cab. We might not shoot it, though.

When people say to me, "Movies are so glamorous," they have no idea. I have a stand-in who takes my place when the crew blocks out shots and checks the lighting on scenes, but it's still a ton of waiting around. When I was just getting started, I was lucky enough to have to stand there for all the set-up too. It was painful.

I'm better at the waiting now.

"Stop wiggling. You're terrible." Amanda elbows me.

"What?"

"Put in your headphones and do your I-think-I'm-Michael-Phelps thing."

"Funny."

Amanda likes to tease.

"Really, go ahead. I need you in the zone when you walk down the street with me. What if you're not in character? The real you walks goofy."

"No, I don't."

"You don't even walk in a straight line. Remember that time in Aspen when you bumped into that rapper, what was his name?"

"Easy Cheez."

"Not even close. I thought you were street. You're supposed to remember all the rap names. Hang with them. Get a grill, tat up, you know."

"I don't remember his name. I do remember that he wanted to kill me on the spot. I wasn't even drinking."

"But you can't walk in a straight line."

"Fine, you win." I make a motion for my headphones, but Amanda touches my arm.

"We had fun, though, didn't we?" She smiles.

"Are we reminiscing?" I try to keep the tone light, but I don't think we should go there. It's territory best left in the past, as far as I'm concerned.

A tiny, tiny crack in her confidence flits through her eyes. "You don't like remembering?"

"It's not because of you, Amanda. It was a long time ago. I'm a lot different now."

"You've got a family now."

I start a little, until I realize she's not talking about baby-to-be. She doesn't know, unless I screw up and say something so she guesses.

"Yeah, I guess I do."

"I've seen pictures of the boys. They're older. What's that like?"

"What do you mean?"

"Do they like you?"

"Yeah, I think they do."

"Isn't it hard, with their dad, well, you know — gone?"

"It's hard for them, and it's hard for Kelly. I just try to help as best I can. They're great boys."

"Maybe you'll bring them onto set. I'd like to meet them."

"No, you wouldn't. You hate kids."

Amanda tugs at whatever small thing serves as an undergarment underneath that tiny skirt. "You're right, I do. But I'm dying to meet these boys. They must be magical."

"Why?"

"To tame you. To send you to rehab, turn you into the law-abiding Andrew Pettigrew. No more dancing on the tables, no more sex in the stalls at the club, huh? I remember liking that." She skims a hand over her blazer, smooths the hem.

"Okay. I'm putting my headphones in. And Amanda?"

She licks her lips. "Yes?"

"Let it go. Not interested in skanky club sex anymore."

She yawns. "Where's the fun in that?"

McDougal saves me. He walks up and waves me to the curb. "Let's walk through the cab hailing real quick. I want to make sure you hit your marks."

She *is* as terrible as I remember. Things'll probably get thrown at me. Unless I chuck something at her first.

PAINT IT BLACK

The boys have been here for a week, Andrew's in the swing of filming, and me? I think I am best described as "at loose ends." I miss Tessa. I miss Boise. I miss Ditto, who has been claimed as a hairy, smelly dog "stepbrother" by Tessa's three daughters and is staying with them until we come home to Boise.

I miss Andrew. Yes, he's here. But he's a million miles away. He's happy, most days, and I love seeing him in his element. But I'm just not there with him. He's so smart, and I can see that mind, those gears turning, as we sit at dinner, or watch a movie together. He's with me, but his brain is on set, in the script, in the heart of that movie, that character.

The boys are happy to be here, and I love showing them around. But they are boys too. They are content with sleeping in until noon and watching videos and eating cereal out of the box. They are willing to go with me and explore New York, but they just got here, and they want to veg out too, not just play super tourist with their mother.

So, that leaves me. I'm still a little queasy, and I'm bored. I don't do well with bored. Maybe I used to, a long time ago, but now I fret and worry and pace and other annoying stuff that doesn't endear me to anyone.

This morning I get up with Andrew just to see him a minute before he heads to the set. I pop a ginger ale, my new best food friend, and shuffle into the master bath to see what he's doing.

He's shaving. Watching a man shave—watching *my* man shave—I love it.

"Hey, it's Queasy Girl." He runs the razor under the tap, gives me an air kiss. I avoid the urge to kiss that soapy face, shaving cream or no. I would, but there's a strong possibility it would make me hurl.

"Good morning. I'm Semi-Queasy Girl this a.m. I keep waiting for the morning sickness to decide if it's done kicking my ass or not."

"How much longer before it's officially in the rearview mirror? You're, what, fourteen weeks in?"

I shrug. "A tender stomach is a tender stomach. I wish it would have miraculously cleared up when I made it to the second trimester, but sometimes morning sickness hangs on. Just like it's not always just in the morning."

He nods. "Total false advertising. But look how far we're into it. That's a fringe benefit of the surprise pregnancy. Your first trimester flew by."

He knows this is a sore subject. It pisses me off that I was so clueless and went almost two months before I realized what was up. It makes Andrew grin. He grins right now.

"Ha ha. Don't tease me. I'm not awake yet."

"Why are you up? An early call for me doesn't mean early call for you."

"I wanted to see you before you left." I scoot up behind him, slip my arms around his waist, bury my nose in between his shoulder blades. He smells like chlorine and Ivory soap.

"I have a razor in my hand. Careful there, pet." He pauses for a minute to wrap an arm behind him and give me a little squeeze.

I hold still and peek around his shoulder, watch him draw the razor down his strong jaw.

"I like this." I tighten my hold around his torso a bit.

"Fifteen minutes ago I could have gotten into all sorts of trouble with you. But five minutes from now Janus and Tucker will be waiting for me on the other side of our door. You must not throw off the Apotheosis production schedule."

"Or what?"

"Or suffer the consequences." He flicks a little water on my head.

"Sounds terrifying."

"I don't care about that, but I do have a plan to be the movie MVP. You'd throw a wrench in my plans."

"MVP, eh? Any particular reason?"

"To spite Amanda. It won't be very hard. She's temperamental. Likes to live up to her ginger reputation."

"So, you're feeling a bit competitive?" I let go of him and come to sit on the counter.

"She doesn't know it, but yeah. I have no desire to draw any diva comparisons with her."

I don't say it, but I wonder if since rehab, it's also important to Andrew to prove he's a reliable, bankable, worthy investment. Not a risky chance to be taken.

When he was drinking, he told me, he never messed around on set, but he showed up hung over plenty of times. I think he feels strongly that he make up for any stains on his rep left from back then.

"I need a plan for the day."

"Soon you can come hang with me. We still need to firm up the sitter for the boys, but they can always come hang in my trailer too."

"They can't watch videos in their pjs-slash-underwear in your trailer."

"True. But I like to see them. I miss all of you on the long days."

I run a hand down his forearm. It's still moist from the shower, and I feel the veins and the muscles tense under my touch. "I miss you too."

"Now listen, we just had this conversation. You're too tempting."

"I have no control over my irresistible charms." I smile and sip my ginger ale.

"Why don't you go hit a museum? Maybe Jeremy can hang with the boys today. He can use my office, and he knows Hunter will play *Call of Duty* with him if he asks."

"I don't know. I don't know how I feel about Jeremy King, world-class agent and, oh yeah, babysitter."

"Jeremy is an LA boy. He doesn't know what to do with himself here in New York if he doesn't have meetings. I don't think you get that he'll eventually be the adopted uncle-slash-third, no, wait, fourth

son in our family. I promise you, he's lonely. I'm texting him now."
He picks his phone up and sends Jeremy a message.

I smile. "Poor lonely Jeremy King. And my money was on Todd
to be our extra child."

Jeremy was maybe at the bottom of my list when we first met.
He's still a Hollywood agent, but he stayed at Andrew's side when
he went through rehab, and he's proven to be very loyal. I'd even
hazard a guess and say Andrew might be his best friend. Maybe
his only friend, but still. And he is steadfast and bulldog-tenacious
about protecting Andrew from anyone who might try to take him
off a sober path, so I appreciate that about him. And he's around
anytime Andrew's doing business, so he's been growing on me. He
even was, dare I say, fun to hang out with at the Golden Globes in
January. But I'd never tell him that. His ego is insufferable as it is.

Andrew dismisses the mention of Todd. "Too many groupies in
Todd's line of work. He's a busy, busy man."

"If Jeremy comes over, I think I'll go to the museums."

"He's on his way. And *all* the museums? I'll see you next year."

"Yes, all of them. I'm renting a Rascal scooter and hitting all
of them."

"Really. Well, where first?"

"I think the Met. I want to see the Monets."

"Good choice. By yourself?" He wipes the last of the shaving
cream from his face with a washcloth, and I think I see two seconds
of worry cross that perfect, smooth canvas.

"Maybe I could ask that girl I met. I don't know what floor she
lives on, though. Guess I can't knock on doors all day."

"The runner?" He asks before he sticks his toothbrush under
the faucet.

"Yeah."

"Hang in the lobby when I leave. I've seen her the last three
mornings coming back at about the same time."

This cheers me. But I can't help it, I chuckle. "Are you stalking her?"

"I figure it's her. I thought I might broker some sort of running
buddy program between the two of you. I'm a giver, you know. I do
these things all the time."

I can't help it, I'm excited. "Let me brush my teeth too, and I'll go down to the lobby with you. Set something up. Have you said anything to her?"

"No. I'm trying to keep a low profile, remember? Mr. Movie Star, you know. Don't forget, I'm all kinds of famous." He raises an eyebrow ironically, but he's right. If he wanted to put the two of us together, he'd have to have one of the guys do it. No one knows he's in this building yet.

"Stealthy, that's you. All right, I'm putting on a bra and going down with you."

"Those are such disappointing words. I'm supposed to inspire the removal of undergarments."

"You shut me down not ten seconds ago. You decided you've got to be the punctual brown-noser. You can't be seductive at the same time."

He snaps a towel at me as I leave to find the rest of my clothes. "Tonight, it's all hotness," he calls. "Just you wait."

A few minutes later, I hustle along behind Andrew, trying to appear casual and not too geeky. But oh, I'd like someone to hang with. Mari seemed nice when we ran into each other at the High Line, though she did leave sort of abruptly...I haven't seen her in the building since, and I've been looking.

"Calm yourself, woman." Andrew throws an arm around me as we wait for the elevator.

"What?" And here I thought I was being cool.

"You're spinning the key ring around. A lot." Tucker points to my keys.

"Fine." I cross my arms over my chest and pout.

We get in the elevator, and Tucker moves into business mode. They've got another location shoot today, outside a diner. "I heard from Aaronson last night. He texted me and said the Dubai boys are on set today. Don't let him distract you. You do your job and follow the shooting schedule the way McDougal set it up."

I don't understand why Tucker sounds so peeved. "What would Aaronson try to do?"

Andrew shakes his head. "He's moved scenes around before, screwed up the shooting schedule, just to shoot something flashy for investors."

Tucker rolls his eyes. "Last movie he produced, the second-unit director quit because he meddled so bad. He's such a—"

"Dick?" I offer. "That's his nickname, huh?"

"Jordan the dick. Sad, but true." Andrew steps off the elevator in the lobby. "Okay, Kells, we gotta go." He checks his phone. "She came back in the building right about at this time last couple of days. Keep your eyes peeled." He kisses me quickly and heads toward the front doors. Tucker whispers into the cuff of his jacket, which means someone else is bringing a car around. Probably Janus.

Tucker waves. "See you tonight!"

And then they're out.

I stand in the lobby for a minute, feeling sheepish. What's my plan? I guess I can go sit in one of the chairs by the big fireplace and look at my phone. I should've brought a book.

Just then, Jeremy strolls in. Ugh. I always prefer to have Andrew on hand when I deal with him.

"Gorgeous! Look at you!" He sweeps over to me, takes my hand.

"It's too early in the morning for the sycophant stuff, Jeremy." I stand, and he gives me little air kisses on both cheeks.

"Glowing. Positively." He arches an eyebrow. He loves having that secret.

"Thank you for keeping an eye on the boys. I need to firm up my plans, and then I'll be up to get ready. Maybe you could head on up there?" I point to the elevator as encouragement.

He nods but still grins impishly. "Mum's the word. Or, maybe I should say *mom*'s the word. See you upstairs." He waves over his shoulder and gets on the elevator. I worry for a split second about how he'll get into our place. Then I remember he's Jeremy, and he's always one step ahead of me.

Back to my reconnaissance mission, I sit and pull out my phone, trying to look engaged and busy. I keep one eye on the front door.

And then she walks in. She's clearly been running; she's wearing the same outfit I saw her in on the High Line. I look up and try to figure out how I'm going to get her attention when she sees me and glides over.

"It's Kelly from the South. Hi." She comes to the chair next to me and sits, like we've been friends forever.

"Hi. Mari, right?"

"Yeah, and you said it right too. How's it going?"

"Good. I was hoping I'd run into you."

"Really? I thought I'd see you out on a run."

"I've been running later in the day."

"So, what are you up to today? A run later?"

"No. Actually, I was planning on hitting the Met." And now I have to figure how to ask her to come with me. I feel like I'm dating again. And I always sucked at that.

"Oh, I love the Met. Are you going alone?"

"Well, yeah."

"Want some company? I don't have class today."

"Yes, yes I do." Look at that. I didn't even have to ask her. How perfect was that?

"Well, I obviously need to shower, and you're looking like you just rolled out of bed too, so why don't we get ready and meet down here in an hour and half?"

"Sounds great."

"I can show you how to ride the subway."

"Now, just because I'm a newbie, don't assume. I've already done that."

"Good for you. And it's noob. That's what all the cool kids say nowadays."

"Thanks for reminding me I'm not a cool kid."

"It's okay. Cool's overrated."

I smile and get up. "I'll see you in a little while, then?"

She nods. "I'm going to get my mail from the concierge's desk and then head up. Meet you down here."

"Just come by my place. Sixty-one twenty-nine."

"Okay. I'll knock."

I get on the elevator, excited. As I press the button, I have one minute of regret. I just told her my condo number. Was I supposed to keep that a secret? I shake it off. She doesn't know who my boyfriend is. A normal friend, I'd let them know where I live. Actually, the friend's still normal; it's me that's not anymore. Oh, I don't know—I probably never was. But anyway, I have to check myself more closely. I don't know what strangers might be wanting with me anymore. Mari's fine; she doesn't know who I am, or who Andrew is. But still, my days of no guard up are over.

I hustle upstairs and walk in the condo to be greeted by Jeremy, who is sitting at my breakfast bar, eating my cereal.

"So? You have a date or not?"

"How'd you get in?"

"I've had a key to the place longer than you have, sister. Where are the spawn?"

"If you're referring to Hunter and Beau, they're sleeping."

"I'm so excited. I'm trying to figure out what you're going to owe me for this."

"Ever the generous friend, Jeremy. Leave it to you to turn a favor into blackmail."

"Naw, I'm kidding. I don't have much to do today. I'm supposed to take Amanda out for dinner tonight, so this'll work out."

"*Amanda* Amanda?"

"Sure. I want her as a client."

"Why? I hear she's awful."

"She's never boring, and she's making bank. I'd like ten percent of that bank."

"I didn't know you were in need of new clients."

Jeremy snorts. "I'm the top agent in the business. My list is long and all grade-A talent. Sure, your Andy sucks up most of my time, but I'd be more than happy to attend to Amanda's needs. I can always farm her out to one of my junior agents later, but she'd be a good addition. Plus, I know this movie's going to turn her career dial up to eleven, so now is the time."

"Dial to eleven? I didn't figure you for a *Spinal Tap* fan."

Jeremy waves a hand. "I don't know what you're talking about. It's just an expression."

Figures he doesn't know the reference. Mr. Literal. "Well, you're here, so feed my children when they get up. I'm off to take a shower."

"I could come wash your back."

"I could have Andrew kick your ass."

He slaps the table. "There's a little gumption from the missus. I love it."

I go to shower, and, yes, I lock the door. He might have been kidding, but he *is* an agent, and you just never know.

Two hours later, Mari and I are on the train, headed toward Central Park and the Met.

"Have you ever been before?" She sits next to me. She's got her pale hair pulled into a messy topknot, and she smells faintly of jasmine. Her running clothes are gone, and she has a pair of high-waisted shorts matched with a striped blue and white top. She is darn cute. I feel a pang of jealousy. I was never a fashion school contender, that's for sure. And my widening body looks blobby compared to hers.

"No. I'm sure it's typical tourist, but I want to see the Monet exhibit first, if that's okay."

"It's my favorite. You'll get no complaints from me." She pulls *The Great Gatsby* from her big woven purse.

"Are you reading that? I love that."

"Right now I was looking for my phone buried underneath it, but yeah, I'm reading it. I've read it before."

"That one's my favorite. I couldn't ever get into *The Beautiful and the Damned.*"

"*Gatsby's* the best. You can't beat his character. A young, beautiful man who comes up from nothing and invents this gorgeous, mysterious life. Find me a man like that, and I'll be in love." She's found her phone and pops the book back in her bag. "Sometimes I just re-read a chapter at random. And I draw scenes or copy down lines into my sketchbook, for inspiration."

"Like what?"

"I like the eyes watching over the ash pile."

"The all-seeing eyes. Nice and ominous." The train skids to a halt at our stop. "So, we both like to run, and we both like *Gatsby.*"

She leads me off the subway. "And we both like Monet. I wonder what else we have in common." She looks at me, like she's looking for another clue, before she chuckles and breaks into a grin.

"Let's go."

The Metropolitan Museum of Art is a true feast for the eyes. It's huge, built on a grand scale. Forget other museums; there's no way to even get a look at all the amazing stuff in just this one museum in under a week.

"You know this is the equivalent of a fly-by. We're only skimming the surface of all the art in this building." Mari hands me a map to the exhibits and leads me past gallery after gallery. I crane my neck as we hustle past, trying to catch a glimpse of so many works of art.

"At least I know I can come back. Another day this summer, I could do a more methodical visit."

Mari shakes her head. "No, no, don't attack it that way. Art is visceral. You let it draw you in. Let it call to you. Let the muses pull you in the right direction." She closes her eyes for a moment. It looks like she's listening for something. I stand there, waiting for something to happen. A couple of teenage boys walk by with their skateboards in hand and give Mari a weird look. I shrug, like I'm agreeing that there's no explaining her.

She opens an eye and cocks an eyebrow. "Well?"

"Well, what?"

"What's calling to you?"

Oh. I hadn't been listening. "Um, the Monet exhibit?"

She frowns at me. "You're no fun. We need to work on that intuition of yours. Let the muses in, Kelly from the South."

I check the map, and we start down the wide hall to the wing of the museum with the French Impressionists. "I don't have anything I need inspiration for."

She looks at me, worried. "What do you mean?"

"I'm not working on anything. I'm not a creative type."

"What do you do?"

Ugh. I've always hated that question. First, I didn't relish the discussions when I was a teacher. People always commented on "summers off" and "done by three every day," and that made me want to punch them in the throat. Teachers work hard. Don't get me started.

Now, though, since Peter died, I hate it because I don't have an answer.

I swallow. "I raise my kids. Right now I hang with my boyfriend."

She smiles. "You don't need to sound defensive. Those are plenty. Unless…" She leaves off.

"Unless what?"

"Unless they aren't enough for you. You know, unless you don't feel fulfilled. You know what I mean?"

My heart sinks a little. I do know what she means. She may have struck a tiny tender spot in my ego.

Always, always, I prided myself on purpose. I was my own person. I finished college, went out on my own before Peter and I were married. I had my own career.

And now, most days, I am fine with the fact that I'm not a teacher anymore, that I'm concentrating on this new thing with Andrew, and on taking care of my boys.

But…I look at Mari and wonder what to say about this. She's unaware, strolling along toward the gallery, looking at the art. She has no clue that I'm chewing on her last comment.

Now there's a baby coming. I can't help but feel a gnawing worry. I'm a mom. I'll be a mom to a baby, which is all-consuming. And this is a noble profession, raising a child, but I didn't do a great job of content, peaceful mother when the boys were little. At the end of a day of poopy diapers and spit-up and colicky crying, I always felt stir-crazy, and I had a hard time not fantasizing about night nurses or tropical beaches where little babies slept through the night and never fussed.

She slows. She's noticed that I've yet to respond. "Kelly?"

"Yeah."

"Are you with me?" She smiles and touches my arm, like she's shaking me out of my reverie.

"I was just remembering when my boys were little. No, I'm with you. Yeah, I'm fulfilled. We're so busy right now, all of this is plenty enough."

She nods and walks on. "You don't need to convince me."

I don't know if I've convinced myself, though.

After a day of art, Mari and I part ways in the condo lobby late in the afternoon.

"That was fun." She smiles and sips the last of her tea.

"Yeah, it was."

"We should do more stuff while you're in town. You're only here for the summer, right?"

I can't remember when I told her that. "That's right. I was thinking about taking the boys to the zoo, the one in Central Park. Would you want to go do that with us?"

She smiles. "Sure, I'd be game. Let me know when, and I'm there—if I don't have class, you know."

She takes a step forward and gives me a hug. I'm a little surprised, but it's sweet—a spontaneous gesture, channeled in my direction.

"I'm so glad we're gonna be friends. It's really good this way." She gives my shoulder one more pat and turns to the door to the stairs. "See you soon!"

"Plan on it!" I give her a little wave. She's gone.

I smile. I have my own friend in New York. What a nice surprise.

CHELSEA WALLS

At the end of the week, the boys are ready for a field trip too.

"Can we do the zoo today, Mom?" Beau calls to me from the kitchen.

I try to swallow hard, keep the bile down in my throat. So much for running to start the day. Today I can't walk from the bedroom to the living room without wanting to hurl. I can't wait to feel human again. My second trimester with both boys was a breeze, so I keep waiting for pregnancy number three to get easier too. I'm almost to four months, but every time I think the morning sickness is easing up, I have a morning like this one.

Beau has a carton of orange juice in his hand, and he's waiting for an answer.

"Sure, love. I think it's supposed to rain today, and that should bring the animals out. Not so hot."

Hunter raises a hand from the couch. "I get to take the camera."

"That's fine." I can't talk. Ugh, I have cotton mouth in the worst way. "I need tea desperately."

Beau raises the teapot. "I just poured you a cup, Mom."

Bless this child. I give him a hug.

"Okay, guys, I'm going to invite Mari."

Hunter stands up and comes into the kitchen. "Who's she?"

"She's the new friend I made."

Hunter growls. "Must be nice. I used to have friends."

I take a nice cleansing breath. "Yes, you've mentioned that a time or two thousand." I hug him and plant a smooch on his cheek, much to his dismay. "Soon we'll be home in Boise, and your social life can resume."

Beau's lost interest. He changes the subject. "I want to eat somewhere good after the zoo."

"Somewhere good. Got it." Andrew's going to have to help me out on that one. I make a mental note to text him and ask where we should eat.

Andrew. That reminds me. "We need to pow-wow for a minute. Come sit."

Hunter sits down at the kitchen island. "What?"

"If Mari can come, we need to keep Andrew a secret."

Beau furrows his brows. "What does that mean?"

"Mari lives in our building. No one knows that Andrew lives here yet. It's why things are so quiet so far."

"Things are always quiet in Boise, Mom," Hunter offers. I resist rolling my eyes.

"It's different in New York. Lots of photographers here. And the longer they don't know we're in town, the longer we have some peace."

"So what?" Beau digs through the fridge.

"So, don't go telling Mari that my boyfriend is a big movie star. Can you both do that, please?"

"I thought you were his fiancée." Hunter points at the bubblegum prize on my finger.

"Sure, yes. I'm his fiancée. Still needs to be a secret."

Beau grabs a drink out of the fridge and heads down the hall. "My lips are sealed. Let's get this zoo thing figured out before I die of old age."

A tween and a teen in my house with gigantic attitudes. I'm doomed.

Mari's free in the afternoon, and I'm psyched. The boys'll be able to run around together, and I can have someone to chat with. After lunch, Andrew calls. He's worried. "Janus needs to drive you."

"No, he doesn't. And he's with you and Tucker on set, anyway."

"So, how are you getting there?"

"I think we're taking the subway."

"And this Mari is coming?"

"Yes, she is. Is that all right with you?"

"I guess. It's good to have people to hang out with."

I clear my throat. "I wasn't actually asking your permission. You're my boyfriend slash fiancé, not my boss."

"Slash fiancé, huh? That sounds like a quasi-designation."

"You yourself stated that you were campaigning. I don't want the effort on any of the upcoming proposals to slack. You've gotta work for it." I admire the bubblegum ring on my finger as we talk.

"I could make a bad comment about last night and working it, but I won't."

"I think you just did. I'm gonna go; we're meeting Mari downstairs in a minute. Have a good day."

"I will. Have fun."

"We will."

He hangs up, and I marshal the troops.

The boys are gracious and close-lipped when they meet Mari. The subway ride is without incident. I only feel nauseated twice on the walk to the zoo from the subway, and the weather's uncharacteristically cool and wet. This has all the makings of a great afternoon.

We stroll around the park in the mist, enjoying the antics of the animals, who seem to be playing in the rain. Hunter and Beau wander out in front of us, and I'm enjoying having an adult, a girlfriend no less, with me.

Mari sips a Coke and chews the straw thoughtfully. "Why are you all in town? Visiting relatives?"

"No, for my boyfriend's work."

"What's he do?"

I suck at lying. Here we go. "He's got a project that wraps up end of September, but we're just staying till school starts."

"Is he a project manager for somebody?"

"No, he's more of a consultant. They bring him in on jobs, and he takes his direction from the project manager. Kind of a hired gun."

"In IT or what?"

"Media." That isn't a complete lie, I guess. I call to Beau to change the subject. "Beau! Don't get so far in front of us."

He turns around and taps his foot impatiently.

Mari chuckles. "He's cute. Reminds me of my brother a little."

"Oh yeah? How old?"

"Oh, younger than Beau." She looks a little lost for a minute.

"Does he live on Long Island with your folks?"

She shakes her head. "No, I don't get to see him anymore."

There must've been a divorce. I don't want to pry. "That's a bummer. What's his name?"

"They named him Cameron. I didn't like it at first. I like it now. I miss him."

I nod. Her tone strikes straight to the quick. That kind of melancholy always makes me miss Peter. "I know that feeling."

"Uh-huh." She points to Hunter. "If you ever want to go out, and you need a babysitter, I think I could handle these guys. They're really grown-up."

I love it when people compliment my kids. "I like them. Most of the time. And I might take you up on that. I was going to go to work with Andrew one day maybe next week, and then there might be a reception we need to go to."

"The offer stands. You should have my number anyway, in case you get locked out of the building ever."

We're in front of the penguins. The boys are both crouched down, watching them swim and dive past the glass. Mari and I exchange numbers.

For one second, I consider that I've opened a door—just a tiny crack, but she's got my phone number, and she knows which condo is mine.

But she doesn't know Andrew. And if I met her anytime B.A. (before Andrew), I'd have done exactly what I just did. Be social. Try to make a friend.

No reason to do that any differently that I can see.

The penguins are putting on quite a show, chasing each other through the blue water, skimming up against the wall of the tank, giving the humans on the other side of the glass a thrill. Hunter and Beau are transfixed.

And the wave of nausea hits me, out of nowhere. "Mari, can you keep an eye on the boys? I need to…" I leave off and make a beeline for the nearest park bench, conveniently located next to a trash can.

Please don't puke, please don't puke. I sit and put my head between my legs for a second, peel off my light raincoat, and try to take really deep breaths.

Mari rounds up the boys and comes over to me. "Is everything all right?"

Beau pats my back. "She's having a baby. Major morning sickness."

Well, there goes that gigantic secret. I look up from between my legs to give him a death stare.

But I'm taken aback by the look on Mari's face. It's ashen, and she frowns.

And then, just as suddenly, her expression morphs into a wide smile, and she plops down on the bench. "Wow! That's great news! When are you due?"

"Ahhh…in February."

Hunter pulls me up. "We should go sit and eat dinner. I don't want a puking mom on the subway. I don't care how big New York is; even with strangers that'd be humiliating."

Mari hops up too, nodding in agreement. "There's a fun place we can go eat just outside the zoo."

Hunter cocks an eyebrow. "Are you vegan? 'Cause you look like you could be vegan."

"No. The place is called the Burger Joint. It's in the Parker Meridien hotel. It's on our way out of the park, toward Chelsea."

Hunter considers for a moment. "Hotel sounds too frou frou, but the restaurant sounds safe enough."

Mari pats his shoulder. "Glad it meets your approval."

Beau loops his arm into mine and guides me back toward the entrance. "Let's go eat before Mom embarrasses us."

Hunter walks in front of us with Mari, chatting, and Beau nods his head toward them. "I'm glad you met someone in New York, Mom. She seems cool."

"She does." I smile. I hope she's cool, because she now knows one of our two secrets.

OUT OF THE FRYING PAN

A new week brings one new thing I'm psyched about: Kelly can come to set with me.

I wasn't sure how it was going to go. I was fully prepared for the boys to hang in my trailer. I stocked the fridge and tricked out the Xbox One. But a morning alone with their mom sounds like a whole lot of fun too.

How did this happen, getting her alone? Kelly, bless her, met a friend, and it's a friend who can babysit.

Tucker background checked her, of course, and Kelly hasn't told her who I am yet. I don't know how long we can keep that secret. It's been my experience that when some people find out I'm in the mix, they find ways to ask for favors or money or influence or other things. It makes a person cautious. But for now, new-friend Mari serves my purposes. She's taking the boys down to the pool in our building and maybe on a walk over to the piers if they get really adventurous.

We get to set, and I introduce Kelly around to a few people. She says hello to Mallory, and I give her the very short grand tour. My first scene isn't until later. We've got some time on our hands, and that's all I'm going to say about that, because things'll get real inappropriate real fast if I explore that train of thought.

Yesterday on set was long and boring. There was a complex series of shots, and the waiting around dragged more than usual. Tucker and some of the sound guys and my PA, we started to brainstorm ways to pass the time.

So, this morning Kelly and I have an assignment. A job to do. I lead her to my little RV away from home.

I pull her up into the trailer with me, snap the door shut behind her.

"What?" She smiles broadly.

"I'd like your help." I raise an eyebrow.

She rolls her eyes at me. "And what kind of help would that be, Mr. Pettigrew?" She bats her eyelashes for effect.

"Listen. I want you, of course. I always want you. But I also want to bug the holy hell out of Amanda. And she thinks you and I are a boring old 'married couple.'"

I've piqued her interest. "She does, does she? We're not even officially engaged yet."

"Next proposal I've got trained lemurs and a Marilyn Monroe impersonator on deck. I'm working on it. But that's beside the point."

"What's the point?"

"I want her to walk by this trailer, which she's due to do in about—" I look at my phone "—oh, forty-five seconds. And I want her to be shocked."

"By?" Kelly sits on one of the couches, props her feet on the little ottoman, rubs that adorable belly absently.

"By us. Loud sex. Wild, trailer-rocking sex." I can feel a wide grin spread on my face. That's fun to say.

"Andrew, I love you, and the concept is smoking hot, but is that what you want the whole crew to be talking about?"

"No, of course not. Actually, in a passing moment, yeah, because I'd be big stud on campus, but then I'd die of embarrassment. On the other hand, it'd be amazing." I have to pause for a moment. I run a hand through my hair, take a nice deep breath. There are guy impulses, and they threaten to overcome me right now. I may have to ravish her on the spot. She's got this little curious gleam in her eye, and it's fantastic. I shake myself out of it. "You're getting me off-track. We're pranking her. The whole crew's in on it. You're the last conspirator."

Kelly reaches up, takes me by the hand, and shoots me a sly look. "I don't know the details, but I do know I'm in."

"Well, by all means, let's get this party started, then." I pull her up off the couch and look around for a prop. I pick up a badminton racket.

"What in the world do you have that in your trailer for?"

"Moments like these, I guess." I raise an eyebrow, raise the racket, and give the leather seat behind her a good whack.

She giggles and calls out loudly, "Yes! Andy!" She grins ear to ear.

That's my girl. She knows how to get up to some trouble, this one.

"Hold that thought. I should probably see if she's even anywhere nearby." I grab my phone to call Tucker, the lookout.

Kelly picks up the racket, climbs up on the couch. She holds on to a grab rail and starts jumping.

"What're you doing?"

"Trying to rock the trailer. I don't know if this beast of a land yacht will wiggle at all."

My cell rings. "Yes?"

Tucker's on the line. I put him on speaker. "She's headed your way. Repeat, Red Herring is on the move."

"Red Herring?" Kelly looks like a tween at a slumber party, bouncing up and down on the couch.

"Hey now, don't fall off. You're supposed to be taking it easy, Kelly Belly. And, yeah, we call Amanda Red Herring."

"You and your nicknames. Does she know you call her that?"

I jump up next to Kelly on the leather couch. "She'd throw a fit if she did. She's coming. Let's get wild, shall we?"

Kelly hands me the racket and hollers, "Yeah, baby! That's the way I like it, daddy!"

I can't even. She's so silly. I snort out loud.

She elbows me, whispering. "C'mon! Someone's outside the door! Don't chicken out."

Man, she's fun. I grab the blinds and rattle them, whack the couch with the badminton racket. "That's how baby likes it, don't she? Huh, baby? Huh?"

Kelly crosses her eyes. "Get the Crisco! Ride 'em, cowgirl!"

And then the trailer door opens, and Jordan Aaronson steps inside.

Kelly and I freeze.

"What in the actual fuck, Andy?" His eyes go to the badminton racket.

Kelly and I are out of breath. "Just hanging with my girl." I step down and turn to help Kelly down from the couch as gracefully as I can. She smooths out her clothes, takes the racket from me, and hides it behind her back.

"Jordan Aaronson, this is Kelly Reynolds, my girlfriend." I look at Kelly. She's biting her lip hard, trying not to laugh. "Jordan runs Apotheosis. He's in charge of this production."

Jordan shakes Kelly's hand. "This circus, apparently. What are you two doing? The whole crew's sneaking around, hiding in the bushes outside." His mouth puckers into a sour-lemon pinch.

"Aw, Jordan, we're trying to prank Amanda. A total harmless gag."

"And a total time-suck. We're burning more than daylight. We're burning profit margin."

Kelly looks at her toes. She's a pleaser.

On the other hand, I am not. "It'll all be just fine, Jordan. You should keep morale up, you know. A happy film crew is a productive crew."

Jordan runs his tongue over his front teeth and cocks an eyebrow in irritation. He pulls out his phone and checks it. "You and Amanda are due on set in ten." He shoves the phone back into the pocket of his coat. "Nice to meet you, Kelly."

He turns around and walks back down the trailer's steps, snaps the door shut behind him.

"Isn't he a total ray of sunshine?" Kelly looks at me.

Tucker opens the door and yells, "You guys!"

I take Kelly's hand, and we go out on the pavement. About twenty crew members applaud.

I look at Tucker. "Did Amanda even walk by?"

Tucker laughs. "She did not. Pretty sure Jordan was within earshot for the Crisco remark, though. Classic."

I give Kelly a hug. "We aim to please. Don't tell Jeremy. He'll lose it."

"Lose what?" Jeremy's sitting on the bumper of his New York-rented Benz.

"Ruh-roh, Shaggy." Kelly gives me a peck on the cheek and retreats into the trailer. "Call me when it's all over."

I look at Jeremy. "I can explain."

Jeremy smiles. "Jordan's a dick. Amanda would've been more fun, but if you're gettin' the trailer rocking, Jordan'll work in a pinch too. Let's go talk about how you're gonna make me money today, son."

He claps me on the shoulder, and we walk toward the set.

The rest of the day drags. Kelly has to go, and I envy her. Amanda's being a real pain in the ass. Kelly got to miss all of her antics. Probably good that she did—I'm not too keen on Kelly crossing paths with Amanda. Right now we're shooting dialogue-heavy scenes, and Amanda keeps screwing up her lines. Little flubs, nothing big, but Chase McDougal is not an ad-libber. He co-wrote the script. He expects it memorized. The actor hits his marks, says his lines. Granted, they're good lines, so I'm okay with it, but on a film like this, the actor isn't the boss. Not even close.

Amanda will never cop to being unprepared, so she's been stalking around, looking for someone to blame for her mistakes. No one has made eye contact with her since we came back from lunch—they're terrified of getting stuck as the scapegoat.

When Chase's PA calls a wrap for the day at four that afternoon, and I swear to God I hear someone yell out "Hallelujah," like we're in church. It's all I can do not to laugh out loud on that one. Whoever said it deserves a huge bonus.

Tucker picks me up after the makeup trailer. "Good God and gravy, that was a long one."

"Don't say a word. Until I'm at the condo, I'm terrified someone's going to call me back to set." We pick up our pace and meet Janus, waiting with the car.

We drive back to the condo, and I scan the outside of the building. "No tails yet."

"They tried to follow us back from set." Janus looks at me in the rearview.

"Really?"

Tucker nods. They seem to know everything the other one knows, and all at the same time. Maybe they've done a mind meld.

"I lost him at the turn to the underpass."

"Where's Jeremy?"

"Don't you remember? You and Kelly are due at the Frying Pan. Investors. I think the crew from Dubai."

"Oh joy. Do I have time to change?" I wore a T-shirt to set this morning. I'd love to shower before we go. "Amanda's going to be there, isn't she?"

"Sorry." Tucker has less patience for her than I do.

I rush up to the condo, grab a shower, put on a clean shirt, and stuff a grilled cheese sandwich Kelly's made me in my mouth. She waits for me with Tucker. They chat about all sorts of stuff, and I hear her giggle. The boys are in the media room with Janus.

Apotheosis is sending someone from a nanny service over, at my request, but Aaronson insisted that security stay put too since the nanny service wouldn't fax over a cleared background check. Poor Janus didn't realize he was babysitting tonight. Kelly asked Mari first, but she begged off with some excuse about a date. Luckily Janus likes Halo as much as the boys. They're knee deep in some covert-ops level when we leave. The nanny from the service sits in the kitchen looking nervous.

Tucker drives, and I sit in back with Kelly. We wind through traffic over to the piers.

Kelly's curious. "What's this place we're going to?"

"It's cool. It'll be perfect tonight. Nice breeze off the ocean. It's on a docked old fireboat. They serve buckets of beers and clams." Last time I ate here, I was not sober yet. I shake what potential memories could come back by resting my hand on Kelly's knee.

"Clams?" She makes a puke face.

"Nice cool fresh breeze off the ocean and river. Not going to make you puke, I promise."

"Boat, rocking on the water?" She looks dubious.

I stroke her knee a bit. "I'll keep your mind on other things." I raise an eyebrow.

She leans over and kisses me, nipping my lower lip to finish the kiss off. Now she raises an eyebrow. "I like the sound of that."

Huh. Maybe this pregnancy hormone thing does more than just make Kelly throw up.

She puts her hand on my knee now, and she's dangerously close to driving me nuts when we pull up to the pier. Now I don't want to go. I want to stay in the car and get her out of these clothes. No time like the present.

Tucker, ever the psychic, announces our arrival. "Time to get out, Pettigrew."

"Fine." I kiss Kelly, lingering just a bit too long, and climb out. Tucker offers her a hand.

We get on the ship, and Kelly excuses herself to look for a restroom. Jeremy introduces me to a few people before I see Jordan Aaronson approaching.

"Yay, here comes our favorite person." I plaster on my acting face.

Jeremy fakes a smile. He's not a good actor. He's lucky he's an agent. "Aaronson."

"King." They compete for the firm handshake award. Jeremy looks like he might twist Jordan's arm and make him cry uncle.

"Jordan." I give a normal handshake—I'm not getting sucked into their game.

"Hey, Andy. Where's your lovely girl?"

"Good question. She's been fighting a bit of a stomach bug lately. I better go look for her."

I don't know if she's sick, but she did slip away. Now I'm worried. I find the door to below deck and follow the narrow gray metal stairs to the belly of the ship.

I stand around for a second. The ladies' room is to the left, and there are thick velvet curtains draped around the entrance. I'm tempted to edge a little closer and call for Kelly, but I don't want anyone else to come see what's up. This is close quarters, and the "Hey, you're Andy Pettigrew! Wow, can I get a picture while outside of a bathroom?" is one of my least favorite fan encounters.

I whisper to the velvet curtains. "Kelly? Are you in there?"

"Nope." She stands behind me.

I jump out of my skin.

"Jesus!" I grab her around the waist, ready to scold her for the scare. Instead, her lips are on mine, and she kisses me hard.

"Come this way." She takes me by the necktie and pulls me down a narrow corridor behind us.

"Are you dragging me to the brig?"

She kisses me again. "Just a little quiet, velvety spot I found when I was looking for the bathroom."

She pulls me around a corner, and it's a dead end. Wow. This is scorching hot.

"I enjoy this side of you, Kelly."

"It's way better than puking." She teases me with little kisses on my neck.

"Hormones that don't make you vomit. I like it." I snake an arm around her back, press my hips up against her.

"Are you up for this?" She doesn't sound like it's totally out of the question. I think she's really asking. My God, this is suddenly my favorite investors meet-and-greet in the history of meet-and-greets.

"Why not?" I loosen my tie. I'm about to work on the buttons of her shirt when there's a loud noise behind us, between us and the stairs.

"What was that?" Kelly turns her head.

"I don't know." I kiss her behind her ear, brush a hand down the front of her shirt to below her waist. She wore a skirt. The heavens are smiling upon me tonight.

She turns back to me, but there's a clatter of metal on the floor of the hall. We both turn this time to see the back of someone disappear around the corner, hear feet going up the stairs to the deck.

"Andrew. We had an audience." Kelly's eyes are wide with fear.

"Yeah, that's creepy."

She squeezes my hand. "Good feeling gone." She shrugs.

"We better get back to Tucker." I curse whatever peeping Tom it was. That could've been epically sexy. Now the night just got typically bland. Maybe my luck's not so great after all.

LIVING PROOF

That night I lie in bed, taking stock. I realize I haven't had a nightmare since we came to New York, almost a month and a half ago. No more nightmares. Maybe having someone I love in my bed helps with that. And here Andrew is, in my bed right now.

He fell asleep while reading *For Whom the Bell Tolls*. Hemingway was my thing, but then Andrew started reading him too, so now I guess it's our thing. I set the book over on his bedside table when he drifted off. Now I'm wide awake. I consider picking the book up to see where he stopped. Instead, I just stare at my guy, my movie star.

He's got his arms sprawled up over his head. His chest and stomach are pale in the moonlight. I really want to reach out and run my hand over the planes of his body. He's a light sleeper, though. It wouldn't be fair. I sigh. He's so lean—his muscles are taut, sinewy even in sleep—and here I am next to him. Miss Softie, maybe spelled Softee, like white soft-serve ice cream.

That's what pregnancy does to my body. I widen at the bottom, and my boobs and stomach start to merge into one pile of flesh. Yuck. But just as I am ready to sink into the depths of self-loathing, I feel it.

It's a tiny, tiny flutter, but I know exactly what it is. The baby moved. The baby is moving. I feel it again.

"Oh!" It's not a kick to any part of me—he's still too tiny for that. He's swimming around, dog-paddling and dolphin-kicking in his still-spacious hideaway.

Andrew stirs.

"Andrew! Hey!"

"Hmm?" He turns his chin toward me, but he's still asleep.

"I felt the baby move. He's moving."

Andrew opens his eyes now, luscious long eyelashes blinking sleep away. I hope the baby gets those. He'll be adorable.

"What'd you say?" He sighs, sinking back into sleep again.

"The baby's moving."

He sits up on one elbow.

I turn on the lamp. "He's moving. I can feel him moving."

Andrew puts a hand on my stomach. "Can I feel him?"

I shake my head. "He's still too little. It won't be long, though." I grin. It feels real and good—the baby reminds me that there's a payoff to the dead, heavy fatigue and nausea and spread of cellulite. His check-in is well timed.

Andrew keeps his hand on my stomach and lies on his side. "You keep calling him *him*. What makes you so sure?"

"I don't know." I keep doing it, but I don't know why. Habit, I guess—that's all I know is boys.

"What if he's a she?" His eyes close; he'll be asleep again in a minute.

"Good point. I guess we'll know for sure tomorrow." I put my hand on Andrew's, lace my fingers between his. "That'd be nice too."

"She'd be my little girl. Daddy's little girl." He smiles, and he's asleep, the smile drifting away as he falls more deeply.

I let go of his hand, and he turns over.

There's one more little flutter, and then I remember—hiccups. Baby hiccups. When I was pregnant with Hunter, he got the hiccups in utero all the time. Maybe this is baby's first case.

"Is that it?" I ask baby quietly. "You have the hiccups?"

He or she is my little hiccup, that's for sure. Certainly wasn't part of our regularly scheduled programming. But this pregnancy is no calamity. On this journey Andrew and I get to take together, it's just a bump in the road.

"Hiccup. That's your gender-neutral nickname until you arrive, darling." I pat my tummy and turn off the light.

The next morning we're up and headed to the baby doctor. I'm excited, I won't lie. I like the ultrasounds. Andrew hasn't seen this before. I know he'll love it. Sharing this with him will send him into orbit about the baby.

I watch him jiggle his leg and check and recheck his phone.

"You're nervous."

"No, I'm not."

"There's nothing to be nervous for. This is the fun part. It doesn't hurt me, and I don't have to give up any bodily fluids for it, either."

He nods absently. "I just know to know he's in one piece. Everything's where it's supposed to be. All that developmental stuff."

"I've never for a second worried about it. I think he'll be just fine."

"So, we need to have the talk, though."

"If we'd had that, we wouldn't be in this position." I point to my belly.

"Ha ha."

"What are we talking about?"

"Do we want to know that he's a he? For sure?"

I hadn't thought about this. With Hunter and Beau, eighty million years ago, it was kind of obvious in the ultrasounds that they were boys. They weren't shy. "I guess we could ask not to see, if he's showing off."

"What?"

"Sometimes, when the tech is taking measurements, it's hard not to notice. But it's also kind of early, so the tech might not even be able to tell."

"Well, let's do this differently. I want to be surprised."

I'm touched. He so often defers to me on decisions. He lets me be the one with strong feelings. How nice that it's reversed on this one.

"And you're convinced he's a he, anyway, so it'd just be confirming what you apparently already know."

"Okay, Andrew. You take the lead. I just want to be clear what this does for baby gifts."

"What does it do for baby gifts? Do tell."

"We'll get a ton of green stuff. People will go crazy for the sage green baby stuff. Our baby will wear soft celery onesies for an eternity."

"I can deal with that. I could spring for some different-colored ones when the baby comes, anyway."

"Oh, you'll be able to afford them. But when you'll have the time to actually acquire them is a different story."

"We'll send Jeremy out. To a baby store. He deserves to have to go to a baby store."

"That does sound fun. He should have to buy butt cream. Ooh! No, nursing pads. He needs to ask someone in Babies 'R' Us where the nursing pads are."

"I like how we bond over making Jeremy squirm. But do I want to know what a nursing pad is? Maybe it'll make *me* squirm."

"All part of breastfeeding. What a joy. Then you'll know all about nursing pads, and liniments, and hopefully not thrush, which sucks more than almost anything, and mama when baby won't latch on right, and when baby gets teeth. Yeah, can't wait."

"So, breastfeeding sucks is what I'm hearing."

"Pretty much. Someone else might've liked it, but I was taking one for the team when I breastfed the boys. They're geniuses now, so I guess it was worth it."

"Time to change the subject. I can only take the dirty, gritty details in small doses." He goes back to fidgeting.

Janus drives the car around the block, checking for tails. We really, really don't want pictures going in and out of the doctor's office. I don't relish looking like the beached whale next to gorgeous Andrew. Tucker doesn't want anyone to know where the office is—or, you know, that we have a reason to visit such an office. Tucker, always with the security over the vanity. What a guy.

After his circuit, Janus seems satisfied, and we park in the garage. Andrew texts the front desk, and as a result, we're led through the reception area straight into an exam room. I giggle inside because the look on some of the pregnant ladies' faces in the office when they see Andy Pettigrew is priceless. I'd bet most of them convince themselves it wasn't him. Why in the world would he be strolling through their OB's office?

The room is different than usual. It's the ultrasound room. It's dim, and I'm tempted to take a nap. Except that I was good and followed orders and drank a large amount of water before I came. I can't sleep when I might float away.

"Time to find out what you're having!" The tech breezes in and goes to the sink to wash her hands.

Andrew straightens up. "Not exactly. We want to be surprised."

"What?" She smiles. "I'm Stacy, by the way. You sure?"

"Yep. I want to be surprised. Miss Psychic over here thinks she already knows."

"Oh yeah?"

I nod. "Mother's intuition."

"What are you thinking?" Stacy has pretty black ringlets of hair almost to her butt. She tosses them when she asks this, almost like a challenge.

"If I told you then you couldn't be trusted. Your face would give away what you saw."

"Hmm…you've thought through this. I like it. Okay, well, let's get to it."

She has me lie back, and we get rolling.

Andrew sits next to me, watches my face. "You're okay?" This is the first visit he's been able to come to. I've been a good patient, taking the initiative to find a doctor in NYC (with Dr. Joe in Boise's blessing, of course), making all my appointments. Poor Andrew, this ultrasound is nothing. He's going faint dead away during delivery—talk about the ugly, dirty truth.

"I'm completely fine. Watch the screen." I point to the monitor.

Stacy adjusts the wand on my belly a bit. "I'm trying not to have the little one give you a show. Let's measure head to butt." She drops and drags a dotted line, marks, types the measurement into the computer. "Yep. Okay, let's get a head measurement."

She angles the wand, presses a little. "I need to get him to turn a bit."

Andrew perks up. "Him?"

"Or her. Don't know yet." Stacy looks at him and smiles. "I promise. I won't give it away. I've done this a time or two, you know."

"You can call him Hiccup." I offer this up to be helpful.

"Nice nickname."

"I'm not wild about it." Andrew runs a hand through his hair. He hasn't relaxed yet.

"It won't stick. Don't worry, nicknames like that don't stick. Usually." Stacy chuckles. She's teasing him.

I like her. She has not one bit of shyness or weirdness given who Andrew is. She's just got moxie.

She gets a few more measurements and prints a picture of the head, looking like a creepy alien baby head, and a cute one of the foot, and one where it looks like baby is waving. The boys will love that one.

"Okay, last chance to check out the goods. Any takers?" She looks at me, then Andrew. "What willpower. Well, Dr. Sorensen will get a look at these, but I feel safe saying it's all systems go. I think your due date of February thirteenth is pretty on-target. And everything's looking good."

"Healthy? Ten fingers, ten toes?" Andrew asks.

"Yep."

"Except for the tail." I can't help it.

"What?" His face goes blank.

"Gotcha." I slap him on the arm.

"Wow. That was hysterical." He stands up. "I'm going to take my baby pictures and leave in a huff."

"Let me get my shoes on." I sit up.

"Fine. Still going to be huffy." He puts a hand out to Stacy. "Thanks for your help. And thanks for not teasing me like my terribly cruel significant other here."

"You're welcome. Have a great rest of your stay in New York." She leaves the room, and I get my stuff together.

Andrew fidgets, sitting on the doctor's stool, flipping his phone over and over. I'm mostly ready, but he keeps looking at me. "Are you done yet?"

"Are you in a hurry?" I stand up and pull on my coat.

"I was waiting to do this." He pulls a small box out of his coat, takes my hand.

"What're you doing?"

He pops the lid. It's a ring pop, shaped like a pacifier. "Proposing again."

"A ring pop?" I shake my head.

"Wait, are you saying no? Is this my first no? I was going for a four-peat."

I kiss him, pull him close. He answers with a strong kiss of his own, his hands sliding under my coat, around my waist, and all of a sudden I've forgotten the doctor's office and the ultrasound and everything else.

He breaks the kiss and the mood. "I'm taking that as an unspoken yes. And now we need to go home. This is not the place for what we're about to get up to."

We leave the office, and Janus has the car running at the door of the garage. He's out of the car and has the back door open.

Andrew stiffens. "Uh-oh."

"What?" I don't see anything.

"Janus is rolling."

"What's that mean?"

"It means someone texted from the doctor's office, and there are probably photographers in the garage. Let's go."

He holds his coat up in front of my face, and he propels me through the garage doors.

All of a sudden, the garage is filled with echoes, shouts, and men. Janus gets a hand out in front of one guy with a video camera who steps in front of me.

Andrew puts a forearm into the guy's chest, pressing him out of my space. "Move."

Then we're in the back of the car, but I'm startled by a smack, smack, smack, on the glass of the car window. Paparazzi press their camera lenses flat to the glass, and flashes rapid fire as they try to get a shot inside the car.

I sit paralyzed.

Janus guns the engine and peels out.

"What just happened?" I don't even have my seatbelt on all the way.

"The magic of our interconnected world. That's all it takes. One tip-off about where Andy Pettigrew is. One tweet lets loose a feeding frenzy."

I don't know how he stands it. And then I wonder how long I'm going to have to stand it. "That kind of stuff makes me miss Boise."

"You and me both. Let's go get lunch. Janus, drive us all around Manhattan and ditch these losers."

"No problem." Janus turns out on to Seventh Avenue and guns it. A town car, two scooters, and a BMW give chase.

MAKING PLANS

The summer's been nuts. I've been putting in sixteen-hour days on set, we just had an ultrasound for the baby, Kelly and the boys are due to go back to Boise for the start of the school year, and yesterday someone tipped off the paparazzi that we were at the doctor's office. The last thing I want to do right now is spend lunch with Jeremy talking about me and my film career. But I know Jeremy's right. We need to sit and have a strategy session.

Someone in Hollywood once said, "You're only as good as your last picture." That's bullshit. You're only as good as the next project you have lined up. And it better be financed, locked and loaded, and starting pre-production. Second unit better be gearing up to start location shots, or you've got nothing.

I'm white hot right now. That's not vanity; that's fact. And if I don't capitalize on it, squeeze every last deal out of it while I can, I'll turn around and find the offers for *Dancing with the Stars* and VH1's *Where are They Now* and Lifetime Christmas movies as the only game in my town.

I'm not ready for my fifteen minutes to be up. I love acting. I like the challenge. I want to get better. I need to work to get better.

And yes, I won a Golden Globe, but I haven't gotten one of those little golden guys that make every actor salivate.

I want one. I'm ambitious. This town would have eaten me alive ages ago if I hadn't been hungry, willing to push myself, and willing to expect more from myself every single time.

So, Jeremy sits with me at lunch at the Lion in the Village. Lucky for me, as one of the best agents in Hollywood, Jeremy King's not just hungry; he's downright bloodthirsty. He'll die making a deal for me if he thinks it'll get us closer to the prize. He wants an Oscar for me, sure, but he also wants me to have my pick of projects, and he wants the projects I pick to get made.

Easier said than done in our business.

"Let's talk about *Flat Rock*," he begins.

"Give me the update."

"Daniel means well, but I swear he needs to not talk to the money guys at Paramount. Every time he does, they call me, and I have to promise that we can control him and that, no, shooting will not take 'as long as it needs to take.'"

Daniel is the best director for this picture, but he gets lost in the art. Movies are about money, plain and simple. If you want to shoot a period piece with horses and special effects and a star like me, you better serve up a budget and a tight shooting schedule and lots and lots of promises that the movie will be loved by every demographic group from twelve to sixty-four.

"Just keep telling them it's a four-quadrant movie," I tell him. "And keep reminding them that the production company can squeeze a nickel from a turnip."

Jeremy crunches a celery stick. "I don't think that's the saying."

"Whatever."

"He who pays the piper calls the tune — that's a better saying for that."

"Don't make me get out my phone and Google pithy money aphorisms. I'll do it."

"We just need to keep Daniel on track, son. I smell a hit, and it has the appeal across all four quadrants, so, yes, I'll keep telling them that. Now you help me by keeping the drama of your life out of your work."

"There's no drama. Everything's fine."

"Really? Let's take stock. Your girlfriend's pregnant, and you'd rather no one know about it yet, but you just got ambushed outside the baby doctor's office. Amanda keeps making googly eyes at you on set. Your new sobriety is not even two years old. Yeah, that's quite the boring life."

"And there was a weird thing."

"Weirder than normal? Do tell. Why am I not on blood pressure meds yet? Why? Oh, that's right, I still drink."

I raise an eyebrow.

"Not in front of you, Andy. I'm as considerate as the next guy."

"You're waiting until I hit two years, and then you'll drink whatever you damn well please in front of me. And consider taking up smoking just to irk me. I know you."

"Too well. It's all out of love, only love. What's the weird stuff?"

"At the Frying Pan, below deck, someone was watching us."

"So? You're you. Someone sees you; they watch you."

"No, someone sees me; they come over and want a picture and ask me to sign the back of their iPhone case and see if I will call their aunt in Hoboken and tell her yes, OMG, it's really Andy Pettigrew on the phone. Someone does not stay hidden and run away when we hear him."

"Okay, that's weird. Did you tell Tucker?"

"Yes."

"What else?"

"That's it. Can we talk movies now? My palms are sweating." Even now, thinking about that rattles me.

"Fine. What do you want to work on next?"

"After *Flat Rock*?"

"Before that. It's not till May. It's barely September, and we wrap end of the month. You could squeeze three projects in before May. You'll have post on *The Bull and the Bear* and *The Whatever-the-hell-else*, but reshoots shouldn't be too bad."

"I have a baby coming in February, Jeremy. I'm not jumping into another project. Not yet."

"Really." He snaps another celery stick in two.

"Really. Baby. Baby being born. Kind of a big deal."

"You'll have more than enough time to play Daddy of the Year when your streak cools off. Don't lose your momentum. Eight months is an eternity."

"You have a cameo in something? Something supporting? I could probably do something if it was in LA."

"Only if you're planning on living in LA for a while. You can't just drop in on a set if you're going back to Boise after this."

"The boys start school in Boise, and I'm already going to leave them alone for almost a month."

"That's the boys. Kelly's a pro at taking care of them on her own. She's done it before, if you recall."

"And now you're starting to piss me off. I get it, Jeremy. I need to be where the business is. But I am also a top-earning actor. I can use some of my 'star power' to leverage the life I want."

"What if we found a really awesome new house in LA? That way we could see about squeezing in some projects before the baby comes. The whole family could be together in LA. You keep your momentum with a couple new projects, and then, boom, you're home in Boise to hang the tinsel for Christmas. And I have another script you could check out for filming in January — just three weeks in LA on your own, then home to Boise for the babypalooza."

"Kelly wants to be in Boise for the semester. It's bad enough they have to start the school year without me."

Jeremy looks at me, stops chewing. His face is dead serious. "Maybe now's the time to have the you're-the-almost-wife-of-a-working-actor-in-Hollywood talk with the missus. Andy, you can't miss this chance. You know it as well as I do. Why not have a place in LA? Why not have the kids out of school for a semester? There's such a thing as a tutor. I think you can spring for one."

I sit quiet. I take a sip of water. He's got me on this one. He's right.

"You know I'm right, son. You know you have to capitalize on your heat. Now. And I have a director who's dying to work with you."

"Who?"

"Oh, I don't know, someone who's won Best Picture. And not in Cannes, and not at the Globes. I'm talking the big leagues. The full-on Academy Awards."

"Now I think you're lying."

Jeremy looks left and right and pulls out a pen. I hate it when he's dramatic. Whenever we have business lunches out, he refuses to talk names out loud—he says someone screwed him on a deal once when they heard him discussing it at Nobu over lunch. I really think it's that he wishes he was a spy. I swear to God. He pens the name of the director on a cocktail napkin and slides it over to me. Below it is a huge dollar amount.

"This script—I can shoot it to you this afternoon. You don't have to audition, the money's solid, the director's attached, and the deal's locked down. And that number? The one with all those zeroes? Yeah, that's just the beginning number for negotiations. It's the most anyone's ever offered you for a leading role. Serious folding money, brother."

I shake my head. "You can't put a deal like that together this fast. There's no way it'd shoot until after Christmas, at least. And anyway, Mr. Director-Who-Shall-Not-Be-Named is about to start filming in LA next month on another movie, *Out of Range*."

Jeremy smiles, ear-to-damn-ear. "I know. And his star just came down with pneumonia. Dropped out."

Well, shit. If this is true, Jeremy has me exactly where he wants me. I'd have to be certifiable not to jump at an opportunity like this. That director's worked with DeNiro, Damon, Clooney, Hanks. My pulse revs at the thought of getting a part like that.

I nod. "Yes, I'm interested."

Jeremy fist pumps in victory. "I knew you'd come to your senses. Andy Pettigrew, you're as dog-with-a-bone about this as I am. Don't deny it. We both want the top of the pile, number-one spot. Badly. You've worked your ass off for it."

I sigh. "All right. You can cram October to January with as much as I can humanly do. Make this deal happen; see what else is out there. But come February, it's full-time babyrama."

"For how long?"

"I want to be home with Kelly, in Boise, till we start on *Flat Rock*."

"God, Andy. That's a long, long time."

"Yes, it is. That I want to spend with my family."

"Fine. In May, it's *Flat Rock*. Then you can take the whole family on location for the rest of the summer. You get quality time with them, you shoot a big action movie that I happen to have a lead on, and the kids get to play in the lovely waters of the Mediterranean."

"Where?"

"Croatia. Cheap labor. Warm waters. It's actually not a shithole. I went there once with Brunhilda."

Brunhilda is Jeremy's ex—not her real name of course. Jeremy never refers to exes by real names once he breaks up with them. She's a gorgeous woman who ate men for a living. They were a match made in heaven. But she moved on to an eighty-year-old Israeli producer with a very small immediate family and a very weak heart.

"What's the movie?"

"Let's just say someone is aging out of a particular franchise, and you look great in a tux."

"I'm not British. There'd be a riot."

"Not that one."

Something occurs to me. "What's the shooting schedule for *Bull and Bear* the last two weeks?"

"Why?"

"You've got to clear it with Aaronson that I'm in Boise for Hunter's birthday."

"How adorable. When is it?"

"September twenty-fifth. I can't miss that. Even if I have to borrow Jordan the Dick's jet, I have to be there for that."

"How old will the whipper-snapper be?"

"Fourteen."

"Only four more years till he's out of the house. Good for you."

"You're a douche. You know that, don't you?" I throw a crouton at him.

"Yes, I do. You pay me very well to be *your* douche. So there." He throws the crouton back at me.

YOU SPIN ME ROUND

Even though the doctor's office paparazzi spooked me, I still want to do what I want to do. The boys and I only have a few days left in NYC before we go back to Boise. I want to savor the big city in our time left, do the things I like. Mari and I have taken the boys on lots of strolls in Central Park, and we went to the top of the Empire State Building on a rainy day. Mari even took us on a tour of the Fashion District and pointed out all the boutiques where she wants to have her designs featured someday.

Besides getting to know the city, one of the simpler things I like to do is spend too much money at the Whole Foods in our building. It's so convenient, it's dangerous. Today I sneak with Tucker from the delivery entrance of the condos through the front doors of the store. He hangs out in front with the carts, looking as casual as he can. No one seems to notice me. No one recognizes me without Andrew by my side.

This time I buy red cinnamon bears for Andrew, avocadoes for the salad tonight, and juice and pop for the boys. Hunter has decided he's going to "eat clean," and Beau has decided to do exactly the opposite just to goad his brother.

Hunter hangs around Tucker too much. They've been talking about lifting and CrossFit and all sorts of manly things lately.

When I'm done, we head up to the condo. I get the key in the door and swing it wide, carrying my bag. Tucker always wants to carry it, but I'm pregnant, not an invalid.

Tucker calls out, "Honey, we're home!" Since we've been in New York, Tucker lives with us, camped out in the guest room. I'm surrounded by boys, but I like it.

Andrew strolls out from the study. "Hey." He claps Tucker on the shoulder; Tucker gives him a strong handshake.

Hunter and Beau materialize from the far corners of the condo to dig through my bag. They're dressed in swim trunks and have towels. They live at the condo pool.

"Don't drink those till dinner," I call.

"Fine, Mom," Beau answers as he turns back toward wherever he came from, tailed by Hunter. They look likely to be ignoring me.

"I don't even know why I bother." I sigh.

The boys return to the great room and turn on the TV, too loud as usual.

I have twenty million things going on at the same time in my head.

Andrew comes over. We haven't even said hi yet. "We need to talk," he says.

"What?" I can't sort any of the noise in the room. It's too much.

"Never mind," he walks away. He seems stressed, worried about something. But he's not giving me much of a chance.

Ugh. I swear. "Hey, I just didn't hear you."

"Can you listen?" He purses his lips. The annoyed look. This should be fun.

"I'm trying. I have ten things in my ear right now."

Tucker notices us, smiles at me nervously. Double ugh.

I really want to scream, but I won't. "Let's go in the study for two seconds." I breathe deep. I feel snappish. I shouldn't be snappish.

"Okay. It's not that big of a deal," Andrew says.

"It's big enough that I need to attend to it, and right now Beau's infatuation with *Antiques Roadshow* is cramping my listening style."

We head down the hall into the study. I exhale. My brain feels a hundred times better without the barrage of continuous noise. "What's up?"

Andrew plops down in the overstuffed leather chair behind his desk. I take a spot on the edge of the desk.

"So, you know that I need to stay in New York until beginning of October."

I don't know if all girls do this, but as soon as this sentence is out of his beautiful, pouty lips, I start trying to figure out where Andrew's headed with this. "Yeah. And?" What's he getting at?

"Well, after that, I was supposed to come join you guys in Boise."

"Supposed?" My jaw tenses.

"Jeremy got an offer."

"Jeremy? You let Jeremy get you another job? We're supposed to be in Boise, together, for school. We talked about it."

"Can you please let me finish?" He pushes back from the desk and runs his hands through his hair.

I bite my lip.

"It's not just a job. It's the most I've ever been offered. Ever. Eight figures."

I can't help it. I go on the attack. I want to scream in frustration, but instead, I go for the jugular. "Money? This is about money? How long are you going to be gone?"

Andrew stands up, and I take two steps back. He's mad now too, and he's tall and kind of intimidating when he's mad. "It's not the money. It's the point of the money. That's a lot of power in Hollywood."

"Power and money, some super-awesome family values. Awesome." The sarcasm drips from my words. *I* don't even like the sound of them. I sound mean.

"You need to slow down and breathe, Kelly. You've gone from zero to raging in two seconds."

I walk to the window. I know I need to back off, but I still feel like I want to go in for the kill. I want to punch the crap out of each of the carefully tufted pillows on the stylish suede couch in front of me. *Yikes.* "Why is this so important to you? What's special about this besides the money?"

"I'd be in very good company. Best Picture company."

"How long are you going to be gone?"

"I thought we'd live in LA until Christmas. We could pull the boys—"

I don't even let him finish. "Pull them out of school? Are you absolutely crazy? They'll freak. Boise is home, Andrew. You said it was your home. Now I don't even know. Maybe you didn't mean that."

"Of course I meant that. Jesus, Kelly. Don't make this about everything. We need to actually have a real talk, not a hormone-driven blowout."

Now I do kick the leg of the couch. Twice. Really. The second I do it, I feel like the biggest freak of pregnant nature. "You're making me crazy! I can't do this right now. I won't. Leave me alone."

I attempt to turn on my heel and go back down the hall toward the laundry room. But the swift turn sends my head into a spin.

Everything gets hot, I feel like I'm about to puke, and the room goes gray.

"She's coming to. Andrew, get off the phone! If you call dispatch, everyone and their sister will be shouting about this across all the internet and TV stations in five minutes." Tucker pats me on the cheek. "Kelly Jo Jo, open your eyes now."

I do as I'm told. "What?"

He's above me. I'm on the floor. "You fainted."

"Is she conscious?" I hear the squeak of sneakers on the hardwood floor. Andrew's head is over me now too.

"I feel like I'm going to puke." My head throbs.

"You're a lovely shade of green. Did you eat recently? Does your head hurt?" Tucker always sounds so calm. I like him so much. Maybe we should name the baby after him.

"Did I crack my head?"

"Did she?"

Tucker runs a hand gently over the back of my head. I wince when he rubs a forming goose egg. "Yep."

"Then we're going to the hospital. Go get the car." Andrew smooths my hair with one hand, slides the other one under my shoulders.

"Wait a second there, cowboy." Tucker rests a hand on Andrew's shoulder. "She's awake. She fainted, but she didn't lose consciousness from hitting her head. People faint."

"Yeah, people faint." I chime in. I feel the need to contribute to this discussion. I also might contribute by puking, but you know…

The two men stare at each other for a minute. I don't think I've ever seen them fight. Interesting.

Andrew raises an eyebrow. "You sure about this, Tuck?"

"No hospital. Not now. We can watch her." He smiles at me, pats my hand. "You want to stand up, Miss Kelly?"

I don't know. My number-one priority is not vomiting. I hate throwing up. "Um. Maybe I'll just hang out down here for a while."

The guys act without any more discussion. Andrew has me by the shoulders, then the world is upright again. I'm on my feet for less than a second when he sweeps me up into his arms.

"I don't want him to carry me. I'm still mad."

Tucker laughs. "She's fine."

"And he'll throw his back out. I'm not some teeny movie girl. I'm big and pregnant."

Andrew doesn't even look at me. He still looks at Tucker.

"He's all hopped up on adrenaline, Kelly. His back'll be fine." Tucker is calm and cool. I think he might be trying to calm Andrew down.

Maybe I should follow suit. "Are you implying that I'm heavy?"

"I've seen the snacks you've had in the name of 'eating for two.'" Tucker's eyes twinkle with mischief.

"Are you two done?" Andrew has carried me down the hall to the bedroom door. He nods to Tucker, who swings the door open for him in response.

"I feel better, Andrew. I promise. I just want to be alone for a while."

He carries me to the bed. Tucker stands at the doorway and gives me a little salute. "I'll go make sandwiches to start."

Andrew puts me in the bed, pulls the covers up, adds a pillow behind me.

"I'm not tired. I'm pissed. And I was going to make dinner. It's, like, five thirty, you know." In most cases, I'd love the idea of being swept off my feet, but we haven't finished talking about this movie.

"I did this." He sits on the edge of the bed and stares at the floor.

"What?" I'm confused.

"I upset you, and you fainted. You could have a concussion. It could have put the baby in danger."

"Hiccup's fine. I have a lot of padding around him. And I passed out because I was tired and spun around too fast, and I probably should have eaten more at lunch. This is not emotional distress. I'm not Rhett's lover…you know, the one from *Gone With the Wind*."

"You don't remember her name?" Andrew's eyes are aflame with worry.

"Pregnancy brain. Not concussion brain. Andrew, it's okay."

"What's her name, then?" He looks like he's going to cry. His blue eyes are deep and wet.

"Jesus. Scarlett. Scarlett O'Hara, okay? I couldn't remember for a second. It's more likely Alzheimer's than a brain injury. I promise." I take his hand. "Listen, the boys and I can manage in Boise alone. We've done it before."

"No. I'll turn down the movie. I don't care about it."

"No, you do care about it. You've worked very hard for a very long time to make this happen. You deserve it. My job as your almost-wife is to cheer you on. I should trust you enough to believe in you."

"I'd be in LA until Christmas, probably."

Tears come up in my eyes. That sucks. I hate being away from him. "We could manage. Make hay when the sun shines, right?"

"You're just repeating stuff you've heard Jeremy say."

"If I was doing that, I'd be cussing and insulting someone, possibly saying something sexist." I squeeze his hand. "It'll be fine. I'm tired and pregnant, and I worry. But we've gotten through lots worse. It'll be fine. It's not even for very long."

He takes his hand back and runs it over the back of my head. He pauses on the bump, and I resist the urge to smack him. Yes, I have a knot on the back of my head. Stop touching it, everybody. Geez.

But I don't smack him. He leans over and plants the softest, most tender kiss on my lips. "Nothing can happen to you. You, the boys, the baby. He has to be safe. You guys all have to be okay."

"Ha! See, I got you to call Hiccup a him. I'm winning the gender war."

"Hiccup. Ugh." He smiles, just a little. Maybe I have succeeded in distracting him.

"It's cheesy, I know. He had the hiccups. It was destiny. And if it's a girl, then it's gender neutral enough for her too."

"I'm not kidding. Your safety is first. If anything happened to you…" He stops talking and tucks the blanket tightly in around me.

"Same for you, Andrew. You know that. Life is precious and short. You're talking to the expert at that, remember?"

He kisses me again, taking me by the shoulders. His intensity stirs me, and I kiss back, wanting him closer. I pull his shirt, tug him toward me.

"Slow down there, Cochise." He lifts his head and breaks the moment.

"You started it."

"I love you, and I want you to rest now. Humor me?" He tucks a strand of my hair behind my ear, kisses me again, this time on my forehead.

I sigh. "Fine. Tell the boys not to drink what I bought them yet. They'll never eat dinner."

"I'll handle it. They were going down to the pool last time I checked. I'm glad they missed all this. They worry about you too, you know."

"Enough worrying! I'll take a nap. Go handle dinner."

"I'm looking in on you in about ten minutes. Call me if you feel sick again."

I push him. "Go. If you hover, I will be sick from all the fussing."

He stands, and his hands go deep in his pockets, his shoulders shrugging up. "I know, but—"

"Stop!" I throw a pillow at his head.

He ducks. "I'm going." He smiles and slides out of the room, pulling the door shut behind him.

I stare at the ceiling. I'm not tired. I feel fine. I don't even feel sick anymore. But for Andrew to worry, that gets me worrying too. I'm the master at it. I've spent my life with real, unreal, big, and little fears eating at my gut.

The man I love is a movie star. He's a natural target. I'm pregnant, and I know every single terrible sad story I've ever heard about lost babies by heart, since they linger stubbornly in the crevices of my brain. I have two beautiful young men I love more than my own life, and they're about to be in the prime bad-choice-making era of their lives. I know what it's like to lose a loved one. It's happened once; it could happen again.

All of this could tear me apart or paralyze me. Fear of the unknown.

Strangely, today a peace settles over me. For right now, for this moment, nothing is wrong. I can't know what will happen tomorrow, but there is no sense in worrying about it tonight. I wonder where this calm came from, but I am thankful for it.

Maybe it's the knock to the head. Perhaps some sense found its way in.

I close my eyes and am surprised to feel drowsiness settle on my limbs, warm and heavy. For now, I will sleep and know that the ones I love are safe.

TOO CLOSE

Jesus. I step out of the limo, and there it is, as usual — the roar.

As usual. I sound like a total douche. I can't believe I just thought that. Here I am, about to be interviewed on a national morning TV show, and I'm Mr. Blasé.

But I want to be at home with Kelly right now. Last night, we argued, and she fainted, and it scared the hell out of me. I'd rather keep an eye on her than stand here and listen to people scream their heads off at the sight of me. Now I really sound like an ego-maniac.

I do have my absolutely neurotic moments: "They aren't squealing as loudly as they used to." That's the thing about going after fame or acceptance or whatever this craziness is — it's so cliché, but there's never a point where it's enough. Because really what a narcissist like me — a fame whore, an actor — is looking for, we're not ever going to find out there. Until we're enough inside, all the success and magazine covers will just whip people like me into a weird, insecure frenzy. We need to get another hit, score another deal, more more more to get the same buzz we used to get from less attention. That sounds utterly familiar, doesn't it?

Why couldn't I be a normal addict and transfer my addiction to something like Saint Bernard-size plastic cups of Mountain Dew? I shake off nicotine and alcohol, but fame, man, it tastes so damn sweet.

Facing the crowd, I breathe in deep and bite the insides of both of my cheeks as I stand tall. This deep breath and slight twinge of pain helps to center me, sure, but Sandy, my publicist, also taught me to do it for the red carpet, for appearances. It makes the cheekbones pop.

Wow, this stream of consciousness is getting dangerously shallow, isn't it?

Anyone who thinks photogenic people were born that way haven't been through media training with a major movie studio.

"Hey, handsome." It's Amanda.

"Amanda." I'm gonna be hoarse. It's loud out here. The concrete canyons of the city bounce all the sound of the crowd back to my ears. Again I wish I was back at the condo, still in bed with Kelly since she goes back to Boise soon.

Amanda pokes me on the arm. "I'm here to save you from taking yourself so seriously."

"Uh-huh." I eye the sidewalk between us and the stage door to the television studio. On one side, a large group of people is contained against the building by a metal crowd-control fence. On the other side, the sidewalk is supposed to be clear for us and for anyone who hopes to just walk down the street, but people have heard the commotion and are starting to mill around to see what's up. The limo I just got out of pulls away, and Tucker joins us for the short walk from the fire lane up the city sidewalk to the back door of the building. We're taping a spot to promote the movie on the morning show I hate, the one with two people who despise each other with a passion but who pretend to be besties for the sake of sagging mid-morning ratings.

Tucker hustles us along, his hands out to clear a path through the gathering crowd. We have to edge closer to the street, avoiding the looky-loos.

"Let's go in. We could hold hands." Amanda gives me a sly look.

"No, we couldn't."

"'Cause we're not going steady? You could give me your ring. Or pin me."

"'Cause I'm in love with someone who is quite clearly not you and who wouldn't be caught dead wearing jeans with that amount of shit on the back pockets. What, did you tie one on and get crazy with the Bedazzler?"

"Suck it, Pettigrew."

"Always the lady, Amanda."

Right now I only mildly hate her, and most of the time on set it's been more reminiscent of Arthur and D.W. than Hepburn and Tracy. She's the pesky cartoon kid sister—if D.W. were into cupping and fish pedicures and colonics and whatever other weird beauty nonsense Amanda is doing to herself lately.

I look to my left as she takes a step ahead, just in time to see Tucker lunge toward me.

At that exact moment, someone shoves me from behind, hard. I'm off balance, turn a bit in my bid to regain my footing, and am thrown back on my heels. I'm going over, about to be off the curb.

Except that there's nowhere for me to go, no pavement on which to be laid out flat, because this isn't the bowed-in fire lane next to the studio alley. Moving north, the flow of traffic is right on me. Behind me. About to take me out.

Tucker's hand has me by the neck of my sweater, roughly, and he yanks. My head comes up, sending the trajectory of my body in a direction away from the New York City traffic. But as he gives me a serious neck burn, I also feel sharp, clean pain bite hard into my shoulder blade.

I hear a crunch, a pop of plastic, and hope that crunch was glass or something else besides my scapula. Noise—a yelp—escapes my mouth, and for a second I'm self-aware and proud of not letting loose a huge chain of filthy, angry pain words.

But I also hear a sick gasp come collectively from everyone witnessing what just happened. There's an eerie half-second of quiet, then girlish screams of concern.

I'm listening, but really what I'm doing is being dragged by one arm and my lapels. Tucker pulls me through a door.

"*Oh shit oh shit oh shit.*" I hear myself repeating it, like a panicked mantra.

Tucker shouts, bellows, and now I look at linoleum and the glare of fluorescent lighting, and I hear, I think, the heels of my shoes squeaking and squealing on the tile because Tucker's not done dragging me yet.

I wonder when he's gonna stop when all of a sudden he does.

We're in the back of a kitchen, by a prep sink. He's on the cell phone, and he's put himself between me and anyone else. There's a small crowd of wait staff and cooks hovering behind him, but navy-sport-coated burly guys form a human barrier between him and them. They must be network security.

He talks to me. "Andrew! Andrew!"

"Huh?"

"Are you all right?"

"What?" I have no idea what the hell's going on. Everything's just now coming into focus. "You shredded my neck."

He turns me around, away from him. I look at the sign above the sink: *It's New York State Law, Wash Your Hands Before Returning to Work.*

He barks again. "Someone get me scissors. And give me a status report on the driver of the SUV. I want the actual statement he gives to the police."

I feel something hot and wet on my right hand. It's blood. It's my blood. "My shoulder?"

Someone's gotten him scissors. "Jesus, Andrew. What happened out there?"

"Someone shoved me. It was like a dirty play from that Burt Reynolds movie, the one where the prison guys play football."

"*All the Right Moves?*" There's loud ripping of fabric.

Jacket's ruined. Probably the sweater, too. Jeremy'll be pissed. He got Escada to dress me for today. Now it's all gone to hell. "No, not *All the Right Moves*—that's Tom Cruise. Good God."

Tucker works on the back of me. "Oh, I know. *The Longest Yard.*"

"Yeah, that one." I watch my blood drip into the sink. "Tuck, the blood thing. You know how I do blood."

"Your own, not well. How do you feel right now?"

To tell the truth, right now I can bet money—oh hell, I'll bet that sweet flat screen I was going to give Jeremy for Christmas—that I've been struck by a car. I know logically that I took most of the hit to the right shoulder blade, which laid the flesh above it wide open, probably clean down to the bone.

But shock's a wonderful thing. I don't feel anything, not yet, except for the warm, wet river down the right side of my back.

"Janus, come put pressure on this," Tucker says. Janus comes to my side. Tucker leans around, looks me in the face. "Ambulance is one-forty out. They'd be here right now, but the traffic is a cluster. Police shut the whole block down. EMTs are driving the last half-block down the sidewalk."

Something comes to me clear and bright, like a yellow balloon in a blue summer sky. "Tucker, that was on purpose."

Tucker looks me straight in the eye as he turns me around and helps me sit on the edge of the stainless steel sink that's now covered in my blood. There go the six-hundred-dollar pants. My shoulder decides to start throbbing in a hey-there's-some-trauma-going-on-here rhythm under the heavy-fisted pressure Janus's putting on it.

Tucker nods gravely. "It was definitely on purpose."

WORST THAT COULD HAPPEN

When the phone rings, I answer right away, expecting Andrew. He left insanely early to tape a morning show segment. He's even less of a morning person than I am, so this is a grouchy phone call, probably.

"How's Mandy?" I ask in greeting.

"Kelly, I'm on the way over there." It's Jeremy.

"What?"

"I'm on my way, be sure to buzz me up fast." I've never heard him sound like this. His voice is brittle, like gray driftwood on the beach.

"What's wrong? Where's Andrew? What's happened to him?" My heart is pounding.

"Stop. He'll kill me. He didn't even want to tell you yet. He got clipped by a car on the way into the studio for the taping."

"Clipped? What does that mean?" My voice is high and tight.

"A car grazed him. He took it on the shoulder."

"Oh my God, Jeremy. Where is he?"

"Getting stitches. Getting checked out at Roosevelt Hospital, since Jordan the dick won't rest until he knows his investment is in one piece. The studio doctor could've handled it, but no—"

"Jeremy! Why are you coming here? I want to go there and see him."

"Ah, that's just what he said you'd say. I've been told to come over there and prevent you from going anywhere. Tucker and Andrew will come home shortly. You are to stay put. End of story."

"That's crap. I'll get a cab."

Jeremy exhales sharply. "Kelly, for chrissake. Just do this, for once. Don't flip out. This is hard enough on him." Jeremy is always one for the tactful, gentle comment.

"How badly is he hurt?" I ask.

"Lots of stitches. Nothing else as far as I know. It'll hurt like a bitch, though. No pain meds for Mr. Clean."

I turn circles in the kitchen. Judging by the other night when I fainted, I need to proceed with caution — too much spazzy aimlessness on my part and I'll probably keel over again. I sit at the kitchen island.

"I'm here. Buzz me up." Jeremy hangs up.

I'm on my feet again. I try to stay quiet. Hunter's still asleep. He stayed up late last night watching movies. Beau's in his room reading. What are we going to say to them about this? It'll scare them. They'll worry for Andrew.

There's a loud rapping on the door. I check the peephole and let Jeremy in.

He's got a bag in his hands. "I brought food."

"You stopped to get a bite to eat? Who does that?" Sometimes Jeremy's absolutely callous demeanor makes me want to push him off a cliff.

"I stole it from the green room at NBC. It's the least they can do. Fuckers almost got my favorite client killed." He dumps out cartons of milk, juice boxes, bagels, croissants, doughnuts.

I can't help it. I laugh. "Jesus, Jeremy."

"Tucker's expected to do all the crowd control? By himself?" Jeremy waves a bagel around in his zeal. "Did it not occur to them that one of the biggest stars in Hollywood was coming by? They couldn't even close the stupid sidewalk for thirty minutes while they did arrivals?"

"What happened?"

"He was walking into the studio, the crowd surged, he got pushed almost into traffic. You owe Tucker big. He swiped him out of the way, before anything worse could've happened."

I sit down again. "My God."

"Hey, hey now." He finally seems to remember that I'm Kelly the widow, Kelly the lady who knows death. He sits down next to me, grabs a doughnut. "Listen, Tucker was right there. No big deal. He'll have a good story to go along with the scar."

I can't say anything. He hands me a chocolate milk and takes my hand, pats it.

We sit like this for a minute. It's the nearest to compassion Jeremy gets. When he's quiet, that's a very big deal.

"You know, it's probably best if you don't watch TV for the day," he says after a moment. "They'll have coverage of it for a while."

"I just want him to come home."

He lets go of my hand and starts walking around the kitchen. He finds the butter and slathers it on one of the bagels. "He'll be here. I'll hang with you till they come. It's going to be fine."

"I just want to have a peaceful day or two with him. Is that too much to ask?"

"He's Andy Pettigrew, Kelly. Yes, it's too much to ask—at least until he's not so famous. That'll happen, sooner or later. Right now, he's on fire. So, no, no peaceful stuff quite yet."

He pats my hand again. "C'mon. We'll go sit on the patio and sunbathe. Maybe you can suntan that expanding belly of yours. Tan fat is better than white fat, you know."

Even with my spinning head and pounding heart, I would rather sit with him than be left to my own devices. "All right. But if you call me fat again, I'll cut your heart out with that butter knife. Do not mess with a pregnant woman."

"Got it." He leads the way to the patio.

I spend the whole time, three agonizing hours, waiting for Andrew and Tucker to come home. I'm drenched in sweat, chewing my lips, trying to breathe in nice and slow, and at least for the baby's sake, trying to stay in control. I will not cry. This is not my moment to be all shaky and wimpy. I don't know how badly Andrew's hurt, and he's going to need the TLC, not me.

I hadn't thought about the pain meds, not till Jeremy said something. Andrew will hurt. That sucks. "Ice. We need more ice, I bet. I should check." I make a move to get up from the lounge chair Jeremy's parked me in.

"You have plenty. I had Hunter check." Jeremy went in and talked to both boys. I suspect he made it sound all very nonchalant. I guess I'm thankful for that. There's no way I could have told them without crying, and they'd freak out. When I had to tell them their dad had died, it was one of the worst times in my life. I suspect I would have a similar look on my face, and both of them probably would get taken right back to that moment. No need to drag them back through that.

I hear voices in the hall and jump to get up. Jeremy grabs my arm again. "Slow down, sister. Let him come out here."

I hate Jeremy—have I said that? I sit impatiently.

Tucker appears on the patio first. His face is passive, no emotion on it whatsoever.

Andrew's behind him, his arm in a sling. He is pale.

I jump up, run over to him. "Andrew, oh, Andrew." I stop short.

He puts the free arm out. "I can't tell you how good it is to see you." He hugs me.

I reach up and touch his face, search his eyes for clues. "Are you all right?"

"Yes. My shoulder hurts like a mother. But I'm fine. Tucker was right there."

Tucker nods. "The crowd got a little out of hand. Nothing we haven't seen before. It's just that there's nowhere to go on a New York City sidewalk. Andrew stepped back off the curb, and the car caught his shoulder. Police questioned the driver, but he just had nowhere to go, couldn't get out of the way. Felt awful about hitting a huge movie star. He's terrified Andrew will sue him or something."

Jeremy gets up. "What's the damage?"

"Sixty-seven stitches."

"That's gonna leave a serious mark." Jeremy shakes his head. "Did you at least get pain meds while you were in the ER?"

Andrew shakes his head in return. "I told them no. They did numb the area with local. It wasn't terrible."

Tucker disagrees. "Yes, it was. There was some whimpering."

"You or him?" Jeremy gives Tucker a nudge.

"Both, to be honest." Tucker walks a perimeter of the patio. He scans the surrounding buildings. I can tell he's rattled. His heightened awareness equals nerves.

"If you guys don't mind, I'd like to go lie down. You all can leave now." Andrew looks at both of them.

Jeremy waves him off. "Oh, no you don't. We're the support team. I'll crash out on the couch in the media room. I have to run damage control, and I'm answering all of your calls—your cell and Kelly's cell. Sandy'll be over tomorrow to help."

Andrew rolls his eyes, points at Tucker. "You're already in the guest room. Are you part of the hovering too?"

"I'll keep the press off your back. They've set up camp out front. I can keep them out of the building. And then I want the building swept. Apotheosis is sending extra guys over. I told them fine as long as I get to coordinate it."

"One big family, eh?" Andrew leans his good hand up against the wall of the patio, defeated.

"I'm kind of glad. It'll make the boys feel better. They like having the guys around." I take his hand, wrap my fingers around his. His hand is clammy.

"Fine. I want to go close my bedroom door and talk with my fiancée. Does everyone approve of that?"

Jeremy perks up. "What? Fiancée? Since when?"

I haven't heard Andrew use the word, either. I thought we were keeping it on the downlow. "What?"

"Look, Kelly and I are getting married. Maybe we've been joking about the proposals up till now, but now that I've had an opportunity to take stock—while I lay on my stomach for an hour getting stitches—I don't care if I haven't had a chance to propose properly. You're my fiancée, and that's that. The rest is details."

My chest feels warm. I give his hand a squeeze. "I agree completely. Details." I kiss him gingerly on the cheek. "Why the sling?"

Tucker takes the question. "No movement. It'll pull the stitches in his back out."

Andrew laces his fingers into mine. "Come with me."

Jeremy holds a hand up. "Not to dwell on details, but are we going public with the fiancée thing?" Jeremy tries very hard to keep a neutral face, but I can see the excitement spark in his eyes. This news would set things on fire for Andrew in the press in a good way, not in an almost-died-when-hit-by-car way—for a couple days, at least, until the twenty-four-hour news cycle lost interest and moved on to something else.

"Let me sleep on it, Jeremy."

"It'd be great to get them off the car thing." Jeremy flips his phone over and over in his hand. The man is a caffeinated terrier.

"I hear you, J. But I said let me sleep on it." Andrew walks right by him. "I think it's fair to say I've already had a long-ass day, don't you think? Don't force me to decide about it now. I want to lie down for a while."

"No problem." Jeremy steps back.

Andrew pulls me by the hand down the long hallway to our bedroom. I stay quiet. He gets us in the door and pulls it shut.

"I was going to give you this when I got home tonight. Proposal number five. It was going to go in your piece of pizza." He pulls a slim silver band out of his pocket. It has a tiny red apple made out of rhinestones on it.

I feel tears slide down my cheeks. "It's so cute. Yes." I slip it on, try for a joke. "I probably would've accidentally swallowed it if it'd been hidden in the pizza. It's better that you're just giving it to me."

"Tucker bought it yesterday from a guy on the street. He's always looking out for me, you know." He smiles a little, and then closes his eyes for a long pause.

I can't say anything. I watch him. He lets go of my hand, goes to the bed, pulls back the covers. He looks at me. "I want to lie down with you. I want to hold you and listen to your heart beat. I want you to tell me about each little twitch you feel our baby make. I want to fall asleep with my arms around you."

"Okay. Do you want me to get your jeans off?"

He looks stuck. He's gotten his shoes off.

"Yes, damn it. I wish it was because we were going to do nasty, dirty things to each other, but the pain right now…"

"Stop. You're human. Stop trying to be so strong. It was a close call."

I come to him, unbutton his jeans. He steps out of them and kisses me for a moment.

"I don't even want to try the shirt. It was a beast to put it on after the stitches."

"I don't recognize it."

He wears a big, soft gray T-shirt. I help him to take the sling off. He holds his arm folded against his torso, tucked like a bird's wounded wing.

"It's Tucker's. He gave me the shirt off his back. He can't stand that I got hurt on his watch. He might not forgive himself."

I shake my head. "It's nobody's fault. Just an accident. And you're fine. He caught you. Just a stupid accident."

Something dark flits across his face, creases his brow and turns his mouth down. I see the expression, and it's gone, replaced by the actor face, perfectly placid, perfectly neutral. "You're right. Just an accident."

"What?"

"Nothing. It'd just be a stupid way to die."

"We're not talking about that. I'm treading on very thin ice here. You know that. For everyone's sake, we're not talking about death. No one wants me to go there." My voice trembles as I say it, but I swallow hard. This is not about me.

"Enough. Lie down with me." He climbs in and arranges himself carefully.

"I don't know where to go. You can't hold me; you'll hurt your back."

"Stop." He pats the spot in front of him. "Right here, baby mama."

I crawl carefully in next to him. I hold as still as I can. He puts his arm over me, draped over my growing belly. "Is this okay?"

He kisses my neck. I feel his breath on me, and it's shaky. "I love you."

He doesn't say anything else. I lie there, listen to him breathe. Eventually his breathing falls into a rhythm.

Andrew sleeps for most of the day. I keep the boys busy, make them lunch, take them to the pool.

Jeremy holes up in the media room, as promised. He's on the phone to everyone—all sorts of phone calls. I can imagine Aaronson needs lots of calming, and I can tell several are probably strategy calls to Sandy, the publicist, about what's going to be said to the press.

Tucker also talks on the phone, but I can't tell who he speaks to. His conversations are much more secretive. More than once, I think he steps out on to the patio to spare me the details of Andrew's accident.

At some point late in the afternoon, Jeremy comes out of the media room with my cell in his hand. He wasn't lying about commandeering all of the phones.

"Kelly?"

"Yeah?"

"This one you can take. It's your friend? Mari?" He hands the phone to me.

"Hello?"

"Hi, Kelly. What's going on?" Her voice sounds casual, and I want to snap at her, remind her that there's a lot going on, thank you very much.

And then I remember I haven't told her about Andrew yet.

"It's a little crazy over here. How are you?"

She breathes in a little. "Good, I guess. What's going on?"

I don't know how to lie right now. I'm so tired, and the adrenaline of the day is wearing thin. "Tonight's just not a good time to talk. Can we catch up tomorrow? I might need a babysitter this week. Something's come up, and I could use your help."

"Sure, that's fine. Let me know." She ends the call.

I feel weariness settling into my bones. I scavenge the refrigerator and make sandwiches for everyone to eat. Beau, ever the helper, takes food to Tucker and Jeremy.

I take dinner into the bedroom for Andrew.

He's reading Hemingway, holding the book with his good arm. I've propped him up with every conceivable pillow I could find, but he still looks uncomfortable.

"Dinner?" I hold up the plate.

He makes a face. "I don't have an appetite. Maybe some tea?"

"You have to eat. Your body needs to heal. You need fuel to heal up." I sit on the edge of the bed facing him. I fight the rising uneasy feeling tightening around my chest.

"I promise I will tomorrow. Tonight, I'm just hoping to fall asleep."

I wonder how he will, with the pain. "I'll get you new ice."

"You know what? Just tell me some stories. Tell me about when the boys were born." He sets the book down.

"I'm no Papa Hemingway."

"He and Robert Jordan are gearing up to blow up a bridge right now, but you don't have to try to compete with that. I want to think about what it's going to be like to see my baby born."

So, I lie down next to him and tell him all the ins and outs of when the boys were born. He's able to manage some chuckles, especially when I tell him about mowing the lawn when I was overdue with Hunter.

He eventually falls asleep.

I get back up and check in on everyone, get Hunter and Beau to bed, straighten up the kitchen. Then I come back to Andrew, trying to slip in between the covers as gently as I can.

And then I stare at the wall all night; thank God over and over again.

The sun dawns pale in the sky as I cry silent tears of gratitude.

FLOAT ON

The next morning, Tucker takes the boys out for the day. Bless him. He sneaks them out one of the back freight elevators and down to the parking garage, where they take a car one of the security guys from Apotheosis dropped last night. They're able to slip out of the building without anyone being the wiser.

Andrew sleeps. The production will "shoot around him," producer Aaronson declared last night. He won't have filming stopped, not for Andrew's injury, not for anything. Jeremy spent a long time last night making sure McDougal could pick up scenes that didn't involve Andrew for two or three days.

Before he left, Tucker, expert on trauma, gave me a list of to-dos to help Andrew recover on a quiet day alone. "Have him take the ibuprofen for the pain, but also to clear the adrenaline out of his body. It helps the body process it."

I feel like I've been run over by a truck, so I can only imagine how Andrew feels. I want a cup of tea and decide on chamomile and green. I need caffeine, even just a little bit, but I also need something to calm my jagged nerves.

I didn't sleep. At all. I know this isn't good for the baby. I will nap later, I promise myself.

I decide to swim. It's early, but it's a weekday, so no one should be at the little indoor pool. There aren't enough people in the building who use it very much. It has an adjoining workout room — gym might be what the concierge calls it, but two treadmills and a couple weight machines might be pushing the definition of *gym*. We might be the only interested tenants. The boys come down to swim and are usually by themselves.

I pull on my suit. What an exercise in total humiliation. The pregnant body in a swimsuit is not a thing of beauty. Wow. I think Jeremy's remark about tan fat might have been on the mark.

I am careful not to wake Andrew as I leave a note on the pillow next to him. I don't want him to wake to an empty condo and flip out.

I sneak out and take the elevator to the pool level.

It's quiet. No one else is swimming. The water laps its blue tongue against old, 1920s-style black and white tiles. The room smells of chlorine, and the humidity curls the hairs at my neck.

As I slip in, the warm water welcomes me. I forgot what a relief this is. My hips thank me immediately, the burden of a spreading midsection off of their bones for a moment.

I warm up with a couple easy laps, the breaststroke letting my shoulders and legs stretch out.

At the deep end, I let down my guard and float on my back. The water fills my ears, and I enjoy the cocoon. I open my eyes to someone standing on the pool deck and jump out of my skin, inhaling water in the process.

"Andrew!" I sputter and cough.

His arm's in a sling. He wears trunks. "Morning. Thought I'd join you."

"You can't swim with your shoulder all torn up."

"Why not? The sutures are all covered with that thick steri-tape. They said I could shower." His voice sounds tired.

"Come in, then." I'm not fighting him today, on anything. The person who was almost run over wins all the arguments.

"No, you're right. I should probably keep it out of the water." He walks to the stairs and eases in, careful to come only waist deep. He coaxes his arm out of the sling and puts the sling aside.

"Careful." I swim toward him. I'm timid. I don't want to touch him for fear of hurting him.

"I know." He's not protesting. I think he's hurting enough to proceed carefully.

I watch him take another step, a little deeper in the water. He's still for a moment, testing, keeping his arm close to his body.

"Are you all right?"

"It's fine so far." He takes some slow steps, stands a little straighter.

I just want to wrap him in my arms and hold him for the day. Or the week, or the rest of my life. I don't want to let him go.

I duck my head under the water before the tears come. I don't want him to see me upset by this. He'll take it personally, beat himself up for upsetting me, which is ridiculous.

I come up for air, slick my hair back. I'm closer now, and I stand in the shallows next to him.

"Are you okay?" He scans my face for the emotion there.

"I'd be lying if I said I was fine. But I'll be fine. I just want you to heal, not to hurt too much." I want to touch his chest, feel his strength, and reassure myself that he's still strong, still vital. "And I've decided: we're staying here in New York with you, till shooting's done. Then we're going, as a family, to LA. We'll get a tutor for the boys for the semester."

"Are you sure?" He looks relieved.

"I'm positive. I'm not letting you out of my sight."

He leans over and kisses me without moving his arms. I am careful to keep my body away from his. When he speaks, his voice is thick with emotion. "I want you so badly. I need to hold you, to lose myself in you."

He kisses me deeply, hungry and scared. I open my mouth to him, but I try to keep in control. The tears, sobs, are right under my thin skin, and I don't want to cry. This is my time to support him.

"I want you, Kelly." He wraps one arm around me, pulls my hips to his, urgently. I kiss him hard, and now my hands go to his neck, almost instinctively.

He jumps. "Careful."

"God, that hurt, didn't it?"

He shakes his head. "It's okay. Kiss me."

I put my hand on his cheek and kiss him. He breathes heavily against my neck, his good hand grasping the small of my back and pulling me closer.

"I want you." His arm between us drops without him checking it. He sucks a breath in. "Christ." He releases me and pulls the arm close to his body. He ducks his bad shoulder, trying to escape the pain, which I'm sure is carving a long, thin line around his shoulder blade.

"That's it. We need to call a timeout before you pull your stitches." I kiss him and turn him around to check them. They are angry and red, but still safely intact under the clear, thick steri-tape.

"We should to go up to the condo." He sounds tired.

I want to salvage the moment. "Wait a second. Let's just float for a minute. It can't be any worse than a shower. Hold my hand and lie back."

He leans back and floats. I hold his hand, float next to him, let the water fill up my ears.

I feel his hand in mine, and I look up at the ceiling, listening to my blood pump. As long as I can touch him, I feel peaceful. I can feel new tears slide down my face, joining the pool water, but they are tears of relief. I could have lost him. I can barely think about it without dissolving into panic. I try to push the what-ifs into the back of my mind. I feel the water lapping over my skin and breathe slowly, calming my thoughts.

I don't know how many minutes we lie there, floating side by side. It's sheer peace.

Then I sense a shadow at the door to the pool. I sit up and slide under the surface, swimming under water to the side.

It's Mari. She's in workout clothes, wears earbuds, has a towel draped over her shoulder. I smile. She has *The Great Gatsby* open, reads as she walks.

Andrew's next to me. "We should have left."

"It's okay. It's just Mari. She must be cutting through to the gym." I wave at her. "Mari!"

She looks up and takes out the earbuds. "Kelly! Hey! I didn't see you there."

"Mari, I don't think you've officially met my boyfriend." I try to sound nonchalant.

Andrew gives me a nervous sideways glance. "I'm Andrew. I'd shake, but I'm soaking wet."

"And he tore his rotator cuff. Shoulder surgery. Sling and no handshakes." I swim to the ladder and pull myself up, go get his sling and his towel.

Mari nods. "That sucks. Good idea rehabbing in the pool, though."

Andrew climbs out at the steps rather than the ladder, and I hand him the towel. He conveniently pulls it over the scar and over his head, accomplishing a hoodie effect.

"I'm headed up. Nice to meet you." He turns toward the door to leave.

"See you. It was nice to meet you, Andy." She continues into the gym as we're walking out the door.

Down the hall, I finally make a comment. "Nice acting. I don't think she made the connection."

He looks at me. "Nice lying. You've been hanging around me too much. But she knew exactly who I was."

"Why do you say that?"

"She called me Andy. I introduced myself as Andrew."

"The Andy Pettigrew giveaway. Very astute of you."

"Now let's go upstairs. We were in the middle of something."

"Tearing out your stitches. You need to lie down and rest."

"Not my plan." He stoops a bit and kisses me.

He's going to be hard to resist, stitches or no.

We board the elevator. Andrew still hasn't pulled the towel from his head. He broods.

"What are you chewing on?"

"I don't know about this Mari girl." He keeps his eyes on the carpet of the elevator as it climbs to our floor.

"What do you mean?" I take a step a little to one side, trying to get a look at his face, read his expression.

He shakes his head, just barely. "I just, maybe it's because of the accident, all the attention now, the media outside the building." He leaves off as the doors of the elevator open and walks out into the hall.

"Are you going to finish that thought?" I take two long strides to catch back up to him and walk next to him in the hallway to our door.

"I think maybe you should keep some space between you and her."

"Why?"

"Because we're targets now." He says this, and I feel a chill. The words come through as short, clipped, dangerous.

"What do you mean? You've been hurt. I get that. But what could Mari do?"

Now the towel comes off his head, and he stops walking. "She knows who I am. The accident makes us a target. People want in this building. They want information. I just…She makes me feel uneasy."

I look at his face. He means it. There's worry in his eyes.

"I hear you. But I don't see it. I want to trust her. I need a friend here. Maybe now more than ever, Andrew. I don't see it." I'm frustrated. I've made one friend. *One*. And now I'm supposed to give her up.

He touches my arm, takes hold of me gently with his good hand. "I don't want you paranoid. I'm not saying that. I don't know what I'm saying, I'm so exhausted. Can you hear me, though, that my gut says to be wary? Can you at least acknowledge that I'm getting a weird intuition off of her? Humor me a little?"

He's not ever been one to be paranoid. Or a worrier. That's my claim to fame. "I get it. I hear you, Andrew. Yes, I'll be cautious. And I get why we're a target. I do. Let me be cautious, but let me have a friend. I need someone. But I'll be smart about it."

"I don't want you lonely. But, yes, trust your gut. And mine. Please."

I reach up and kiss him gently one more time. "My gut tells me Jeremy's on the other side of that door, and I'm going to want to punch him in under an hour."

Andrew cracks a smile, the first one I've seen this morning. Maybe the first one since he was hurt yesterday. "That's not intuition, that's just ears that can hear."

On cue, I hear Jeremy yell on the other side of the door. "Tucker! Where's my cell charger? How am I supposed to save the world with a dying phone?"

I'm not lying when I say we spent a minute or two debating going inside.

HURTS SO GOOD

Coming back on set sucks. It's been three days. I'm not scared—more anxious. But the big issue is the fuss everyone will make over me.

It's bad enough, the way people kiss my ass when we make a movie. Everybody, from the set dresser to the PA for the cinematographer, treats me like I walk on water. And it's such transparently suck-up-ish behavior I could smack somebody. The second I cool off on the STARmeter on IMDb, all of these people will evaporate into thin air.

But injured? Oh lord, people here don't know the meaning of "too much drama." What an opportunity to win my approval: by kissing up to my injured ass.

It's too much to bear.

Jeremy, though? Jeremy is a godsend. He's in the car when I get to it in the garage, on his phone. Tucker gets the door for me, and I climb in gingerly.

"Hey, pussy," Jeremy says.

"I have sixty-seven stitches. Sorry I didn't hop in the car."

"Okay, baby. Next time you want to play in traffic, pay better attention."

See, that may seem cold, but I love it. Jeremy treats me like crap no matter what. I don't think he even comprehends how to kiss up to me. He calls it like he sees it. If I'm being a jackass, I know Jeremy will tell me straight up.

Tucker rolls the car out of the garage and slides into traffic. Today we're shooting in Battery Park. It's been locked down. Jordan and his Apotheosis crew spent serious dime to accomplish that, but he also had to promise the folks insuring the production that I wouldn't get my ass killed, so no expense will be spared to make things airtight today.

I don't mind, to be honest. Whoever gave me that shove into traffic has some serious issues. I'd rather not run into them without backup.

But it's not my job to think about that. In fact, it's my job to shoot five to seven scenes, and right now I'm hoping my head is clear enough to recall the forty-odd pages of dialogue I'm supposed to have committed to memory for today.

I'm usually really good at that. I have a pretty sharp memory. But the crescent moon cut into my back has made it hard to sleep, and lack of sleep makes recall pretty damn hard. And, yes, I've had a couple nightmares. Maybe more than a couple. Maybe the one with the broken glass and the pistol again.

Plus, Kelly won't come near me. She's terrified she's going to hurt me, open my stitches up. What I want to do is forget, and my hands and mouth all over her always seems to make me feel better about everything. A private moment to have my way with her has been damn hard to come by, though, since the condo's been crawling with security and producers and doctors and everybody else in the world who wants to keep me safe because I am part of their earnings ratio on their retirement plan.

Sandy the publicist was by yesterday, trying to convince me to do an interview with *60 Minutes* or *Dateline* about the car thing.

No one but Tucker and I knows there was a push. A shove. I don't want to talk about it at all. Someone wanted me road pizza and failed. I'd rather not go on national television and tell them, "Hey, bastard, you blew it. Wanna try to kill me again?"

I think poking the homicidal bear with a stick seems like a bad idea.

Thank God Tucker bent Jeremy's ear about it already. He put the kibosh on Sandy's idea and sent her on her way.

When I got up this morning to try to shower before I left, all I could think of was pulling Kelly in there with me, letting all the fear and pain wash away, cleansing my soul with a little time close to her skin.

But she was sleeping so soundly. She finally looked relaxed. She's looked so exhausted since the accident, and I just couldn't bear it.

The car stops at the entrance to the parking lot of Battery Park, and all of a sudden, Jeremy has his phone to his ear. "Give me five minutes, that's all. Then the rest of the day is yours." He ends the call.

"What was that?"

He loosens his tie. "I want to talk with Jordan the dick. Before your day starts. Before I turn you over to these leeches."

Do I detect a hint of a protective streak? "I can handle him myself, Jeremy. I'm a big boy."

"Look, Andy, you pay me a nice cut of your earnings to do things for you. This one is all mine. I expect you to make it to the end of this shoot in one piece. Jordan only needs you for this movie. I need you to keep working for a long, long time."

I nod grimly. "Teslas don't pay for themselves, after all." I don't like talking about my own longevity.

"You're my friend. Everything aside, he can't screw you over with this. It's not your fault this happened, and I don't want you exhausted. We know how getting overworked wrecked you last time."

He's referring to the beginning of my long slide into rehab — a media tour and an anniversary I don't like to revisit resulted in pneumonia and all hell breaking loose. I don't like to remember it. I almost lost Kelly forever because of it.

"Fine. Do your thang, Jeremy."

Tucker chimes in. "Go get 'em, Tiger."

"Shut it, Tucker." Jeremy gets out and motions for the both of us to stay put.

Tucker goes over the shooting schedule for the day, and I check my phone. I'd text Kelly, but it would wake her up.

A few minutes pass. Jeremy jumps back in the car. "On to makeup. You're golden. I'll stay close today, make sure they treat you right."

I nod, and Tucker gives me the signal. High alert today means I don't make a move until he tells me to. I step out of the car to him waiting by the door, and he provides close coverage until I'm in the makeup trailer. There's another security guy covering the door, Janus again. Tucker stands just inside, talking into the cuff of his shirt from time to time.

Mallory, my lovely makeup artist, looks over at him. "No chit-chat today, huh?"

I shake my head. "Tucker's all business until he can see that no one's planning to lay me out flat again." I reach for a stick of gum.

Mallory ushers me to the chair. "We're all glad you're okay. How's it going to be to sit back?"

"It's going to hurt." My back protests the feeling of pressure as I say this.

"Tell you what—let's try it another way." She looks around the trailer. "Tucker, can you grab that stool?"

He comes over with it and plunks it down, returns to his station. Tucker post-accident is absolutely no fun.

I sit on the stool and thank Mallory profusely. It still hurts, but it's not agony.

My phone buzzes just about the same time Amanda sashays into the trailer.

"Yes?" I say to the phone—not Amanda.

"Hey, it's me." Kelly sounds sleepy.

"Hey, beautiful! How'd you sleep?"

"Until you left, okay. I don't like not knowing where you are."

"You knew I was going back to set today. Time to get back up on the proverbial horse." Amanda waves at me, sits down in the chair next to me, and pulls off her sweatshirt. She's in a bra. "I have to go. Mallory's improvising a bit. She needs to use the trowel on me. Even out the fatigue and wrinkles, you know."

"Love you."

I look right at Amanda. "Love you too. Go back to sleep, baby mama."

"Okay."

Amanda can't leave it alone. "You are simply adorable, you know that?"

She runs a finger under the strap of her bra, readjusting. Bullshit. She's trying to get some attention. I have zero patience for her games right now.

"Cut it out, Amanda. This is a big day. Let's try to stay focused, you know?"

"Oh, I get it, Andy. You're brave to even be here. I'd be so rattled. You look like you haven't slept. Good thing Mallory's a whiz, isn't it?"

"Uh-huh." I close my eyes and try to find my happy place. The Coast: walking on the beach with the boys and Kelly.

"How's Kelly taking all this? She's so new to all of it; she's not used to it like you and me. Bet it's hard on her. Wonder if she can hold up under the reality of your life, you know?"

"Uh-huh." I have an idea — that house, the one Kelly was staring at last time we were in Oregon.

Mallory taps me gently on the shoulder. "Andy, I'm so sorry. I need to go find Justine. She's got the wardrobe for the scenes today. Two-minute break, is that okay?"

"Sure." I'm grateful for the chance to stand up and give the shoulder blade a minute to rest.

Mallory scoots past Tucker. Amanda is out of her chair too and comes over to me. "Can we have a word?"

I nod. "Sure."

She takes me by the elbow. "Over here. I want a private minute."

We stand in the corner. "What, Amanda?"

She puts her hands on my forearms, comes close, whispers, "I was so scared."

"What?"

"So scared for you. I thought, *what if I'd lost him?* and it shook me to the bone."

"What?" I look over her head at Tucker. He's talking into his cuff again. He really needs to get over here and deal with this crazy woman.

"I want to try again, with you." She touches my hand. I resist the urge to snatch it away from her. "I think you feel it too. We both want each other. Remember the sex, Andy? We were amazing. We could be again."

"Amanda, are you on drugs? I mean, right at this moment, are you high?" I take a step back.

"What do you mean?"

"At what point in the weeks we've been shooting have I given even one tiny indication to you that I am interested in anyone but Kelly?"

"Well, I just thought, with your near-death experience, you'd be done humoring her. You'd want to get back to living the life you want, with your kind of people…"

"Kelly's my kind of people. She's having my baby. I love her."

Mallory comes back. Thank Jesus. I walk away from Amanda before she can even respond.

I expected people sucking up to my wounded self. I did not expect that.

I pick up my cell and call Jeremy. "Jeremy, there's a piece of property I want you to check out in Oregon."

Amanda almost looks upset. I close my eyes. Lord, get me through this day. Tucker can protect me from the danger of the street, but who knew I'd need someone to hold Amanda at bay.

HOUSE OF THE RISING SUN

D ay four post-accident, I get up early. Really early. I want to run alone. I need it. This morning when I woke up, I felt something that had been gone since Andrew and I have been together. It's the anvil, the one that was formerly camped out, pressing down on my chest from the moment my sweet husband Peter died until the moment Andrew and I kissed in the rain on the condo steps a year ago last June.

I don't know exactly why it's back, but it scares me. Depression is my Achilles heel. I can't go back to it; I just can't.

When the boys were born, I was fine. I count myself lucky that postpartum depression didn't visit me. But the depression of losing a loved one, and the time I sent Andrew away while he suffered through getting sober alone — those times were terrible. I hate the feeling.

And it seems to want to creep up on me.

So, I'm going to run away from it. I'm going to push my body and feel my lungs burn and breathe in. I will fight back, and I will say, "No, I won't go away like this. I have people who want me here."

I have a baby who wants me here.

Andrew's accident has thrown me for a loop. I know logically that I should chalk this melancholy up to the scare. But I thought, for just a second, that I could be stronger than that, that I could move forward and be fine, be grateful and live in the moment.

The anvil weight on my chest tells me it's not working.

I slip out of the bedroom to the kitchen with running shoes in hand. The sun is just starting to peek into the tall windows of the condo. Down in the concrete narrows, it's probably still pretty dark. I think I can get out of the building without paparazzi. They do actually go to bed sometimes too. I won't put my headphones in on the street. I will stay alert and hustle to the High Line. Then the sun will touch me, and I will run this funk out of me.

"Good morning, sunshine." Tucker sips a Frappuccino. Not only is he already up, he's already been out and back. There's a green iced tea on the kitchen island for me and one for Andrew.

"What are you doing up? You all aren't shooting until late tonight I thought." I pick up the tea and sip it. Oh, it tastes so good. "I love you for many things, Tucker, but right now I love you for this tea."

"I'm up because I get up this early almost every day. I can't help it."

"Night shoots and nights out with movie stars necessitate sleeping in sometimes, don't they?"

"Sometimes. Most times, no. What are you doing?"

"I'm going to run."

"Good for you. I'll go get my shoes." Tucker points down the hall. Jeremy's practically living in the media room too, but he goes out places at night and stays who knows where. He's put his other clients on with junior agents at his agency, turning all of his attentions to his star. Which means he's here. All the time. I feel sometimes like the dorm mother. I like having them all here, though. Might as well have every important person in my New York world in one place.

"I was going to go out on my own. I'll be fine." *I need the time alone*, I add silently.

"Nope. Andrew wouldn't forgive me if something happened to you and Hiccup. You get an escort."

"I could see if Mari wanted to come with me. She's probably running early this morning anyway."

"I'm going. End of story." He trots off after patting my head.

I sip my tea and get my sneakers on. So much for alone time.

Tucker's back. "I can do the official bodyguard thing and run behind you. I do that for a lot of my female clients. They get nervous with me running next to them. Say I'm too fit."

"I don't care about that. I've been in a funk, and I need to shake it off. I don't want to slip into depression. It's not a pretty place for me to be."

"Let's go whip up some endorphins, shall we?" Tucker smiles and jogs a little in place.

"Let's."

We get out of the building without incident, but almost immediately I'm happy Tucker came along. The street is relatively quiet. It's also awfully shadowy. Dumpsters and parked vans and construction scaffolds throw large, dark squares on to the sidewalk.

We jog along next to each other and don't say anything.

I feel okay, but it's getting more and more uncomfortable to run. The baby is tucked in his safe little floating fortress, but his palace and all the extra cushion around it are getting awkward to tote around.

Then we get to the stairs to the High Line. I don't even try to jog them. I just want to climb, slow and steady. Every time I step up, the pain stabs behind my kneecap. The clicking is back too.

"Kelly Jo, is that your knee making that sound?" Tucker looks at me.

I stop. I have to stop. It hurts too bad. "Yes. It hurts, Tuck."

"So, don't climb up any more stairs. Let's just go back to street level."

"I want to get up there, though. It's what I need." I start to cry.

"Why are you crying? It's okay. Things change while you're pregnant. The ligaments are probably off. Pulls your kneecap too far to one side. No big deal."

"I need this. I have to run. I can't be that sad again. I'm supposed to be strong for Andrew right now."

I sit on the step and just let it go. This verges on the infamous ugly cry.

Tucker stands next to me. He rubs my back for a minute. "There, there, Kells. Just breathe."

I suck in a deep breath and stand up.

"There's an elevator two blocks over. Let's go do that." Tucker points down the block. "Less pain, same pretty view."

"Tucker…" I can't finish.

"Hey. You have my word. I will help you through this. No one else has to know. Not even Andrew if you're worried about worrying him. I swear, the two of you spend so much time simultaneously trying to protect each other, it's exhausting to watch."

He wraps an arm around my shoulder and squeezes. "I know a guy who can check out the knee too. That part Andrew is going to want to know about. But again, no big deal. We can do this. Okay?"

"Okay." I wipe my face on my sleeve and edge back down the few stairs I've made it up. The kneecap clicks with every step.

This sucks. I don't do well without running. We're about to find out how poorly it's going to go this time.

The next morning, Tucker announces our visit to the doctor as we eat scrambled eggs around the kitchen island. His voice is so neutral, I almost miss it.

"So, Kelly and I are going to swing by NYSMI today." His look tells me to go with it.

Andrew raises an eyebrow over *The New York Times*. "What?"

"Columbia Orthopedics. Her knee's bugging her a little, so we're going to get it checked out. We should be back in time for me to take you to set." Andrew can't drive with his shoulder all torn up. He rarely drives in New York, anyway. Tucker handles it. Janus rides shotgun for backup. Tucker says he's the one decent guy on Apotheosis's payroll, and I think he's including Jordan Aaronson, the dick.

"When did this happen?" Andrew looks at me.

"It's been clicking for a while, when I go up and down stairs especially. Since we got to New York. It's starting to hurt more just lately." I leave out *it's more of a deal now that I have to run to survive the way I feel after your accident.*

Hunter shovels eggs into his mouth, holding the plate level with his face. "You need to lift, Mom. Strengthen the muscles around the knee."

Tucker speaks up. "Nothing to worry about. The guys will take a peek at it and may tee up some PT too. Don't want the little mama hobbling along with the waddling."

I smile. Tucker is a saint. "I'll go get my stuff."

We leave the parking garage in a nondescript Camry. Our car changes almost every day, now that the paparazzi have camped out since Andrew's accident. Tucker's taken to driving a different rig when it's just me or just the kids. Before, if Andrew hadn't been spotted in it, the car didn't draw much attention, and we could actually keep it for a week or two. But after the accident, each one of us seems to be a heightened target.

No one follows us from the building this morning, thankfully. The orthopedist's office is by MOMA, south of the park. We park in the adjacent parking garage.

Ironically, there are steps. Tucker walks next to me down the long parking garage stairwell. "There couldn't be an elevator working. Of course." His voice is sympathetic. He pats me on the shoulder.

By the time we get to the office, my knee screams in protest. The receptionist ushers us into an examination room right away. Tucker insists upon it, for the privacy. He still gives people too much credit. I really don't think I'm recognizable on my own. I don't get approached in stores or on the street. Unless I've been in Andrew's immediate company, I'm still luckily anonymous.

I sit on the exam table and fill out paperwork. "Tucker, you don't need to be in here with me. Despite the disaster I've been lately, I do normally take care of myself. I did it for quite a long time before I met Andrew, you know."

"I know. But isn't it nice to not have to? Just once in a while?"

The man is a psychic. The ability to abdicate, on a few things, feels nice. It feels nice to be taken care of. Maybe not the most "I am woman, hear me roar" attitude, but I had to roar for myself, lonely and afraid, for two long years. I know I can do it, and I've proven to myself and everyone else I am strong and I can handle the big, bad world all by myself. It's not a terrible thing to let it go and let someone else handle it. Not a bad thing at all.

"Just once in a while," I tell him. "You're right. And I want you to know how lucky Andrew and I both are to have you in our lives. I'm sure you know, but you're so much more than a bodyguard. I mean it, Tucker."

"Don't get me all verklempt in the doctor's office. Rudy will come in, and I'll be embarrassed."

"Rudy?"

"He's my bud. Your new doctor. I know he's no best-friend's-husband Joe, but he's the best at knees on the East Coast. He fixed me up almost ten years ago."

"What happened?"

"Nothing big. I got tackled by a crazy fan onstage at a client's concert. The dude took me out sideways, at the knees. Tore my right meniscus all to hell. Man, did it hurt."

"You weren't covering Andrew."

"No. This was back when Andrew was a normal famous guy, not a nuclear famous guy. He had some soap opera fan club crazies, but they usually just wanted him to sign underwear. I didn't have to do crowd control everywhere he went. It was usually just appearances or movie premieres. I had other clients then."

"Do you miss that?"

"Not a bit. I've worked for some other sweet people, but there are a lot of celebrities who need the most protection from themselves. I could tell you stories."

I don't get a chance to ask. The door to the room opens, and Rudy appears.

Rudy apparently was a wide receiver in a former life. He's as tall and wide as Tucker. I feel puny next to them. I may even feel compelled to go lift some heavy things just to fit in.

"Good morning! How is everyone today?" Rudy gives Tucker a hearty hug.

"My man, my man. Long time no see!" Tucker glows. Clearly these men are made for each other. I wonder if Rudy's interested. Tucker should have a boyfriend. He never lets me set him up. Part of that could be that I don't really know anyone to set him up with, not anywhere except Boise.

"And this must be the fabulous Kelly. How are you?" Rudy shakes my hand, holds on to it for a moment.

"I'm okay."

"Tucker tells me you're not so hot." He's still holding my hand, but reaches behind him to pull up a rolling stool and sits in front of me on it.

"My knee is bugging me. And I really like to run. It keeps me sane." I shrug.

He looks at Tucker and smiles. "She is adorable. You were completely right." He laughs. He's a big laugher, with his head tilted back and his mouth wide, eyes crinkled shut.

Tucker looks at me. "I only said adorable things about you. I promise."

Rudy chuckles again. "You're in the right place, Kelly. I want to take a look at it and see about maybe an MRI. Then we can decide what's next."

"MRI? While I'm pregnant?"

"It's the safest alternative. Way safer than a CT. We'll get one good look before I decide if I need to scope it or not. But I'm getting ahead of myself. Let's have a look."

I pull up the leg to my yoga pants, and Rudy tenderly probes around my kneecap.

"You know, the way your body weight gets redistributed when you're pregnant, just that might be enough to set this off. Your hips spread a bit and the angle from knee to hip changes."

"The clicking didn't really start until I was here in New York."

"Lots more stairs to climb. Subway, buildings, you know. Plus everything here is paved. I bet you ran on trails mostly in Boise. Nice healthy dirt."

"You're right."

"Well, let's schedule the MRI, and lay off the running until then. When I know more I'll give you some specific things to do to build the muscles around the knee, but I want to wait until I see what's up."

I will not cry, I will not cry. I breathe in. "No running?"

Tucker looks at me, smiles. "You can do this, Kelly."

"Yeah, unfortunately, no running. What's in your building? You have a swimming pool? Do that, and maybe an elliptical, but if it feels funky on the knee, don't do that."

"This sucks." I can't be all chipper about it.

"I know. Tucker tells me it's really your go-to stress reliever."

"It's how I combat depression. Number-one way."

"I feel you. I get SAD every year. The time change and short days suck the life out of me."

He's the happiest person I've ever seen. I don't believe it. "You personify sunshine. You're Rudy of Sunnybrook Farm. Come on."

"I lift, I run, and I do yoga. I get acupuncture too. You should try that. I have a guy I really like. That might be something you can do with Andrew too. He should get after that in a couple weeks. It'll help with the nerve damage on his shoulder blade."

"I don't know if he's even gotten that far. That sounds like a good idea." I know Dr. Joe at home is all about the acupuncture.

Tucker stretches. "I'll go with you. My knees could stand some poking too."

"Kelly can do it for knees and for depression. That means extra needles." Rudy laughs again.

"So, no running." I sigh.

"Nope." He hands a slip of paper to Tucker. "We'll do the MRI in-house. See you next week."

I don't know about this. No running. I chew the inside of my cheek while I process this on the way to the car. Tucker's quiet.

"Well, Miss Kelly, should we hit the tea shop before we get home?"

"Sure."

"Hey. Remember, we're going to do this together. No big deal."

I nod.

He stops short at the bottom of the stairs. "I have a brilliant idea. You're going to love me for this."

"What?"

"What about some girl time?"

"What?"

"Tessa and the terrible triplets. Think of all the fun you could have with your best friend and her three little monsters. The American Girl store, Natural History Museum, carriage rides around Central Park, dress up and Madeline's tea at the Carlyle. Let's invite them to visit."

"Yes. I'm all about that idea. I love it, Tucker. Let's call Tessa from the car."

Tucker takes my hand to help me climb the stairs. "This is why I am the man. You might love that Andrew guy, but I am a genius and truly the man."

"I completely agree," I tell him. "You rock."

I'M NOT THE ONLY ONE

just want to lie down. Really. I could wish for a drink, or a smoke, or to be wrapped up in Kelly's arms, but as of right now, on set, the only thing that's attainable, that's allowed, and that won't get me fired or on the path to ruin is to lie down and take a nice, long nap.

"Tucker, if McDougal comes back, just whistle twice, one low, one high, and I'll jump right back to my mark." I turn away from the group of people I'm standing with and start inching my way to the low green velour couch that someone on the crew dragged over to the area by the food. I have no idea where in New York City this couch came from, seeing as how it's now appeared in the middle of our trailers and set, but I don't care. I don't even care if it smells. My shoulder hurts, and I want to lie down.

"Are we in a secret club? How about I just say, 'He's coming!'" Tucker even gets pissy from time to time. Between the two of us, we've probably had maybe fifteen hours of sleep in the past three days.

"That works too." I sit down on the couch and think about the best way to spare my torn-up shoulder when I fall into blissful slumber.

"Andy!" I hear him before I see him. "Andy, aren't you about to run through this scene?"

Aaronson. He powerwalks over to me. I was so close.

"McDougal paused us for a minute. He wanted to ask the second unit DP something. I think he just stepped into that trailer over there." I point in the direction my director went, hoping to send Aaronson away.

He stands over me, looking down. "I don't want him. I want to talk to you."

I sigh. "Okay." I stand up and try to look more awake. "What's up?"

Aaronson looks up to the heavens, takes a deep breath, lets it out, looks me straight in the eye. "Are you okay?"

"My shoulder, no. Me? Sure. I'll be fine." I stand up tall.

He nods. "Good. Let me know if you need anything. Glad to hear you're fine."

He turns and strides back the way he came. I look over at Tucker. Tucker just shrugs.

"Tucker, I'll be in my trailer. Come get me. Tell McDougal I needed to change the dressing on my shoulder."

"If that's a legit thing I'm telling him, I can send someone in to help you fix it. The on-set nurse knows how to dress a wound. Her name's Angie. She's nice."

"It's a lie. I'm going to go nap. I must lie flat."

He knew that before he asked me.

I get in my trailer, and I'm so happy to be near a couch to lie down on, it takes me a minute to realize something is wrong.

Lots of things are wrong. So, so many things are wrong.

The inside of my trailer looks like it's been attacked by a French whore. A classy, high-priced one, but still. There are swaths, miles and miles of fabric, all pink and gold and shiny, draped over the windows and covering the table—and the little trailer bench seats. There are candles lit everywhere. I smell perfume, something familiar and spicy, and hear music playing. Something I've heard before.

My blood goes cold.

"Amanda?" I call out.

"In here, Andy."

As soon as the smells and sounds registered in my brain, one word came to mind: Cannes.

Cannes the film festival. Cannes the place where Amanda and I hooked up and broke up.

"You're not in the bedroom, are you?"

My trailer has a tiny bedroom at the back of it.

"Of course I am. Don't be an idiot. Come here."

I walk back to the door of the room.

Amanda has a lighter in her hand. She touches it to the tips of the candles in a huge silver candelabra in the middle of a little table, set for two.

"Stop." I close my eyes in the hopes that she will disappear.

"What?"

"I don't know what you're doing, or thinking, but stop. Get out of my trailer, Amanda."

"I thought you'd like a little Cannes right here in New York. Remember our room? The balcony, where the sea air drifted in at night, the way the curtains billowed up with the breeze off the Mediterranean?" She gestures to all of the decorations she's added.

"I'm not interested. I don't want this. I don't want you."

Amanda lights the last candle and looks up, straight into my eyes. "I don't believe you. You're trying to 'remake your image,' and I'm not buying it for one second."

"Get out of my trailer. I don't care if you believe it or not. I don't want to be a drunk. I don't want to get wild in a Cannes disco bathroom with you. I definitely don't want to have sex with you. Anywhere. Anytime." I hold her gaze.

She picks up a plate from the table and throws it at me. I duck left as it flies by. Then she flips the table and storms past me. "If that's true, then go fuck yourself, Andy Pettigrew."

The door slams shut. I stand still and look at the wreckage.

The door opens again, and Tucker pops his head in. "Did you get a nap?"

"You've got to be kidding me, Tucker."

"What? They need you on set."

"I'll fill you in between takes." I grab my sunglasses and follow him out of my trailer.

His first job is to put a lock on that door.

BAD NEWS

It's been two weeks since the accident. Now the world knows where we're staying in New York, and somewhere in there, the word got out about my pregnancy too. The suckage meter is at full tilt. I guess I'm getting used to the chaos when I leave the building. If Andrew's not with me, it only lasts for twenty seconds, anyway. Tons of screams and lights popping, followed by, "He's not with her," followed by no lights popping, followed by one or two rude questions shouted at me, usually along the lines of "What's it like to share Andy with Mandy?" or "When's the shotgun wedding?"

Sometimes there's a knock about me being too old to carry the baby. I love that one. That's my favorite gem. I suspect the wish is that I pass on one of these remarks to Andrew. Then he might get incensed and come out and pound on someone. Boy, then those would be some choice pictures, wouldn't they?

But I chuckle because I prefer to imagine me going hoss on one of them. The crazy pregnant lady comes out swinging — maybe pulls a few ninja moves. I say nothing to Andrew about it. It actually doesn't bother me at all, weirdly. I think there isn't any real feeling behind the statements, so no reason to react with feeling.

The bustle for Andrew, though, it's scary. *Bustle* isn't the best word. Frenzy. If we try to go out, he holds my hand tightly as we dash for the cab. There's a sustained yelling and the flash of the cameras, and sometimes the doormen (there are two now) and even Tucker have to push back a wave, a wall of people who press closer to us. That physical swell of bodies can get intimidating.

And then there are one or two guys on scooters who dart in and out of traffic and follow us through the streets of New York.

It's too bad, because the streets were supposed to be our anonymous hangout. Now Andrew can only go to set and back to the condo. The rest is crazy. We try to go out to eat, but it's just not worth it. With his shoulder all torn up, he could really get hurt, and he only takes that risk to do his job.

Tonight, though, he's home from set early. We're going to tell the boys about no Boise. It's going to really suck. I'm not thrilled, but there's no way we're going to be apart from each other for longer than a weekend. Not with Andrew hurt. I'm not leaving him alone to go through this. And this opportunity he has in LA, it's too amazing for him to pass up. He even let me take a peek at the script, and I can tell it'll be huge for him. It's about a mobster who goes into hiding at a cattle ranch in the middle of nowhere. With a meaty role and a high-powered director, Andrew'll be one step closer to the ultimate prize in Hollywood: one of those little gold guys.

The only concession I think we need to make is Hunter's birthday. He turns fourteen next week, and he wants to be in Boise with his friends for that. There's no way he'll abide another four weeks in New York and the rest of a semester in LA if we don't get back to say goodbye to his friends.

I'm making tacos to soften the blow. I cook very basic stuff, but the boys have always liked my tacos.

Andrew comes in the kitchen from the study. He's been on the phone with the super-top-secret director for the mobster picture, *Out of Range*. He looks tired.

For the past two weeks, he goes to set every night, usually for thirteen-hour shoots. Then he and Tucker go hit physical therapy right after that, usually around six or seven in the morning. Then he comes home and sleeps.

I don't sleep. At night, I worry. I watch the boys sleep. I pace. Sometimes I go down to the pool to swim, but at night, it's kind of a creepy place—lots of echoes and drips and shadows. Plus I've been doing it without Andrew and Tucker knowing, and if they get wind of it, they'll go ballistic. The guilt of that limits my trips to swim.

During the day, when Andrew is home, I try to nap with him. But I spend a good chunk of time afraid I'll hurt his shoulder when I try to turn over or something. The other part of the time I spend watching him breathe.

I remember the first night home from the hospital with Hunter when he was born. I just watched him breathe, all night long. I was amazed at how tiny he was and terrified he wouldn't take his next breath. But *that* worry ebbed after the first few nights. I got used to having a little baby around, and he was so tenacious and vocal (he was quite the crier) that he put me at ease.

Andrew, he looks so vulnerable right now. He has deep circles under his eyes, dark and worrisome. He's lost weight since getting hurt. The pain wears on him, and when his actor's face is slack with sleep, it shows through. He whimpers, lets down his guard when he's sleeping, and I can tell how much he hurts.

I respect why he's not taken anything more than an Advil. But the pain is slowing his healing.

So, I worry and watch him sleep.

I absentmindedly stir the taco meat. He comes to me, script in hand, and kisses me. We're both tentative, more tender than usual, but it feels so good to be in his arms.

"You look tired." He kisses my forehead.

"So do you." I wrap my arms around his waist, rest my head on his chest to hear his heartbeat.

"You'll burn your tacos." He rubs my back for a minute.

"The peace offering can't be burned. Bad karma." I let go of him to check on the simmering ground beef.

"What peace offering?" Beau strolls in.

I give him a squeeze and then turn him in the direction of the hall. "Andrew and I need to talk to you and your brother. Can you go get him?"

Beau looks at me and turns toward the bedrooms. "Hunter! Mom needs you!" he screams. "Hunter!"

I roll my eyes. "I could've done that."

Beau's brow furrows. "The last time we had a 'talk,' you told us about Hiccup. What is it now?"

Hunter shuffles in. He wears soccer slides and his board shorts and that's it.

Fourteen. He's going to be fourteen. His feet are almost as big as Andrew's. He looks more and more like his dad every day, though he didn't inherit the black curls. That's Beau's claim to Peter's side of the family. How did we get these young men from those tiny babies I held not so long ago?

I feel a little twinge of the sadness, but it's a warm melancholy. Peter would be so proud of his boys.

Hunter breaks my reverie. "What's the big deal?"

I have plates out. "Let's do the tacos buffet-style. Then we'll talk."

"Uh-oh." Hunter squints at me. "Is everyone okay? Is Ditto all right? I don't trust those girls with him. They're going to let him out of the backyard. They live in a busy neighborhood. He's gonna get hit."

The conversation isn't going to get any easier. I plate up the tacos for the boys. "Here. Just sit, and then we'll talk."

They do as they're told. Andrew sits at the end of the island. He looks at me. "Kelly?"

"Fine. Guys, Andrew's got a chance to work on an amazing movie in LA. And since the accident, I'm not keen on us being apart. I want all of us in the same place."

"And?"

"So, we're going to stay in New York a little longer."

Beau jumps up. "Awesome! We get to miss the start of school. I love it."

"Actually, you'll do school online this semester, or maybe with a tutor. We're going with Andrew to LA after he's done shooting here."

Hunter's up out of his seat. "No way. My birthday is this month. In Boise! All my friends. I told all of them I was having a party."

Andrew stands too. "You still are, bud. We'll all be in Boise for your birthday. But we're going to stick together."

"You can see why, with Andrew's hurt shoulder, and the baby, you can see that, can't you, Hunter?" My voice sounds squeaky. It doesn't sound like much of an idea. Or much of a reason.

"No." Hunter picks up his plate and dumps it in the sink with a clatter. "No. I'll live in Boise with Tessa. You can't take me away from my friends, away from Boise. No."

He storms down the hall, and I hear the front door of the condo slam behind him.

I rush to go after him, and Andrew catches me. "I'll have Tucker go check on him. I bet he went to the pool."

"I need to go tell him, explain it to him."

"What is there to explain? We promised him his life wouldn't change that much, with me coming into it, and here it is, changing." He lets go of me and rubs his hands over his face, frustrated. "Give him some time. And I want to be the one to talk to him. I'm the one who lied to him."

"You didn't lie. How could we know? We can't be apart, Andrew. We can't."

"He's almost fourteen. It's how it feels, so it's true. End of story." He stalks out of the room.

Beau sits at the counter. He eats his tacos. "It'll be fine, Mom."

"Why aren't you mad? What makes it okay for you?"

He shrugs. "I don't know. I'd have Mr. Kissinger or Miss Bideganeta if we were in Boise. They're both supposed to be mean. Maybe I'm dodging a bullet."

I give him the biggest hug I can manage. "Beau, I love you so much right now I can't stand it."

"I'm still in the market for a phone. Maybe there's a phone in my future if I stay mellow." He wiggles his eyebrows suggestively. He polishes off the last of his taco and goes into the great room to watch TV.

I sit at the island and look at the pile of uneaten food. That went well.

EVERYBODY LOVES ME

After Kelly and I break the news to the boys, I decide to take care of some unfinished business before we have to leave New York. We've only got a few weeks left. It's stupid, I know, but I call Tucker and have him set it up anyway. I can't protect Kelly, can't keep the boys' lives calm, maybe I can't even keep my ass alive long enough to provide for this new family of mine, but I sure as hell can shut Tiffany's down and get Kelly the biggest diamond my money can buy. Eye of the Tiger all the way here, people.

Tucker humors me. Jeremy declares he's coming along. Mostly, I think, because I usually don't like to spend money, and here — in the course of what? Two weeks? — I've asked him to buy a house on the Oregon Coast for me and now I'm after a huge piece of jewelry. Maybe he's worried I'm losing it.

Maybe I am. I'm tired. Mind-numbingly tired. I hurt. My damn shoulder. There is no way, absolutely no way to sleep without it hurting. It gnaws at me mercilessly.

This trip to buy a "real ring" gives me a couple minutes alone with Tucker and Jeremy to put my theory out there too. Somebody put a target on my back. Amanda is acting completely insane. Maybe she has something to do with this.

I'd be lying if I said I wasn't scared. But I'm scared for Kelly. For the baby. For the boys.

My folks called, and they feigned concern for two seconds. Maybe it was real concern, but no one offered to come down and stay with us, or take the boys up to Pennsylvania. Mom lectured me about my "lifestyle choice," which I think means she thinks acting is a poor career move, but I've never once heard her say a good thing about it, so now certainly won't be the time when she's supportive. And I don't think she's very supportive about Kelly and me. She's trying. I think she and my dad are trying. But not "Send your family up here, and we'll keep them safe for you" trying.

Kelly wouldn't go, anyway. I think I might feel the same way. I think she'd be safer away from me, but I can't stand to think of her anywhere but here. My selfishness wins out since it coincides with her stubbornness.

When she goes out for groceries now, I insist that Tucker goes with her, and I'm at loose ends until they get back. And on set is almost impossible. I don't know how long any of us can maintain.

I keep telling myself we just need to get to LA. Back to a routine. Jeremy's scouting for a house in a locked-down neighborhood. High walls, 24/7 guards at the gate, the works. I'll get to work on *Out of Range*, the press will forget about the baby, and we'll put some distance between us and cars that want to run me over and costars that want to sleep with or kill me, I can't tell which.

I brood and flip my phone over and over in the elevator. Janus is with me. He'll deposit me in a big armored Suburban and get himself back upstairs to my family. Jeremy and Tucker are already at Tiffany's. They insisted on meeting the advance team together.

Some Apotheosis driver picks me up in the garage. He's bald and looks a lot like Oddjob from the Bond movies. I almost smile at the thought, but he could definitely kick my ass, and it's been kicked around quite enough already.

It's late, after the store closing of seven p.m., and, no, I didn't cheese out and go to the flagship store. Jeremy probably salivated about that photo op for at least a second, but I want privacy, not Aunt Mae from New Brunswick snapping photos from the sidewalk.

So, it's the SoHo store, and as Oddjob drives down Seventh Avenue, I sit back and try to focus on what I need to tell Tucker. Jeremy will just have to be an accomplice.

The car turns left onto the store's small street, and the tires hum over the cobbles. Oddjob pulls up to the curb and jumps out to get my door. He's pretty light on his feet, as big as he is.

No cameras. No one. He hustles me to the front of the store, where a man in a black suit holds the door open, then promptly shuts and locks it behind me. I watch the Suburban pull away and disappear down the dark street.

The store is quiet for a moment. Then Jeremy hollers. It's what he does.

"My whipped friend! Never thought I'd see the day, brother!" He stands with Tucker and a girl with a bright Tiffany blue blouse and black skirt, her hair short and her lips very red.

"The less you talk tonight, J, the happier I'll be." I come to them and shake Tucker's hand. "Did you scope out some contenders?"

"Lupita here pulled a tray together for you." He nods to the girl. She smiles with very white teeth in between the red lips.

"Can I get you anything to drink, Mr. Pettigrew?" She reminds me of a flight attendant.

"You know, Lupita, I'd love a water."

"Still or sparkling?"

"Surprise me. I need to have a few words with my team for a minute, before you come back with that water."

A tiny crease in her smooth brow pops up and then disappears. She smiles widely again. "Of course. Take your time. I'll be back."

She glides away, her heels clicking on the polished floors. The man at the door stands guard. The street is still empty.

Tucker looks worried. "What?"

"I wanted to talk, and I can't figure out how to get you alone in the condo or on set, so here we are."

Jeremy shakes his head. "Wait, we're here to talk privately? You couldn't ask for a moment alone with your security staff?"

I pinch the bridge of my nose. "Shut up for a minute. You'll get it if you actually listen."

"Go on." Tucker leans in.

"Amanda. I think you need to look at Amanda for all of this."

Jeremy opens his mouth again. "For what?"

"Jeremy, I'm serious about the shutting the hell up part." I'll punch him, I'll do it.

"Yes, sorry."

Tucker's gears are already turning. "Tell me."

"She was with us on the curb."

"She was in front of you."

"Wait, that wasn't an accident?" Jeremy's blabbing again. "Somebody pushed you? What in the—"

This time I ignore Jeremy and continue. "But she has people. She could've hired someone. In the makeup trailer, she was seriously weird. Then the hiding in my trailer and dish throwing, that was full-on aggressive. I just say look at her for it."

Tucker nods, and he motions to Lupita, who waits with a carafe. "You can come on over."

Jeremy looks disappointed. "That's it? That's what all the cloak and dagger was about?"

Tucker looks straight at him. "Do you not hear what we're saying? This isn't an accident. Someone wants to hurt Andrew. On purpose. Kill him."

"So, get the FBI in, get law enforcement. Get it handled." Now Jeremy's gone from lost little puppy to killer German Shepherd.

Tucker finishes the conversation. "They're in the loop, and now so are you. Keep your mouth shut on this one. This isn't some casting rumor."

Jeremy nods. His lips are a grim line. "Fine." Lupita hands me a glass of water, and Jeremy breaks out in a smile. "So, let's get a big fat diamond, why don't we?"

He's about to clap me on the back, like he always does, when he remembers the chunk taken out of my shoulder and stuffs his hands in his pockets.

Lupita goes behind the counter and pulls out a velvet tray. "What do you have in mind, Mr. Pettigrew?"

"Something in line with my agent here: ridiculously overpaid and too big for his britches."

"You got that right, son. I'm a living Eye of the Tiger."

She pulls a large diamond out of the tray. "Something like this?"

I take it from her. It fits on the first section of my ring finger. It's actually quite beautiful, a bit yellow in color, and set in a thicker gold band.

"I love it."

Jeremy looks at me. "You do?"

"Sure. What's not to love?"

"It, no offense, looks like a hooker ring. You'd buy a prostitute off with that ring after a nasty night in Vegas, one she needed to not blab about."

Who knew Jeremy would care? "Good eye," I tell him. "Tucker, what do you think?"

"We're picking a ring out for Kelly here because?"

"The grand gesture. Life is short. I want to spare no expense, and she deserves something for putting up with me." My voice cracks at the last of the sentence. I swallow.

Tucker looks straight at me. "She needs you as much as you need her. You know that."

I shake my head. "No, not so much. She doesn't need to be near me. What all of you would advise her to do, if you were smart, would be to get the hell back to Boise and the hell away from me."

Tucker takes me by the elbow and turns me away from Lupita. "Don't."

"Don't what?"

"This is self-pity. This might be a tiny bit about her. But mostly you're tired, and you're wishing your life wasn't what it is."

"Maybe. But maybe I don't deserve her, Tuck."

He rolls his eyes. "That's not your decision to make. She's made hers. And here she is, in New York, pregnant with your baby. She thinks you deserve her. Be worthy of that."

"I can't keep them safe. I can't give them the life they need."

"Yes, you can. That's why you have me, and God, I hate to say it, but why you have Jeremy. I can keep you all safe, and he can help you get where you want to be, give them whatever kind of life you want to give them."

I cover my face with my hands for a minute.

"Take a deep breath. Think about that smile of hers, the one she has when she's with you. You do that. You've made her happy. You both stuck together. You're here. Own it."

I nod. I know he's right. "I'm just so damn tired, Tuck."

"Yes, you are. Let your heart tell you what ring to get, and let's go home. I want to watch SportsCenter, and you want to cuddle with your almost-wife."

Jeremy butts in. "Are we doing this?"

"Definitely." I answer, suddenly clear again about my reason for being here, my reason for being anywhere.

"When are you giving it to her?" Tucker asks me but keeps his eyes on the front door, as a group of people walk by outside. He hasn't settled down since the accident. It probably didn't help that I told him how Amanda's been acting.

"I'm not sure yet. I want to tell her about the house in Oregon. Maybe we can get away. I could give it to her up there."

Jeremy sighs. "And you're going to squeeze the being-an-actor part into your busy schedule when exactly?"

I ignore Jeremy. "Let's look at something different, Lupita."

Lupita picks up another ring. "Vintage, perhaps? This is an antique from an estate sale."

I finger the delicate band, look at the emerald-cut diamond. Much more Kelly. "I like this. Jeremy?"

"Classy. Much better." He nods. "Kelly's a good girl. You're a lucky man." He says it with a softness that's not usually his style.

"You're right." I look at Tucker, who smiles back. "You're right, J. I'm a lucky, lucky man."

NEW YORK STATE OF MIND

Tessa can't come to visit any faster. We have two weeks to go here in New York. Hunter's still mad. Andrew's exhausted. I'm going crazy without running. The only people who seem halfway their normal selves are Beau, Tucker, and Jeremy—and that thought scares me. When Jeremy starts to seem like a normal person, and worse, like a normal member of the family, that's cause for concern.

The diversion that is Tessa will be good for all of us. Tucker, bless his soul, made all the arrangements for her and the triplets. He even wrote up a little itinerary, and Beau, bored because he's one of the few people not hurt or pouting or both, helped him make a poster of the plan for their visit. Then Beau taped it with duct tape to the side of the Viking fridge, which just about sent Jeremy into orbit, since this condo is a rental. Because Mr. Multi-Millionaire Andrew couldn't pay for a sticky mark on an expensive refrigerator, I guess. At least Jeremy's careful with Andrew's money.

Tucker and Beau are the receiving team for the girls. They drive a big Suburban to the airport to collect them for their four-day visit. It's not very long, but Joe couldn't get away, and traveling with the girls on her own, Tessa is brave to stay as long as she is. I owe her for coming.

Andrew went with Janus to set and is due back at a somewhat reasonable hour. Night shoots wrap up next week, which'll be a relief.

Rudy did the MRI on my knee last week, and I haven't gotten results back. Right now, I sport either an ice pack or a heat wrap on the offending knee every minute Andrew isn't in the condo. When he's home, I ditch it. He doesn't need to worry more than he already does.

We share that. I sleep for the baby, because of the baby—but if I didn't have to, I'd probably be awake and worrying most of the time.

Hunter shuffles into the kitchen. He dressed today, even took a shower after swimming laps this morning. He wears a polo over his board shorts.

"Are they on the way?" he asks.

"Do I detect a hint of anticipation?" I tease. But I tease him gently, because he's burst into tears and/or tirades three times at the drop of a hat since the news about Boise. I tread lightly.

"I want to see Tessa. I like Tessa, Mom." He finds a box of Life cereal and digs a hand into it, pulls out a fist of the squares.

I pull him into a hug. "I'm sorry about how things are working out, Hunter. I know you miss Boise. I do too."

"Maybe Tessa will reconsider me staying with her."

Tessa shot that idea down without even having to ask me, but it was because she knew I'd kill her if she took him under her wing.

"Maybe. At least we get to go to Boise for your birthday. Fourteen. You're getting so big."

He drifts away from me. "I get it, Mom, you know."

"What?"

"I know why we need to stick together. I wouldn't want to leave Andrew, either."

"Really?"

He looks up at me with cheeks full of cereal and nods. "I like him. I don't want him to be sad. I worry about him. And you."

My heart sinks. "We need to offer stock on the worrying going on around here. Our initial offering would blow the roof off Wall Street. Too many brains around here worrying."

"We need a designated worrier. We could each take turns." Hunter smiles. I haven't seen that in a while.

"I like you smiling. You're my handsome boy. You need to smile." I hug him again.

He gets up to dig in the cereal box. "Whatever." He gives me a kiss on the cheek, mouth still full.

"Please don't slobber on me."

The door swings open in the front hall, and all of a sudden there are high-pitched squeals, a tangle of little-girl voices.

"Here we go. Pink princesses attack." Hunter heads to the foyer.

"Hunter?" I stop him.

"Mom?" He looks over his shoulder.

"I'm sorry again. I love you."

"Life happens, Mom. We need to be together. I get it. But I better get the most amazing Boise birthday party known to young man."

"Bet on it." I take his hand, and we go to meet Tessa and the girls. Everything seems just a little bit lighter.

Moments later, it's chaos. I feel bad about how unruly Beau and Hunter can be, but when Tessa and the terrible trio roll in, I feel less bad.

"My girls!" I call to the triplets: Genevieve, Josie, and Jasmine, little black-haired, half-Japanese, half-Italian dolls.

They all run to me, dropping carry-on bags, toys, purses, all sorts of little-girl debris. "Kelleeeee!" I get three hugs around the legs and try to stay on my feet in the enthusiasm.

Tessa comes behind them. "Lord, look at you! You're really preggers!" She peels kids off of me and kisses my cheek.

I want to cry. Seeing her is a relief. Someone I know, I trust, someone from my old, mostly predictable life. "Look at you, not pregnant! Lucky thing." I hug her a long, long time.

"I missed you, Kelly Jo. Are you okay?" She gives me the Tessa look, peering into my eyes for the truth she's sure I won't share willingly.

"I'm okay. Especially now that you're here."

"The accident. How terrifying. I just immediately knew you'd be distraught."

I bite my lip. All the kids are still milling around the entryway. Beau is at the I-love-listening-in-to-grown-up-conversation stage. I appreciate that he still acknowledges my existence, but he doesn't need to hear how I really feel about Andrew getting hurt.

Tessa takes the cue, looks at the boys, and points her finger in command. "Hunter, Beau, your mom and I are gonna do the girlfriend catch-up thing. Can you take the girls in the kitchen and feed them whatever didn't get smashed in their carry-ons? There should be gold-fish and juice boxes."

Hunter rolls his eyes. Beau smiles. He loves to be in charge. "Let's go, kiddos." The girls grab on to parts of him and head to the kitchen.

"Show me some extravagant room," Tessa says once they've gone. "Do you have a salon or a parlor or something? Isn't that what rich people have in their houses?"

I smile. "Would a study do?"

"Does it have overstuffed leather furniture?" She smiles slyly.

"Of course."

"Lead the way."

We sneak down the hall and open the door to the study. She nods appreciatively and plops down in Andrew's leather chair.

"So, toots, what's up?"

I sit across from her on the couch and put up my feet. "Tessa, I'm pregnant, for crying out loud. My knee is rebelling. Poor Andrew is a mess. Hunter threw a fit about not getting back to Boise for the semester. What's *not* up?"

She sighs. "You're certainly cornering the lots-of-shit-going-down market at the moment."

I look at her. "It's not terrible. Everybody's tired. We get to come home for Hunter's birthday. It'll get better. I love New York, but it's a zoo at the moment."

"You should swim. Joe said to tell you to swim. It'll help while you can't run. And he'll work you in when you get home. Rudy's been sending him copies of your charts, like you asked, so he knows what's up. Nothing a little rehab won't cure."

I nod. "When's it going to stop, though?"

"What?"

"The craziness. I feel like Andrew and I keep waiting to fall into a rhythm. It's not happening."

"Give it time. You have a whole life together. Everything ebbs and flows."

"What if we don't?" I choke up a little.

She gets up. "Oh, hon, now I know where you're going with this. Of course, of course, you're going to think about that. After Peter, how could you not? But Andrew's okay. He's safe. And you? You'll be fine. You can't sit around and wait for the other shoe to drop. That's no life." She sits down and puts an arm around me.

"I'm so glad you're here. Let's do lots of stupid New York tourist stuff that my movie star boyfriend is way too cool to endure."

She pats me on the back. "Stop one is the American Girl Place. There will be a princess riot if we don't check that off the list."

"Hunter and Beau may die, but maybe Tucker can take them somewhere else, and we can meet up."

"I was counting on a three-on-three adult-to-triplet ratio. We need man-to-princess coverage."

"I could ask my new friend, Mari. She's nice."

Tessa raises an eyebrow. "You met someone?"

"Why do you always doubt my friend-making abilities?"

"'Cause you suck at meeting new people."

"Well, she's nice. She's a design student. She's even babysat for the kids."

"Wow. She didn't do an Andy Pettigrew freak out?"

"No. Though I think she's figured out who he is. But everybody in New York knows he's here, so why should she be any different?" I consider Andrew's words of warning. I get what he means, but I like the feeling of having someone here in New York. I hold back sharing Andrew's worries with Tessa.

Tessa pats my arm. "I think it'd be great to meet your New York friend who sounds way too hip for either of us. Let me guess — she's young too, huh?"

I nod. "Young and really adorable. And tiny skinny. And blond."

"Great." Tessa stands up and pulls me off the couch. "Just keep her in front of you, like a big handbag. She'll disguise your belly. They do that on TV shows all the time."

The next day Mari comes along on our New York tourist bonanza. Tessa is right; three adults seem almost essential to keep her little pack of ravens in line. Hunter and Beau try to help, but when faced with the American Girl storefront, they can't run away fast enough. I think even Tucker is relieved to not have to go in.

No photographers tailed us on the way out of our building, and for now, in the store, we don't seem to be drawing anyone's attention. I almost feel normal.

The girls are all dragging around the dolls they already own. Tessa has promised them either a new doll with an outfit or some accessory for the old one. Currently Josie is trying to convince Tessa that a horse and stable and extra doll all count as an accessory for her old doll.

Mari sits with me and the other two girls on the couch centrally located in the store. The girls are fading. Genevieve sucks her thumb and leans into Mari's shoulder. The little girl's basically asleep, and her sister Jasmine, on my lap, is close.

"Tessa's nice. Thanks for bringing me with you all."

I give a little elbow. "I'm rubbing off on you. You almost said *ya'll*."

She pats the small black head bobbing into slumber next to her. "I like kids. I miss being around them."

"You mentioned your little brother."

She closes her eyes for a second. "I miss him. It's hard to talk about."

I don't want to push. I never like when people press for details about Peter. It always feels like they're looking for gossip. "I bet. I lost my husband. Did you know that?"

"Yeah." She looks at me. "I think Hunter mentioned it. Is your boyfriend now okay with that?"

"You can call him Andrew. I think you know which Andrew he is too." I smile, try to tell her with my expression that it's okay.

Her eyes cloud for a minute, and then she smiles. "I recognized him at the pool. But is he okay with your past?"

"You mean with me being a widow? I think he is. He seems very understanding."

"What about Boise? Is he okay with Boise?"

"What do you mean?"

"Hunter told me you were supposed to move back to Boise after this shoot, but now you're not going. Do you think Andrew ever really wanted to move back to Boise, live there?"

I'm not following her tone. "Sure. Why wouldn't he?"

"Oh, I don't know. I just can't imagine an actor feeling established enough to take a risk with his career like that."

Huh. This feels a little sore. It's a dig? Does she mean to be hurtful? "We both love Boise. That's where we started dating. It's our special place." I sound a little defensive, maybe.

"Oh, well then, ignore what I just said. It's probably a refuge for him."

"Yeah, I think it is."

"But I get what we were talking about before more now, knowing about the Boise thing."

"What were we talking about before?"

Her eyes and nose crinkle, like she's got a whiff of New York garbage. "You know, how you were worried about finding your purpose. At the museum."

"Oh, yeah. That's tough."

"Well, and if you love Boise, and Andrew needs to be in LA to work, I can see how being disconnected from what you know, and where you've worked before…I can see how that would leave you feeling a bit like you're tagging along."

"Sometimes." I shift. I don't know if it's because Jasmine is getting heavy as she drifts off, or if the conversation makes me uncomfortable.

"But Andrew's great. I can tell, you know, from what you say about him. I can tell he's terrific." Mari smiles and touches my elbow, and her expression is so soft and full of concern. I like this. I have a new friend and an old friend, and for the first time in a while, I feel safe. Like people care about me. It's a good feeling.

"You know how you saw us swimming that one time?" I ask her.

"Yeah?"

"I'm supposed to swim. I can't run anymore. You want to swim with me, until I have to go to Boise? Like every morning?"

She considers. "Water and I have a complicated relationship. Kind of love/hate." She looks down at the floor for a minute.

"Really? When you saw me and Andrew at the pool, I know you were cutting through to the gym, but I thought maybe swimming was something you did."

"It was, but you know, I don't always…" She lets the sentence peter out, looks at the floor again. "I'm supposed to get past it, get used to things, but it's hard."

I jump in, eager to smooth things over with her. "If you don't want to, it's really no big deal. I didn't mean to put you on the spot."

I look right at her, and she seems to relax a bit. "But maybe I could make you feel more at ease in the water, and you could help me rehab this pesky knee. What do you think?"

She shrugs. "Yeah, I'd like that. We could help each other out."

I give her a squeeze. "Then it's settled. We swim while we can. Maybe in the mornings, early before you have class? Then I get to Boise for a weekend, then on to go do my housewife of LA routine until the end of the semester."

"And before you know it, you'll all be back in Boise. One happy family."

"Yep."

Mari looks down at the sleeping girls. "Happy families. What a nice thing."

We make it home later that evening. After we met back up with them, Tucker and the boys insisted on visiting stores in Times Square that were more boy and less pink, and everyone insisted on eating mac and cheese and milkshakes at Schnipper's. Now, with the crew thoroughly wrung out, Andrew greets Tessa and me at the door.

"Is there anything left in Manhattan to buy?" He gives Tessa a little peck on the cheek, wraps me in his arms and squeezes me, the hug still lopsided from the injury.

Tessa smiles as Tucker carries in Josie and Genevieve, both fast asleep, one over each shoulder. Hunter follows with Jasmine, who's awake and on her feet, but just barely. "Everyone is thoroughly shopped and touristed out. There's still stuff left, but nothing in pink."

Andrew waves to the kitchen. "We brought takeout home. Did you eat?"

"We grabbed a bite after the Empire State Building. The girls couldn't wait." Tessa sets her purse down. "I'm going to lie down. I don't get peace like this very often."

She drifts down the hall to the room we've put her and the girls in. The condo might be the height of luxury, but we've packed it like a tenement house. The boys are squeezed into one room now (and arguing about it), Tessa and the girls are in Beau's room, and there are Tucker and Jeremy about like always. One big cozy family.

Andrew leads me into the kitchen. The boys must have retreated to the TV room. No one is around.

"This is eerie. I don't think it's been this quiet since we moved in." Andrew gets me a glass with ice in it, pours a bottle of tea into it. "How was the day?"

I sit at the island. "Nice. Mari and Tessa seemed to like each other. And the jig is up. We talked about you."

He shakes his head. "You took Mari with you?"

Here it comes. He's going to be mad at me for not keeping my distance. "Tucker was with us. She's nice, Andrew. I know you think she'll sell us out to the paparazzi or something, but I don't think so."

He shrugs. "I'm not so worried about that."

"What's the worry, then?" I don't know where he's going with this.

"Nothing. She didn't make a big deal out of me?"

I want him to relax. "Not at all. I think it's going to be fine. Really, Andrew."

He tilts his head a little, and it feels like he might be letting go of something. The shoulders shrug up again. "She already knew about me at the pool, the day after the accident. Not hard to figure out, I guess."

"She won't say anything to anybody. She didn't say anything about you back when she saw us at the pool. I like her. I feel like she needs somebody, like I need somebody."

"What makes you say that?" He sits next to me at the island, rubs my hand in circles.

"Her needing me or me needing her?" I'm tired and not making sense.

"Either." He tips his head a little. That's his close-listening mode. We haven't had much chance to sit and really listen to each other, not for a while.

"I needed someone in New York. We're going to swim a ton before I have to leave too."

"What'd Rudy say about the MRI results?"

I frown. "Still no running, probably for six weeks. Joe'll double check when we're in Boise, but I think Rudy's probably right."

"That's tough."

"I'm worried, Andrew. I know depression, and I don't want to do it. And pregnant is one thing, but add postpartum to no exercise, and it scares me."

He nods. "I know. I promise to keep a close eye on you. I do."

"But you shouldn't have to. You've got enough. You're hurt. That's enough to think about."

"Let me decide what I worry about. I'm a man. I'm all tough and stuff. Don't worry about me."

I touch his cheek, and he leans over and kisses me. At first it's just a peck. Then he lingers, and I find my hands moving over his body. The kiss deepens, and I like the feel of my pulse racing in my arms, neck, my blood quickening.

"Andrew."

"Kelly?" There's a glint in those blue eyes of his.

"'Spose we sneak off to the master bedroom to continue this discussion."

"Is that what we're calling it these days?"

"If you're up to it, yes."

"I'm not going to walk through that wide open door of a joke you just gave me, but, yes, I'm in."

"Your shoulder'll be okay?"

"Beyond okay. Who cares? I don't." He stands up and takes my hand. I follow him down the hall on tiptoes.

He whispers to me before we sneak to our room. "Remind me to send you out shopping more often. I like this end result."

"Don't spoil it by waking napping beasts." I place a finger to my lips.

He kisses me, over my finger, nods silently, and disappears behind the door.

Naptime rocks.

BRIDGE OVER TROUBLED WATER

The pool room is humid this morning. I fight against the uncomfortable closeness of the air. It feels heavy as I draw it into my lungs between strokes. Mari's due to meet me in a minute. It's been a few days since the American Girl store adventure, so I texted last night to make our first "swim date."

She comes through the door now, towel wrapped around her slim waist. She has on a pretty emerald green two-piece, kind of retro.

I pause and tread water to say hello. "I like the suit."

"Thanks. I wanted to wear it to show off my new present to myself."

She slides into the water and kicks over to me, tentative. *A complicated relationship with water*, that's what she said. She moves carefully, as though on guard.

"What is it?"

We're in the shallow end, and she turns her back to me.

On her shoulder, from the top down to the bottom of her shoulder blade and twisting underneath it, is a tattoo.

And what a tattoo it is: a pair of disembodied eyes, floating over a sea of emerald green. Lights from a carnival and Ferris wheel float between.

The eyes are full of tears, and one tear drips out of the left eye and into the ocean below.

"Is this a Gatsby tattoo?" It's still pink around the edges. She must have just gotten it. I just saw her the other day, and it hasn't even scabbed over yet.

"How perceptive of you. I love the eyes."

"It's like the cover. I can't tell if these eyes are a woman's or a man's, though."

She bobs up and turns around to face me. "They might be a boy's."

"It's beautiful. What's the occasion?"

She swallows hard. "Just 'cause, mostly. It's partly an anniversary and partly a new beginning. Feels like things are falling into place for me—things I've been patient about for a long time."

"Things?"

"A thing. Maybe a person."

"So, a tattoo to celebrate a person?"

She shrugs. "I don't mean to be vague. It's about two people. Someone I want to remember. And there's someone I've liked for a long time, and it feels like finally we might be together."

"What's holding you back?"

"I might be holding myself back, you know? I think every girl needs to be strong. Not needy, especially if the other person's going through a lot. I'm working on being the kind of girl who's not a burden. Takes care of herself. Isn't clingy. I think that kind of stuff drives men away."

"Being strong is never a bad thing."

"I know the guy I like; he's got enough going on. He doesn't need drama from me."

I can't help but think of Andrew. This is why my whining about my knee, whining about being pregnant, it needs to stop. He's got enough going on. He's in pain. Real pain. "I hope things go right for you with him."

She dips her head back a little and pulls her wet hair over her shoulder. "I try to bring good things into my life now. Maybe the tattoo is a good luck charm." She touches it, hand over her back, and her eyes focus on a spot somewhere far away. Then she shakes herself out of it. "Or it's just a tattoo I want because I want it for me. Doesn't have to be a big thing, does it?"

I turn on my back and float a little, looking at the ceiling. "Well, I think those are all good reasons for a tattoo. And you're allowed to do something just for yourself. I like that."

She pulls her goggles down on to her eyes. "You should try it sometime." She smiles, then tenses for a moment and slides under the water, headed to the other end of the pool.

"Funny." She's already swimming and can't hear me. I blow out a big breath and let the water swallow me up too.

The next day, on Tessa's last night, Andrew takes all of us out to dinner. I worry, of course. It seems like a huge risk. And there's chaos with all our kids together under normal circumstances. Adding New York and the paparazzi to the mix? That's just crazy.

Tucker pulls Janus along for the fun. We all pile into two black-windowed SUVs and head up toward Central Park.

Andrew seems so self-assured about the whole thing. I sit next to him. Beau's on the other side of me, but he's turned around, making faces at Jasmine, who's in love with him. He's in heaven, of course.

"Where is this place?"

"It's by the Met."

"I could've had lunch there with Mari when we went to the museum."

"But tonight it'll be ten times cooler, because you're lucky enough to eat there with me."

I crinkle my nose at him. "Mr. Ego. Nice."

He slides an arm around me carefully. "It's called Crown. There's a hidden private room."

Beau turns around. "What?"

"The restaurant. We're eating in the private dining room. It has a hidden entrance, behind a marble staircase."

Beau nods in approval. "That's cool."

"And that's why you're so smug about us eating out, huh?" I wrap my hand in his.

"Basically, yes. They're expecting us."

I lean over and kiss him. "Thanks for taking such good care of us."

His expression changes. "I wish I wasn't the reason you needed taking care of."

"Don't be silly. It's not your fault."

"Yeah, let's not talk about it. I want to have a nice, peaceful night out with my family."

Jasmine lets out a giggle at this same moment and hucks a My Little Pony from her car seat up toward Beau. Beau ducks the flying Rainbow Dash.

I smile. "I wouldn't count on it, Mr. Pettigrew."

Then, barely twelve hours later, here Tessa and I are again, saying goodbye at an airport. I drove with Tucker to drop her off.

We sit in the backseat as the Skycaps pull lots of pink luggage out from the back of the car.

"It was too fast," I say, hugging her tightly.

"I know. But you'll be in Boise for Hunter's birthday, so we might as well not even say goodbye."

"Okay." I try not to cry.

"Everything has a way of working out. You know it will. You always make it through."

"I know." I don't seem to have much to say.

"And I like Mari. She's someone good to know. Maybe she can come out and visit in LA while Andrew's filming—if she doesn't have school."

I hadn't thought about that. "I wish you could come."

"You know I'll be there for your shower."

"You know I don't want a baby shower."

"You know I'm Tessa, and I'll do what I want. I'm throwing you a shower. Your mom would botch the whole thing up. I have the party skills."

She's right. Tessa plans parties with deadly precision. Birthday parties for triplets have honed that skill.

"Okay, one more smooch. I've got little wombats to herd." She plants a big kiss on my cheek and smiles at me. "Take care of yourself. Baby Movie Star needs a happy mama."

I nod. I can't talk.

She scoots out of the car and hustles to the curb, gathering up the girls. I see her thank Tucker and say something else to him. She's probably giving him orders to spy on me.

Then she and the girls disappear through the doors into the terminal.

I sit next to Tucker and try harder not to cry. I'll work on the happy mama thing tomorrow.

BETTER BE HOME SOON

"Mom?"

"Yeah?" Beau and I sit at the kitchen table in our Boise home. It's the end of September. What a relief, to be in our house. Ditto the dog keeps sniffing at us, either put out by our absence or trying to figure out who the heck we are.

Beau puts paper cupcake holders into the tins. "Who decided what size muffin tin holes would be?"

I look up at him. I'm waiting for Andrew to text, to tell us he's on his way for Hunter's birthday party tonight. It's the end of filming on *The Bull, The Bear, and The Dragon*, and Andrew's catching a flight to Boise in an hour or so. He'll just make it.

"What'd you say?"

"Was there a Geneva Convention ruling or what? How come the papers always fit the tins, no matter what brand you use?"

I pull him to me and kiss the top of his head. "That brain of yours amazes me. And I don't know the answer. You better Google it."

He gets up and drifts off to somewhere else in the house. My phone buzzes.

It's a text, but it's Mari, not Andrew:

Tell Hunter Happy Birthday. Kisses, Mari

It's been a few days since we came home. Hunter's happy, back with his buddies, though he's definitely milking the "I have to go to LA for the rest of the semester" angle. Beau's milking the "I get a tutor in LA and haven't had to go to school yet this semester" angle. That makes me really nervous, but Andrew promises we'll get a top-notch tutor to make up for the late start.

Beau and I went to the party store and got all manner of streamers, centerpieces, and balloons. I want to make this a good birthday for Hunter. I know things haven't worked out the way he wanted them to these past few months. He invited about eight good friends for the party, and the big plan is to wear out the Xbox One and eat pizza. Thank God for boys. He didn't invite a single girl, didn't even think about it, and didn't want a big production, as much as he talked about it. He was thrilled to open the Xbox early this morning, since that was on the top of his birthday list.

I get the cupcakes into the oven, and there's still no text from Andrew. Now I start to worry. Surprising, I know. "He's going to miss his flight." Ditto looks at me, like I'm talking to him. "Maybe I'm talking to Hiccup, did you think of that?" I give my belly a little rub.

Finally, finally, I'm into the decent stage of pregnancy here in month five. The morning sickness is gone, and so is the life-sucking fatigue. I'm not quite big enough to start with the swollen ankles or terrible heartburn at night, though that's coming soon. For now, I feel decent.

I saw Dr. Joe, Tessa's husband, yesterday, and running is still out for me, but PT is working, and it looks like I won't have to have my knee scoped. I can stand that, I think. I just need to get to LA, and I can figure out a morning workout that doesn't hurt and keeps me from going crazy.

"Knock, knock, not really." Tessa strolls into the kitchen.

"How'd you get in?" I never lock the doors in Boise, but Andrew told the boys he'd pay them each twenty bucks if they kept them bolted. He's been protective, more so since the accident. He says he doesn't trust that a stray paparazzo won't try to wander in if we're not vigilant.

"Beau saw me. If he was supposed to help you, you're down a man. He went off toward the school with Hunter and some other kid to shoot hoops."

"And they didn't let me know. Hunter thinks he'll get away with murder just because it's his birthday."

"I'm supposed to tell you. Don't shoot the messenger, crabby pregnant lady." Tessa gets into the fridge and finds a bottle of water.

"Tell me you're hanging out with me until the party." I give her my best pitiful look.

"You're in luck, actually. Joe's taken the girls out for some playground time, then lunch and fro-yo downtown. He'll swing by with them later. You've got me all to yourself."

I clap my hands. "Yes! I wish we could have a glass of wine or something."

"Um, you're pregnant, you never drink, and it's, like, ten in the morning."

I check my phone again. "This isn't good. Andrew's supposed to be at the airport, headed through security. His flight's at eleven thirty. If he misses it, he can't get in until, like, eleven tonight."

"Have you flown with him? I doubt he has a leisurely walk down the concourse. How's he supposed to text you until he's in the lounge or on the plane?"

This is true. Airport security bows to no man, and when Andy Pettigrew goes through airport security at a major US airport, every man, woman, and nosy puppy dog knows he's on the move.

Tessa drags me out of the kitchen and into the living room. "Come on. Let's hang up balloons and stop fretting."

No text, and it's eleven forty-five. Tessa and I take Ditto for a walk.

At twelve thirty we have lunch, and I call. His phone goes straight to voice mail.

It's one p.m. If he's not on the plane, he won't make the party.

At two thirty I'm at my wits' end.

At five, Tessa has her cell out. We've tried Andrew's cell, Jeremy's, and Tucker's. No luck. Either there's some massive power outage in New York, or they all made it on the plane but never bothered to check their phones beforehand.

"I don't like this. If he's still on set, I'll kill him." I can feel my jaw tighten at the thought. "He promised. He promised me, and he promised Hunter."

Tessa waves a hand. "Listen, something's up. He wouldn't just blow this off. Let's just get the pizza ordered and go about our business. Watched pot never boils, you know."

I have to laugh. "That's the lamest saying. But I've managed a few birthday parties on my own. I'm a smart woman. This is no big deal."

"No big deal." Tessa smiles when she says it, but the smile doesn't reach her eyes.

And if Tessa's worried, then we do have a problem.

At seven p.m., it's crystal clear Andrew's not coming to the party. But no one knows where he is. Tessa, amazingly resourceful bestie, gets in touch with Jordan Aaronson, of all people, and he reports that Andrew and company finished a production meeting early in the morning and headed to JFK, en route to an on-time eleven thirty a.m. departure.

My hands tremble a little. "This is where I usually call Tucker. But he's with Andrew. Where are they, Tessa?"

She shakes her head. "I really don't know."

I have a moment. What if they did something stupid? Got drunk in the airport lounge, hooked up with a couple star-hungry girls, headed back into Manhattan to paint the town red?

My brain's not working. No way Andrew would do something like that. And Jeremy might, but Tucker sure as hell wouldn't. And the three of them are together.

Hunter comes into the kitchen. The party's in full swing. The boys play Xbox One, eat pizza, do boy things like burp loudly. They're having a good time.

"Mom. We want to open presents. Can we?"

I glance at the oven clock for the millionth time. "I wanted to wait for Andrew."

Hunter sighs. "Obviously something happened. Let's do presents."

I relent. "Fine. Tessa, will you take pictures?"

She throws an arm around me. "You know I will."

We go out to the living room. We're not waiting anymore, and it breaks my heart.

The guests all go home at eleven. No Andrew. I want to call the police, but Tessa told me not to. She's right—it'd just set off a huge media frenzy. Even if I called dispatch on the non-emergency number, someone would still get wind of it, and what a mess that'd be. She and Joe and the triplets went home at ten. The little girls needed to sleep in their own beds.

"I'm going to bed, Mom." Beau gives me a big kiss and leaves me alone at the kitchen island. We've waited up, with no word, and it's now eleven thirty p.m.

"Me too." Hunter comes up behind him. He kisses me on the top of my head. He's so big, so grown-up.

I start crying. I can't help it. He's fourteen. This is a big deal. And the person we've all come to rely on, he's not here. "I'm so sorry, Hunter. I don't know what to say."

"It's okay, Mom. It's not your fault. I still had a good birthday." He hugs me and heads off to bed.

I put my head down on the granite countertop. I don't know if I want to sob or give up and fall asleep.

"Hey."

It's Andrew. He walks into the kitchen, luggage slung over his good shoulder. He sets the bag down and comes to me.

"Where've you been? What happened to you?" I don't sound calm. The words are loud against the kitchen tile.

He pulls me into his arms. "Long story."

I push away from him. "Hunter wanted you here. Not just me. You disappointed him too." I grit my teeth to keep my voice down. I don't want to alert the kids to this fight.

"What are you talking about? Do you even want to know what happened?"

I shake my head no. "I don't want to hear the excuse." And suddenly, a strange, resigned calm comes over me. This might be the end of our relationship, and I need to be the bigger person. "I can bet you got stuck on set. And it's fine. I know I backed you into a corner. This was insta-family. It's not very fair. I get it."

"Stop it. Stop it right now." Andrew steps to me and takes me into his arms again. "I'm here. I'm late, but I love you and the boys and our baby. Stop it right now."

He kisses me on the lips, hard. I look at him, try to read his eyes.

"Kelly. Kelly, listen to me. We got to the airport, and Tucker and Jeremy got through security just fine, and then they checked my bag. They swiped it for residue, and it came up positive. *Positive.* Why in the hell it did, nobody knows. But if your bag tests positive for traces of explosive materials, you can bet that you and the party you're flying with — well, none of us went very far for a very long time."

"What?" My whole body shakes. My teeth chatter. All this information shoots the adrenaline straight into my heart, and it pumps in a crazy panic.

"Kelly, somebody tampered with my bag. Someone wanted to make sure I missed my flight."

I cry out. I can't process this. I can't stop sobbing.

"Okay, it's okay. Breathe." Andrew rubs a hand down my back. "Please, Kelly, please. I'm fine. We weren't ever in danger."

The tears don't stop. Andrew rubs both hands over his face. He pulls out his cell and dials.

"Tessa? Hey. I know. Long story. Listen, can you put Joe on? Kelly's pretty upset."

There's a pause. I put my head down on the countertop, the shudders and heaves of my chest shooting pain through my entire torso.

"Joe? Hey, it's Andrew. Yeah, I know. So, Kelly's really upset."

He walks out of the kitchen. I can't hear the rest of the conversation.

He comes back in and takes my hand.

"Can you come with me?"

I nod through my sobs. I try to catch my breath. The tears just keep coming.

Andrew leads me into the master bedroom, through to the bathroom.

He turns on the shower, then turns and looks me straight in the eyes.

"Kells, I think you're having a panic attack. Here's what we're going to do, okay?"

I nod.

"We're going to get into the shower. I'll hold you. Just close your eyes."

He steps back for a minute and strips off his shirt, shoes, and steps out of his jeans. He pulls my T-shirt over my head and helps me step out of my pajama pants.

We're both still in our underwear, but he pulls me into the shower anyway.

I can't stop crying. I feel the hot water run in rivulets through my hair, down into my eyes.

He pulls me close to his chest. "It's okay. Just breathe."

I listen to his heart. I try to breathe.

Finally, and I don't know how long we've stood there, I can catch my breath. He rubs my back in small circles with one hand, the other holding me tight to him.

He murmurs into my wet hair. "Is it getting better?"

I nod.

"Come on, then." He turns off the water and gets me a towel. He wraps me up and helps me into bed. He climbs in behind me, pulls the covers tight around us, and holds me close.

I shudder a little. I must've been hyperventilating—my fingers and toes slowly uncramp. I didn't even notice.

Andrew pulls me tighter to him. "I'm taking you away tomorrow. We're going to go somewhere quiet, and I will make this better for you. No one's going to hurt us. I promise."

I close my eyes and fall into a dreamless sleep.

OCEAN AVENUE

Kelly's very quiet on the plane.

Yes, I borrowed Jordan's private jet. I called last night after Kelly finally fell asleep and cashed in a very big favor from him. He's a dick, but he's a dick with a plane, and I need to help Kelly shake off this dark shadow that has such a grip on her.

So, here I am, doing the big, crazy proposal. She's not throwing up, and she's not in labor, so I think I'm allowed to propose for real. With all the proposals and since I already told her she's my fiancée, I guess I took her part out of it, but oh well.

The big plan is to surprise her with the Oregon house, show her the ring, and hopefully skip down the beach hand in hand like two happy, crazy kids.

That's all I've got.

Tucker gave Jeremy the heads up that I wanted to do something nice to show Kelly the house and surprise her, so maybe he got a little more creative than I did. But he's Jeremy, so I don't know if that's a good thing or not.

"Are we there yet?" Kelly looks at me sleepily. She's been sleeping on and off for the past couple hours. I expected her to throw a big fit, not knowing where we were going, but she just smiled and said she was curious.

This is not her. She never makes things easy, and she never just lets things happen. This passivity is unnerving. I want my Kelly back. This is a little like Stepford Wife Kelly. I don't like it.

"We're descending now. Wanna know where to?"

She nods. This quiet stuff's creepy too. She's never been a woman of few words.

"Portland, my pet."

"Really?"

"Yes, really. Then a little car ride. Then the surprise."

"A private jet, just for the two of us. I'm impressed. Must be some surprise."

"Come here." I motion her to my seat. She takes her seatbelt off and slides over. I put my arms around her. "You're worth a very big surprise." I kiss her, and I feel her mouth on mine, but she's soft, and she gently takes my kiss without returning it. I run my hand along her body, tracing my fingertips across her warm skin. She leans into me and closes her eyes, but again, she's accepting my touch, not reacting to it. "Are you okay, Kelly?"

"I will be. Getting away with just you will be good. Thanks for this. I'm sorry."

"What for?"

"You're the one who got hurt. I'm supposed to be strong for you. I'm being ridiculous. I know it's been a burden to you."

"What in the hell are you talking about? It's not a burden. Jesus. You had a panic attack, rightly so, and you think I'll lose my patience with you?"

"Sometimes it happens. Mari and I were talking about it." She ducks her head.

"It's not happening right now, so stop thinking about it." I pull her closer. I wish I could kiss that kind of stupid, lethal thinking out of her head. How can she think I'd find her tiresome?

"Sorry."

"Nope, no more apologies this whole trip. I don't care if you accidentally push my ass down the stairs, you won't be saying sorry for anything for the duration of our stay in Oregon. Are we clear?"

Finally, finally, I see her smile. She seems to relax a little into my embrace. "Crystal." She leans forward and kisses me this time. I want to unleash all of it on her, turn her to straddle me, get my hands all over that gorgeous blooming body of hers, but she's drifting off again, eyelids drooping.

"Why are you so tired?"

"I don't know."

"Do you sleep when I sleep?"

She shakes her head. "No. I watch you. I worry about you. Watching you breathe feels calm, peaceful. I just wait to fall asleep, but lately, the sun comes up, and I'm still watching."

What would she be like if Tucker and I had told her the whole truth about the car accident? What a mess.

I don't know who put the fear of God into her like this, but it needs to stop. It's unacceptable.

We land in Portland, and I actually get to drive for the trip out to the place on the coast. No paparazzi tailing us, no bodyguard—not that I don't love Tucker—no boys—not that I don't love the boys. Just us. The two of us. I think back to the last time we were alone, and I can't put my finger on when it was. We've been sleeping with someone next door for too many months to count. This shoot turned into summer camp. Camp Pettigrew. How sad.

"I get to pump my own gas," I say to the dashboard. Kelly's dozing in the seat next to me. This trip I rented a fun car. Kelly always gets a Prius. I got an Escalade. Normally Kelly would think that was silly, and she'd probably sing rap songs at me, ask me if I was riding dirty, give me all sorts of grief. Not this time. I don't like it. She's not herself.

I pull into a gas station to top off the tank and get out. In LA, I can't pump my own gas—too much commotion. In New York, I wasn't doing my own driving. Here, for just a minute, I'm normal. Crazy thought, huh, to be psyched to do something like pump my own gas? But I swear I miss regular stuff. I miss Target. I liked Target.

I haven't been in a box store in years. Actual years. The mob scene it'd cause—and I'm not saying that to be douchey. It'd be a frenzy.

I stand with my credit card and gas nozzle at the ready. A guy comes out from the store.

"Hey, you can't do that," he tells me.

"What?" Has it been so long that I don't know the right way to pump gas?

He shakes his head. "Oregon. You don't pump your gas. I do."

I sigh and step out of the way.

On the plus side, he doesn't recognize me.

All done. I get back in and pull away. Kelly still sleeps. She didn't even wake up for the stop.

Finally, I pull off 101 after the business loop for Tolovana. Now Kelly stirs and sits up, curious. Her eyes seem brighter than they have in a while. Maybe in the time since my accident.

"Where are we going? A bed and breakfast? Is it the Whale's Perch?"

"Nope."

I edge the car around a couple deeper potholes. The house has sat empty since we saw it at the beginning of the summer, so when I bought it, I made a point of getting an interior designer in from Portland to furnish it, clean it, the whole deal. By the looks of the tall grass on either side of the drive, the house might have been for sale for a while before that.

Kelly's figuring it out. "Wait a second." She punches me in the arm. "You didn't!"

"I didn't what?" I can't help it. I grin. I'm not much good at surprises.

"You bought the house I love, the one on Silver Point! This house, the one at the end of this driveway!" Now she bounces up and down on the car seat like a ten-year-old. That's my Kelly.

"Okay. I totally did."

"Shut up!" She punches me on the arm again.

"You shut up!" I park the car. I bet she's never seen the house from this point of view. She always just stared at it from afar, admiring it from the beach on her runs.

I win. I made her smile, made her happy.

I'm a happy man.

I get out and come around, open her door for her, walk her to the front door. Jeremy had the agent stash the key under the mat.

It's Oregon, people. Until someone gets wind that I live here, this is a very safe place.

"I can't believe this. I can't wait to see the inside!" She takes my arm and squeezes it. Suddenly her limp is barely there. I swing the door wide, and she pushes past me.

"This is really the first time either of us has seen it. Kind of weird, huh?" I hope she likes it. God, what if it sucks inside? I hadn't thought about that.

She walks down the corridor, following the daylight. I know from the pics online that the big payoff is the great room, with its floor-to-ceiling windows overlooking the ocean. I feel for the ring in my coat pocket. Here we go.

"Andrew, come look! It's gorgeous. Oh, what did you do? Awww..." She's fawning over something. What did I do? What did Jeremy do? Please don't be something sick. Jeremy's idea of romance is edible panties.

I walk in. The whole wall I'm facing is windows. It's spectacular. And the east and west walls are all rock, with a huge two-story fireplace on the west side.

But Kelly is over at the kitchen sink. I join her.

"This is so romantic. I love it." She turns around and wraps her arms around me.

I peek around her to see what the fuss is about.

The deep farmhouse sink is filled with ice, and there's a bottle of sparkling cider in it. And two or three dozen long-stem red roses chilling as well, all tucked in one by one around the bottle. And a note that says "Welcome to your new beach house, Kelly," on one of those florists' picks. For once Jeremy had some class.

"You deserve it." I kiss her deeply. This time, she returns the kiss, and I realize that we're alone, truly alone.

"I love you."

"You feeling more awake? I think there's a bedroom up those stairs." Hell yes, I'm seizing the moment. I want to be with my girl.

She nods and kisses me again, her tongue teasing mine before she turns away and goes to the stairs. "You need to give an assist on the stairs part. Bum knee here, you know."

Here's my chance. I cover the space between us in two strides to pick her up in my arms. "I'm on it."

She puts her arms up. "No, no you don't. You'll hurt your shoulder."

I ignore her and sweep her up. "I got cleared from *my* physical therapy, unlike some slackers I know." I feel a twinge of pain over the scar, but no way in hell will she know that. I kiss her and begin up the stairs. "After this, you need to give me a little assist. I need some help with something. In bed."

She laughs loudly, and it echoes off the rock walls. "Your double entendres suck. Carry me up the stairs, and let's get to the 'assisting,' big boy." She uses air quotes, even.

Maybe she's out of her funk.

JUST SAY YES

I lie in Andrew's arms, finally happy. I haven't felt like this since the accident. This house, the quiet, no one here but us—it liberates me. The anvil, my unwelcome companion pressing down on my chest, has lifted. Hopefully it's gone for good. I feel calm and safe.

"Happy?" He strokes my hair, kisses my head.

"Definitely. Relieved."

"About what?"

"I wasn't sure if I could shake this off. But I think I feel better."

"Good. In LA you should keep up with the PT. You could get scheduled as soon as we're there. You won't miss me—I've got meetings back to back to back after being in New York for so long."

"Yay."

"I know. But you can hang with your folks."

"It'll be fine. And the weather rocks. I can wear your hoodie all the time!"

"Then what will I wear all the time?" he asks.

He's a good sport.

"I think it's time I just get you a real wubbie, and you admit that you never wanted to give up your fuzzy teddy bear from when you were two."

"You know me too well." He nips my earlobe and dips his head to nibble on my shoulder.

"How's the back?" I worry about him. What we just did, that could pull something.

"Fine. Thanks for asking, now that you've already had your way with me. When we were busy, you didn't seem too worried about my state of health." He kisses me on the cheek.

"A woman has needs. Then she can feign concern for your well-being."

He tickles me in the armpit. "Cold. That's cold."

I wriggle away from him. "Ooh!" I sit up.

"What?"

"That was a good swift kick from Hiccup. He's not keen on our shenanigans, apparently."

"A kicker? I'll call the private soccer coach when we get to LA. Probably a waiting list, like the preschools."

I roll my eyes. "This will not be an LA kid. No showbiz brat. There's a reason we live in Idaho."

"I know." He sits up and picks up my hand, kisses each fingertip.

I can see that this comment hurts him a bit. This stay in LA, he's taking it personally.

"Now come get dressed," he says after a moment. "I want to check out the rest of the house. We didn't even go out on the deck."

I grin. This is my house. My house with this amazing man, who right now is slipping his old jeans over his amazing body. This feels good, relaxed. All the worries are set aside for now.

I slip on my clothes and skip the shoes. He walks me around the other bedrooms, helps me back down to the main level, and then strolls to the deck door. "Let's check the view out, shall we?"

I follow him out. It's breathtaking. Andrew turns the fireplace on, and it warms the deck outside as well as in. I stare at the beach below. The black, forbidding rock spreads out from underneath the house, its fingers reaching down to the water's edge before it dives under the surf, only to rise above seventy-five feet out to sea, a huge dark monolith.

"Silver Point. It's gorgeous."

Andrew comes up behind me. "You like it?"

"Of course. You saw me drooling over it in June. You're sneaky."

"I pay attention. I want to know the things I can do to make you happy, you know." He turns me around and kisses me.

"You make me happy. Just you is good."

"Oh, then I can give the house back. Good."

"Now let's not be hasty. The house makes me happy too. We can keep it."

"Oh, all right. I want to talk to you about something real for a minute." He shifts on his feet a little. His hands go into his front pockets, and his shoulders shrug up.

"What?" I know this look. It's his uncomfortable, nervous stance.

"I'm not sure how to do this."

"Do what?"

He takes me by both hands. "Come stand right here."

I do as he says.

He comes up behind me. "Close your eyes."

"Okay."

I feel him wrap his arms around me. "Open them."

I open my eyes. He holds a ring box in front of me. "Here."

He lets me go, comes to stand in front of me. "Marry me."

"What? Is this the real one?" I open the box. It's an old, emerald-cut diamond, set in a delicate band.

"Tucker and Jeremy helped me pick it out, believe it or not. It's antique."

"It's gorgeous. I love it."

"Is that a yes?"

"What?"

"Are you saying you'll marry me?"

"You're already calling me your fiancée. You've proposed ninety million times."

"So, is that a yes?"

"Yes. Andrew Pettigrew, I want to marry you. Thanks for officially asking me." I kiss him. He holds me tightly, kisses me playfully on the jaw.

"I really wanted to do another super proposal, but doctors Rudy and Joe both advised against skydiving this far into a pregnancy. And the elephant got a cold."

"I consider this to be a very elaborate, extravagant, and perfect proposal. I love it."

"Good. Maybe when we renew our vows somewhere down the line, the elephant can get involved."

"Sounds fair."

"Are you hungry? I want to eat, devour you a little more, and sleep. And then possibly repeat."

"All of the above. I'm hungry for all of that. You heal my heart, Andrew. Thanks for sweeping me away. I needed it so desperately."

"My pleasure, Mrs. Almost-Pettigrew." He kisses me one last time and slips inside.

I follow eagerly. I have an almost-husband to attack.

I NEVER PROMISED YOU A ROSE GARDEN

After the blissful time in Oregon, I fly alone to Boise to meet the boys for a few days, then it's on to California to catch up with Andrew for the rest of fall semester. When we land in LA, Tucker picks us up at the airport. No fanfare at LAX today, since it's just me, Hunter, and Beau. Tucker is always on guard here, though.

"They tail you to your house. Then they park someone at the gate twenty-four-seven, lie in wait. They're complete predators."

Beau chimes in. "I'd say more like vultures. They circle and keep their distance, then swoop in when you're vulnerable."

Tucker smiles. "Beau, you're absolutely right. Creepy birds with red heads, that's them. Definitely." He pulls the SUV away from the curb.

"So, are you going to spill the big news or what?" Hunter has turned a Beats headphone around so he can converse. I guess it's nice, the large cups over his ears, because, boy, when he turns one around, it means we better take notice: he's actually entering the land of the conversant. I don't say much about it because I very clearly remember wearing out my Walkman when I was his age. There's a way to play a tape so much you can hear the other side of tape when playing it.

"Who's going to spill what big news?" Beau looks around at everyone.

Tucker shakes his head. "How do you know anything, Hunter?"

"I just texted Andrew that we're here, and he asked how far into the drive we were. Then I asked him why, and he said 'you'll see.' I figured something was up."

"You text Andrew all the time, do you?" I know he does. I think it's cute.

"Mom, get over it. What's the surprise, Tucker?"

"No, no, I'm not caving. You just sit tight, mister. All will soon be revealed." Tucker takes a turn north on the 405 and just smiles, quite Cheshire cat-like.

The boys needle him relentlessly for who knows how many more miles. I'm about to my breaking point when we cruise right past the turn-off for the 10.

"Where are we headed? That was our turn. I thought we were going home." Beau practically hops up and down in the backseat.

"I have been sworn to secrecy." Tucker grins. He clearly loves being a part of this. It makes me happy.

When we turn north on Santa Monica Boulevard, I am truly stumped. "Tucker, I do need to let you know that the baby sits squarely on my bladder, so if this is an unscheduled sightseeing trip, I'm going to need to take a pit stop." I'm only partially kidding. One of the joys of pregnancy: the constant bathroom breaks.

"Kelly, dear, you're as bad as the boys. We're almost there."

We roll through Beverly Hills. As we pass Rodeo Drive, I'm truly confused. This isn't our part of town. Sure, Andrew has to come here all the time, to meet with producers. But I take comfort in the fact, daily, that he breaks out in as much of a rash as I do when it comes to this excessive display of wealth. One, I don't have that kind of wealth to display (Andrew does, but still), and two, if I did, I'd like to think I would put it to better use than buying ridiculous things. Andrew has kept his charitable business very quiet, and I like that very much. He does what he does to help people, not to schedule a photo op through Sandy.

I fidget. Tucker takes us farther north, and the car climbs out of LA and into the dry hills. This is a pricy neighborhood, and the lawns and shrubs and mailboxes all are perfectly tended and perfectly expensive.

The boys point at one house after another, wowed by the displays of wealth. They're kids, and they still get impressed by the showy side of LA. Money doesn't start to stink until you see what it does to people over time. It's the houseguest who has outstayed his welcome, but the boys are still too young to bear witness to that.

"Tucker, seriously, I need to stop soon. And traffic is slow. Is there a point to all this?"

He turns right as I say this. "You'll see soon enough."

He pulls to a stop at a guard house. A guy with dark, thick eyebrows and sideburns steps out. Tucker lowers the window and flashes a pass. The guard nods and steps back in, and the gate ahead of us swings wide.

"Tucker—"

My phone rings. I answer, "Andrew, what's up?"

"Look to your right." He sounds like a little kid.

I look right, and Tucker slows the car, pulling into a short driveway. "What is this?"

It's a house. A big house. A different house than the one Andrew's rented the whole time I've known him, the one we've all come to know as our place when we're in LA.

This is no rambling 1920s Spanish-style home. This is a mansion; there's no other word for it.

The door is a huge arch detailed with ornate, curving wrought iron. The face of the house is large white stone, with just the right amount of ivy curling up the sides to meet the balconies above—two on each side of the arched front door.

Beau jumps from the car and runs to the porch, where Andrew waits. "Dude, what the what?"

Andrew hugs him. "New digs for the Pettigrew-Reynolds clan." He looks to me. I make sure my face is neutral, putting my tongue to the roof of my mouth.

We step into the front hallway, and I catch myself before I say a word.

A marble stairway curves to the second story, and a sparkling crystal and brass chandelier dangles above our heads. The floor is diamonds of white and black marble.

It's ridiculous. I wait for Scarlett O'Hara to sweep down the stairs, calling for Rhett.

"Whoa, this is a rich person's house!" Beau races Hunter up the stairs.

"What is this?" I look at Andrew.

"How about, 'Hi, darling, dashing father of my child, how I've missed you'?" He comes to my side and kisses me on the lips, wraps his arms around me for a moment.

"Andrew, really. What is this?" I feel my bottom lip quiver a bit.

"If you say that one more time, I may have to assume you've had a stroke. Um, I wanted to surprise you. It's the new house. Our lease was up, and I wanted a place with beefier security. You know, like how we talked about after all the stuff in New York."

"Please tell me you didn't buy this." My voice sounds wavery.

"No, of course not. The only house we own is in Boise. That's our home. Well, now at Silver Point as well. This is a place we stay when we need to be here in LA. When I'm working." He exhales loudly, looks like he's losing his patience.

I take a huge breath in, trying to maintain calm. Tucker looks at me and makes a beeline for the front door, closing it behind him as he goes outside.

"You're not going to cry, are you? Why in the world are you upset?" Andrew rubs a hand across his forehead.

"This house, Andrew. This isn't me at all. I thought it wasn't us. But you chose it. *You* did. How could you think it was actually right for us?"

"You know what? I'm going out back. I will chalk this up to a hormonal moment, and then you can come on out, and I will explain why I did something as dastardly as pick a house that is safer by a mile than our old one here in LA, and one with a pool so you can rehab your knee. How I thought you'd get a kick out of the handprints in the cement by the pool out back, the ones with Ingrid Bergman's signature. But right now I'm going to give the baby mama a moment, because I don't feel so gracious."

He disappears down the hall. I sink down on the first step of the ridiculous stairway, feeling two inches tall, and try not to dissolve into tears.

I suck, as usual.

I shake myself out of it. I need to fix this before it gets out of hand.

I head toward the back of the house, looking for Andrew. The other rooms are ostentatious, to be sure (there are two dishwashers, two ovens, two prep sinks, and a Subzero fridge the size of a minivan in the kitchen), but nothing as outlandish as the *Gone With the Wind* staircase foyer. Maybe it's not so bad.

I come out of the house to the pool area. It really is lovely. There are old, painted-white wrought-iron fences, detailed and intricate, like a balcony from the French Quarter. There's a beautiful view of the city. The shrubs are large, old-growth holly bushes. In the center is a kidney-shaped pool, not gigantic, with a diving board on one side. It's perfect for the boys. All of this is much more modest than the entryway.

Andrew sits on the pool deck, khakis rolled up, feet dangling in the pool. He looks out at the view, the city stretched out below. "This would be a perfect time for a smoke." He looks up at me.

I rub my tummy. "No, it wouldn't." I come to him, kick off my shoes, sit, and ease my feet into the water. "It's cold."

"It's in the shade most of the morning. And I haven't figured out how to turn on the heater yet."

"Doesn't it come with a pool boy?"

"No. I don't want anyone to get any ideas about the lady of the house, my *mamacita*." He elbows me a little.

I put an arm around him. "I'm sorry."

"I'm sorry too. I know it's a little much. I should've asked you first."

"The proposal, the Oregon house, I loved it. But this decision just caught me off balance. You know, I can't run, I'm losing my mind a little bit with the panic attack and all, and we aren't in Boise..."

"And?"

"Well, what makes me who I am?"

"I don't know. What do you mean?"

"I feel rudderless. I'm a runner. Now I'm not. I live in Boise. Except right now, I don't. I'm the person who everyone else relies on, except now, since I'm falling apart all over the place. I don't even have a job."

"You're about to have a baby. You don't need a job. You'll be plenty busy."

"I know. I'm about to be mom of a newborn baby for the first time in years. I think, Andrew, that what I know about me right now is not very much."

"I think I see where you're headed. What'll help?"

"Maybe I need a project. I'm smart. I like to use my brain. Or help. Help someone."

Andrew takes my hand, rubs his thumb across my palm. "I can go get some of those big Post-it charts. We could make lists. You like lists."

"I just need to think about it."

"And breathe. You still have me. You still have the boys. You have Tessa and Joe and your mom and dad. And Tucker loves you unnaturally, if you ask me. Maybe you're defined by the people you love. The people you take care of." He splashes me a little. "You don't need it all figured out this minute. Give it some time to gel."

I look in his eyes. "What about you? Are you okay? Are we okay?"

"I'm fine. I'm working hard and looking forward to meeting this little one. I like my projects, and I know this amazing girl, and this amazing family. They seem to like me. I, as they say, am sitting pretty."

He leans over and kisses me.

I smile. "I really want to do this one thing right now, though."

"What?" He looks straight into my eyes, ever the good listener.

I push him in the pool.

He splashes up to the edge, a surprised smile on his face.

"You did not just do that." He takes me under the arms and pulls me in along with him.

"That is so, so, so cold!" I shiver.

He goes under, comes up in front of me, and shakes his head like a dog, whipping his hair out of his eyes, smiling with a wide white grin. "Go cry to the pool boy about it."

COME AS YOU ARE

I like routine. I like that we have a routine. And I can't tell Kelly this, but I like our little family life in LA.

Almost three months of peace. I was crazy busy on Mr. Oscar Bait movie, *Out of Range,* but how often do I get to play a mobster in hiding on a huge film? And then drive home to the missus every night. Shooting in LA has a lot of advantages. We spent Christmas with Kelly's folks, we hired a tutor for the boys, we found an almost normal (I didn't say normal, I said *almost*) rhythm, and I watched Kelly settle into the pregnancy.

But that movie's wrapped now. Jeremy took me at my word, in my moment of weakness, and booked me straight through, so now I'm prepping for the next movie. And prep for my next movie right now means working out. Running.

I have to run. Kelly loves to run. I don't. But Christmas with Kelly's folks, I ate anything that was put in front of me and anything else that didn't move. I loved it. But now I'm on to my next project, *Leave No Trace*, and I'm not ready for any comparisons to Brando or Elvis or anyone else who ate fried sammiches and porked out.

The script for *Leave No Trace* packs in the action and the mystery. A man and his girlfriend go camping, and the girl goes missing in the middle of the night. As the hero, I'm expected to run around and look fit while finding her and saving the day. And it's too indie a movie to do any digital touch-ups of me shirtless, so here I am, getting ready to run.

Hunter will run with me, though. That makes it worth it.

I stand in the kitchen, drinking the disgusting green shake thing that Tucker talked me and Hunter into adding to our diets. It's not even a green color. It looks like green-gray baby puke. I choke it down.

"That face is priceless." Kelly walks in. "I wish I had my phone. That's a moment right there." She comes over and waits for me to be done.

"Your son's been drinking this sludge too."

She nods. "You're both crazy."

I set my drink down and take her into my arms. She's big now. We're in the home stretch, just six weeks to go, and I love the way she leads with her stomach.

She *doesn't* love it, so I try not to say much about her expanding belly. But that's my child in there. What's not to love?

"Where's Hunter, anyway? We're supposed to go run," I ask her. I have just a few days off in these next weeks. I try to pack as much family bonding as possible into each of them. Soon the movie will wrap, and I'll be done until *Flat Rock* in May. I keep calling it paternity leave, mostly because Jeremy looks like he'll throw up each time I do.

"Hunter!" Kelly yells for him.

"Mom! I'm right here. Hang on, Andrew. I just need my earbuds. Have you seen them anywhere, Mom?"

You know how everybody says people expect the mom to know where everything is? It's true. Here's the other part: she usually does. A guy can't help asking, under those circumstances.

Kelly points to the island. "Hold still for a minute right there, in front of the counter. They'll jump up and bite you."

Hunter turns around and stares at the island for a minute. Then he plucks the earbuds off the placemat right in front of him.

"I don't know about the sarcasm, Mom. I don't think it's good for your mom-ly image." He gives her a hug.

"I can't help myself sometimes." She kisses him on the cheek.

"Hunter, go on out," I tell him. "I'll be there in a minute."

"I'll get Ditto. Where's his leash?" He looks at Kelly.

"Look in the garage. I'm going to start charging for locator services. You get two more free asks."

He shrugs and goes out the door.

"Come here, Mrs. Almost-Pettigrew." I fold her in my arms.

"Yes?" She leans her head against my neck.

I breathe in her smell, fruity and clean. She's never worn perfume. I like that. Almost all of the women I've worked with smell strongly of some Oriental perfume, or some "essential oil," which I have no idea about, except that they make my eyes water when we have to do love scenes.

Kissing people I don't like is weird. But there's a point where it's the ultimate acting—if I can make an audience believe in my "love" for someone like Amanda, for instance, then I'm really pulling one over on them.

Right now, though, this girl, this woman, I *want* to kiss. I lean over and kiss her softly. She smiles under my lips. I'm pretty sure that's code for *not so fast*. She pushes me away.

"Get going, mister. You've got a teen and a dog waiting. They're not a tolerant bunch." She pats me on the butt.

I leave her in the kitchen and cut through the garage.

Hunter jogs around the circular drive. Ditto bounces around next to him.

The air's cool. In LA, people pull out sweaters and wool coats in weather like this. When we went to visit Boise for New Year's, it was sixteen degrees for the high, and Joe, Tessa's husband, still wore shorts. Today in LA it's probably sixty.

"I wonder if I need my jacket." I look at Hunter. He has a short-sleeve shirt on.

"It's fine. Let's go."

We jog to the gatehouse of the neighborhood. It's been quiet since we got out here in October. Kelly and the boys were supposed to go back to Boise for spring semester, but the boys came to us after New Year's and told us they wanted to stay together, stay in LA.

Devon, their tutor, might be part of the reason they're okay with sticking in LA with us. He's young and smart and knows a lot about music. He's been really creative with the lessons he designs for the boys, and he knows what makes each of them tick. He took Beau to the La Brea tar pits for a science lesson about heat and thermal energy. Hunter actually read a few books without a huge fit, mostly because one of them was about Pelé, the soccer legend, and the other was about the music scene in Seattle in the nineties.

I watch Hunter now. He jogs in front of me with the dog, bobbing along, all legs. He's grown a ton, just since I met him. I can't believe it. Kelly comments on it all the time, but it's hard for me to think that the boys were ever tiny babies. I'm psyched to experience that with the new little one coming. Going from tiny and helpless to this big gawky teen kid. Kelly gets a misty look in her eye when she talks about it.

She's been doing better. And nothing else weird has happened — nothing like the shove or the baggage tampering. She swims in the pool every day, and her knee seems better. Her smile is back. I can breathe a little now. When she had the panic attack, it just about killed me. Almost three months of peace has been complete heaven.

Ditto sits down on the sidewalk to the left of me. Damn dog. He's old, and he's fat and lazy. More than that, he knows our path is about to go up into the hills above our development. He doesn't want to go.

Hunter stops with him. "I could just go back to the house with him."

"No, that's not fair. Listen, I'll run back to the guard house with him. If Larry's there still, Ditto can hang out with him till we get back."

"I'll come with you. If I stay here, he won't go with you."

We brought Ditto back with us from our New Year's visit, when we decided we were staying in LA until I was done shooting *Leave No Trace*. He's punishing us for kenneling him and putting him on a plane. And he sheds everywhere. I've never been home long enough to have a pet, and I don't know… The dog's cute enough and always seems chipper, but he's a pain. I'm still deciding if pet ownership is worth it or not.

We jog with him back to the guardhouse. Larry's still there. He's one of the guards, but what Hunter doesn't know is that he's the one Tucker hired. I'm paying for the additional guard on duty at the development. It's one of the things we set up when we picked out the new place.

We leave the dog with him and get up into the hills. It's good to run with Hunter. His youth beats my lukewarm determination every time. I keep up with him, but just barely. I'm motivated by fear of humiliation.

The first two miles are uphill. Hunter sets a mild pace out of pity for my advanced age. I'm proud to keep it under fifteen minutes. We turn around at the top and head back down, LA spread out in front of us in the valley below. It'd be pretty, but there's a brownish smog. It hangs over the city even in the January weather.

With about a mile left on the way down, a woman jogs up the trail toward us. I know who it is before I can even see her face.

"Hunter, don't stop running, even though I do."

"Why?" He's next to me.

"This is Amanda Walters. You do not need to meet this piece of work."

He makes a weird face. "Okay. I'll take your word for it."

We run downhill and closer to her. Her red hair is tied up in a red bandanna, all piled on top of her head. She kind of runs.

I grit my teeth. "I'll bet you money she came out here to try to run into us."

"Why would she do that?" Hunter asks.

"To be a pain in the ass. Because we haven't seen each other since we wrapped in New York."

"Doesn't she know you're with Mom?"

God, I love this kid. I could kiss him. "Yeah, doesn't she?"

He looks at me one more time, looks at the woman in the doo-rag and shiny running tights. "Good luck."

He picks up his pace and flies down the path, not even looking at Amanda.

Which leaves her to me. The last time we were alone, she chucked a plate at my head after breaking, entering, and redecorating my trailer. I wonder for a minute if I shouldn't bring Tucker on these runs. What if she really is certifiable?

"Amanda. What're you doing here?"

"Same as you."

"Except I live right down there." I point toward our house.

"So I've heard. How's Kelly? Was that her boy who just ran by?"

"She's fine. And yes, that's Hunter."

"How cute. A little daddy bonding."

This chafes me. She's an insensitive bitch. "Nobody'll take the place of his dad. We're just friends. He doesn't need another dad."

"That's sweet." She doesn't give a crap. "I heard your fiancée's having a shower?"

"You've heard a lot of stuff lately."

"Am I invited?"

"What do you think?"

"Aw, c'mon, Andy. Let's kiss and make up. Friends?" She puts out a hand.

"Amanda, listen. You're a terrific actress. We have a history together. Let's leave it at that. Can we just quit while we're ahead? Please?"

She smiles slyly. "You know I love it when you beg."

This woman. I can't even believe her. "Clearly that's a no, so I'm going to finish my run. I'll see you around."

I take off down the hill. When I get back to the guardhouse, Hunter informs me that's my fastest mile split yet.

Maybe I should have ex-girlfriends chase my ass around the Hollywood Hills more often.

"Field trip today. Wahoo!" Beau announces this to the whole house from the kitchen table the next morning.

Devon stands behind the boys with his messenger bag slung over his shoulder. "Wahoo. But Hunter needs to hustle it up, or we'll spend the day looking at the back of a Geo Metro on the 405."

Beau laughs. "Funny." Then he turns his body, just barely, and yells again. "Hunter! Let's go!"

Kelly's out back, swimming laps. All of us in the house were supposed to be leaving by now. She's already said her goodbyes, and it's probably good, because this yelling thing is one of her mom pet peeves. I try to curb the behavior all by myself. Andrew, the cool but sensible adult, to the rescue. "Beau. The yelling. Devon and I want to retain what hearing we still have."

Beau nods. "Fine." He gets up and pulls on a baseball hat with zombies on it, grabs his lunch bag and backpack. "I'll be in the car, Devon. I just want to make it clear that I am on time, ready to go."

Devon points to the car. "Duly noted. Go get in the car."

I look around for my phone. Tucker's due any minute to take me to set. "Are they behaving for you?"

Devon grabs three water bottles out of the fridge and tucks them in his bag, folds the flap over and buckles it. "These two boys? I wish I could clone them. So very different from the usual LA clientele."

I'm proud of them. "Good."

"Probably all the more reason not to settle down in LA for too long then, huh?" He smiles.

If he only knew the arguments Kelly and I had about that in NYC. "Absolutely."

He points to the copy of *For Whom the Bell Tolls* on the counter. "Kelly's reading that?"

People assume movie stars are idiots. Usually we are. "No, that's me."

He shrugs. "Huh." He shifts uncomfortably. Maybe he's embarrassed he assumed. "What do you think of it?"

"I like it. The whole book feels sun-baked." I regret saying that. I could say that to Kelly, and she'd get it, but maybe not everyone. I try to continue in English. "It's full of good stuff. Robert Jordan, the hero, in the part I just read was talking about living a full life in the now, in a moment. How one person's few hours can be as packed as someone else's whole life." I stop. Kelly could explain it better. She gets it. She lives that way.

Devon gives a small nod. "That's cool." He sounds very noncommittal. Maybe he hasn't read it.

Hunter finally strolls in. "I'm ready."

Devon turns to the door. "I don't see a backpack."

"Damn!" Hunter sprints back out of the room.

"Mouth!" I call after him.

But he's gone, back to his room to retrieve the backpack.

I grab my Hemingway and my phone, which is buzzing, and answer it as I walk. "I'm on my way out the door, Tuck."

Today's sure to be a long one. I hope to text Kelly, read my book, and maybe nap in my trailer in between blocking the next action sequence.

"Have a good day on set, Andy." Devon waits for Hunter to return.

"Take care of my boys, Devon. And have fun sitting in traffic."

SNAP OUT OF IT

We are a month out. It's mid-January in LA, about sixty degrees, and I'm sweating. Partly because it's warm, but mostly because today is the baby shower. Baby showers are all well and good when they're someone else's. But when it's a shower for me and Hiccup, well, let's just say I'm less than thrilled.

"Where's the Play-Doh?" Tessa rushes into the gigantic kitchen. Yes, she made good on her promise, and she swept into LA last night with bags and bags of stuff.

It's kind of silly. We don't have a lot of family here. My mom, yes. She'll be here today. But I don't have any sisters. And Andrew's sisters live back in Pennsylvania. And Mari, from New York — we've texted and talked on the phone, but she's a grad student. There's no way I'd expect her to come out here just for a baby shower.

Now that we're in LA, I hang out with my mom and dad, the boys, and Andrew when he's not working. It's nice to have family in town, because I haven't really met anyone here. Our house, super Fortress of Solitude that it is, is in a development of similar fortresses. I think the next door neighbor is a rap producer. I've seen him backing out of his driveway twice. I take walks and mostly run into the guards at the gatehouse. I guess the whole point of our subdivision is seclusion.

So, guess who's coming to the shower? Sandy, Andrew's publicist; Mallory, Andrew's makeup artist; my mom; and Tessa. That's about it.

Tucker enters the kitchen. "Did you look in the living room with your other bags? I don't think it'd be out here." He's been recruited into helping get ready for the shower.

"Should I ask what the Play-Doh is for?" I sit at the kitchen island, following orders. I don't disobey Tessa, not when she's in this kind of mood. I'm not foolish.

Tucker shakes his head. "No, you shouldn't ask."

Baby showers seem to revolve around humiliating the mama-to-be. Predict how big she is with this piece of string! Find the goofiest or weirdest baby or new mama equipment! Take pictures of her ginormous belly for all posterity!

I think it's clear why I'm less than thrilled. I'm about a month out from my due date, and, yes, I'm huge. The Miss Softee soft serve ice cream cone look is just about complete. The added touch is that Hiccup likes to press out a foot or hand and distend my tummy in weird, alien-like ways. So, I'm an alien-infected soft serve ice cream cone. Even better.

Tessa disappears into the other room, then shouts "Found it!" to no one in particular. Andrew rolls in with a glass of iced tea in hand. "Why don't you go out by the pool? It's nice out there." He comes to me, gives my belly a rub, kisses me behind the ear, one of those spots that I love to have kissed.

"Tessa's having the shower out there in an hour. I'm not allowed."

"It's a surprise baby shower? I think you already know you're having a baby." He sits next to me.

"The decorations. She wants to surprise me. It's an awful lot of effort for, like, six people."

He sits with me for a minute, sips his tea. "That's Tessa. Indulge her."

"I am, which is why I'm in here."

He goes to the fridge, opens both doors at the same time. "What's in here that's good?"

"Hey, Mr. Movie Star, you're shooting a shirtless scene tomorrow, remember? Stay out of the corn dogs. They're for the boys."

He rolls his eyes. "You're no fun."

I smile sweetly at him. "Just trying to be helpful. You can have a slice of cake from the shower if you want."

"Oh, there's not a cake. That's so passé." Tessa's back. "You ready to go to your shower?"

I stand up. "I thought it was in an hour?"

"Surprise! We're ready for you now, Kelly Jo."

"Okay."

Andrew takes my hand, and we follow Tessa out into the backyard.

It's more than six people. It's closer to thirty. Holy cow.

"Surprise!" Everyone yells at once. People clap.

I scan the crowd. Both of Andrew's sisters are here. Several of Tessa's friends, who by default are mostly my friends too, are here. And Mari from New York is here.

"You got people to come! How'd you do that?" I give Tessa a big hug.

"I'm pretty persuasive. And your husband-to-be helped fly some people out. Mari, for example."

I make a silent note to thank him. He was wary of her when we were in New York, but bless him for respecting the fact that I so desperately needed her as my friend when I was down and lonely.

I see Mari walking toward us. "Hey! I'm so glad you could be here!" I tell her.

She gives me a hug. "You're so pregnant. How close?"

"A month or so. Both my boys were overdue, so I'm not holding my breath yet."

"I have news too." Mari smiles and holds up her phone. There's a picture on it.

"What's this?" I take the phone from her. It's a picture of a non-descript apartment building.

"I'm moving out here! I signed a lease on this apartment today."

I'm surprised. I'd never have the guts to move across the country—use a plane ticket for a baby shower as the impetus to make a huge change like that. I give her a hug. "That's huge news. Why? Are you done with design school already?"

She shakes her head no. "I might defer for a semester, maybe a year." She points to her shoulder. "Remember the tattoo?"

"Yeah."

"Well, the guy—the guy that was the future person, not the past? I think it's going to work out. I moved out here to be closer to him."

"Wow. He's here now? That's huge news, Mari. What about money?"

"I might sell my car back in New York. And I've got student loan money still." She waves her hand, dismissing the question.

"Well, selfishly, it's awesome for me, 'cause you can come over all the time now. Much better than just texting to keep in touch. And I hope the move will be what you want for you too," I add, still trying to figure out her impulsive decision, wondering what Andrew will say about it. "And at some point, I want to hear all about this mystery man."

Tessa comes over. "I hate to break up this chat, but we've got the first game to play."

"Fabulous." I take Mari's hand. "I'm afraid of the Play-Doh. Don't let them do terrible things to me."

She laughs, a big, open-mouthed laugh. "Only if I'm helping!"

The party moves along at a nice tempo, with Tessa running the guests through several ridiculous games (the Play-Doh was to make a model of the baby, which resulted in ludicrous sculptures). Tessa got a doughnut pyramid, made from blue-and-pink-frosted Voodoo Doughnuts she had FedExed in from Portland. She knows we always try to stop there when we're headed to the coast from Boise.

We open presents, and of course there's plenty of *ooh*ing and *aah*ing over adorable little outfits.

The boys—all of them—are scarce. Andrew piled everybody into the car and took them miniature golfing. Even Jeremy went with, though thankfully he's not living with us anymore.

Mom comes over with a big box. "This last one is from me and your dad. We never thought we'd be welcoming another grandbaby into the world—not from you, at least." Mom's always hopeful that my brother will give her more grandchildren, but he and his girlfriend are currently traveling in Southeast Asia, and the chances look slimmer with every grand trip they take.

I pull the blue and pink wrapping paper off the box and lift the lid.

It's a sage green quilt. "Mom, it's beautiful." She made quilts for both of the boys too.

"I wish it didn't have to be green, but oh well." She hasn't been keen on not knowing the sex of the baby.

I give her a big kiss. "Thank you, Mom." Other guests applaud. It's the last big gift. People begin to drift away from the circle of chairs and loungers Tessa has set up. Some wander into the house, or over to the snack and drink table.

Mom lingers, takes my hand. "Oh, Bug. It's been so wonderful having you in town. I know the boys will want to go back to school in Boise, but maybe with Andrew's career, you could make LA your second home." She sounds hopeful. She's always wished we could live in the same town.

"We'll see, Mom. I've stopped trying to predict the future. It never seems to want to go the way that I plan it." I give her a smooch on the cheek.

Tessa appears. "Just a couple more cards, and you can be done with this ordeal." She hands me two thick envelopes.

"It's been much less painful than I thought. Thank you, Tessa. Honestly. You're great to do this."

She waves me off. "Anything for the baby mama."

I open the first envelope. It's a gift certificate for a massage from my auntie in Tennessee.

Mom sighs in relief. "Thank goodness. She was sure it wouldn't make it in the mail in time. I'm going to go in the house and call and tell her." She gets up and goes in.

I'm left with one more envelope. Tessa and I sit together in the loungers, our feet up. This envelope has no return address, but it came to the house yesterday. On the back someone's stuck an "Open on Shower Day" label, complete with blue and pink balloons. I tear it open.

It's a greeting card. It looks as though it had a picture of a teddy bear on a horse on the front of it. But it's been carefully blacked out. The whole image is black.

And inside is a folded-up piece of stationery. I unfold it. It's a letter. In a hand I don't know. I read:

To Whom It May Concern:
Or, to the Lady in His Bed:

You probably want to go on your merry way, live your merry life. Don't assume that the bells aren't tolling for you, or for him, for that matter.

My hands go cold. I can feel my expression fall.

"What is it?" Tessa looks at me.

"I don't know yet. A letter. Let me finish it."

Insinuation isn't pretty. A vine, even a pretty flowering one, even a morning glory, is still a parasite, and when evening comes, closes its eye to the dark.

When the host is sucked dry, when you take his vitality and plant it elsewhere, who is left at the harvest?

Think about worth and worthiness. You cheapen something, you wash that value away. Temptation is then followed, and you destroy who you seek, who you want so very badly. So think on it: you reap what you sow. What you are, you turn him to. Gold turns to brass. All things float away, washed away in your cheap, ceaseless current.

Note it.

I sit still for a minute, and then I crumple up the letter.

"What the hell was it? Why do you look that way, Kelly?"

"It was a letter written by some crazy freak. And it's not worth upsetting anyone over." I toss it into the pile of shredded wrapping paper.

I'm surprised, because I would've predicted that I'd get a letter like this and be terrified.

No, I'm just pissed.

We've had a calm, enjoyable life out here. Three months of almost-normal existence. Sure, the boys aren't in school, but Devon, the tutor, he's been great. And I feel better, swimming every day. And Andrew's shoulder is mostly healed. There hasn't been the frenzy we felt in New York.

He's busy, but life has been good.

Now this.

I stand up. "Let's go in and say goodbye to the guests. I know some people are getting ready to leave."

"Aren't you going to do anything with that?" Tessa stoops over to pick up the card with the blacked out front, the folded letter.

"Leave it. It's meaningless. I refuse to give it any power over me or my family."

"What?" Andrew walks up from behind us. *Shit*. He's going to freak out.

"A dumb anonymous letter. From someone who thinks they're all literary and deep."

Tessa does pick it up now, hands it to Andrew.

He scans it and looks up into my eyes.

I don't waver. I refuse to panic. I won't let someone do that to me again.

He nods. I think he can read me pretty loud and clear. "Okay. I'll let Tucker see it."

I speak up. My voice sounds loud, confident. Hearing it makes me feel stronger. "Tomorrow. Don't give it any more weight than that. Fear is only fear when you allow it to be."

He pulls me to him, kisses the top of my head. "I agree. For now, I have the rest of a doughnut pyramid to eat."

Tessa shakes a finger at him. "Shirtless, tomorrow at eight am."

"You two are such nags, I swear."

She punches him on the arm.

And life returns to normal, at least for now.

POISON IVY

We survived the baby shower, and now, a week later, I have to survive The Ivy.

Jeremy and The Ivy. You'd think Mr. Hip Agent Guy would have nothing to do with such a Hollywood cliché. The Ivy was the place to be seen probably twenty years ago. And the inside looks like Laura Ashley threw up. Stars who want to be sure *US* or *People* get a good shot of their toned asses in their yoga pants sit out on the terrace, in full view of the street and God and everybody.

I don't want to sit outside, and when J texts, I tell him as much. He says okay, probably because of Tucker's high alert. I suspect Tucker will pass along the letter Kelly got at the shower to law enforcement, and his vigilance has notched back up. Jeremy respects that. He can tell when Tucker is worried.

And The Ivy, besides being so frilly, is so high visibility, he couldn't have thought it was a good idea. It had to have been someone else's.

I see the someone else as Janus and I pull up to the front of the restaurant. Amanda. Jeremy is so very close to snagging her as a client. After seeing her on the run in the hills, I haven't seen or heard anything more from her. I wish she'd hurry up and sign with him.

He asked about the trouble with her, asked what my "comfort level" was if he took her on as a client. I told him it was fine. There's no reason for my troubles with an ex to keep him from a major deal. Once he had my okay, he's been relentless. He's like a nervous little dog, all yippy and trembling. He might even pee a little on the carpet when he sees her next.

As Janus lets me off out front, I chuckle to myself at that thought.

"What's so funny?" Amanda stands on the picket fence-lined patio.

"I'm hysterical. You missed it."

She puts a cheek out to me, to be air-kissed. A photographer on the sidewalk snaps away behind us. I ignore both of them. She probably called him and told him we'd be here. "Was the joke at my expense?"

"Surprisingly, no. All Jeremy this time. Where is he?"

She points a long shiny nail inside.

"You're not having lunch with us, are you?"

"Oh, God no. My two favorite men, it's tempting, but I just had Jeremy drop some papers to my lawyer. My lawyer and I were here for brunch. Jeremy wasn't invited."

"I'm not one of your 'men.'"

"Whatever." She tosses her head like she doesn't care. The photographer snaps her picture. Another paparazzo parks his scooter at the curb, pulls out his long lens, ready to join in. "And tell Jeremy to stop texting me — it makes him smell desperate. I don't do desperate."

I nod and get inside, done with the photographers and Amanda. Poor Jeremy. I hope she doesn't get her claws into him in any way other than business. He hasn't earned hearts and flowers, but he deserves at least a couple steps up from female praying mantis biting his head off.

I weave through the floral arrangements and wicker chairs and people trying to wave me down and find Jeremy sitting at a table covered in a pineapple tablecloth, pineapple plates, and pitchers full of petunias and geraniums. He sneezes.

"Sit down, for Christ's sake, before I go into anaphylactic shock. I need a Benadryl."

"Amanda's playing cat and mouse with you. You don't need her as a client this bad. Since when do you meet her lawyer here to drop off paperwork? You're not her errand boy."

"I know." He yanks a red and white checked pillow from behind his back and tosses it on the ground.

"But what?"

"I had a very big carrot to dangle, and I'm not talking about my own generous anatomy."

"You need to quit with the overcompensating talk. We've talked about this before. You've clearly got an inferiority complex."

"I'm blowing off that burn. I have a four-page spread and cover for her in a certain fashion mag if she signs with me."

"Which one?" He's good. She might take that bait.

He looks for a napkin to write on. The only one he comes up with has big roses on it. He gives up and leans forward. "Editor likes sunglasses. A lot. Might have a movie about her, one with devils and fashion brands."

"Anna Wintour. *Vogue*. I get it."

He looks around. "Hey, let's not let the bob-haired cat out of the bag."

"You're too paranoid." I look desperately for a waiter. I need an iced tea and something to eat.

"Speaking of paranoid, what's new at Casa Pettigrew?"

"Kelly got a letter."

"What?"

"Someone sent her a letter, sent it to the house, which means someone knows we're staying there."

"That's definitely stalky. What'd it say?"

"It was pretty bizarre. I think the message was to keep a close watch on me. It mentioned temptation. And the letter was clear that the author doesn't think Kelly is worthy of me."

"Was it threatening?"

"Kind of. Tucker hasn't decided if he's going to pass it along to the FBI or not."

"Whatever he decides, keep me posted."

"I will. So, why did I have to be here?"

"I didn't care where we ate, and I was already meeting her here. No offense, but you're a done deal. I don't go back for seconds on meals I've already had, so impressing you with some hip restaurant wasn't a priority."

"I'm your client. Not a conquest. And we've been together for nine years, so you're more old married man than one-night-stand material. You like to think you're all sex and danger and trampolines, but you're one step away from twin beds."

"This metaphor is all sorts of used up." Jeremy looks in danger of sneezing again for a moment. "I don't get why Amanda was still out front when you got here, though. We were all finished. She could have left."

"That's weird." I nod. "Don't you think that's weird?"

"Kind of. She does get an odd look when she mentions you."

"Odd?"

"I don't know. I think she's waiting for you to get tired of Miss Idaho Home. Thinks you'll end up back in her bed."

"But you know I'm never doing that."

"I know that, but she doesn't. I don't know. Amanda's always been a little crazy. She drove that one producer's car into the swimming pool when he dumped her, remember that?"

"I guess. I don't like this conversation. You're telling me she's nuts and that she hung around waiting for me to show up today. I don't think that feels right. And you know what I think?"

"What?"

"I still think she's capable of all this shit someone's been doing to my family. Maybe I should go."

"I think you should tell Tucker again what you think about her. And not give her one inkling that you might suspect her, so stay put. She could still be out there."

He may have a point. I don't get up.

"While she preens and poses for whatever slimeball with a camera is out on the curb, let's talk about your little indie *Leave No Trace* movie. How's the shoot going?"

I'm formulating an answer when the fire alarm goes off. "Saved by the bell." I hop up, happy to be done.

"We're not through with this discussion. I want you to work this movie into two more after we're done with *Flat Rock*. At least three of the exec producers you could get a commit out of. You gotta make hay while the sun shines, my friend."

"Weird. Someone else said that to me not too long ago. I get it, J. I do."

We move to the fire exit, and we're about to walk out when Jeremy grabs me.

"Don't." He pulls me away from the door and shows me his phone. There's a text from Tucker.

Come to the house. There's been a break-in.

"What the hell?" I check my phone. Tucker's text pops on my screen too.

"We'll take my car. Let's go out the back way." Jeremy leads us out through the kitchen to the back alley.

"I don't like any of this, Jeremy. Someone's put a target on my back."

"Tucker'll get to the bottom of it. He needs to send that letter to the FBI."

We make it to his car. Janus runs up behind us. "You two need to get in and clear the area."

"Now what?"

"Fire alarm was pulled from a pull station at the front of the building. I left the car to check on the situation. It was a false pull, so I went back to the car."

"And what?" Jeremy has the driver's door open.

Janus puts a hand on his shoulder. His lips are set in a firm line. "And the tires were slashed."

"Jesus. Jeremy, let Janus drive."

Jeremy hands him the keys. He doesn't say a word. He's never at a loss for words. He is now.

I break out in a cold sweat.

THE FEAR

Five minutes ago, everything was normal.

The boys and I piled out of the car, Tucker handing the boys bags of groceries to carry to the front door. I was thinking about texting Mari to ask her to go on a walk with me. We've been trying to get together since she moved out here.

"Listen, I still say you shouldn't drink your calories," Tucker counseled Hunter. They've been lifting together, and Hunter listens to his advice. He chooses lean chicken and has been known to actually touch a green bean because of Tucker's influence.

"I've decided I can't let go of pop. I just can't do it, Tucker. Let me have this one thing." Hunter used his melodrama voice.

I put my key out, but the door swung open.

"Tucker." I tried to keep my voice flat. The boys were right there with us.

He looked at me and looked at the lock. "There's a key broken off in the lock."

"What?" Beau looked at Tucker.

"Andrew must've accidentally broken his key off in the lock," Tucker continued without missing a beat. "I'll call the locksmith in a second. Or I know, why don't you and the boys call from the car?"

"Sure. We'll leave the groceries with you." I handed him my bag.

"I can just go put them in the kitchen." Beau made a move to the door, but Tucker grabbed him by the arm. "It's okay, kiddo. I'll do it."

In the most innocuous five minutes, the world turns upside down.

Tucker texts three people right in a row. One of them is sure to be a cop. Tucker looks over him at me. I know. He's going to sweep the house.

There might be someone in the house.

"Let's go wait in the car, guys. Tucker might even be able to fix it without calling a locksmith."

The boys aren't dumb. Hunter takes one of the bags. "What's going on?"

I swallow, trying to keep the fear out of my voice. "It's probably nothing. Let Tucker do his job, Hunter."

I put a hand on Beau's shoulder and steer them both back to the car. We get in, and I wait at the wheel, looking at Tucker.

After a moment, he turns around and jogs to the car. "I've got someone coming. Why don't you all go get a snack?"

I'm not leaving him here, not until there's someone to help. "We'll wait until someone comes to give you a hand with the lock."

Tucker grits his teeth. "You don't need to do that."

"Then don't go in until someone else gets here."

"Kelly, don't be stubborn. You know that I know what I'm doing."

We don't have to bicker any longer, because a police cruiser pulls up.

"Now will you go?"

"Where's Andrew?"

"He's with Jeremy. They're finishing up lunch. Go down the street and get something to eat."

I start the car. "Text me."

He pulls out his phone, and suddenly he takes my arm. "Scratch that. Wait here for a second."

He walks over to the cruiser. The officer gets out, and the two of them look at Tucker's phone, then the house, then at us.

"What's going on, Mom? Is everything okay?" Beau asks.

"I don't know. Everything's fine, I think."

Tucker comes over. "I want you to drive to the police station on Rexford. Straight shot down the hill into town. Ten minutes. Can you find it from here?"

"And do what?"

"Pull into the parking garage. There'll be an officer waiting for you. You don't have to do anything; I just need you to wait for me there."

"Where's Andrew?"

"He's fine. He and Jeremy and Janus are together. I'll have Andrew give you a call in a while."

"I don't like not knowing what's going on, Tucker."

"Neither do I, Kelly. If I knew what was up, we wouldn't be having this conversation. Now please go."

I pull the car out of the drive and head to the gate of the subdivision. As we pull through the gates, another police car pulls in behind us.

"We have an escort, Mom." Hunter looks behind us nervously.

"It's all going to be fine. You know Tucker. He's being cautious. It's his job."

No one argues with me. Both boys are quiet. I appreciate that we're all keeping our worrying to ourselves. Because Tucker is cautious, but none of us are dumb—something is wrong.

I keep my hands on the wheel and continue to check the rearview for the police car for the whole drive.

My phone buzzes. It's Andrew.

"Hunter, grab that, would you?" I can't talk to him right now without bursting into tears.

"Hey, Andrew, it's Hunter. Yeah, Mom's driving. Tucker sent us to the police station. We're almost there."

He listens for a moment.

"I'll tell her. See you soon." He puts the phone down.

"What? What did he say?"

"He's headed to the house, but he wants you to call him when you're at the station. When you can talk."

At last we get there, and the cruiser behind us wheels around in front. An officer at the parking garage entrance waves. I drive by, and he nods at me as I pass.

Inside, the driver of the car waves me into a spot next to him. I park, and the boys get out.

A young, clean-shaven officer approaches us. "Ms. Reynolds?"

"Yes."

"We're going to have you come this way, ma'am."

I hate being called ma'am. Beau takes my hand, and we walk through the doors into the station.

"Can you please wait here?" The young policeman leads us to a small conference room with one window in the door. Maybe it's an interrogation room. I don't know. I've never actually been in a police station.

Hunter and Beau won't sit at the table. They pace around, looking out the window.

"Call Andrew, Mom."

I want to, I really do, but I don't want to call in front of the boys. What's going on, I have no idea, but I want a second to process it before I pass it along to them. I have no poker face. I'm no actor, and whatever I hear on the phone, they'll both see in my expression.

"I'm going to go find someone and see what's up. You two wait here for me, you promise?" I give them the mom stare.

A tall woman with long, blond hair pokes her head in the door. "Kelly Reynolds?"

"Yes?"

"Phone call for you. You want to take it at my desk? I can wait here with your sons." She whisks me out of the room and points to a desk, closing the door on my boys at the same time.

"Thanks."

"I'm Sergeant Ridley. I'll wait with them, and then I can give you an update when you're done. Line two. Just press the red blinking light." She smiles through perfectly peachy lips.

I watch her walk back to the room where Hunter and Beau are, and I pick up the receiver. "Hello?"

"You okay?"

It's Andrew.

"We're fine. What's going on? Are you at the house?"

"Yeah. Tucker has the police here. Looks like whoever broke the key off in the door didn't really do much inside. We just walked around, and I couldn't really see anything out of place or stolen. Tucker wonders if he ever even got inside, maybe got scared away by a neighbor instead."

I exhale. "I hate the idea of someone in the house."

"Well, Tucker will check the security camera footage from the guard house and the ones at our doors. If there's anything, he'll follow up with the police."

"Did the alarm go off?"

"No. It wasn't armed."

I silently curse my forgetfulness. Stupid pregnancy brain. "Do we need to stay here, then?"

"Well, there's one other thing we're following up on."

"Yes?"

"We had a fire alarm pulled at the restaurant, and it looks like it was to get us out of the building."

"Why?"

"Maybe to make me a target."

"And when you went outside?"

"Jeremy and I were all sneaky and went out the back to his car, not ours. Janus came to check the alarm, went back to the car, and the tires were slashed."

"Jesus, Andrew. This person's getting worse."

There's a long pause on the other side of the phone. "It feels like that, doesn't it?"

"Who could it be?"

"Well, the police's job is to figure that out. But I'm sending Janus down there to get you."

"I love you. I'm scared."

"I love you. And I'm scared too. But we'll be okay. I promise you that. I won't let anyone hurt my family. It won't happen. I'll see you soon."

"Okay." When I hang up, I watch Sergeant Ridley walk out of the conference room and back over to me.

"Is he coming to meet you?"

"He's sending someone. If he showed up here, it'd be a mess."

She nods. "True. Let me fill you in. We like a friendly for this."

"A friendly? What's that mean?"

"Someone who has access to your inner circle in some tangential way. A maid, a housekeeper, a personal assistant."

"We don't have any of those."

She raises an eyebrow. "That's not very Hollywood of you."

"We don't live here. We like Idaho."

She smiles. "I could see that. Fair enough. We're going to recheck backgrounds, look at phone logs. We'll start with any personal employees, then folks on the last couple of Andrew's movies. Is there anyone else we should look into?"

I rack my brain. I can't even fathom knowing someone who would want to hurt or scare us. "I can't think of anyone. I haven't made a lot of enemies. I don't think Andrew has, either."

"Well, your employees are a place to start. We'll keep you posted."

I get up and turn to collect my kids from the conference room. Janus is standing there waiting for me.

"Are you driving us home?"

"Yes, ma'am." He takes a step forward. "Would you like me to drive your car back? An officer drove me here."

"Janus, you never call me ma'am. Don't start now."

"Okay, Ms. Reynolds. Are you ready to go?"

"Yes."

We get the boys, and I spend the first part of the drive explaining what little I know to them. Beau's eyes widen at the idea of someone in our house.

"Are we going to have to stay there? I don't think I'll be able to sleep." He shivers.

My heart tightens. "Beau, honey, you can sack out with your brother in his room. I bet you that right now Tucker is getting extra help for watching the house too."

Hunter chimes in. "Yeah, we can pull my mattress off the loft bed, and drag yours in. It'll be slumber party central." Hunter's never wanted to have Beau in his room. Maybe he's a little spooked too. I know I am.

The boys relax a little with a plan, and Janus looks up in the rearview. "You need gas. Should we stop and fill the tank?"

"Sure."

We pull into the station, and Janus gets out to pump gas. I get out to stretch my legs. My back and knee are aching. The baby has been living up to his name and hiccupping for the whole ride back, shifting around and pushing into my ribs, doing an all-around great job of making me uncomfortable.

"I have to tell you something," Janus blurts out. He looks shaken.

"Janus, what?" I've never even heard him talk this much.

"I heard the policewoman mention phone checks on your employees."

"Yes. I think they're doing that."

"Ms. Reynolds, I'm so sorry. Please don't fire me."

I swallow hard. "For what?"

His eyes tear up. "I've got a mom back in the Philippines. She's really sick. Her meds every month…" He trails off.

"Janus, tell me what you did." My heart pounds.

"That day, in the doctor's office? When the paparazzi ambushed us in the parking garage?"

I remember that, of course. Hard to forget when your boyfriend has to drag you out through a gauntlet of screaming photographers. "Yes?"

"I called them. A website offered me five thousand dollars if I tipped them off."

Holy hell. That's a ton of money. "I'll tell Tucker. I'll talk to him about it. That's not what we're worried about right now, anyway."

He hugs me, right there by the gas pump: a huge crying Filipino security guard holding on to a massively pregnant Softee ice cream lady.

We get back in the car, and Janus drives us home. No one says a word.

There is nothing about this life that makes any kind of sense.

LET'S GET THIS PARTY STARTED

I think having a party is madness, particularly a party at our house five days after a possible break-in. Kelly's been silent about it. Tucker thinks we should go ahead with our lives and not cancel things that are important.

But this party isn't important to me. It's important to Aaronson. It's not even a good idea in Jeremy's opinion, and the whole stalker thing usually is no big deal to him. He used to think of stalking as a sign that I'm popular and said it "comes with the territory," but he said *no way* to this party after the latest incident.

But the one thing that made us go through with it was Tucker's idea: flush the guy out. Make the stalker show himself. Bust him. Get him out of our lives.

And I can't argue with that. The sooner the bastard's in jail, the better. Kelly's not sleeping again. The boys are sleeping in one room, and they're worried about Kelly, picking up on their mom's distress. No matter that we told them the whole business with the police station was a precaution. They're not stupid.

So, let's get this guy arrested and be done. I can be bait for a night if that's what it takes.

It's a grand affair, in celebration of the Independent Spirit Awards and Aaronson. He's getting a producing award. As soon as he sees me, he wants to talk about *The Bull, The Bear, and the Dragon*, of course, which is deep in post-production and due to release in late March. Eventually he gets around to asking about my current project, and I have to choose my words carefully. The indie I'm shooting, *Leave No Trace*, I hate. When I took it, it was fine. Now, not so much. It's about a man and his fiancée who go camping. She steps out of the tent in the middle of the night to go to the bathroom and never comes back. The whole thing's a mystery about who took her and what happened, and it sets my teeth on edge given current events. Art damn near imitates life, and I don't like it one bit.

Tucker's got every Apotheosis security guy on the job tonight. We picked this house because of the gated community and the high wall around our property. The guys crawl all over it tonight, and there's a SWAT team from the city too. Some of them hide in the shrubs behind the swimming pool. I pity the poor schmuck who tries to sneak off to smoke a joint. If he doesn't get his head blown off by the snipers on the roof of the house, he'll be lucky not to be pummeled senseless by the guys in the bushes.

On the other end of the bizarre spectrum of tonight's festivities: Sandy and Jeremy hired Quique Fox, the biggest party planner in LA. Quique is a diva. He demands a huge paycheck and perfection.

When he suggested a 1920s theme, I nodded. I don't give a rat's ass. Kelly doesn't care. She did shut down his several ideas about live animals. But the rest, Quique ruled over. There are Packards parked by the swimming pool. The band plays Cotton Club jazz. Martini glasses fill tables where lilies are piled in high clusters. I said hell no to dressing in costume. Kelly said yes, mostly because the boys agreed to it too. But the servers are all in twenties attire: robin's egg blue uniforms straight out of a Ziegfeld Follies film. Lots of guests wear flapper dresses or pinstriped suits.

I stand over by the bar, a long, heavy wood ordeal under a canvas tent, and wish I had a drink in my hand. A real drink. I want one tonight. Badly. It's the strongest temptation I've felt since rehab.

And if not a drink, then I want Kelly in my arms. I wish for a dark corner to pull her into. I want to have my way with her.

But our life's not cooperating with this idea. The last time I saw Kelly, she was sitting rubbing her feet. She looked tired. She needed to lie down. I can't ravage her when she looks so pale and worried.

I'm the host, the all-powerful Andy Pettigrew, Mr. Newly-Minted Earns-Eight-Figures. I can't get a drink, and I can't get laid. Oh yeah, and someone wants me dead. Great party.

So, I walk to the top step of the stairs to the deck, and I watch over the mayhem.

There's a girl in a lemon yellow flapper dress. She's wandering along the back wall of the yard, a young guy in a beanie trailing along behind her. She keeps picking up on some line of a song and singing just that line, before her voice breaks, like she's going to cry. I swear I see her look around to see if anyone is paying attention.

Stupid actress. I have zero patience for this kind of bullshit drama. For an actor, I'm not a very good fit in Hollywood. LA gets so old sometimes I could spit.

Instead of spitting, I decide to look for a cigarette. I want one.

But then I see Hunter run across the lawn, laughing with Beau. I sigh and thank the universe for the reminder of why I'm not smoking anymore. I go to find a toothpick instead.

I start to turn the corner to cut through the garage door when I hear Amanda's throaty laugh. "Yeah, I know. Andy's like that!"

Oh God. I have to see Amanda. Jordan the dick must've invited her. I didn't vet the guest list; Jeremy did. Figures.

I walk around the corner of the house.

There she is, holding court in the side yard by the recycling. She is smoking. There are three men sitting at her feet. I kid you not.

"Like what?" I walk up to them.

Amanda jumps, drops her cigarette. One of the men scrambles to pick it up for her, but curses as he catches the lit end of it in his palm.

"Andy!" Amanda rushes over and throws her arms around me.

I peel her off. She reeks of booze. "Like what?"

She shifts nervously, waves a hand to the men, who are now all on their feet. "You know, we were just talking about how you're always trying to be perfect."

"Huh." I narrow my eyes at the men. They blanch, look anywhere but at me, and start to inch away from Amanda, eager to escape.

Amanda stands next to me and smiles. "We're alone now."

Shit. That wasn't where this was headed. "You mean you're alone now. I'm leaving." I turn to go.

She takes my arm. "Wait, Andy. Please."

I stop for a second. "I need to find my fiancée."

"Aren't you bored? Rumor is you're bored. Ready to admit what you really want." She's still holding on to my arm, pulls herself close to me.

I try to step back. "I don't know what you're talking about. *You* don't know what you're talking about. I'm going, Amanda. You need to let go of me."

She makes a weird little noise, and if it were anyone else, I'd say it was crying, but Amanda's always been cold as a snake in my experience.

The lemon yellow dress girl comes around the corner just then, staggering and yelling, "Watch out! I think I'm gonna be sick." She makes a beeline for the recycling bins.

This is my life in Hollywood in one shitty little nutshell.

Yellow girl pukes her guts out, and I peel Amanda off of me again. "Please, Amanda, leave me alone. I don't want to go back to anything that was. I do know what I want. I want Kelly. I don't want you. Please."

Amanda makes one more swipe, pulling me by the arm close to her, trying, I think, to kiss me. She's stinking drunk. Otherwise she'd never put herself out there for this kind of rejection, not like this. Whether she admits it or not, she has to have gotten my message.

"Jesus. Amanda, stop. I'm walking away." I push away from her and take three large strides across the side yard to the garage door.

"Are you Andy Pettigrew? Did she kiss you? Holy shit." Yellow dress girl has her head up out of the blue recycling bin. "Where's my phone?"

Amanda lets out a sob and throws herself on the ground. The girl plops down next to her and pats her on the back, like she's petting a puppy.

I need to find Kelly now. This is getting out of hand.

I walk through the garage, and Tucker greets me, not Kelly.

"Good, I need you. Come back out here." He takes me by the elbow and steps into the garage.

"Wait, is this night about to get worse? Of course it is."

"Maybe not. We have a suspect. A good one."

"Amanda just threw herself at me. In a pretty certifiable way."

Tucker's brow wrinkles. "Yeah, she's still on my radar. But it looks like somebody else."

"Who?"

"Devon. The tutor."

"What in the hell?" My stomach heaves. The guy who's been in my house, taking care of my kids…

"They'll take him for questioning tonight. It's not rock solid, but it looks good. He was in New York at the right time; he has a record."

"No, he doesn't. You checked."

"He lied."

"Then throw his ass in jail. I'm ready to be done with all of this."

Tucker claps me on the shoulder and steers me into the house. "Me too. Let's go find Kelly."

IT'S MY PARTY

Aaronson's party sucks, but I didn't have a better idea. I just called all hands on deck for help and moral support, and I was relieved Mari could make it. She's just gotten a reception job down at the Sony lot, but I've tried really hard to make time to see her. She's new in town, like me, after all.

She stands next to me as we survey the party, now in full swing. Andrew has disappeared somewhere…

"A Gatsby party. Huh." Mari watches two teetering flappers flap by.

"What's the huh?" I look at Mari and pull my gloves back up to my elbows.

"Does that mean I'm the Jordan to your Daisy?" she asks.

"Then does that mean Andrew is Tom, Daisy's rotten husband? I don't like that thought."

She twirls her pearl necklace. "No. No, he's definitely Gatsby."

Her eyes, her expression, go to some faraway place for a split second — like she's remembering some distant place with a green light of her own. Her face is slack, dreamy, for just that moment, and I'm about to break her out of her reverie when we both turn in the direction of a commotion.

An angry man yells, "This is bullshit."

"You need to come with us, sir." A different male voice, flat but firm.

"This is total bullshit. Don't you see that?" The angry man sounds louder, angrier.

At first I can't see, and Mari and I press through the crowd toward the pool.

There are two uniformed officers, one with a hand on his gun, like that's how he casually stands, and the other with a hand up, showing the way to someone, reasoning with him.

It's Devon. Devon the tutor, who we invited to the party at the boys' request. He shakes his head vehemently about something. Tucker and Janus are both standing to the left of him.

Mari touches my shoulder. "What's going on?"

I lead her around the pool, over to the group of men.

Jeremy catches my arm before I make it very far. "Hold up there, cowgirl. Let Beverly's finest deal with him."

"What's going on?"

"Maybe Andrew better fill you in, but I'll give you the short version. Your tutor there? He's the one scaring the shit out of all of you. He's your stalker."

"What? How can that be?"

"The security guys at Apotheosis found out he lied on his background check. He had a previous conviction, under a different name in Texas."

"For what?"

"Harassment. Broke an ex-girlfriend's no-contact order. Threw a rock through her window."

"But he did all of the stuff to us?"

"He was in New York when Andrew got pushed, and he was in LA for The Ivy and the tires, so it looks like it."

"Hold up. Andrew got what?"

Jeremy's face falls flat. "Andrew hasn't told you that part. I'm dead." He turns and watches the cops lead Devon away, then walks after them, in a hurry all of a sudden.

Andrew walks up.

"Jeremy told me. You lied, Andrew."

Mari touches my elbow. "Kelly, take it easy. Think about Hiccup."

"Mari, can you go find the boys? Help them get ready for bed. It's late."

"Kelly."

Cold as ice, I stare at her. "Please, Mari." She nods and leaves.

Andrew's hands are deep in his pockets. I'm suddenly aware of my stupid 1920s outfit and stupid wig, and I start yanking things off: feather boa, elbow-length gloves, necklaces.

"No one told me someone tried to kill you. You said it was an accident. You lied."

"Tucker and I thought it was best. We weren't sure what was going on."

"You weren't sure you were pushed?" My pulse intensifies.

"No, we knew that."

"And you think it was Devon? All of it?"

"It looks like that, yes."

"I can't do this." I kick off my stupid shoes.

"Kelly, what are you doing?"

I turn my back on him and get a good look at the crowd that's been watching me scream at Andrew. Deep shame and fear rush through me. I feel faint, sick, and furious.

Raging, I throw my shoes over the garden wall instead of taking one of the onlookers' heads off. "Party's over. You all don't give a crap about him anyway. You're sycophants, and you don't care if he lives or dies, so long as you get to come to the party. Get out of my house!"

I scream so loud my voice goes hoarse, like blown-out speakers at a concert. I wipe my mouth, wet with tears and rage and spit.

I run inside. I don't know what's going on, and I'm humiliated. I'm trying to understand that I know the person who was scaring us, and he wanted Andrew dead—all while he sat at my kitchen table, helping my boys with their homework.

I get to the master suite and rush into the bathroom. I throw up, retching until I'm empty inside.

"Kelly?" It's Andrew at the bathroom door.

"If anyone comes in this bedroom tonight, I swear I'm getting in the car and driving away. Don't you push me tonight. Don't do it."

I don't hear a response, just footsteps down the hall.

I finally am able to take a deep breath, wipe my face with a washcloth, go into the empty bedroom, and crawl under the covers in my stupid flapper dress.

Thank God for blind rage, because I can't even entertain what all this new information means for me, my boys, my baby, Andrew. I cry angry, terrified tears until I fall asleep exhausted, wrung dry.

I do not dream.

I wake up to the sound of my boys' voices. They giggle in the kitchen, and I hear Mari's melodic voice mix with theirs. The pale light of morning filters through the windows.

I'm awake, and my boys are okay.

I think back to my last thoughts and feelings, and they're there, but they've been muted by the heaviness of sleep.

I need to talk to Andrew. I need to set my head straight. It was Jeremy, after all, who told me about New York. He might be completely wrong.

But Andrew didn't correct me when I asked. He said he didn't know what to do.

I need to talk to him.

I hate how mad I was last night. I hate that I was that mad in front of people.

If I was on his side of that screaming lunatic last night, I'd be done, I'm sure. I can't constantly treat him like dirt and chalk it up to the hormones of pregnancy. There are plenty of pregnant women who are kind and pleasant and balanced. I'm acting crazy, and if I want him to be mine, I need to knock it the hell off.

I will lose him. I will drive him away.

And he'll go away somewhere where I can't make sure he's safe. And then I will lose him like I lost Peter. Forever.

My heart pounds, and I hear my breath. I'm hyperventilating. I just told myself that any more crazy behavior would put him over the edge, and here I am having a panic attack. Again.

I sit up in bed. I try to take deep breaths. I keep as quiet as I can.

"Kelly?" Andrew's on the other side of the bedroom door.

"Uh-huh?" It's all I can get out and still sound normal. I gulp at the air, trying to get a grip on my racehorse heart.

"Can I come in?"

He can't. He'll see that I'm still a ridiculous crazy mess. "Let me come out. I'll be out in a minute."

"Okay."

I jump out of bed and put both arms out to brace myself, my head spinning. I get to the sink when the bedroom door opens behind me.

"Sorry, I'm not waiting. I'm worried about you." He comes up behind me and turns me around to face him.

"Just give me a second." I try to get another deep breath.

"Kelly, you had every right to be mad and scared."

He looks at me for a moment, as I'm unable to respond, then takes me by the shoulders and looks me straight in the eyes. "This is a vicious cycle. Break it."

He stares at me, steady as a rock. His blue eyes are clear, calm. He searches mine. He waits.

I breathe in again. And out again. I close my eyes and concentrate on just breathing.

"Better?"

I open my eyes. I nod. "It's too much, Andrew. There's too much to think about."

He knows. He nods too. "I know. Tell you what; right now there are an amazingly annoying number of people who make money because of me, worrying about a hell of a lot of our business. Let's let them."

"But you didn't tell me."

"I didn't. I didn't know what to do. Tucker didn't, either. I'm sorry."

"You have to be one-hundred-percent honest with me. We have to be on the same page. I start wondering why you aren't telling me everything. I wonder if you're overwhelmed, if all this is too much."

"Give me a little bit of credit. I'm insulted, actually. How many times do I have to propose to you before you believe that I want you? I want you. The you that threw her shoes over the wall into the neighbor's yard, by the way."

He smiles. He grins and shows all of those white teeth, and his eyes crinkle up. I love his smile, his real smile that crinkles up those eyes.

"C'mon. It's funny. I don't even know where you chucked that wig."

I take one more big deep breath, and he pulls me into a strong hug.

"I know it's scary. I'm scared. But we're here together. We can do this."

I look up at him, and he puts a hand on my stomach, smoothing his palm over what is probably Hiccup's heel or elbow.

"Andrew…"

"Stop. Let's just be for a while." He kisses me, covering the rest of my sentence before it can be spoken. "We can slow all of this down until we both feel stronger. Deal?"

I hold both of his hands in mine. "Deal."

I take the longest shower known to man, throw some yoga pants on, and get the dog's leash. I can't run, but I can go on a good, cleansing walk.

In the kitchen, Mari's still here, helping the boys with their homework. Without Devon, I don't know how we're going to finish their school year.

And with all this craziness, I don't know how we're going to make room for Hiccup to enter the world. Little babies demand a lot of attention. He's going to have a hard time.

But maybe…if Devon is the person who did all that crazy stuff, maybe our lives can quiet down now.

I still can't wrap my head around Devon being the stalker. I should say attempted murderer. He tried to push Andrew into traffic. I can't believe it.

"Mari, come walk the dog with me."

She looks up from Hunter's homework. "Okay."

We get outside. Janus walks behind us, about twenty paces. Tucker's still not taking any chances, not until the police piece all of it together and bring charges against Devon.

Poor Janus. Tucker and he sat down for a very difficult talk about the tabloid tip. But I pleaded for him and Andrew to give him another chance. And they did. He's been silent and stone-faced, but Janus is still on the Apotheosis security team, and essentially our team now.

"What's up?" Mari walks close to me, her elbow grazing mine from time to time.

"I wanted to apologize for the party. You tried to talk me down."

"Yeah."

"I'm sorry."

"You just don't appreciate what you've got sometimes, you know that?" Her tone verges on angry.

"What?"

"It's nothing. I just think Andrew—you're lucky to have him."

I feel ashamed. She's right. "He didn't tell me the truth."

"Nobody's perfect. You're not, are you?" She looks at me with those cornflower blue eyes. Right now they look watery and faintly bloodshot.

"Far from it."

"I'm just saying." Her voice cracks a bit.

"Are you okay?"

She pulls her hair out of its ponytail, shakes her head a little, takes a deep breath. "You know the brother I mentioned? His name was Cameron."

"What about Cameron?"

"I was watching him. Mom and Dad were out for the afternoon, just running a few errands. Two hours at the most."

My stomach clenches. "Mari, what happened?"

"We were watching TV. He got out the back door, and I was busy getting cereal. I went to the bathroom, and I wasn't thinking that he wasn't watching TV anymore."

"Oh, Mari."

"He went into the backyard and fell in the pool. When I found him, he was floating face down. I called nine-one-one, pulled him out, did CPR the best I could."

We continue to walk. Tears stream down her face.

"Oh, Mari." I put an arm around her shoulder.

"I talk to him every day. I sing to him at night when I can't sleep. My dad wouldn't speak to me for a year after Cameron drowned. We lived in the same house, and he wouldn't even say my name."

"He had no right to do that. You were just a kid. It was an accident. Nobody's fault."

She stops and pulls her hair back into a ponytail. "I've stayed alive, wondering what the point to staying alive was. And then I met this man. The future. My future."

"The one you followed out here?"

"That one. But I don't know. I don't know if he feels the same way. I'm afraid he's going to be changed."

"By what?"

"Circumstances. When I was in New York, something happened. I thought maybe I couldn't stand to be with him, when I found out what he'd done. I wanted to hurt him back, maybe even make him go away for good. But I couldn't stay away from him. I couldn't help but forgive him. When I thought he might be gone, for real, it hurt me."

I don't know how this girl can even function. Her resolve, her strength must be frighteningly deep. "But now?"

"Now, I think if I can see him alone again, without the influence of these circumstances, the things that have him backed into a corner, I think he'll be himself again. I see the light at the end of the tunnel. I believe we can be together, finally."

"You sound confident about it."

"I think I am."

"He must be a good guy."

"He is." She gets that faraway look in her eyes, but the tears have stopped.

"Mari, I'm honored you told me about Cameron. That must have been the worst moment of your life. You're very brave to share about it."

"I'll see him again one day."

I look at her profile closely. I don't see distress, but I don't like the way she just said that. "Things will work out with this man," I tell her, hoping it's true for her sake and resisting the urge to ask more questions. It doesn't seem like the time.

"What about you?" she asks.

"What do you mean?"

"Are you ready for this baby?"

"Honestly? No. The party was too much. I wish I could have a little peace before the baby train rolls into the station."

"Why don't you go to the house in Oregon? Take the boys?"

"I don't know. It's almost February. I have three weeks to my due date."

"You said yourself both the boys were overdue. You have time to sneak away."

"Los Angeles weather doesn't make it seem this way, but the weather on the way up the coast could be horrible."

"So, check the weather. I think you should go."

I watch Ditto sit down on the sidewalk. He's done walking, I guess. "I don't know."

"Do something for yourself for a change. Take care of yourself."

"You really think I should?"

"You need to be out of the way somewhere. It'll get rid of the distractions. Things will come into focus. The truth will be clear then."

"I don't know about all that. I can see myself in front of that amazing fireplace, though, drinking tea and reading."

"And think how secluded you'd be. If Devon's not the one, who could find you up there? Who could hurt you if you were up there?"

"That's a point. I just don't see him for the stalker. He's not got any good reason."

"I don't see it either." She scratches Ditto behind the ear. "I guess we need to head back, since Ditto's done."

"I guess. I like this idea. I think I'll probably go, Mari. You win."

She smiles. "Good. I like it when things go my way."

We walk the rest of the way back home in silence. She's just revealed a major trauma from her childhood to me. It feels somber, and I struggle for words.

We're almost to the front door. "I wish I could make it better for you, Mari."

She smiles at me. "Who knows? Maybe you just did."

I give her one more hug.

Andrew and I lie in bed. All afternoon I turned Mari's ideas around and around in my head. I don't know that Andrew would let me go. With everything that's happened, I think he wouldn't want us apart. But I'd have peace. It'd be a strong move, taking the boys somewhere safe until all of this blew over.

Andrew wouldn't be able to join us, not until *Leave No Trace* was done…maybe four days until he could come up and join us. But it could work.

My phone buzzes. I look at the clock. It's ten. No one texts me this late.

Thanks for the walk and talk today.
I hope you find peace up north this week. Do it.

Mari. Her words nudge me to make a decision.

I think you should come with. Could you get off work?

I shoot off another quick text to Tessa, letting her know a trip to Oregon might be in the works. Then I check to see if Mari has responded yet. I text her again.

It'd be good for you and me, Mari. Think about it.

"Who are you texting?" Andrew looks at me over the top of his script.

"Mari. She told me something today that makes me really worry for her."

He sets his script down. "What was it?"

"I think she told me in confidence. But a thing like that, it'd shake you to the core. Transform you. Worse even than what I went through with Peter. I'm worried she might do something."

"You can't say stuff like that and not tell me what's going on. That's way too dramatic. Fill me in."

"She got blamed for a tragedy. By her father. He didn't speak to her. I just wonder when it's all going to come back to the surface for her. People suffer and hurt themselves over less painful stuff. You and I both know that."

"I know. So, see, this stuff…"

He looks hesitant. I press for more. "Yeah, what about this stuff?"

He sighs. "I can't help it. The moment I saw Mari at the pool in New York—I mean, I'd seen her come and go in the mornings. Remember, I was the one who thought you might run with her—"

"I remember that," I encourage, trying to loosen his tongue.

"But when I saw her at the pool, alarm bells went off for me. Maybe this is why—maybe she's carrying all this trauma around. Just be careful."

I sit up on an elbow to get a better look in his eyes. "But you flew her out here for the baby shower."

He nods. "Yeah, I did, but I didn't know she was going to drop everything and move here. And now you're saying she's troubled. If she needs help, you need to be careful, Kelly. I worry that you'll take it really hard if you can't help her."

"I get it, Andrew."

He's quiet for a moment. "Plus…"

"Plus what?" I am gentle. He seems reluctant to say whatever this is.

"All this weird stuff."

"Yeah?" I'm not sure where he's headed with this. "But the police arrested Devon."

He nods. "I know. But even you said it didn't sit right with you. What about Mari?"

I consider. "I don't know. She's been nothing but kind. I like her. And Tucker did a background check on her."

He runs his hand through his hair, sighs. "I know. But now anyone does any little thing, and I can't help but wonder if there's more to it than we think."

I touch his arm. "I love that you're worried. But we can't let it eat us alive. Stay in the moment, right? You're the one who helps me do that."

He leans over and kisses me. "This moment requires that I finish reading the script Jeremy sent me." He picks the script up and adjusts his pillow before lying back again.

I feel a sharp tightening. "Hey, that was a contraction."

"Are you sure we have three weeks?" Andrew sits up, concern in his eyes.

"Probably closer to four. The boys were both overdue."

"Maybe baby Pettigrew's on his own schedule. Sleep now and stop trying to solve all the world's problems. Remember, we're slowing things down. If we're living in the moment, let's slow down."

I consider this, turn it over in my mind. "Andrew? What would you think if we went to Oregon? Took the boys? Maybe I could invite Tessa? Maybe Mari if we both feel okay about it?" We'll go to Oregon, and take Mari, help her heal.

Andrew chews his lip. "I don't know. It feels like we're so close to baby."

"There's a hospital in Seaside, but I promise, both boys were late. There's no reason to think this one is coming early. I could take everybody now, and then you could join us on the weekend."

He sighs. "Let's decide in the morning."

"Okay. I think it'd be peaceful; it'd be good."

"Sleep now, and we'll talk about it."

I can do this.

I wake up early, shower and dress, make tea for me and Andrew. Poor guy has another early call, and tonight he might not even make it home.

He comes in the kitchen, hair wet, eyes barely open. "I am so tired. This movie needs to be done."

"Just wait—the baby will make this look like a leisurely pace. Both of the boys waited until they were about a year before they slept through the night."

He wraps his arms around me and kisses me. "A baby is at least cute in the middle of the night. The crew looks like a legion of zombies right now."

I turn to face him. "So, what do you think about my road trip idea?"

He stretches, rolls his shoulders before they shrug up. "I worry. What if you just wait for me to be done, and we go together? I'd feel a lot better. Tucker could come with that way too."

His lips thin into a worried line.

I can't push him. We've made all these efforts to be together, so it seems dumb to argue about being apart. "I can see how you feel about it. I can wait. I'll let Mari know."

His shoulders soften as soon as I say this. "After everything, playing it safe just seems smart."

I nod. He's right. "All right, Mr. Movie Star, I'll wait for you. Give me a kiss."

He gives me a smooch, and I breathe in the smell of clean Andrew: shampoo and shaving cream. I love it.

Later that morning, when I text Mari to tell her, she doesn't text back. I start to worry right away. What if letting the secret come to the surface was too much? I don't want anything bad to happen. There's been too much already.

I have the day to myself. Mom and Dad came by after Andrew left, took the boys and the dog for a "nature sleepover." Mom, bless her, stills campaigns to make LA and California seem more appealing. She's hoping to turn my boys to her side. I don't know if inviting comparison between the great outdoors in Boise vs. LA will be the way to do it. But she and Dad have them for two days full of hiking and fresh-ish air.

So, I enjoy the day. I nap, I watch some soap operas and Judge Judy/Mathis/Somebody shows, I take a bubble bath and paint my nails. I make a note to have someone else paint my toes — it's too awkward with my baby belly to reach them at the moment. I try texting Mari again and get no response.

After a lovely warmed-up-leftovers dinner, I call my folks and say good night to the boys, and text Andrew to say good night. I don't even bother to try to call him. I know they're pushing hard to wrap this movie, and the next three days will be almost non-stop filming for him.

The house starts to get a little quiet. I miss everyone, and the stillness feels weird. But I know I should enjoy it. I remember the pace a new baby will set. With an infant in the house, getting showered is sure to become a major accomplishment.

There's a knock at the door. It's ten p.m. I look through the peephole. Mari.

I open the door, and she stands in front of me, her eyes red, her hair wild. It looks as though she's worn the same clothes for several days straight. Her car's not out front. I don't know how she got here.

"Mari! You didn't text me back. Are you all right?"

"I thought we were going to Oregon. I packed and everything." She points to a duffel bag at her feet.

"Andrew wants us to wait for him. That's why I texted." I shift a little, feeling the hairs on my neck start to prickle.

She points to my car. "I'm going to put my bag in the back. I'll wait while you go get your stuff."

I shake my head. "No, Mari, we can't go yet. Why don't you come inside, and I'll get you something to eat. We can rest up, and you can stay with us."

She turns and carries her bag to the car, plunks it down next to the passenger door.

I start to tremble. I've never seen her like this. She's a ghost, not really aware of me. "Mari."

She comes around the car. For just one second, I see a glint of steel in her hand, but she slips whatever it is into her pocket.

She pushes the sleeves of her hoodie up a little. There are bandages around her wrists, and long, deep red streaks up her arms.

"Mari! What is going on? What did you do to yourself?" I step toward her.

She shakes her head. "Kelly, please. I'm really upset. It'd be so nice if we could just go. You know, leave? Like we planned it." She pushes her sleeves back down.

"Fine. Let me call Andrew." I pull my phone from my back pocket.

"No. Don't call." Her hand goes into her pocket, and she shakes her head again. No, no, back and forth as though she's trying to get something out of her head. "Can we just go? I think we need to just go." Her voice rises, tight and small. "When I think about staying here, it starts to hurt so bad…" She leaves off and both hands go into her pockets.

It's a gun. She has a gun in her pocket. I can see the outline of it. I'm sure of it.

"Mari? Let's get you some help. Please, let me help." I try to smooth my voice out, soothe her.

"Let's just go. Please? Please, I just want to go."

I breathe in through my nose, try to slow my heart down. I still have my phone in my hand. "Mari, I can't leave right now. The boys will wonder. I can't leave without them. Andrew will worry." I start to text him.

She snatches the phone out of my hand and backs up. "No. I can't wait. I can't stand it. I need for us to go." She slips my phone into her pocket.

There is a gun in that pocket. She's already tried to harm herself. I can't call for help. I swallow hard. Things are unraveling.

I rush to pack something while Mari follows me around, her eyes wide and wild and watchful.

I keep praying that Andrew will come home from set, that Mom and Dad will cut the "nature sleepover" short and bring the boys back. But it's after ten, and no one's due home. I told Mari I had to pack. I try to buy time, stall, but she watches my every move.

I don't have much of a plan if she forces me to leave. Get in the car and drive and keep driving through the night. She'll fall asleep. She looks exhausted. Then I can call 9-1-1, get her help. Let Andrew or Tucker know where we are.

"Kelly, we need to go." She ushers us back out the front door. I stand on the front step. "We're going. Get in the car."

"Mari." I whisper. "Please."

She looks me in the eyes. "We have to go. I can't stay here another second. Please." Tears stream down her cheeks.

I get in the car, and we drive.

She holds my phone in one hand, keeps the other hand deep in her pocket. We drive north. My phone beeps once before she turns it off.

"Was that Andrew? I should text him. He'll be worried."

"No. It was Tessa."

"Let me tell Andrew where we're going. He should know we're going to the Oregon house. He'll be so worried."

"We just need to get there, and I'll feel better. I know it." She looks at me again, and I see that her pupils are wide with adrenaline.

I am in danger.

I'M SO INTO YOU

Tucker calls me in my trailer. I left yesterday at six a.m. to wrap up this shoot. We've got three days left. Last night we shot until midnight, and I collapsed here on the couch. Kelly knew not to expect me. My call was at four thirty this morning. It's three p.m. now. There's no point in even trying to go home when the hours are whacked out like this. We've been shooting for fourteen to sixteen hours straight most days/nights to push and finish on time.

I get up and pace while I talk. But there's not much room. On this indie movie, my trailer really is a trailer. Someone lent the production company an old Airstream. It's nice, but I'm used to multimillion dollar budgets, not shoestring. I've gotten spoiled. I hate to admit it, but it's true.

"Andrew, I think your gut instinct might have been right all along."

"What?"

"Amanda."

"What about her?"

"After two days of investigation, nothing panned out on Devon. He was in NYC when you got pushed, but he was uptown tutoring a Broadway star's little twins. He has an airtight alibi for the incident at The Ivy too. But guess who didn't?" Tucker's eyes are wide.

"Amanda? She was there, Tucker, because she was there with Jeremy."

"The paparazzo just rolled. She paid him to slash your tires."

Holy shit. "You're kidding."

"Not a bit. Police questioned him again about the fire alarm pull and the tires. I guess he claims she pulled the alarm, and he did the tires. It's looking good."

"Unbelievable." I shake my head.

"Totally believable. As you know, she's been crazy since you started filming *The Bull, the Bear*."

"So, what next?"

"Why don't you go home early to that almost-wife of yours and let her know the case is close to wrapping? She'll be thrilled, I bet."

"The press will freak when they find out about this."

"It's not going to leak anytime soon. There's a mountain of investigation still to do. They have to tie her to all of it, if they really want to throw the book at her. No way do they want all the media to muck it up while she's still under investigation."

I stand up. "I think they need to throw a very thick book at that woman. But right now, I need to go home to my woman."

Tucker laughs. "I'm hanging up. I'll call you later if I know more."

When I open the door to the house, I can tell something's not right. After so many years of living alone, with Kelly and the boys in my life, usually I can feel the extra bodies in the house. And I love it. I grew up with two sisters, and I liked a big crowd, so the cavernous LA houses I lived in after I found success sucked.

But the house is empty. I know the boys are with their grandparents. But where is she?

"Kelly?" I call up the curved staircase. No answer. I walk out the back, to the yard, thinking she's out at the pool.

After a two-minute walk around the rest of the house, I dial Kelly's number. None of this sits well. Something is wrong. Kelly can lay claim to women's intuition all she wants, but this is my time to tell something's bad. My heart pounds as her phone rings.

And it goes to voice mail. That's not right. She answers. She always answers my calls.

I call Tucker. "Tuck, where's Kelly?"

"What?" He sounds relaxed.

"She's not here. Have you talked to Kelly?"

"Is her car in the garage? Maybe she took Ditto on a walk."

"No, Kelly's parents took the boys and the dog. Kelly should be home." I jog to the garage. Her car is gone. "No car."

"Andrew, there's a million places she could be. Call her."

"I did. She's not answering. I have a bad feeling about this, Tuck."

"Why?"

"Kelly told me night before last that she was worried about Mari. She got some texts from her."

"About what?"

"She said she was dealing with very traumatic stuff. She hinted that Mari might hurt herself."

"And what are you thinking?"

"What if we're wrong about Amanda? What if it's Mari? What if she wouldn't hurt herself—but she might hurt someone else?"

"Andrew, where do you think they are?"

I run back up the stairs, into the bedroom, and pull open the closet door. Kelly's closet is in disarray, clothes all over the floor. Her suitcase is gone. "She's gone. Tucker, I think this is bad. Kelly and I talked about going to Oregon. She wanted to go alone, take Mari, maybe Tessa, but we decided to go when I was done shooting. She wouldn't just up and leave after we decided. And she wouldn't leave without the boys. No way."

"I'll be right there. Try calling Tessa."

"Why?"

"If she had changed her mind, she would have told you, right? If she couldn't tell you, maybe she talked with someone else before she was in a position not to talk."

"How could this happen? She'd tell me if she'd changed her mind."

"Which means something happened that kept her from doing that."

"Jesus, Tucker, get over here. We've got to find them. She's thirty-seven weeks pregnant!"

"I'm coming right now. I'll get California Highway Patrol on board. We'll find them, Andrew."

"Hurry, Tucker. If anything happens to her, my God…"

I can't even finish. I end the call and race from bedroom to bedroom, check the bathroom. Whatever happened, it was rushed. Her closet is a mess.

The coast. Up the coast to Oregon. Oh my God. Mari is fucking crazy, and my fiancée is headed up Highway 101 with her? Is Mari holding her hostage? What the hell?

I replay the conversation from night before last. *I'm worried she might do something.*

Kelly offered up the house in Oregon as a place to gather Mari's scattered self. A quiet place. But she wouldn't leave by herself. We'd decided. We talked about Mari, talked about my worries specifically. I know Kelly. I know she wouldn't leave while the boys were away, and I know she understood how I felt.

I try Kelly's cell again. No luck. I text her again; no response.

I check the weather. It's clear right now, but there's a huge storm coming in. There are winter storm advisories all up and down the Pacific coastline.

Kelly is in danger, and a storm's bearing down on her.

If anything happens, I don't know what I'll do.

I call Tessa. No answer.

Desperate, I look up the number for Joe, Tessa's husband, at his practice in Boise. If Tessa's not answering, maybe he knows where she is.

The receptionist answers and reluctantly patches me through when I lie and say Joe is waiting for me to consult on a patient of his.

"This is Dr. Ogata."

"Joe, this is Andrew Pettigrew."

"Well, hi, are you lonely already? I'll probably start missing Tessa tonight when the bed is cold." He chuckles.

"Where are they?" I sound crazy. Maybe I am.

"Is everything okay? Tessa left super early this morning. They were meeting at the house on Silver Point."

"I don't know, Joe. Who was going?"

"Tessa mentioned that Kelly's friend Mari needed a change of scenery. Kelly texted Tessa, told her to meet her."

Maybe Mari doesn't know Tessa is coming too. This could be good.

"Andrew? Is everything okay?"

"I'm working on it. This friend, I don't know how stable she is. I just have a bad feeling about it."

"It *is* a little late for Kelly to be road tripping. You all have a baby coming, you know."

"I know, Joe. Thanks for the help." I end the call.

My mind's spinning. I call Tucker again.

"Yes?" He answers with an urgency.

"They're going to the coast. Tessa's meeting them there today."

"Andrew, I have to tell you something."

"What?"

"Sergeant Ridley called. The super of your building in NYC called her an hour ago. Ridley contacted him when Devon looked good for it, left her card with him. He wanted to follow up with her. He said the mail was piling up for one of the units. Turns out it was the one where Mari had been staying, supposedly as a housesitter. It doesn't look good. Her family's been looking for her. She wasn't supposed to leave New York—she had a psychiatrist, was on meds. Of course none of that would pop in a background check. That's all confidential information. She's gone off the grid. She hasn't contacted her family since she left New York."

I want to smash the phone into a million pieces on the tile in the foyer. "Fuck, Tucker. Fuck my life if anything happens to Kelly and the baby."

"Nothing will, Andrew. You and I will make certain it doesn't."

Tucker's in the driveway in ten minutes. I've called Kelly's folks, and Tucker's sent Janus and an Apotheosis security detail to wait with them and keep them informed. He's already alerted CHP, and now we'll meet a plane at LAX and fly to Portland, where a car is waiting to take us to the coast. We'd take a helicopter, but the weather's already getting dicey, and just making it into Portland will take a miracle. Luckily Tucker has friends, and one of them happens to be a former Navy pilot. He'll take us to Portland. We'll take it from there.

Tucker hangs up the phone. "Her credit card was used for gas at six a.m. at the One Stop in Red Bluff."

"Why didn't she call me?"

"I'm sure because she couldn't. When did she tell you about Mari?"

"Two nights ago. She knew I'd be working two, maybe three days straight."

"We can get officers to the house and intercept them."

"I hope so."

Tucker's phone buzzes, and he answers. "Caldwell." He listens intently, and I watch as his frown deepens.

He pulls over to the side of the road. My heart's in my throat. If he's about to tell me the worst news of my life, I don't know what I'll do. I can't live without her.

He doesn't look at me. "Fine. I'm checking it now. That plane better be ready to taxi when we get there. Call Sloan. This is an interstate thing now. FBI needs to get on it. They swing the biggest stick; they need to be incident command on this one."

He ends the call and swipes his cell. I can't tell what he's doing. Then he hands the phone to me. "The super went into the Chelsea condo and called NYPD." He hands me the phone and pulls the car back onto the freeway, gunning it to get into traffic.

There are pictures. I swallow bile as it rises in my throat.

The living room walls in the condo are plastered in pictures. Pictures printed off, cut out of magazines, poster-sized pictures.

They are all of me.

"Tucker."

"I know, I know. Don't say anything. Just keep breathing."

I swallow hard. I want to scream, to beg God and any other higher power that might be listening for this not to be happening, not to my Kelly, not to my baby. *Please God, please God, please God.*

I'm about to start my bargaining, my pleading, my promises to never work again, to move the family to Canada, to give my life for theirs, when Tucker stops me cold.

"Andrew, I know how you feel right now, but I need you to help me. As much as you want to panic right now, you need to tell me everything and anything that Kelly might ever have told you about this Mari."

It might be better to have something to do. To focus on. I shake my head, try to physically clear the ugly panic from my brain. Focus. I can do this. I can play this part, if only for a little while. Let me disappear into this job. Maybe if I do my part, it'll save Kelly.

The lump in my throat won't go anywhere, and my pulse still pounds at my neck, in my ears, but my brain clears a bit.

"She met her running. She went out one morning, and Mari left the building at about the same time. God, I actually suggested they be friends."

Tucker nods. "That was her way in. She probably IDed her when you moved in."

"How'd she get in the building? How'd she pull that?"

We drive around the main terminals now, headed to the terminal for private jets. Tucker's all business. "Don't know how she figured out the leasing agent you went through, but then she just watched and waited for a lease to pop close to when you were to start filming. She found an empty condo in the building and wheedled her way in, offering them a free housesitter — told them she was in fashion design school. She even had references."

"She's just one of my psycho fans? All of this is about me?"

"I don't know, Andrew. FBI is on it. They're looking for her family right now. She's only twenty-two."

The guard at the gate to the private hangars must be expecting us. He swings the gate wide as we approach, and we race through. On the open tarmac, Tucker floors it, and we race across the pavement to a sleek white jet waiting, door open, stairs down.

Two men who look like plainclothes cops meet us as we screech to a halt. One with a robust red beard and glasses jogs next to us, boards with us as we get on the jet.

"The storm's screwing it all up, Tucker. We tracked them into Portland, got Oregon State Police on the trail of Kelly's car."

"And what?" Tucker's been handed a file folder. I don't know if I want to see what's in it.

"And then the storm started in on the coast. At about milepost seventeen, the visibility's down to half a mile, the roads are starting to accumulate an ice and snow mix, and I don't know how many officers we can put on it. The road between Seaside and Cannon Beach is close to washed out right now. Local law enforcement consists of one county deputy in Cannon Beach, and the cell tower is down, so we haven't made contact with him yet."

"What are we flying into, then?" Tucker looks at him. The flight attendant has pulled up the stairs and closed the door, and we are taxiing.

"Frankly?" The man looks straight at Tucker.

"Yes."

"A cluster. Honestly, if it were Portland, we'd be fine. They're stranded on the coast. You'll be lucky if you make it through."

"We have to. I can't leave her there alone." I say this, and I sound frenzied. "I won't leave her there. Something's going to happen, and I need to get to them."

Tucker raises a hand. "Get a truck. Talk to fire and get one of their wildland vehicles." He looks at me. "We'll do this." He pulls out a yellow pad. "Andrew, remember. I need every detail you can remember. We need as much intel as we can get."

"I need a drink." I look at him, level my eyes on his.

"No, you don't. Be here. Be present. Live in this moment, as awful and terrible as it is."

"I know." I feel tears threaten and shake my head, refuse the emotion. No more fear, whatever the outcome might be. Just strength and determination. Kelly deserves at least that.

I take his phone from him one more time, pull up the pictures. Not a single one of them is with Kelly. There are some where it's clearly me walking down the street with Kelly, or playing in Central Park with the boys and Kelly, but Kelly's not in the pictures. They've all been cut carefully. Some are taken with a camera. Some come from magazines. The hair on the back of my neck stands up. Comments from conversations with Kelly begin to drift back into my brain as the adrenaline clears. Her worries about pushing me away. Her remark about the insta-family, me wanting my old life back. "I think Mari was gaslighting Kelly."

"What does that mean?"

"You ever heard of that movie? *Gaslight*?"

"No." He's scribbling on the pad. "Short-cut it for me."

"Charles Boyer convinces his wife, Ingrid Bergman, that she's going crazy. Those times when Kelly's really fallen apart, she's mentioned talking about us to Mari. Mari kept telling her not to be so clingy, not to drive me away. Then all the other stuff—the note at the shower."

"Mari wrote it." Tucker seems to say this before he realizes who he's saying it to. "She'll push Kelly into labor if she can, force delivery, steal the baby. She's trying to take over Kelly's spot in your life. Or maybe erase everything you care about—" He leaves off. "That was totally out of line."

"No. Kelly's said a couple things. Like that she's driving me away with the way she's acting."

"Mari's been calling her attention to it. Mari's ready to slide in and take over. She's been convincing Kelly *and* herself. Auditioning for the job. Lots of these kinds of people swing between wanting in on your life and wanting to end it."

The plane lurches. The guy in glasses nods at me. "Sorry, Mr. Pettigrew. We're going to hit some serious turbulence."

"Who are you?" I don't know when we picked this guy up.

"Paul Prescott. FBI. I'm communications manager on the incident, until someone with bigger credentials takes over."

Tucker shakes his head at him. "No one else'll make it in this storm. We're the last flight out of LAX going north. And the Portland airport is on the verge of shutting down altogether. You're it."

The plane shakes again, lurches up and then to one side.

Prescott looks sweaty. "Your friend the Navy pilot?" he asks Tucker.

Tucker doesn't look up from his phone. "He can land in weather like this on an aircraft carrier. He flew into hurricanes, on purpose. Let him do his job."

"Sorry." Prescott ducks his head in apology.

Tucker's phone buzzes again. "This just gets more and more insane."

"What?" I ask.

He hands the phone to me again. "We pulled the data from her phone. Look at the picture."

It's the back of someone. In a suit. In an Escada suit, as a matter of fact. "She's the one who shoved me into traffic."

"That crazy bitch." Prescott shakes his head. "Sorry again."

"Insane." Tucker's brow clouds. "Andrew, I should've seen this coming. This is sloppy. I got too comfy, too close to you and the kids, to Kelly. If I'd been at a distance, I would've seen this coming."

"No, you wouldn't have. She's smart."

"Why do you say that?"

"Because she never pushed too hard. Kelly wanted a friend in New York, but Mari wasn't too overbearing. She gave her some space.

But Jesus, she was always around—when stuff was about to happen or just happened."

"Like?"

"Like the attempted break-in. It happened the week after Mari came out to LA. Tucker, I flew her out for the baby shower. Jesus. I'm the reason Mari came to LA. I led her right to us."

"I wish I was one hundred percent clear on her motives." Tucker shakes his head. "If she wants you, and that's it, there's a big problem. But maybe she likes Kelly. That could work to our advantage."

"Nothing works to our advantage if Kelly's stuck at the beach house by herself with Mari, and I can't do anything to help her."

The plane hops to the side again. Prescott the redheaded guy grips the armrests on his seat and appears to be praying.

Tucker fastens his seatbelt. "We'll get there. Right now we're about to put the plane down, hard. Buckle up."

EVERY BREATH YOU TAKE

When I open the door to the house, the smell of cedar and salt hits me. I walk in, set the house keys on the entryway table, and start turning on lights. Since Andrew bought the house, we've been able to come up a few times, settling in, furnishing it, getting comfortable.

But this visit is different. The day is darkening early, the storm clouds gathering and blocking the sun. I try to breathe, sound calm when I speak. "I don't know how long we'll have power." It's four thirty p.m. Back at the house in LA, someone — Andrew or my parents, with the boys — someone has to have come home by now. I've been driving since ten thirty last night, and I ache all over, from terror and fatigue.

Mari comes in behind me. She's been vigilant. I don't know that she's slept in the eighteen hours we drove. I haven't had any chance to try to get away, or get my phone from her. As soon as we stopped the car in the driveway here, she had the car keys in her hand. Then she tucked them into the pocket, the one with the gun.

I try to keep my voice calm. "We better get the stuff out of the car. We might have to seriously batten down the hatches. It could get ugly out there." I've done all I can to keep every word I say as casual as I can. Mari hasn't made threats against me, nothing outward. She's an unstable person with a gun, but maybe I still count as her ally. Maybe I'm not a person she wants to hurt. I want to keep it that way, keep the baby safe.

The wind howls as I step outside. It's getting serious out here. The salt wind and mist bites at my face. I wrestle to get the car door open in the wind, and when it finally gives, the force of it knocks me over. I land hard on my hip, and it feels like the baby just got knocked too.

"Kelly? Are you all right?" Mari helps me up. Her eyes seem clearer. Maybe her break, her episode is lifting. Maybe she'll be lucid, and we can call Andrew and go home.

"I'll be okay." I rub my hip. That's going to hurt like crazy tomorrow. "We better get inside."

"Are we safe?" Mari's voice is small, like a little girl's.

"Up here on the cliff? No doubt. It just might be a while before we're going anywhere." As if on cue, a contraction tightens over my belly. It's a big one. I take in a breath, try to rub it out.

"What?" Mari looks at me suspiciously. "What was that?"

"Contraction. They happen on and off a lot in the last month."

Inside, I try the TV. It's all gray fuzz. "Satellite's already out."

Mari smiles for a minute. "Nothing to worry about. The storm knocked out cell service too. I can't get a signal on my phone or yours." My heart sinks. She doesn't look upset; she looks happy. Maybe this isn't a breakdown; maybe this is premeditated.

She comes over and hugs me. It's so tight, I feel a little breathless. "We're here now, and inside, safe. I know I'll feel better now that I'm here."

She stares at me, her eyes so intense I feel my skin prickle.

Even if she falls asleep now, there's no one to call.

I start to plot how to escape.

I make dinner, trying to sort through a thousand different thoughts as I stir a pot of soup on the stove. Mari seems calmer. At times, though, she looks straight through me, as though I'm a ghost, and if I call her name, only seems to acknowledge my presence faintly. Just when I begin to consider walking past her, straight out the door and down the lane, she'll have a moment of clarity and circle the room, pacing nervously. Now she stands at the edge of the great room and watches me, hands still in her pockets.

I look again at her wrists, the bandages. Does she want to kill herself? Kill me? What is the gun for? Why are we here?

I sift through all of our interactions, try to find the thread. Every time, I feel blind panic rising from the base of my spine. None of this feels good.

Whatever the case, she's slipped into a dark place.

"Mari, please."

"What, Kelly?"

"You must be so tired. I'm tired. We need to rest."

She points to the master bedroom down the hall. "You should go sleep."

I turn everything over in my head. I'm exhausted. I've been up, drove through the night without stopping, and now, I can feel the exhaustion sit on my spine, press on the baby. "What will you do? You need to rest too, Mari. It could help. Help you feel more yourself."

She nods. Her eyes soften. "I'll sleep. Then we can decide what to do in the morning."

Maybe she'll listen to reason. Maybe after sleeping she'll feel better, be back to herself.

Maybe when she sleeps, I can get the gun away from her.

She watches me go into the bedroom, stands outside the door for a while as I lie there, fear pulsing through me. But the heavy, heavy fatigue climbs up my arms and legs and weighs on me until I am out.

I wake up with a start sometime later. This could be my chance. Maybe Mari's fallen asleep too. Maybe the weather has cleared, and the phone will have a signal. Maybe Tessa will arrive. I texted her the night I invited Mari, and then, the following morning, had every intention of calling and canceling. But then Mari arrived.

Tessa might show up here. I could get away from Mari, slip out with Tessa.

I pray for Tessa to get here. She might not make it today, with the weather, but she's Tessa. She might show up when I need her most.

The hall has a tiny sliver of light from the guest bedroom. Mari's still awake. I can't hear anything as I near her door, but I knock softly.

"Mari? You awake?"

The light on the bedside table is on. I hear water running in the bathroom. She's taking a shower.

I stand still for a minute. Where is the gun? Where are the car keys?

"Mari?" I call to the bathroom door.

No response.

I walk around the bed, looking for the car keys.

"Mari?"

I take one more step and side-swipe the comforter. It starts to slide off the bed, so I catch it. A notebook falls off and lands open on the floor.

It's one of Mari's design books, her sketch book. I can see a long, lean figure of a woman with a soft flowing dress, lines blurred and smudged, on the open page.

I pick it up off the floor. It's got a leather cover, red, with a heart etched into it, a rendering of a real heart, its chambers with items flowing from them like blood: musical notes, small letters of the alphabet.

I turn the page. There's a pencil drawing of a young boy, in color, with pale blond hair, like Mari's. His hair flows up around his head, soft and undulating. His lips are blue.

He's underwater, staring at me from the page. It must be a drawing of Mari's brother. Drowned, still and staring with blue, cold eyes.

I shiver, chilled by the image, and flip the page.

There, staring back at me, are Andrew's eyes. His face. She's meticulously drawn his hair in his eyes, and his hand up, about to push it back, like he always does. The resemblance is unnerving.

I flip to the next page. It's another drawing of him. He's floating in the pool, the black-and-white-tile pool from New York. He has his eyes open, floating with a woman, holding her hand.

But it's not me. It's Mari holding his hand.

I turn the page.

It's Andrew in another pool. The pool at our house in LA. He's floating on an air mattress, and there are currents around him, indicating a slow twirl. And there's a smudge of colored pencil, trailing out from the mattress. Blood.

I look more closely and see that she's drawn a bullet hole over his heart.

Below this image she's copied a line from *Gatsby*, about Nick finding Gatsby dead in the swimming pool, the holocaust being complete.

It's the last page of the sketch book.

I go to the first pages, and all of them are filled with Andrew. Some have little clippings from magazines, and then she's illustrated them, drawing out the news, capturing Andrew's life.

One is of Andrew and me leaving the doctor's office. Except my figure has been shaded black. Pitch black.

The water in the bathroom stops. She's getting out of the shower.

I am in the same house as a woman who wants Andrew dead, me erased. There can be no more waiting, no more caution.

I find her hoodie, and the keys are in the pocket.

The gun is gone.

Suddenly every threat, every moment of fear since New York races through my head, but I force myself up and step as quietly and quickly as I can out of the guest bedroom. I creep down the hall to the front door. I will slip out, escape. The storm is safer than this.

The front door flies open.

It's Tessa. She's made it, and the wind whips and blows the door wide. It cracks against the siding of the house.

"What the hell?" She stands on the step, lost.

"Tessa, we've got to go." I grab her fiercely, keeping my voice quiet.

"Hello?" Mari's voice, from the end of the hall, from the guest bedroom.

I flip the hall lights off and grab the Mag Lite by the front door, which is there for when the power goes out, or for night trips out with the dog. "Tessa, go upstairs, hide. Hide and don't come out." I grab her arm again and squeeze, whispering roughly to her.

I don't think Tessa's ever seen me like this. She's never, ever quiet, and right now she does not speak. Her eyes widen, and confusion crosses her face for a moment, but she nods and puts her hand out for the flashlight.

Tessa races up the landing with the Mag Lite in hand. I can see her in the patches of light from the outside porch that stream in through the windows.

I go back to the door and shut and lock it, turning off the outside light. I can't hear Tessa anymore. She's at least made it upstairs.

"Kelly? Where are you?"

Mari's voice sounds calm, flat.

"I was just headed to the kitchen to get some Tums."

I can see her figure now, silhouetted by the light from the guest bedroom. She's in a bathrobe. It has pockets.

"What are you doing down by the front door, then? I heard a commotion."

"The door blew open. The wind's screaming out there now."

"Oh." She still sounds calm. I can't tell if I sound normal or not.

"You want me to make you a cup of tea?" I ask. "I thought I might have one."

I have to get past her to get to the kitchen. I don't know if I can keep my face calm and still walk by her.

"Sure. I need to put my pajamas on."

"You go do that. I'll get the kettle started."

I walk toward her. She hasn't gone back in the bedroom yet. I hold my breath.

"What's wrong?" she asks as I'm about to pass her.

"Nothing. It just spooked me." As I walk by, a contraction tightens over my belly, and I can't help it, I pause, stooped a little by the surprise of pain.

"What? What is it?"

"A contraction. No big deal." I lean over for a second, breathing. I am just past her, and I can see into the guest bedroom. The sketchbook, the one with all the awful, terrible sketches inside of it, is sitting on the edge of the bed.

But it's not in the place I left it.

"You want to sit down?" She swings the door wider.

"Naw, I'll just walk it off. Meet you in the kitchen in a minute."

I stand up, sucking in and pushing through the last of the contraction, and *will* myself down the hallway.

Mari's shadow disappears.

I race down the hall as quietly as I can. I need my phone. It has to have a signal. It just has to.

I search for it in the kitchen. As I race around the island, I grab the kettle and set it on the burner. I can't find the phone.

I hear footsteps in the hallway. Panicking, I grab two teacups and set them down by the stove. Where am I going to go? If she comes in, I'll have to make a break for the back hall, the one that leads to the TV room.

Mari walks in the kitchen, slowly. She holds up the sketchbook.

"You were snooping while I was in the shower."

I don't know what to do. I stand frozen, my mind racing, and all of a sudden, there's a huge crack from outside, and the house is black. A transformer must have blown.

I run. I run and fly to the back hallway, swing the back door open as noiselessly as I can. Out on the deck, I grab a poker from the fire pit. I slide back in the door and press myself flat against the hallway wall. I can't hear anything except the wind howling.

There's a mad woman in my house. Tessa is hiding somewhere.

I have no idea what I'm going to do.

HIT ME WITH YOUR BEST SHOT

I stand on the wood floor in my bare feet. I can hear the wind outside, still howling, building to freight-train shrieks as it tries to fight its way inside through the seams of windows, the dryer vent, the fireplace flue.

But there's a fight inside already. I have the poker in my hand. I like the heft of it. In the black, I can't really see the whole of it, only if I swing it about a bit, brandish it. I try to do that a little, build up some confidence.

I'm going to connect this piece of wrought iron to the soft of someone's body. I am fully prepared to do it. I don't want to feel the impact, but I will do it.

Another contraction hits me, stabs across the top of my belly, wraps like a boa constrictor around to the base of my spine. I can't help it, I suck in a breath. The air whistles between my teeth.

If I just gave up my position to Mari, I'm going to be pissed. Damn contraction.

I pivot on my heels, make a turn in the black of the living room. Nothing moves.

Somewhere in the house, Tessa hides. She wields a Mag Lite flashlight. It's perfect. When the house is safe, it will show her the way to the car, to safety, hopefully. For now, it could clock someone in the head and render her senseless.

I hear something, from the library, and the hair on the back of my neck stands up.

The piano. Mari plays the piano. The melody makes me cringe. It's something I've heard Andrew play before. I think he learned it for a movie.

"Kelly! I'll burn the house down," she calls. "You know I will."

She doesn't know Tessa made it. This is our advantage.

But she's playing the piano to announce her position. I guess this is it. We're going to go toe to toe. She's calling me out, and I have to answer. She's too unstable to ignore. I don't doubt the threat about burning the house down. When we first arrived, I wasn't sure of her motives. But the sketchbook made everything clear. She is crazy, and she wants to hurt my family. Of course she's threatening to burn down the house. She'll do it.

I walk softly toward the library. The wide, smooth wood floor creaks under my feet. She will hear me coming.

I come around the corner, and I can see her. There's a candle on the top of the piano, casting a soft, warm glow across the room. Books, the couches, the worn white coffee table shimmer in the orange light.

She looks up at me. She rests one hand on top of the piano, dabbles the ivory keys with the other.

I stare at her face. Her eyes are streaked with tears. The pupils are glowing in the candlelight; her blue eyes look ghostly.

She waves me closer, and in her hand is the gun. It's built from gray and golden amber streaks in the light. "Kelly. Glad I didn't have to go any farther with the kerosene lantern idea."

"Don't," I tell her softly. "You need to take a deep breath and slow down. Nothing needs to be so extreme."

"You don't know what I need. You have everything. You don't need anything."

"What do you need?"

"I need to know why someone like Andrew, so worldly, so young, so curious, would settle for you." She points at the gun at me.

"I thought you wanted him to be happy."

"Happy with me. Come on, Kelly. You're a kind woman, but I don't need a friend. I needed to be with my soul mate. I needed to feel his mouth on mine, his hand in mine."

"Andrew is your soul mate?"

"Everything would've worked out. You corrupted it, polluted his mind. You ruined him."

I swallow, hard. Her thinking isn't rooted in fact. And it sounds an awful lot like the letter I got at the shower.

She laughs, brittle and tight. "At first, I thought he was just out of my reach. Then you got pregnant. You insinuated yourself into his world, like a parasite. I was so mad at him for falling for that shit." She snorts. "If he can't see that we're meant to be together, what's the point in him living? But I felt horrible. To see him in pain, it hurt so bad. I hoped he'd wake up from the trance you put on him. Just because you're pregnant. What a manipulative move. Come on, Kelly! You should be a strong woman. You didn't need to do the desperate thing." She smacks the keys of the piano with the gun. I flinch. The gun could go off accidentally.

"I can leave him," I offer, willing my voice to remain steady. "You don't have to hurt me. You don't have to hurt Andrew."

"I'm just so sick of it all. I kept waiting, waiting for him to figure it out, realize you were wrong for him. Then I thought I could get you to leave him, but he fixed things between you each time — even after I made sure he missed the party in Boise. I tried to tempt him away from you, but his loyalty to you is blind. You've ruined him completely."

"The residue at the airport."

"It was me. But Amanda's a good decoy. She does still seem to want him, and she slashed his tires. I didn't have a thing to do with that. I saw her cry into her drink about him, but she couldn't get him to join in. If she'd gotten him drunk, maybe she could've seduced him."

I try to breathe. I feel my hand cramping up around the fireplace poker. If she shoots me on the spot, I won't get a chance to even swing. And if she shoots me in the torso, it could kill the baby, kill him straightaway. But this may be my chance. She's spinning out all sorts of fantasies. If she keeps going, maybe I can edge closer and get a swing in.

"I wouldn't do that to him, you know. You know that, right, Kelly?"

"What wouldn't you do?" *Stall, Kelly. Slow her down.*

"I'd never tempt his sobriety. He worked so hard to get clean. He's noble, isn't he? A hero, really." She rubs her face with a shaking hand. The gun rests in her lap.

"You love him. Why would you hurt him? Why'd you try to push him into traffic?" I inch a bit closer.

"Because he wasn't paying attention, and then I found out you were pregnant. He wasn't ever going to leave you. He hadn't noticed me. And I was so mad. If I couldn't be with him, he shouldn't be with anyone. I felt terrible afterward. But I thought if you were so angry and clingy, maybe he'd see the light and leave you. Then I could have my chance. Now, I just don't know. I don't know how we're supposed to be together. You sunk your claws into him deep, and I don't see how he'll ever be the same."

I take another step. I pause for a moment. I hear something somewhere in the house.

She jumps up, gun clasped in both hands. She swings it around, turns in a circle in the narrow ring of candlelight. "Did you hear that?"

"Yes." I stay still.

"What was that?"

"I don't know. Mari, I need to go home. The boys — Hunter and Beau need me. Please."

"I love those guys. I could take care of them, you know."

"They need me. They already lost their dad."

"Then maybe the original family should stay together."

"Where? Where would we go, just me and the boys?"

"You could be with Peter."

"You wouldn't kill the boys. They're innocent. Just like how you were, before Cameron's accident."

"Don't you bring that up. You don't even know. How do you know how it feels? My dad couldn't even look at me in the eye. It was my fault. Everyone hated me. I loved Cameron so much."

"It was horrible, Mari. You needed someone to love you and take care of you. Your dad should've helped you. It wasn't your fault. It was an accident."

She starts to shake. Her shoulders shudder. She's sobbing. Now is my chance. I should hit her with the poker.

I don't think I can. Her cries are so young. She's such a little girl. "Mari, come here. Let me help you. Please."

She shakes her head. "No. No, no, no, no! It's not right. It wasn't right. I was happy. Everything was taken from me. In one stupid, horrible moment." She covers her face with one hand, and the hand with the gun drops to her side.

The shattering of glass comes from somewhere in the house. Is it Tessa? Is she all right?

"What was that, Kelly? What shit are you trying to pull?"

I take a step to her. "Please. It's just the storm. Please. Mari, let me help you. I'm so sorry."

She looks up at me. Her face is stone cold. "You know, I really don't want your pity." She points the gun and fires.

Sharp pain bites me in the arm, and almost immediately it stings and tears through, registers in my ribs like an electric shock. Black, seething fury floods my body. I want to hurt her, badly. I swing the poker at her, my anger forceful and raging. The shaft hits her across the arms and body. She reels backward, and I swing it again, catch her on the elbow, and see the gun fly behind her, out of her hands. It clatters across the piano keys, and I duck, waiting for it to fire.

She comes at me, but I swing the poker at her knees. She howls in pain and drops to the floor. I jump on top of her. I have her by the hair on the back of her head, and I yank, hard.

"Stop! You are done! You are done, Mari. Do you hear me! Stop it now! No more, no more, no more!" I shriek. I bellow. All my rage pours out of my lungs.

She's still. She doesn't fight me. Now I'm not sure what to do. "Mari, you lie still. If you struggle, I'll beat you senseless with this poker. Do you understand me?"

I feel her head nod, pulling slightly against the death grip I have on her ponytail.

"Tessa!" I call. I hope she can hear me, because another contraction is coming on, and I'm terrified that Mari will try something. "Tessa! Come out!"

"Kelly! Kelly, where are you?" It's not Tessa. It's Andrew.

"Andrew? Andrew! By the piano! Andrew!" I cry.

Shafts of flashlight beams swing wildly down the hallway.

Mari yanks at my grip, jerks her head down, and bites me, hard, on the ankle. I feel her claw at my hands, yanking and pulling on my fingers. I grab her head tighter and smack it against the wooden floor. "Stop now! Stop it now!"

A contraction tears through my lower half, and I feel a strange searing pain as it intensifies and meets with a different pain under my ribs. That pain in my arm, the one under my ribs. That was a bullet. I feel it now.

I hear shouts, and I can't hold on to Mari anymore. The pain under my ribs seizes me, stabbing across my tightening belly and shooting down my legs and up to the base of my neck. I yell from the pain. Mari pushes me off of her, but there are legs and beams of light. I roll onto the smooth wooden floor, and someone catches my head. I feel something wet. I wonder if it's my blood or if my water's broken. There's a lot of noise, commotion I can't sort out.

"Kelly? Kelly? Answer me. Oh my God, please answer me." It's Andrew.

I can't do this anymore. I feel bile rising in my throat, and heat sweeps through my body. The pain closes over me like a wave.

PANIC SONG

"Kelly? Kelly? Answer me. Oh my God, please answer me." Kelly's body goes limp, and she slumps over. Tucker catches her before her head cracks on the floor. Mari pushes out from under her and scrambles behind the piano.

I go after her. She stands up, gun in hand. But I have a flashlight, and I swing it, hard, connecting with the side of her head. She goes down like a rag doll.

Tucker puts a boot down on her arm, points his gun at her head, kicks her gun away.

Kelly lies on the floor, still. I see a tiny glint in the puddle of blood or water, I can't tell which. It's her ring, her engagement ring. I can tell that as I pocket it. Mari must've pulled it off her finger in the struggle.

I slide down to her side, cradle her head in my hand. It's too dark; I can't tell what's wrong with her.

I feel down her side, and my hand comes up wet. I feel a warm, jagged wound, flesh torn and bleeding. Panic threatens to strike me paralyzed, but I force my hand to search and come up with another wet warm tear in the fabric of her shirt under her arm, and there's something sharp sticking out of it, splintered like a broken stick. A rib.

"Tucker. She's hurt. She's not awake. She's been shot, Tucker."

The deputy and Prescott come in with kerosene lanterns from the back utility room. Finally I can really see what the hell is going on.

Tucker calls the deputy over. "Cover her. Andrew and I need to help Kelly. She's been shot."

Tucker is next to me, his fingers at Kelly's throat for a pulse.

"She's breathing. Her pulse is thready, though. She's going into shock."

"We've got to get her out of here, Tuck. The baby."

"I know. We're going to do this, okay? We're going to help her." Tucker points to my hoodie. "Take that off. We'll tear it into strips, tourniquet the arm wound. You'll need to put pressure on the one under her arm. Then we'll move her."

The deputy holds his gun steady and covers Prescott as he pulls Mari upright and takes her back the way they came.

Tucker calls to him. "There are zip ties in the toolkit."

"We'll watch her. We've got it handled." The deputy leaves the room with Mari.

Tucker calls to Prescott. "Go look for Tessa. Her car was out front. She's probably upstairs in one of the other bedrooms. She can help you contact Kelly's family, if you can get the radio or cell working. And call for backup and ambulance."

"I don't know. We didn't have any luck getting a signal just now."

"We need the truck, then. You might be forced to hold Mari here for a while."

"You go, Tucker, and we'll handle it here." He disappears down the hall, calling for Tessa, identifying himself.

I don't know what to say. I stare at Kelly's still, pale face. "Where are we going with Kelly?"

Tucker's thinking. "There's no point trying to get to Portland, probably not even Seaside. That low bridge along the bay was basically washed out when we got past it coming down here. By now it's gone."

"She needs help. And the baby, we need to know about the baby."

"So, the deputy said the fire department runs incident command during a winter storm. We need to get there. Someone'll be on duty, and they'll have enough resources. We can deliver the baby if we have to. EMTs in a little town like this have probably even done it before if they've been around long enough."

"A fireman?"

"All of us will help."

I pick her up in my arms. She's lifeless, limp. I swallow hard and feel my heart pushing blood through my veins, taut with adrenaline and panic. We have to get her out of here. "Let's get her to the truck."

Along the road into town, Tucker powers through standing water and even surf in more than a few spots. I hold Kelly in my arms, talk to her, and hit redial on the cell over and over, hoping to raise dispatch long enough to tell them we're coming.

Kelly shudders in my arms. "She's having another contraction, I think, Tuck." I hold her, try to help her through it, cradle her shaking body.

He looks at his cell. "They're coming pretty close together, but we're still okay. I think it's a good sign that labor's still progressing."

I squeeze Kelly's hand. "Hang on. Hang in there, Kells. We're almost there."

I say this nine million times in the fifteen minutes it takes us to get there. And Tucker is going as fast as humanly possible, I know. We hydroplane a couple times before he can wrestle the truck back into the middle of the road.

We roar into the fire station's drive. Tucker leans on the horn and screeches to a halt. Three men come out in T-shirts, rush to the side of the truck.

Tucker's out and talking immediately, shouting over the screaming storm. "Two gunshot wounds, active labor. Thready pulse, loss of consciousness. It's been about twenty minutes since the injury. We're not sure how long she's been laboring. She's having contractions about a minute apart."

"Inside." A white-haired man points to the doors. There's another man holding the door. "Everybody scrub up."

I carry Kelly inside and lay her gently on the gurney they've brought to the door. She's whisked off to another room. The lights are on here, and I can hear the metallic chugging of a generator outside, earning its keep.

Tucker stands shoulder to shoulder with two of the other men, waiting to wash up so he can help. He looks at me. "Scrub up."

I do as I'm told, soap up to my elbows.

Tucker turns to another fireman. "You need to find all the bedding you can, and start thinking about a way to warm the baby. Assuming he's fine, he's going to need to stay warm."

I break in. "If he's not?"

"We'll cross the bridge when we need to, Andrew. Like I said, babies get born all over the place."

The gray-haired man must be the chief. He nods. "They don't wait for us to be ready. They like to make it complicated. Announce their arrival with some drama."

"If they can find formula, be thinking about that also. You might have to bottle feed him till Kelly's able."

I dry my hands, slip into latex gloves. I can't stop shaking.

This is not how this was supposed to go.

COMING AROUND AGAIN

I see bright, warm light and feel a strong, deep urge to push. Nothing's in focus.

"There she is! She's conscious! Kelly, Kelly Jo Jo, come back to us!"

Tucker. Tucker hollers at me.

"I need to push." That's all I can say.

"Okay, gents, let's help her. Tyler, if you'll lift her head and shoulders up. Mind the left side; that's where the wounds are."

"Where's Andrew?" My voice sounds tiny and scratchy.

"He's right here. Are you ready to push?"

I close my eyes tight and push, hard.

Someone else's voice. "Tell her one more good push. He's crowning already. You all got here just in time."

"Kelly, push again—hardest you ever have—and we'll be done. This guy wants to be born."

The other voice again. "Get ready with support for the baby. We don't know what we've got here. Could need to be vented."

More voices. "Do we have a pediatric vent? Did we find it?"

"Yeah, I got it. I got the peds line ready too."

"Think about where you start fluids on a baby. And if we need a line, it may need to be a mainline. Just be ready. Think on your feet, friends."

"Ready to push, Kelly? Now, hon, push hard, push hard. Push!"

I push again. I feel a stabbing sharp pain behind my breast. "Andrew! It hurts. Andrew!"

And finally, I hear him. I feel his hand in mine, squeezing it, reassuring me. "I'm here, Kelly. I'm here. Push through it. It's okay."

Tucker's voice. "She's got to be done on this one. That rib could be perforating her lung on the other side. I couldn't tell how shattered it was by the bullet."

I push and push, and it feels like forever, but suddenly everyone's voices speak all at once. "Hey, here we go, yes! Kelly, you did it! He's here! Okay, quickly guys. Umbilical and vitals, stat."

An unfamiliar voice speaks up. "Please tell me we can transport. Any word on that?"

"Hey! Andrew! Kelly! Kelly Jo Jo, you have a healthy baby girl!"

I hear this. *A girl!* "A girl?"

"She's talking. That's good. She must be stabilizing a little. We can push fluids hard on the trip to Seaside."

"A girl. She's looking good. She's pinking up." I can tell these things are spoken in my direction.

"Andrew?" I call.

"I'm right here."

"Go hold her. I don't want her to be alone."

As he goes to do this, deep relief floods me, washing over the stabbing pain I still feel in my abdomen and all up my side.

"I'll stay with her, Kelly," he says. "You stay with me."

"She's losing consciousness. Her blood pressure is low. Let's try…"

Everything washes away in a sigh, turning to gray water and tears on my cheeks. The pain ebbs.

SWEET AND LOWDOWN

The nurse wanted her on the warming table, all swaddled up, but I just want to hold her. The tears stream down my cheeks as I look at her. That's me. Andy Pettigrew, master of the universe, king of the box office, reduced to a trembling mess.

I got to bottle feed her already. I have no idea what to call her. Kelly hasn't regained consciousness. Her name's got to be a team decision. The doctors said Kelly'll wake up soon, since mostly it was the blood pressure and lost blood, and they've put four units into her since we got here. It doesn't look like we'll have to airlift anyone to Portland, after all, which is good. The weather's still shitty.

Kelly broke a rib. The bullet broke her rib, actually. But she didn't perforate her lung, like we thought she might have, so we were very lucky.

I look at my little girl without a name. She's fine. She hums, and I love it, but the nurses don't. They say it's a breathing problem. But the humming that no one except me likes, it's starting to subside. Kelly's going to miss it. I tried to record it on my phone. When she wakes up I'll play it for her.

The baby was delivered at thirty-seven weeks and a few days, pretty much full-term, so that was not the biggest concern of the event. No one mentioned it to me until we were back here in the NICU, but baby girl had the umbilical cord wrapped around her neck. Maybe arriving on the scene a little early was good. That situation could have gone all to hell even without any of this crazy drama.

Mari's in jail, but on the psych ward. They had to hold her in the little lock up in Cannon Beach for a night, and the deputy had to clear five boxes of paper towels out of the holding cell to do it. Shows you how often they have trouble.

I need to close my eyes. If the nurse comes in, I'll ask her to stay with the baby. I can just sleep for a couple minutes, then when Kelly comes around I can function.

I don't pray, not usually. But right now I lay myself down on the vinyl of the lounger, and I call out to whoever it is that let me keep my Kelly and my baby, and I say thank you, God. Thank you for the second and third and millionth chances you've given me to figure out my ridiculous, self-absorbed life. Thank you for letting me find these amazing creatures and for not scaring them off, and for being able to keep them safe even when someone wanted to hurt us. Thank you, universe. I owe you. I owe you big.

WAKING UP

I open my eyes, and everything makes sense, suddenly. It's been a fog for I don't know how long. The pain nudges me in the familiar spot under my arm, but it's just a nudge and not an ice pick between the ribs.

The room is cute. There are three quilts hung up, all green and blue and purples. Lots of teddy bears and flowers.

"Andrew?" I call, though not really, because I have no voice. It's all scratch. I look around the room again.

He's asleep in the lounger. Out. He has dark, dark circles under his closed eyes. He's here. I'm safe.

"The baby? Where's the baby?" Again, it's a scratchy nothing. I do a quick survey and find the call button on the side of the bed. I press it once, gently.

A big lady with big hair and very red lipstick strolls in. She wears red and black scrubs. Her smile gets wider when she sees I'm awake. "There you are, lady! Welcome back!"

She glides over and puts her hand to my wrist. She checks my pupils with a little light. I motion to my throat.

"Water. Got it." She gets the pitcher and pours me a glass. "You pushed the call button?"

I nod. "My baby?" It's a peep, a scratchy peep, but I can talk now.

"Would you like to meet her?"

"How long has it been?"

"You haven't missed much. It's been about six hours since you got here. You lost a lot of blood; your blood pressure was low. The doctor sedated you for a bit too."

"Has she eaten?"

"Andrew bottle fed her, but you can try nursing her. You all didn't get to choose how that went down, did you?"

She's on a first name basis with Andrew. I smile. It's good that they like each other. Nurses rule the maternity wing.

"I'll go get her out of the nursery."

She glides out. I love how calm she is.

Andrew hasn't woken up yet. I wiggle my toes. Maybe I can get up and wake him.

But I don't know if I'm in one piece. I take stock head to toe. No C-section scar. That's good. I remember the pushing. Good.

My arm hurts. There's a big bandage. The gun. The searing pain in my arm. I was shot. And there's a big bandage on my side, under my arm. That one I don't even touch. It still throbs and reminds me it's there.

Mari. I don't know what happened to her. But it's quiet here. I feel safe, even though the wounds throb. Other than these injuries, there's just general soreness. And sensations I remember from the early days of being a mother. I take another drink through the straw.

"Andrew?" It sounds better, more like a word. Maybe I should just let him sleep.

The nurse comes in. "Here she is, Baby Girl Pettigrew."

She hands me my baby. She wears a little knit blue, pink, and white cap. She has hair, dark and thick. Her eyes are open, blinking and confused. She and I just got here. We're both trying to catch up to all these other people who know what's been going on for longer.

I touch her tiny fingers. Her nails. Someone clipped them already. That's good.

"You want to try?" The nurse looks at me.

"Sure. I'm Kelly, by the way."

"I'm Regina. Nice to meet you, Mrs. Pettigrew."

"Mrs. Almost-Pettigrew," Andrew chimes in. He's awake. God, I love his voice. I want to squeeze him.

"Please, just Kelly," I say to her, but she's already walking out the door.

"Give the nursing a try. The doctor gave it the okay. I'm going to give you all a minute." She waves over her shoulder.

"I changed her already." He comes to my side. I grab his arm and pull him to me.

"Oh, Andrew." I kiss him, hold him around the neck. "I love you so much."

"Hi, love. I'm so glad to see those bright eyes of yours again." He kisses me deeply.

"Where's Tessa? Is she okay? Where are the boys?" I can't stand to think that someone was so close to us and could have hurt anyone else.

"Tessa's fine. She's here. So are the boys. Tucker has some serious connections. He flew your folks and the boys in as soon as the weather began to even hint at clearing."

He presses his forehead to mine, then leans down and plants a little kiss on the baby's forehead. "Welcome to the family, baby without a name. This is your mama, Mrs. Almost-Pettigrew." He sits next to me. "So, you're doing this? Are you feeling well enough?"

"I feel tons better. I feel awake. So, yeah, we're doing this. Time for baby to eat."

It takes a minute for the little one to figure out it's dinner time, but we get the hang of it. Andrew sits, very quiet, rubs my elbow once in a while.

"See? We've got it all figured out."

"You need to take it as it comes, Kelly. If you need a rest, I've already bottle fed her, so she's not being picky. No confusion. She's brilliant already."

"She needs a name."

"Yes, yes, she does. I know what I want her middle name to be, if that's okay."

"What?"

"Emily. For my friend." He looks straight at me. Emily was the friend Andrew lost right after he left home for Hollywood. Losing her was very hard on him.

"I like that a lot. First name ideas?"

"I got nothin'. I've been busy saving the world. Though I understand you took someone out with a fireplace poker."

"Yes, I did." I close my eyes. I don't know how to feel about Mari. Her brother, her tragedy—she was clearly sick. But that rage and fear, the threat she posed to my family, I don't know when I'll be able to hear her name without a rush of emotions.

"We're safe from her," Andrew soothes. "She's on the psych wing of the county jail. She'll get help. You didn't completely wreck her; we just slowed her way down."

"I didn't know I was capable of that."

"I'll remember not to make you mad." He strokes my hair, tucks a strand behind my ear, kisses me softly on the lips.

The baby fusses. "Time to change sides. This one could be a little tricky."

"Your bad wing. I'll help hold her." He scoots closer, puts a hand under her tiny, swaddled bundle of a body. She's a lot smaller than the boys were. Both of them were overdue. She's my early bird.

"She's light. How much does she weigh?"

"She's holding her own. Five pounds, fifteen ounces." Proud daddy sticking up for her.

"What day is it?"

"January twenty-fifth."

"Three fives. Maybe there's a name in there somewhere," I muse.

"No Cinco Pettigrew."

Hunter and Beau come charging in. "Mom!"

They both climb up on the bed, give me hugs on my good side. I can't shower them with enough kisses. "No one can go anywhere," I tell them. "I have all of you here, safe, in one spot. We're good."

"Did you name her yet?" Beau strokes the baby's hair with one pinky. He seems to love her already.

"We were getting around to it," Andrew says. "Your mom was working on five names."

"She doesn't need five different names. That's too confusing." Beau shakes his head.

Hunter intervenes. "No, names that have something with the number five."

"She was born on the twenty-fifth, she was five pounds five ounces, you know."

"Well, then it should be Quincy." Beau makes little curls with the hair on the top of her head.

"What?"

"Quincy. It means the fifth son, but it's close enough. And it's not Cinco, which is not a good name." Beau tells us this as a matter of fact.

"I like it. I don't know where that came from, Beau, but I like it." Andrew gives him a hug.

Beau hugs me one more time. "Excellent. It's done. I'll go tell everybody, and we can go to the cafeteria."

The boys coo over Quincy for a few more moments, then leave to go get something to eat.

Andrew sits on the edge of the bed, holding Quincy as she drifts back to sleep, full and sated. "I have something to give you, Mrs. Almost-Pettigrew."

"What?" I sit up a little straighter.

He turns and sets Quincy down in her bassinet, gently tucking her blanket in around her feet. Then he comes back to my and kneels by my bed. "Marry me, Kelly."

"My ring? Where'd you get that?" I hadn't noticed it was gone.

"It was on the floor near you. It must have come off in the struggle."

I look at my fingers. They're covered in scratches. I shiver a bit.

"Um, hello?" Andrew's still on one knee by the bed.

"Oh! Yes, I'll marry you. Just like I said the...I've lost track. How many times?"

Andrew smiles, and my skin warms with pleasure. Nothing can replace that bright grin. "I think this is lucky number seven."

"Yes, again."

He stands up and slides the ring on my finger.

I pull him down to the bed, and we kiss.

"Well, enough of that, then. Maybe now we can get to making plans for the wedding. I still have the number for that elephant." He smiles again.

Everything feels settled, after so many months of fear and uncertainty.

"Sleep," he tells me. "I'll run down to the cafeteria and see what looks good."

I watch him walk away and feel at peace.

HEY, MAN, NICE SHOT

Tucker won the bet about Quincy's gender, so here we are at Pebble Beach, playing golf. Tucker, Jeremy, Todd, and me. All because of a five-month-old baby girl who has me wrapped around her little finger already.

"Are you gonna tee off or what?" Jeremy calls from behind me.

"Shut it. I'm trying to concentrate."

Todd joins in. "It looks like you're trying to pass a kidney stone. Just hit it, Tiger."

I connect with the ball, and it soars down the fairway, straight and true.

Tucker's on my side. "That's how you do it, gentlemen."

"Lucky shot." Jeremy checks his phone.

We get back into two golf carts and cruise to our next shots. The fairway is warm in the sun. The cut grass smells fresh and clean. Life is good.

"So, how's life on tour?" Tucker asks Todd as they disembark.

"Lots of moldy hotel rooms, but someone threw panties instead of a beer bottle on the last stop, so that's an improvement."

"Oxford Comma, eh?" Jeremy looks at him.

"Yeah."

"Clever band name."

"We thought so."

I don't know why, but Jeremy and Todd don't love each other. Maybe it's best friend competition. That's such a girl thing to do.

"Let's not squabble, girls." Tucker does his level best to tease both of them at any opportunity.

We make our next shots and land on or near the green. "Last hole, gents. Next up is drinks in the clubhouse." Jeremy twirls his putter and fidgets. The man is never at rest.

"Thanks for your support, J." He knows I hate bars.

"Fine. We'll go back into Carmel for an early, wholesome dinner. Some bachelor party."

Tucker chips his ball up onto the green, edging it impressively close to the pin. "Go hang with other agents if you're looking for the scumbag experience."

Jeremy takes in a deep breath and turns full circle, arms out. "No, seriously, a gorgeous day like this with, dare I say it, my best friends? This is where I want to be, even if it means we don't drink."

Todd nods in agreement. "What're you going to do now that you're a full-on family man, Andrew? We'll never get to see you. Especially when you hightail it back to Boise whenever you can."

Tucker speaks up. "You have to admit, Andrew, it's not on the way to anywhere."

"Exactly the way I like it." I bend over the green and line up my putt. I tap the ball gently. It sails across the green, makes the hole, but lips the cup. "Damn it."

"Sorry, Mr. Woods. You're denied a birdie." Todd marks the score card.

Jeremy speaks up. "No, really. We need to plan something. Otherwise I'll never see you unless we're working."

I smile and watch Todd make his putt. "I have a plan, actually." I walk over to the cart, reach in my bag, and pull out three white envelopes.

"What's this?" Jeremy tears into his.

"Fly-fishing trip. Swan Valley, Idaho, next summer. Best fly-fishing in the world. You three, me, and maybe Hunter and Beau if they can stand so many old guys."

Tucker nods. "Perfect. I want to try out my new reel."

Todd shrugs. "Never fished, but you know I'm down. The band's taking next July off. Damon has to have carpal tunnel surgery."

"It's settled, then." I hop in the driver's seat of the cart.

"What, I don't get a vote? What if I don't want to go?" Jeremy looks pouty.

"I'm about to make you a ten-percent commission on a three-hundred-million-plus franchise movie. You want to go."

"Fine. I want to go. I hate you, though." He gets in the cart next to me.

"I hate you too." I smack him on the leg with a golf glove.

Tucker and Todd load into the cart behind us. The wind comes up off the ocean. The sun begins to sink, lighting the clouds orange and pink and blue from behind.

Jeremy looks at me, looks at the deep emerald green turf, the ocean laid out in front of us. He breathes in deep. "This, son, this is why you and I put up with all the bullshit. Thank you."

"We're almost having a moment, aren't we?"

"Don't ever quote me, but yeah. This is a good time." He looks down at his golf glove, interested in the stitching all of a sudden.

I turn the cart toward the clubhouse. "A good time. Definitely."

Things are all falling into place. And it's a good place, finally.

I like it.

The next week, the way everything is decked out, the Bishop's House is breathtaking.

I know, I'm a guy. I don't get this stuff. But I can appreciate when something is really beautiful. It's a beautiful June day, and I'm getting married.

Initially, I was doubtful about this spot. Kelly dragged me around to all sorts of places in Boise. We knew it had to be Boise; that was a no-brainer. It's our place. It's our home. LA is just where I work.

So, she brings me out here back in February, and everything's dead, it's freezing, I'm freezing my ass off, and, hello, it's next to the old prison? That's a weird symbolism I'd prefer not to associate with my wedding day.

But then we hiked up the path in the back, curling up to Tablerock, and the lights of the city sparkled out in front of us, and the river twisted in a ribbon through the dry hills and down into town, and I thought, *Okay, I guess I can see it.*

She showed me the little side garden, told me about the roses in bloom in June, and I nodded my head yes.

If it made her happy, I was on board anyway.

I guess it was smaller than I expected. I come from Hollywood. Land of the oversized everything. There is no such thing as restraint. Texas is probably the only other place so ridiculous. No shame in a very big game—that's how LA plays it.

Weddings I've been to in the past have been over the top. I went with Jeremy to one of his other client's weddings. It featured a horrible amount of pink tulle: Pepto-Bismol and cotton candy's love child. The swans in the pond at the entrance of the estate had pink tulle bows around their necks. PETA would've freaked.

LA weddings that pretend not to be pretentious are the worst, though. One invite told me to wear a white or cream dress shirt with jeans that were "distressed," and they "preferred" I not wear shoes. Women were supposed to wear "carefree country garden looks." I hucked that one in the garbage at the two-second mark.

Getting ready for our wedding, I was surprised at the small garden, the tiny rooms inside the house, and, yes, the abandoned penitentiary next door. But I was happy that Kelly didn't want anything bigger. I wasn't very surprised about that, though. One of the things I love about Kelly is how down to earth she is. She's not trying to be anything she's not. I can't tell you how desperately refreshing that continues to be, especially after any extended length of time in LA.

And here we are. I haven't seen Kelly for hours. She's somewhere in the Bishop's House. I've been with the boys—Tucker, Todd, and Jeremy—out in the ridiculous tour-bus-sized RV Jeremy rented for us to get ready and "pre-function" in. It has a huge TV inside, which Hunter and Beau love. They've spent most of the day watching *Adventure Time* and eating what I think were supposed to be party favor mints. Hopefully Tessa doesn't notice they're missing off the tables.

Another difference from a Hollywood wedding, Tessa is as close as we get to a "wedding planner." She and Kelly planned it all themselves, and the furthest they went toward a staff was to enlist various female friends and relatives to help out with different little things: favors, centerpieces, decorations, big fabric bows that I do not understand. We had a huge budget, only because Sandy told me what an average wedding costs in LA, and the girls have used a tiny fraction of it.

My only request was music. I got to pick the band for the reception. They are an LA band, and they are going to kill it, if I do say so myself. Todd was going to play with Oxford Comma, but two of the guys are on a trip to Mexico. Kelly asked a friend to play the cello as she walks down the aisle, so that will be pretty. What matters to me is that the reception gets us a noise ordinance ticket. (It would if we'd had it at the old LA house. I know that; it's happened before.)

I'm outside, wandering around the garden. The boys are driving me nuts. Jeremy might be the worst of them. The windows of the house all have a filmy acetate over them. It's very pretty, and it's also smart-man Jeremy's way of discouraging any wayward guests from taking shots to sell to tabloids.

The paparazzi aren't here yet. We've done all the arrangements under pseudonyms, and most of the people are friends of Kelly's or Tessa's, so they haven't said anything, but we sent out a final "party" invitation yesterday, so someone will get wind.

We had a "save the date" invite go out, and we told them it was for Quincy's christening. I'm sly like that. We christened her weeks ago. An old friend of Kelly and Peter's did the honors. Kelly knows everyone in Boise, I swear. But it helps, because no one except the three of us, our folks, Hunter, Beau, and Quincy knew about it.

My mom and Kelly's mom are holed up with Quincy somewhere, and I hope the two of them aren't fighting. I'm also hoping they aren't hitting it off too well. Gwen and Maria do not need to form any kind of mom alliance. I'm proud of my mom, though. It took a lot of prescription medication and more than a few counseling sessions, but she gutted it out and got on a plane with Dad to come for the wedding.

The cellist tunes up in the garden. The guests will be driven over from the church downtown in about fifteen (Tucker thought of that — he's good, that one). The trees and the arbors and the stone walls of the garden are all lit with tiny white lights. It reminds me of the time Kelly and I had dinner when she visited me on set during *The Last Drive*. The memory makes me smile.

But what really takes my breath away is my bride. She stands at the end of the aisle.

"You're not supposed to be out here," she informs me.

I wonder if I should close my eyes. "I wanted to see you before everyone got here. And I'm a rule breaker."

She's amazing. A delicate veil falls down her back from the comb in her thick, dark hair. Her dress is a pale pink. She looks a little nervous, her cheeks flushed. We had a delicate conversation a while back about the way a wedding might feel to her, what it might feel like to put on a wedding dress again.

I wasn't sure how a widow might want things to go. She decided to wear Peter's ring on her right hand. It's her way to bring his memory to the ceremony. It breaks my heart when she touches it. I swear I can see all the hurt and loss in the depths of her eyes. The whole story of losing him unspools in the seconds between her touching the band and her consciously changing course to think of something else.

This only makes me more determined to keep her happy for the rest of her life. She deserves it for so many reasons.

After a lot of consideration, and wondering if it felt right, she decided she wanted to have a ceremony with family and friends, the people we've leaned on.

And so here she stands, in her soft, satin gown, the clean lines hugging her waist and falling to the ground, trailing out behind her. It's simple and purely sexy. I can't stand it. Let's skip to the leaving for the honeymoon part right now, can we?

"Just a quick kiss, and then I better go back in," she says. "The moms will skin me alive if they know I'm out here."

I pull her to me, feel the silky gown under my hands, smooth my fingers down the back with the little buttons at the small of her waist. I could get very lost in the sensation.

"Hello, Mr. Pettigrew, are you with me?" She steps out of the embrace and touches me playfully on the nose.

"I'm here. You're amazing." I lean forward to kiss her.

"Wait."

"What?"

"Before all of this is a blur, and it will be—"

"What?"

"I never thought I'd be happy again. Not like this. I didn't know I could."

Her eyes well up with tears. She looks up to the sky, breathes in.

"I didn't know how to be happy before you." I take both her hands.

"Well, thank you. For fixing me. For loving me."

"And the same to you, Mrs. Almost-Pettigrew." I kiss her, her hands in mine, and the world stops.

"This is some sort of a wedding-day violation." Jeremy claps me on the back. "You two are going to jinx the whole thing. If the vans pull up with you out here, we'll have a tweetastrophe on our hands. The whole point is I get to confiscate cells when they get off. Don't take that away from me. That's my moment...that and the toast."

"That's still up for negotiation. I may have Hunter and Beau handle yours. And Tucker gets to go first."

"Fine. Now go hide. We need to get this show on the road."

My bride lets go of my hand and disappears.

Why have I not killed Jeremy? For the millionth time the question occurs to me. I give him yet another opportunity to live.

BEAUTIFUL DAY

Quincy's fussy. Mom and Maria are passing her back and forth, cooing and humming and trying every trick in the book.

She's probably hungry, and lately, the bottle just doesn't compare to me.

I am in my wedding dress, and if I have to nurse my baby on the way down the aisle, well, that will just be par for the course. I am Kelly Reynolds Almost-Pettigrew, and this is how we roll, my family and me.

"Do you want me to nurse her?" I ask. "We have a few minutes."

Both the moms look at me in horror. "Lord, no, Kelly. This is your day. We can handle a hungry baby." Maria scurries off to find the diaper bag.

I got ready way too early. I wandered around. I sneaked out to see Andrew. Mostly I have just been turning in nervous circles. Jeremy poked his head in about five minutes ago and said there was one more vanload of guests coming from the church, and then it was all systems go.

I am about to say it's on, right now, and one last batch of friends is just going to have to pick up in the middle. It's not like they won't figure out that it's our wedding and not Quincy's christening. I'd say me in a wedding gown and Andrew standing up at the end of an aisle would be a giveaway, but you know, that's just me. Maybe I'm assuming too much on our guests' parts.

Maria returns with a warmed bottle. Quincy relaxes into her arms.

Jeremy's head appears in the doorway again. "It's time."

There's a collective female noise at this news. Maybe it's a happy purr? I wouldn't say squeal. Most of us have been out of the squealing phase of our lives for a long time now.

Tessa comes up and circles me. She tugs on the dress, fluffs the back of it, digs the teeth of my hair comb into my scalp. "You're ready to roll. And I want to apologize for the girls. Joe's got 'em teed up right at the head of the aisle, but he may not get the lollipops out of their hands for the walk. You ask five-year-old triplets to be flower girls, you get what you get."

"They're adorable no matter what. They could pickpocket the guests and still be adorable."

"Don't say that in front of them. They'll do it. They're a mob. They're like a little diminutive French Revolution. They'll throw your rose petals and then go storm the Bastille." Tessa hugs me, hands me my bouquet. "Dan's waiting for you, and he's such a cute father of the bride. This is it, my friend. It's your day, kiddo. I'm so thrilled for you. You got your second chance." She kisses me on the cheek and then has to wipe her lipstick off. Typical Tessa.

The crowd of female helpers clears out ahead of me. I walk slowly out of the house and down the steps. I see Hunter and Beau at the gate to the garden. They have Quincy in the baby carriage now. Tessa found it, a perfect old-school pram, and tricked it out with cabbage roses and tulle. It's lovely. I can see my baby girl kicking her feet up above the rim. Hunter jiggles the handle to keep her distracted. Beau waves at me and holds up Quincy's binky. He's ready for any extenuating circumstance.

They get their cue and push the pram down the aisle, in front of me. I walk through the gate and into the garden.

There it is, my new life spread out in front of me. Tessa's little black-haired girls have just thrown the last of the rose petals and run down the side of the garden, trying to escape from Tessa and Joe, who are in hot pursuit.

My mom stands up at the front of the garden in the front row of guests. Hunter and Beau push Quincy along, and everyone laughs and sighs at the sight of her. My dad stands next to me, arm out to walk me down the aisle.

And Andrew. Andrew stands at the end of this aisle, Tucker and Jeremy beside him, waving the boys up to the altar to join him, to stand as his best men.

He sees me and smiles so broadly. He's always had a million-dollar smile. He looks right at me and mouths, "Love you." I nod and mouth it back.

Joy sweeps through my body. Electricity prickles the hair on my neck, sends chills out to my toes and fingers. The tears come to my eyes, and I look up to the sky. The blue of it is crisp and perfect.

My life could not be more perfect. It's been scary and terrible and lonely and wonderful and filled with love. And it is my perfectly imperfect and wonderful life to live.

I walk down the aisle to meet Andrew, so we can begin our perfect ending.

Together.

ACKNOWLEDGMENTS

First, to my husband: Every day I'm reminded that the team of you and me is the best team ever. And to my boys: Love you madly.

To my Chix: As always and of course.

To Jessica: The editor supreme, Queen of Everything.

To Elizabeth at Omnific and Micki at Gallery Books: Thank you for your continued support.

To my education family: You encourage me in both of my jobs.

To the Anderson, Finn, and Skold clans: All of your support and enthusiasm is invaluable.

It takes a village to grow a writer. My village is very big. Thank you all.

ABOUT THE AUTHOR

Beck Anderson loves to write about love and its power to heal and grow people past their many imperfections. She is a firm believer in the phrase "mistakes are for learning" and uses it frequently to guide her in writing life and real life.

Beck balances (clumsily at best) writing novels and screenplays, working full-time as an educator, mothering two pre-teen males, loving one post-forty husband, and making time to walk the foothills of Boise, Idaho, with Stefano DiMera Delfino Anderson, the suavest Chihuahua north of the border.

Her first novel, *Fix You*, was a RWA Rita® finalist for Best First Book and Best Contemporary Romance. Learn more at:

AuthorBeck.com

←——→New Adult Romance←——→

Three Daves by Nicki Elson
Streamline by Jennifer Lane
The Shades series: *Shades of Atlantis* & *Shades of Avalon* by Carol Oates
The Heart series: *Beside Your Heart, Disclosure of the Heart* & *Forever Your Heart*
by Mary Whitney
Romancing the Bookworm by Kate Evangelista
Flirting with Chaos by Kenya Wright
The Vice, Virtue & Video series: *Revealed, Captured, Desired* & *Devoted*
by Bianca Giovanni
Granton University series: *Loving Lies* by Linda Kage
Missing Pieces by Meredith Tate

←——→Paranormal & Fantasy Romance←——→

The Light series: *Seers of Light, Whisper of Light* & *Circle of Light* by Jennifer DeLucy
The Hanaford Park series: *Eve of Samhain* & *Pleasures Untold* by Lisa Sanchez
Immortal Awakening by KC Randall
The Seraphim series: *Crushed Seraphim* & *Bittersweet Seraphim* by Debra Anastasia
The Guardian's Wild Child by Feather Stone
Grave Refrain by Sarah M. Glover
The Divinity series: *Divinity* & *Entity* by Patricia Leever
The Blood Vine series: *Blood Vine, Blood Entangled* & *Blood Reunited* by Amber Belldene
Divine Temptation by Nicki Elson
The Dead Rapture series: *Love in the Time of the Dead, Love at the End of Days* &
Love Starts with Z by Tera Shanley
The Hidden Races series: *Incandescent* & *Illumination* by M.V. Freeman
Something Wicked by Carol Oates
Chronicles of Midvalen: *Command the Tides* (book 1) by Wren Handman

←——→Romantic Suspense←——→

Whirlwind by Robin DeJarnett
The CONduct series: *With Good Behavior, Bad Behavior* & *On Best Behavior*
by Jennifer Lane
Indivisible by Jessica McQuinn
Between the Lies by Alison Oburia
Blind Man's Bargain by Tracy Winegar

←——→Historical Romance←——→

Cat O' Nine Tails by Patricia Leever
Burning Embers by Hannah Fielding
Seven for a Secret by Rumer Haven
The Counterfeit by Tracy Winegar

Erotic Romance

The Keyhole series: *Becoming sage* (book 1) by Kasi Alexander
The Keyhole series: *Saving sunni* (book 2) by Kasi & Reggie Alexander
The Winemaker's Dinner: *Appetizers & Entrée* by Dr. Ivan Rusilko & Everly Drummond
The Winemaker's Dinner: *Dessert* by Dr. Ivan Rusilko
Client N° 5 by Joy Fulcher
The Enclave series: *Closer and Closer* (book 1) by Jenna Barton
The Adventures of Clarissa Hardy by Chloe Gillis

Anthologies

A Valentine Anthology including short stories by
Alice Clayton ("With a Double Oven"),
Jennifer DeLucy ("Magnus of Pfelt, Conquering Viking Lord"),
Nicki Elson ("I Don't Do Valentine's Day"),
Jessica McQuinn ("Better Than One Dead Rose and a Monkey Card"),
Victoria Michaels ("Home to Jackson"), and
Alison Oburia ("The Bridge")

Taking Liberties including an introduction by Tiffany Reisz and short stories by
Mina Vaughn ("John Hancock-Blocked"),
Linda Cunningham ("A Boston Marriage"),
Joy Fulcher ("Tea for Two"),
KC Holly ("The British Are Coming!"),
Kimberly Jensen & Scott Stark ("E. Pluribus Threesome"), and
Vivian Rider ("M'Lady's Secret Service")

Sets

The Heart Series Box Set (*Beside Your Heart, Disclosure of the Heart &
Forever Your Heart*) by Mary Whitney
The CONduct Series Box Set (*With Good Behavior, Bad Behavior &
On Best Behavior*) by Jennifer Lane
The Light Series Box Set (*Seers of Light, Whisper of Light, Circle of Light &
Glimpse of Light*) by Jennifer DeLucy
The Blood Vine Series Box Set (*Blood Vine, Blood Entangled, Blood Reunited &
Blood Eternal*) by Amber Belldene

Singles, Novellas & Special Editions

It's Only Kinky the First Time (A Keyhole series single) by Kasi Alexander
Learning the Ropes (A Keyhole series single) by Kasi & Reggie Alexander
The Winemaker's Dinner: RSVP by Dr. Ivan Rusilko
The Winemaker's Dinner: No Reservations by Everly Drummond

Big Guns by Jessica McQuinn
Concessions by Robin DeJarnett
Starstruck by Lisa Sanchez
New Flame by BJ Thornton
Shackled by Debra Anastasia
Swim Recruit by Jennifer Lane
Sway by Nicki Elson
Full Speed Ahead by Susan Kaye Quinn
The Second Sunrise by Hannah Downing
The Summer Prince by Carol Oates
Whatever it Takes by Sarah M. Glover
Clarity (A *Divinity* prequel single) by Patricia Leever
A Christmas Wish (A *Cocktails & Dreams* single) by Autumn Markus
Late Night with Andres by Debra Anastasia
Poughkeepsie (enhanced iPad app collector's edition) by Debra Anastasia
Poughkeepsie (audio book edition) by Debra Anastasia
Blood Eternal (A Blood Vine series single, epilogue to series) by Amber Belldene
Carnaval de Amor (*The Winemaker's Dinner*, Spanish edition)
by Dr. Ivan Rusilko & Everly Drummond

coming soon from
OMNIFIC PUBLISHING

The Forever series: *Forever Winter* (book 2) by Christopher Scott Wagner
Twice Upon a Kiss by Jane Susann McCarter
The Ground Rules by Roya Carmen
The Keyhole series: *Keyhole Kinklets* (short story anthology)
by Kasi & Reggie Alexander

www.ingramcontent.com/pod-product-compliance
Lightning Source LLC
Chambersburg PA
CBHW020346120726
47904CB00002B/476